Jane Rawlinson was brought up̲
convent school. and took a deg̲
University. She now lives in Sc̲
their four young children and is̲
Her first. *Cradle Song*. set in Ker̲

JANE RAWLINSON

The Lion and the Lizard

PALADIN
GRAFTON BOOKS
A Division of the Collins Publishing Group

LONDON GLASGOW
TORONTO SYDNEY AUCKLAND

Paladin
Grafton Books
A Division of the Collins Publishing Group
8 Grafton Street, London W1X 3LA

Published in Paladin Books 1987

First published in Great Britain by
Andre Deutsch 1986

ISBN 0-586-08690-0

Printed and bound in Great Britain by
Collins, Glasgow

Set in Times

To D.L. and to Moira

Think, in this batter'd Caravanserai
Whose Doorways are alternate Night and Day,
How Sultan after Sultan with his Pomp
Abode his Hour or two and went his way.

They say the Lion and the Lizard keep
The Courts where Jamshyd gloried and drank deep.
And Bahram, that great Hunter – the Wild Ass
Stamps o'er his Head, and he lies fast asleep.

Rubaiyat of Omar Khayyam
11th century
Translated by Edward Fitzgerald, 1859

Principal Characters

THE GABAYANS
Masoud, a Moslem carpet dealer.
Roya, his wife.
Soraya, his daughter, a university student.
Hussein, his schoolboy son.
Soheila, his daughter.
Ali, an employee in Masoud's shop.

THE BANIYAZDIS
Hamid, an unemployed Iranian Jew.
Aziz, his wife.
Fariba, his daughter.
Shahnaz, his baby daughter.
Mussa, his son.
Three other sons.
Houshang, Hamid's friend.

THE HOMAYOUNS
Fereydoun, an architect.
Theresa, his English wife.
Reza, his son.
Farah, his daughter.
Muna, their servant.

THE KHAKSARS
Shirin, senior civil servant, member of the Bahai faith.
Jacqueline, her daughter.
Dariush, her son.

THE EMANIS
Mrs Emani, member of the Roman Catholic faith.
Jamshid, her son.

THE MULLAH AFSHARZADEH

'In the name of God, the Compassionate, the Merciful, welcome!' Believe me this is not the usual language of your Captain, but there are occasions when, in a manner of speaking, we leave our shoes at the mosque door. Just say to yourself that in the eyes of others we have observances that seem equally strange.

Notre Dame, for example, could learn a lesson or two from this barefootedness. There have been times when I have hardly heard the sermon due to the stench of dog dirt and filth of every description emanating from the upturned soles just below my nose.

Forgive me, I digress. It is an unfortunate tendency of pilots which comes from having one's head in the clouds more often than one's feet on the ground. I develop these little homespun philosophies during the long lonely hours when I find myself nearer to God than to man.

My intention was to explain my rather novel words of welcome. This flight was not my idea. My company asked for volunteers to deliver a Holy Man back to his own people. Due to an element of danger, the financial considerations were considerable, or, as my wife put it, I would have been a fool to say No.

My wife, you see, had her eyes on this old farmhouse down in Provence. The contract is now signed, and in about six hours she will be taking our two children down there on holiday. The fact that she may be a widow by then doesn't seem to have entered her mind.

She's probably right. I mean, who would worry about one old gentleman who talks a lot but won't last long? My

11

gaffer's the same age. Seventy-eight. He can't manage his own flies let alone run a country.

There's hundreds of them back there, you know, like a party of nuns on a picnic. Not the old man, he keeps himself to himself, in the upstairs lounge. One of the other bearded gents – they all look the same – asked just now whether Mecca was still in front of us, to our right, or behind us. I plotted our position and reported back, whereupon they scattered pages of Paris Soir *all over the cabin floor. Before I could open my mouth to protest, I was faced with this seething eruption of black bottoms. One has to be prepared for all types of eccentricities in this game.*

I have already mentioned my little excursions into the realms of amateur philosophy. Let me add a touch of comparative theology. My French father comes of part Jewish stock, my mother, Iranian by birth, remains a devout Moslem. I myself received in the south of England an education in rugger, Christianity, Latin and certain schoolboy malpractices. My wife, I should have mentioned before, is part Chinese. With my background, and seated more often than not a few thousand feet above the earth's surface, I can do no other than adopt a world view.

Are you ready for the next revelation? As I hurtle towards the dawn, I have come to the conclusion that God must certainly be someone of mixed nationality. Someone very like me. In fact the frightening thought has come to me lately that perhaps I am God. Don't laugh, please. Simply step back and look at me up here in isolation, high in the sky.

See what I mean? It makes me laugh to think of the Ayatollah going back. Mohammed's representative on earth, and who is actually steering him towards his destiny? Even God, you see, has a sense of humour.

'This is your Captain speaking. In the hands of God, the Compassionate, the Merciful, we are now approaching Tehran. Would you please fasten your seat-belts and remain in your seats.'

1

Tehran. The Year after Mohammed 1357. February 1st 1979.

'Is it time?' Masoud Gabayan nudged his companion and looked anxiously skyward. He saw with relief the first signs of dawn in the sky. Minus ten degrees centigrade, and he ached with the numbness of a night in the open.

Nearer to Heaven, the Ayatollah emerged from his bedroll on the floor of the upstairs lounge of an Air France Boeing 747. After performing his ritual ablutions, he recited the dawn prayers and the prayers for those who expect to die. Then he ate a little yoghurt.

'Got anything to eat?' Masoud asked.

His friend produced some bread from his pocket, something to chew on, something to do while they watched and waited. To the north of the city the mountain peaks glowed pink. Further east the snow-covered cone of Damavand sparkled in the rising sun.

'Look! A plane!' Masoud screwed up his eyes. From the west came the Ayatollah, his sun already risen, a ball of fire on the rim of the world. The speck became larger, then came the noise. People waved their stiff arms, pointing, shouting. Hysteria spread through the cold, hungry tens of thousands.

'The soul of Hussein is coming back.'

What blasphemy was this, Masoud wondered, clicking his prayer beads between his fingers. An elbow in his ribs, a shrill voice in his ear. 'The doors of Paradise have opened again.'

Masoud lunged angrily sideways and pulled his woollen hat over his ears.

15

The crowd's excitement became an indrawn gasp of horror as the plane swooped low over the runway then lifted its nose skyward again. At the eleventh hour Paradise was eluding the faithful. People shrieked their despair to the heavens.

'Will you please remain seated,' shouted the Captain above the rumpus on board the plane. Journalists, Mullahs and cameramen fought for window seats, slithering on the discarded newspapers which had earlier served as prayer mats.

In a mammoth lumbering circle the jumbo jet turned over the heads of the crowd, back towards the west. The plane had extra tanks with sufficient fuel for the return journey to Paris.

'This is your Captain speaking. Will you please remain seated. We have checked that the runway is clear, we are now preparing to land.'

For the second time the huge belly of the plane plunged towards the tarmac. The Ayatollah landed in a scream of red hot tyres and a roar from his followers.

In a small blue van, protected by Revolutionary Guards with automatic weapons at the ready, the Ayatollah moved slowly towards the city. People fought to get near him to receive the spiritual power conferred at the touch of his robes. They crowded the rooftops, perched on dustbins, hung from fences, anything that might give a better view of the Saviour.

Masoud began to wonder why he had come. He wouldn't see a thing of the Ayatollah. Not in this mob. He'd have got a better view on telly. He shrank back against the pillar of the soaring Shahyad Monument, glad of something solid at his back. The monument commemorated the two thousand five hundredth anniversary of the monarchy which had ended some three weeks earlier with the departure of the Shah.

Masoud looked nervously around, relieved that there was no sign of the army. And the Mullahs were doing their best, he had to admit that, trying to drown the shouts of 'Now is the hour of martyrdom' with a more sedate 'God is Great.' He wished he had stayed at home. It would all be in the papers tomorrow.

By way of the back streets, Masoud made slightly better progress towards the city centre than the Ayatollah. It took the official convoy twelve hours to travel the twelve miles. At pre-arranged points the vehicles stopped while he addressed the crowds from makeshift platforms. Women wept and fainted, for the sacrifice he demanded was great. The Ayatollah wanted their sons, their daughters in his Holy War. 'Blessed be your milk,' he said, and they offered the fruit of their own wombs gladly. Why, they would give their own lives if he requested it. And he did.

Troop carriers, tanks and armoured cars rumbled through the streets. The metal tracks screamed and tore at the tarmac.

'Just a routine movement of troops,' the generals tried to reassure the populace. But Masoud knew better. He shrank into the doorway of a house and felt the walls vibrate behind him.

When a helicopter flew overhead Masoud dived for cover, hid his head in his hands and waited for the burst of machinegun fire. Nothing happened. The helicopter landed a short distance away to collect the hoarse and exhausted Ayatollah, to carry him over the heads of the faithful to the sprawling, single-storied cluster of buildings in the south of the city. The Alavieh School was to become his headquarters.

This is your Captain speaking! Please, wait for me. Since we seem to be heading in the same direction, allow me to be your guide. There are, you see, certain areas where it is inadvisable for a foreigner to go unattended. I do not want to startle you with gruesome details but please, take heed.

For me, it is different. I speak the language fluently, I have changed into some very unremarkable clothes, as you may have noticed, and my physiological attributes make me equally inconspicuous whether in the boulevards of Paris or the alleyways of southern Tehran.

Let us proceed! Do not imagine the bazaar area as you see it now, a mere ghost of its usual self. For this is the pulse of the nation. An area so densely populated that, in my mother's words, you could drop a needle and it would not reach the earth.

The Jewish Quarter crouched beneath a pall of snow; the low houses humps of sparkling white separated by blue alleyways and purple, rectangular courtyards. The Mahalleh in its snow-enshrouded silence resembled some abandoned settlement of long ago.

No more dancing in the streets. No more Shah. No more fuel. No more food. Only freedom! The Imam had returned from the skies like some God of old. His sword blazed red in a fiery dawn. But visions of Paradise lingered elsewhere, far from the children's whimpering bellies.

Many of the wealthier Jews were at the airport among mountains of carpets, where jewels shimmered like early morning frost. Where gold bars gleamed and suitcases bulged with dollar bills.

'We have come to save people, not carpets,' expostulated harassed airline officials of El Al.

The Jews without carpets stayed at home.

Hamid Baniyazdi scratched himself and groaned. The children grizzled. His stomach grumbled. Anything was better than staying at home. Wander the streets. Visit. Anything. Trousers over pyjamas. Jacket over pyjama top. Woollen hat and scarf. Shoes taken from a dustbin, trodden down at the back, guaranteed to fit any size. Fists crammed into pockets, shoulders hunched, he stepped outside.

'Where are you going, Hamid?'

It was only Aziz. He didn't bother to reply. A game of backgammon perhaps. A pipe of opium. Such dreams! No work, no money, no food. Melting snow trickled between his toes, then froze. The bazaar yawned, cavernous, empty. Hamid's spine was permanently knotted, braced against an enormous weight. And the cold. It gnawed through his jacket, biting at his shoulder blades.

'Houshang!' he yelled. 'Houshang!' Fingers rapping numb as the wood against a door in the wall.

'Houshang!'

'Who's that?' A frightened squeak from the other side.

'Houshangja, it's me, Hamid.'

'Anyone else?'

'Only me.'

The bolt harsh in its metal runway, up and down, up and down. From along the alley the sound of feet and voices. Booted feet. Moslem feet. The feet of the self-styled Revolutionary Guard – the Pasdaran.

'Houshang, hurry! They're coming.'

'I'm trying, Hamid. The metal's cold.'

More grinding of the bolt and the footsteps became louder. Hamid shivered, a convulsive shuddering of his whole body. In spite of the cold, sweat trickled down his nose and froze.

'Please, Houshangja. Let me in.'

'Can't you see I'm trying.'

Hamid fell through the door as the bolt drew back. Houshang stood, the bolt frozen to his hand.

'What a time to come visiting!'

The two men leant against the door. Houshang clasped his bleeding fingers between his legs. Chanting filled the

19

narrow alley, the sound spilled upwards and over the compound wall.

'Khomeini-e-Imam, Khomeini-e-Imam.' Laughter and sticks rattled against the high mud walls. An empty Coke can sailed through the air and landed tinny against the stone trough in the centre of the yard.

A small boy ran to retrieve the can. His mother fought to get it away before he cut his tongue on the sharp opening. The child opened his mouth to scream. Hamid and Houshang dived on top of him to silence the howl of protest.

In the city centre, Masoud Gabayan avoided the blood-stained patches on the pavements with reverence. Mothers, fathers, sisters and brothers thawed the snow with their tears. They scattered narcissi to show their respect for the martyrs who had died in the struggle against the Shah.

Outside his shop Masoud paused to savour the usual surge of pride. 'The Oriental Carpet Emporium, Proprietor M. Gabayan', written of course in English.

'Heard the news?' Masoud called to his employee Ali.

'Balé, balé.' Ali grinned and nodded.

'Any customers today?'

Ali shook his head.

Masoud drew the steel shutters across the shop front.

'Off you go,' he said, laughing to see Ali scamper into the crowd like a boy released from school.

Masoud headed for the nearest tea house. 'Salaam aleikum.' Masoud warmed to the cries of greeting in the steamy atmosphere. Seated on a carpet on one of the squat rectangular tables, he clasped his hands round a glass of tea and let himself dream. It was as if the wealth of the entire Persian Gulf was about to be diverted into his very own pocket.

* * *

20

*I would have liked to draw Masoud Gabayan for you.
The face is typical of many, lined with the permanent cares
of trade. Not only in terms of carpets but in the daily
bargaining over his soul which takes place between man
and God. One of the aspiring middle class, one-time stall-
holder made good, he wears the requisite nondescript suit
and a day's stubble about his chin, and permanently clicks
his prayer beads through his fingers like some portable
abacus.*

*Anyone could draw his wife. My children, comfortably
ensconced in the farmhouse in Provence, are probably
drawing something very similar at this moment. The
inverted teardrop of a ghost. A limbless, bodiless veil with
two enormous eyes. Please allow me to present to you
Khanum, or should I say Mrs, Roya Gabayan.*

In her flat in the town centre, Roya Gabayan switched
off the radio. She had to share the news with someone.
Pulling her chador tightly about her face she hurried onto
the landing.

'Did you hear?' she called down. 'Did you hear the
news?'

From the well of the stairway her neighbours looked
up.

'Isn't it wonderful?'

'Just imagine, we are all free.'

'I shall have a new cooker and a three-piece suite.'

'What about a car?'

There seemed no end to the possibilities. Like schoolgirls they slithered onto the icy streets, giggling, clinging
to one another for balance. Arm in arm they swung
along, laughed, chattered and broke into song.

The main streets were packed. Strangers shook hands,
offered congratulations, tea and sweetmeats, or twirled
them around until their veils billowed in grotesque black
shadows behind them.

21

In a shower of rose petals, the whole city danced, until the last red and white carnations were trampled into the slush and the orchestration of car horns fell silent.

But there were others for whom the return of the Ayatollah was no cause for rejoicing. In the foothills of the Elburz Mountains to the north of the city there were those who wept for their betrayal. Their King had abandoned his people.

'Be quiet, can't you!' Theresa Homayoun snapped at her children and turned on the car radio. The wailing recitation of the Koran was more than she could bear. She switched it off again. For two hours she had queued for petrol. At that rate she would hardly make the shops before closing time.

She rubbed her hands together and wished she had brought some biscuits for Farah and Reza, some toys perhaps and a thermos of coffee for herself. She released the handbrake and the car slid into the empty space left by a vehicle that abandoned the queue.

It was nearly half past four. Perhaps it would be better to try again tomorrow, to repeat the whole tedious exercise, but her husband Fereydoun had suggested she should use a taxi for the time being. The thought strengthened her resolve to remain where she was.

'Mummy, I want to do a wee.'

'Not now, Farah. You'll have to wait.'

'I can't wait, Mummy.'

Theresa looked in the mirror at her daughter's pinched face. The child stared back, dumb with misery.

'She's done it,' shrieked Reza. 'All over the seat.'

Please forgive this handkerchief permanently in my hand. The bloodstains bear no relation to revolutions and Holy War. At this altitude I find I am frequently affected by nose-bleeds, particularly when, as now, we move into the foothills of the mountains above the general squalor and clamour of the south.

If you experience any shortness of breath, just take things easy for a while. Here at last is somewhere where Western man can relax. In the shadow of the Niavaran Palace, the comforts are considerable. Accommodation is spacious. There are trees and gardens. The views are magnificent. A swimming pool is taken for granted and of course I need not even mention running water, electricity, central heating and imported furnishings (apart from the ubiquitous fitted carpet which is to be found only among the aspiring middle classes).

Assuming you are lucky enough to obtain a free line, you can dial a telephone number anywhere in the world. Please excuse me while I stop to draw breath, and let us eavesdrop for a moment on Shirin Khaksar, senior civil servant, engaged in transcontinental conversation with her daughter Jackie (named of course after Jackie Kennedy, whom Shirin once met at a cocktail party).

'Of course I'm alright, Jackie darling. Don't sound so worried.' Shirin Khaksar strolled between the telephone table and the window, twining her fingers through the cord as she walked.

'Yes. I know reports are bad but I've spent the last few days working at home and I haven't been into town at all.'

'I do appreciate your concern and it's all very well for the princess to say "You must come and live in New York" but how am I to get there?'

'No. It isn't just the money. The airport is still closed and I am not allowed to leave the country.'

'Darling, please be careful what you say. I can imagine how different things may look from New York, but I am not in any actual danger. Tehran isn't rattling with gunfire. I could do with more candles but otherwise I'm fine – a bit cold but comfortable.'

'Of course there isn't any heating. With oil production down to nil.'

'Electricity? A flicker now and then.'

'How do I keep warm? I wear lots of clothes. You can send me a thermal vest if you really want to, but it's not necessary. How were your exams?'

'Of course I want to know. That's more important than revolutions!'

'No, darling, you mustn't even think of coming home at the moment. Wait until things have settled down a bit. You'd better go now. Think of the bill!'

'No. I'm fine. Stop worrying. No one's been writing graffiti in blood on my walls. My love to your brother if you see him.'

'Yes. Bye.'

You may think it strange for a pilot, but I cannot endure this rarefied atmosphere for too long. Let us head southwards again, I would like to be back in my hotel before dark. As soon as this wretched nose-bleed stops I will put my handkerchief back in my pocket, it attracts too much attention.

Do you know, a man stopped me just now and muttered something about 'blood of the martyrs'. Before I could stop him, he had ripped the hanky in half and hurried off down the street waving his piece over his head like a banner.

There is one person I must point out to you, if indeed it is my luck to pick her out of the crowd. I would rather she did not see me because she has in the past proved an embarrassment, such as the time when she appeared at the airport and presented me with a mammoth-sized pair of hand-crocheted slippers.

'I know men have big feet, it is in their nature,' she said.

I have always prided myself on a certain exquisiteness of build and found this remark hurtful.

Anyway, here she comes. Look over there, can you see her? Look carefully, she is a person who has brought the art of self-effacement to such perfection, she is almost invisible.

Mrs Emani walked along Shah Reza, only she knew it wasn't called Shah Reza any more. She tried to remember the new name. Something to do with the Revolution. The Prime Minister perhaps? Only who was the Prime Minister today? She hoped her rug was ready as she teetered across the icy road, anchoring her headscarf with one hand, gripping her shopping bag with the other.

Inside the Oriental Carpet Emporium, Ali sat cross-legged on the floor in fez and pyjamas.

'It's not ready yet, Khanum.'

Mrs Emani shrugged.

'Farda,' said Ali. 'Tomorrow.' He had said the same thing yesterday and the day before, last week and the week before that. He would probably say the same thing tomorrow, and yet one day, Mrs Emani knew, Ali would be right.

'You see.' By way of explanation Ali gestured towards the rugs and carpets stacked around the room in piles as high as her chin. Of course, Mrs Emani admitted to herself, hers was nothing by comparison. It was only of sentimental value.

Black-massed figures passed between the shop front and the sun, cutting out the light. Mrs Emani shivered and turned away.

'What are they doing today?'

'Today they support the government. They say the Ayatollah has no right to appoint Bakhtiar unless there is a vote.'

'Where is Mr Gabayan?'

'Probably out there somewhere. He looks in morning and evening. He'll come back to lock up.' Ali picked up an enormous needle and returned to his work, shaking his head over the vagaries of his master.

Surely such support for the government could not be a bad thing, thought Fereydoun Homayoun. A good crowd it had been – why, he knew many of them by name. So different from the usual riffraff on the streets. He didn't grudge the people their bit of hysteria. The Ayatollah was simply a nine-day wonder. They would soon come to their senses.

But what could he wear and where would he take Goli tonight? A decent meal perhaps. God, he was sick of Theresa's cooking. Not that she cooked herself but she instructed the cook and the result was as bad. Shortages! He didn't believe a word of it. It was all because she insisted on doing the shopping herself. She might say the servants cheated her but a few rials was nothing to the prices she paid. A kilo of lamb trebled when they saw her blonde hair.

The Xanadu perhaps? A bit of good French cooking. Goli by candlelight with the red lights glinting in her hair. She really understood him and knew how a woman should behave towards a man. Perhaps back to her flat afterwards?

Fereydoun slid the hangers along the wardrobe rail. Not a suit. Sports jacket? Didn't quite suit his mood. Shirt and cardigan? He touched the white silk shirt, soft and clinging, and imagined the touch of Goli's fingers on his shoulder.

Fereydoun lingered in the shower. A good lather under the armpits. The hairs on his chest. His genitals. The steady thrum of warm water, so soothing. What was it that Theresa said?

'But darling, I have to go out. Business.' That should

keep her quiet. Fereydoun stepped out of the shower and wrapped himself in a warm towel. Theresa picked up some good bargains at Harrod's, the local material just couldn't compare.

'I've pressed your suit and put it on the bed,' yelled Theresa.

'Shit.' Fereydoun replaced the suit in the cupboard.

'Thank you, darling,' he yelled. Even Theresa could not spoil his enjoyment as he stood in front of the full-length mirror. A little aftershave to complement the talcum powder. He slithered into the silk. Such an extravagance. Christian Dior – the genuine article. Perhaps he should take Goli on to a disco tonight. How he would shine in the ultra-violet light! Theresa would never go dancing these days.

With a towel over his shoulders, Fereydoun combed his hair. Could that be a touch of grey? He laughed with relief as he flicked away a few flecks of talc. The hairs on his chest combed away from the body gave an impression of greater thickness. Important, he thought, with a style of shirt open to the waist.

Ah yes! Fereydoun reached up into the top of the cupboard and took down a small box. The trousers pinched when he stretched like that. It was all Theresa's ghastly English puddings. The finishing touch – a gold medallion nestling on his chest.

Fereydoun put on his overcoat before he said goodbye, buttoned up to the chin. Theresa sat with her back to the living room door. A quick kiss on the nape of her neck as she bent over some sewing.

'I'm letting out your trousers, Fereydoun, they're beginning to look ridiculous.'

Damn her. She just wanted to upset him.

Theresa wondered how Fereydoun could be so childish. As if she could be so easily deceived. It amused her to set a trap like the suit on the bed. Of course he fell for it, she didn't even need to look. Just because he ran a thriving business didn't mean he could take her in. On second thoughts she went into the bedroom. No suit. She couldn't believe it. Poor old Fereydoun, how she had wronged him. A day in the office and then a wearisome supper.

Theresa went into the bathroom, gathered the trail of discarded underwear, draped the towel over the rail, removed a flannel which hung soggily on one of the gilt taps. She felt behind the shower curtain for the lid of the shampoo bottle. It was like clearing up after the children.

As she carried her husband's dressing gown into the bedroom her footsteps shook open the wardrobe door. There was the suit! She glanced quickly along the rail and knew at once what he had put on. She had even given it a name – his Goli shirt. Not that *she* had ever seen him in it, but there had been that photograph in the paper. So foolish he looked at his age in all those frills and with that silly necklace! Theresa blew out the candles and went to bed.

Mrs Emani blew out the candle and sat in the dark waiting for her son to return home. Candles were important because Jamshid must study. She sat in her overcoat and gloves, huddled into the armchair to conserve heat around her back and shoulders.

Two hours later, Mrs Emani woke with a start as Jamshid flicked the light switches, stumbled against a chair and swore. He lit candles on the dresser, the mantelpiece and the table, then put a match to the fire.

'God, it's cold,' he whined, holding his hands to the brief flare.

'Jamshidja!' His mother ground her knuckles into her eyes, and felt along the arm of the chair for her glasses.

'Jamshidja, are you hungry?'

* * *

Intoxicated with food and drink, dancing and Goli, Fereydoun Homayoun clambered into bed and snuggled up to his wife. She was so fair and soft by contrast. Tired though he was, he was rather proud of his performance.

Theresa was pathetically grateful. After all, he couldn't possibly love two women like that at the same time.

The temperature dropped to minus twelve degrees centigrade. The whole city cowered in darkness as if under curfew. The Shah had abandoned his people and the shadow of the Ayatollah lowered over the metropolis as immense and grim as the mountain range to the north.

2

'If the order is given to fire on you, bare your breasts. Your blood and the love which you show them as you are dying will convince them. The blood of each martyr is a bell which will awake a thousand of the living.'

Even after Roya Gabayan had turned off the radio the Ayatollah's words seemed to sing from every corner of the flat. Her daughter was right. There was a man. A true leader. The Twelfth Imam himself, some people were saying. Roya picked up her broom and attacked the dirt with revolutionary zeal.

Then she shook a rug over the balcony until the dust floated down to lie in a dark fuzz on the street below. The sun shone and the Elburz Mountains were sharp against the cloudless sky. Roya blew out her breath, laughing to see the cloud of vapour slowly disperse in the frozen air.

'Khanum-e-Gabayan!'

Roya leaned out over the balcony railing until she could see her neighbour.

'Salamat, Khanum-e-Nosrat.'

'Roya-ja, you are coming to the demonstration?'

'I don't know.' But fire still burned in her heart.

'The Ayatollah called for women and children. He says the troops will not fire on women and children. They must go first.'

'Well, I don't know. Masoud is going. And Soraya. I'm not sure. There's still the shopping.'

'There will be no shops open today.'

Still Roya hesitated. All this life on the streets. The men not at work. Children off school. Women dragging small children here, there and everywhere, their washing unwashed and their houses uncleaned. But the Ayatollah was a Holy Man of God. A saint.

'I won't be a minute.' She grabbed an extra jumper, put on shoes and a chador and raced downstairs, fearful of being left behind.

The more cynical among us might sneer at the effects of the Ayatollah's words on a simple housewife, but do not underestimate the power of rhetoric. We have been guilty of falling for it in the West. Think of our monarchs, our leaders, our religious evangelists.

My nose-bleeds, you will be pleased to hear, have abated slightly in intensity and duration. I have been taking things easy in the seedy environs of the Hotel Hafez, watching, listening, and waiting for the summons to return to the airport should divine intervention be required to whisk the Imam out of the clutches of the army.

But today I have an inclination to step further afield. As we walk, ignore all beggars and importuners, though a few rials here and there will not go amiss. The profession of beggary is an honourable one. Pitches are handed down from generation to generation. Many are masters of make-up and deception fit to grace the boards of any West End stage.

Out of hours, I am told, they live comfortably enough. The deformities are real, missing digits, hands, feet, limbs, blindness, paralysis, but then we all make sacrifices in the interests of our chosen professions. We all have appearances to maintain in accordance with our chosen way of life.

'The poor you have always with you.' They form an essential part of every religion. Such a comforting thought it is to buy grace at the toss of a coin, an indulgence for so little outlay. In fact, as my mother used to say, if beggary

is such a thriving career, why do some people bother to be poor?

'I'm hungry, Mama,' said Fariba.

But Aziz Baniyazdi leaned back against the wall and said nothing. Hamid had no work. There was no money, no food. Not even free dinners because the school was closed.

Her eyes were closed, her children heaped around her in a squirming mound, like puppies.

'I'm hungry,' repeated Fariba. She wrapped her arms round her knees, hugging them to her body as she rocked backwards and forwards.

The room was warm like a cow byre. Snow had crept into every crevice in the mud walls, the rickety roof and the ill-fitting windowframes, and then frozen. Sealed with such thoroughness the air was stale and heavy with the sticky tang of unwashed bodies, clothing and excrement.

'Mama, what shall we eat?' The corner of Fariba's chador was reduced to a pulp. Chew and suck. Chew and suck. It staved off the pangs for a while.

Aziz shook her head to clear the muzziness.

'Eat?'

A laboured squeaking began in the opposite corner of the room. Fariba watched as Aziz struggled out of the burrowing, whimpering knot and crossed the room on her hands and knees.

Aziz put the baby to her breast and stared into the darkness of the room, wondering when the child would die.

Fariba sucked the corner of warm moist material and envied her small sister. Her brothers followed their mother, regrouping around her. Jostling to get close to her they dislodged the baby's weak hold on the nipple.

'Mama, what shall we eat?'

'Fariba, go to the social workers. Ask for food.' It would be safe for a child. No one would harm a child.

'Take Mussa with you.' At least Mussa had shoes. Fariba and Mussa. Surely they would not be turned away.

'My rug?' inquired Mrs Emani, dark as the shadows beneath the mountain of rugs.

Ali shrugged and threaded his needle. He nodded towards the work that awaited him, like a housewife with an impossible pile of socks to darn.

'I'm so sorry. I wouldn't have asked, only you said . . .'

Ali frowned at the jagged edges of a hole awaiting his attention. Such a priceless rug. People were so careless.

Mrs Emani coughed to remind Ali she was still there. Perhaps if she were to speak to Mr Gabayan?

'Inja nist.'

'When is he here?'

'Today he demonstrates against the government.'

'But I thought you said . . . ?'

'He likes demonstrations.' Ali laughed.

'And you?'

'I have a family.'

Mrs Emani nodded and held up her empty shopping bag.

'I have heard,' said Ali, 'that there are tomatoes in the bazaar.'

Mrs Emani mentally totted up the bus fares and the time it would take and decided she would do without tomatoes.

'Thank you, Ali. When shall I call again?' She hoisted her headscarf on to the top of her head, and it was only as she stood blinking in the sunshine that she realized she had not waited for the answer.

'Farda,' Ali shouted after her.

'Tomorrow.' Khanum-e-Emani waved her shopping bag in acknowledgement.

The marchers swept along the main street, separated from the pavement by the wide jube between tarmac and kerb on both sides of the road. These ditches ran from north to south following the slope of the foothills. Twice a day water poured down, carrying away the garbage of the wealthier districts, to become a stagnant trickle that idled through the slums. If a child survived the first five years of life, it was said, no disease would ever prove fatal.

Protected by the jube, Masoud Gabayan hovered on the kerb. These days provided much food for thought. Under the Shah he had thrived. He had earned an honest wage and shown due deference to his monarch. Indeed his picture had hung on the shop wall. Now, he was told that the Shah was a bad man. All he knew was he hadn't sold a rug since the Ayatollah returned.

'Mar bar Bakhtiar,' called the crowd. First the overthrow of princes, now 'Death to the Prime Minister.' The women screamed, fists clenched, faces distorted by hatred. Masoud was glad Roya was safely at home doing the cleaning, cooking his lunch. Whereas these young women! Plump buttocks squeezed into tight jeans!

'Khomeini-e-Imam. Khomeini-e-Imam.' This was something new. He must ask the Mullah about this. Masoud was not a religious man himself but he was shocked.

'Hey there, Masoud. You coming with us?'

Masoud scanned the crowd for the person who had called out. He was cold and bored. Really one demonstration was much like another. It was too early to go home for lunch. Masoud hesitated, then leapt the jube and found himself warmed by the fervour of a million bodies.

* * *

34

Ten-year-old Fariba Baniyazdi knotted her chador around her waist and skated after Mussa along yesterday's ice-slide. Sun glinted off the ice. She screwed up her eyes and the walls whirled by.

'I got to the end. Did you see me, Mussa? I got to the end.'

Mussa looked up, lost concentration and fell. He wailed loudly and Fariba suddenly became aware of the silence.

'Mussa, shhh. Where are all the people?'

They were frightened by the emptiness. No distant sound of cars. No people. Not so much as a donkey. Hand in hand they ran through the deserted alleyways, glancing fearfully the length of each narrow street. Then at last there were people. Voices. The bang and crash of men at work. Somewhere, not far away, life was going on as usual.

The path gave a final ninety-degree turn to the left and there was the Social Work Office. The shutters screamed as they were torn from their hinges. Glass shattered as it fell from the windows.

'Khomeini-e-Imam,' chanted the crowd. 'Death to all unbelievers.'

Fariba and Mussa shrank back against the wall then melted into the shelter of the alleyways. Hearts pounding they ran over the ice, without a look back, too frightened to think of their empty stomachs, their empty-handed return home.

And there she was, Roya Gabayan, wife of a carpet dealer, ex-bazaar lately risen to Ferdowsi Avenue, leading the mass of chanting humanity the length of Shah Reza and on towards the Majles, the House of Parliament.

'Khomeini-e-Imam,' she shouted until she was hoarse. So many people could not be wrong. Besides, there was something compelling about the man whose eyes held hers from numerous posters.

'Death to the Shah.'

'Death to Bakhtiar.'

Each new cry was taken up and resounded from a million throats. Roya forgot the biting cold, her arms linked with the women on each side of her. Her neighbour? Lost long since, but somewhere in the crowd, Roya knew. Some of the women carried flowers, roses from Shiraz, carnations.

'What are they for?' she asked.

'For the soldiers,' the girl smiled.

'You are from the university?'

She was so like Soraya in the student uniform of jeans and sheepskin jacket, her hair long and loose. Silky and gleaming like polished ebony.

'Do you know my daughter?'

'Mar bar Bakhtiar.' The girl laughed, her teeth sparkled. It was all a game really, thought Roya, just a bit of fun. Death, revolution, religion – what did any of it matter so long as the sun shone and the girl next to her smiled like that.

Round the corner they marched, forty abreast, and there were the soldiers lined up before the Majles. The women halted, uncertain what to do next. The girl beside Roya ran forward and poked the stem of a carnation into the barrel of a rifle. The soldier smiled and his friends giggled.

'Flowers we bring you. Flowers and peace,' called the women above the hubbub. The crowd behind pressed forward. Mothers in the front row snatched up their children for fear they would be crushed.

There were shots and the screaming began. Roya shook the sheepskin jacket of the student lying slumped in the snow and begged her to get up. Echoes of gunfire ricocheted from building to building. Still Roya knelt over the girl, and stroked the shining hair. Then she saw the stain of blood seep across the snow.

36

In the ensuing panic Roya could not regain her feet. On all fours she was sucked along in the stampede to the safety of the alleyways.

Further back, the chanting laughing men pushed forward.

'The Ayatollah said there would be shots,' said Masoud. 'They will only fire into the air, because of the women and children.' He looked up as if he expected to see bullets trace a white arc through the blue sky, just like the cinema.

Roya no longer knew where she was, only that she must run. She had lost her chador. A shoe had come off and she limped along with the snow burning the sole of her foot. Each lungful of air was agony. Yet already the events seemed distanced, as if they were a nightmare, as if such horror could only have been imagined. Her legs were shaking so badly that she hobbled into the shelter of a doorway and sat down. She should have realized before, she told herself, that she was being foolish. Revolutions were not for middle-aged ladies. She would have been better off at home, cleaning and cooking.

Revolutions! We've all had 'em. All stemming in my opinion from weakness at the top, a breakdown in authority. There! You flinch at the very word, don't you? It's not popular nowadays, but where would we be without it? Chaos, that's what you'd get. Total and absolute chaos.

Progress must take some of the blame. Take Tehran for example. All that oil. Such wealth. Who's going to be content with a handful of corn and a mud hut any more? Carry the news to the four corners of the earth that Masoud Gabayan will furnish your every delight from his new Oriental Carpet Emporium, that Ali this and Akbar that have baked beans and whisky for sale and that Fereydoun Homayoun will design and build for you a house that surpasses even your wildest dreams.

37

And what more important profession than architecture in this time of expansion? After all, everyone needs somewhere to live. Everyone without land needs to shop. To be entertained.

Expand! Expand to the background crooning and gurgling of millions of barrels of oil. A job for your son, Your Excellency? Why, of course. We need all the educated help we can get. Eton and Oxford? Couldn't be better. We can't cement brick on brick fast enough these days. A casino, Sir? Would next week suit? More staff. Must have more staff. Can't afford to turn a customer away.

Increase and multiply. Build. Build. A new office? A very desirable site, Takhte Tavous, right opposite the American Embassy. Splendid views right into the compound. The Ambassador's wife sunning herself behind the . . . a prestige site. More staff. More customers. The city's population doubled in size over a ten-year period.

Fereydoun Homayoun looks out over the city he has helped to transform. Why, ten years ago there wasn't a building over a certain height, only a few thirteenth-century onion domes to break the monotony of the skyline. But now! Ah, the magnificent multi-storey blocks, huge and square as tombstones against the Elburz Mountains. Monuments to be proud of.

Fereydoun sits behind his triple-glazed windows, wearing overcoat and gloves. Going home at lunchtime? Not a bit of it. All that oil underground, but someone, it seems, has turned the tap off. Not a drop to warm the radiators, let alone the cockles of the heart.

Poor old Fereydoun! All those wages due at the end of the month. No wonder a cold sweat trickles down his brow. And why should he pay them anything when all they do is sit around the office. Work? Oh yes, plenty of work, the filing cabinets bulge with contracts, but who has stripped the streets of their gold paving?

Doodle, doodle, pencil on pad. A wistful glance at the

Embassy opposite, if only . . . but back to work. To the
endless calculations. If he sacks x members of staff at a
saving of y tomans, how much longer will his capital last
out?

Soraya Gabayan flounced into the empty kitchen, angry
that there was nothing ready for lunch. She helped herself
to some bread and goat's cheese and made a cup of tea.
Mrs Nosrat from downstairs said she had last seen Roya
at the demonstration. The thought amused Soraya: she
found it hard to imagine her mother anywhere other than
in the kitchen.

Today she felt ravenously hungry rather than sick. Now
that the weeks of nausea had passed she was able to
think more clearly about her situation and longed to talk
to her mother. Or perhaps she would call at the American
base and ask to see Peter. Then they would go to the
States, marry and live happily ever after. Perhaps she
could even finish her studies on a campus where students
could hold free discussions without the constant fear of
being reported.

'You alright?'

Soraya jumped. She hadn't heard her father come in.

'Baba, it's you. Were you at the demonstration?'

Masoud nodded.

'Wasn't it wonderful, all those people? You'll see,
Baba, the army will soon come over to our side.'

'Where's your mother? I'm hungry.'

'She's not back yet. Have some bread and cheese.'

'Where is she?'

'At the demonstration.'

They both sat at the table and roared with laughter.

'We must have an Islamic government.'

'But Baba, Islam is only a religion, not a legal system.'

'The only way of life is to follow God's teaching.'

Masoud punctuated each syllable with a thump on the table.

'You've gone very religious all of a sudden. Karl Marx says that religion is the opium of the people.'

Soraya had such a beautiful voice. Roya loved to sit and admire the way ideas came tumbling out of her daughter's lovely head. Not that she understood any of them herself.

'I'm back.' Roya hobbled across the tiles into her daughter's arms.

Fereydoun Homayoun heard footsteps in the corridor. A client? He hastily shoved his piece of paper into the drawer and took out a large ledger.

'You've come about your house?'

The other man nodded.

'I'm afraid I cannot give a completion date. You see, my workmen . . .'

'No. It's not that. It is to say that for financial reasons I am unable to continue with the project.'

Fereydoun nodded. It was only to be expected. He joined his client at the window.

'They claim the Shah killed eighteen thousand people.'

'We both, I think, owed a lot to the royal family. What do you think of these religious fanatics?'

'Who? The Mullahs? I think they might do a lot more harm.'

Fereydoun lit a cigarette and paused for a long time.

'To be perfectly honest with you, I loathe them. And I fear them.'

That night Theresa felt she had hit an all-time low. The children were tucked up in bed. She had made a curry. Fereydoun always liked her curries. The warm smell spiced the flat and mingled well with the softness of the candlelight. It could have been so romantic. To stop herself looking at the clock and rushing to the window each time a car stopped outside, Theresa was trying to read. Her eyes stung from the inadequate light.

Fereydoun had promised to be home early. Just for once. Because she was worried and didn't want to be alone. Today it had seemed as if the whole city was reverberating from gunfire. She had heard the rumbling of tanks moving southwards. From the sitting room window she could see the glow of burning buildings. Police Posts and Guard Posts they had said on the radio. So Muna had told her.

Theresa added water to the meat and decided she would give Fereydoun exactly thirty-nine minutes. By then it would be ten o'clock and she would eat and go to bed.

Three minutes short of the deadline she heard footsteps, a key in the lock. The longing she had felt to fling herself into Fereydoun's arms was replaced by a sudden fury as she smelt the whisky on his breath.

'Darling, I'm sorry,' he murmured.

'You haven't been working at all,' she screamed.

Look kindly on the Homayouns! The Shah has left behind him many little tragedies which cause not a ripple in the deep waters of international concern.

Ladies first. There are many women like Theresa, probably blonde, probably secretaries, who have abandoned their terraced houses for something more exotic. They call their children after members of the royal family, send them to exclusive schools, speak very nicely, and on all social occasions their manners are beyond reproach.

And Fereydoun? Alas, status symbols are subject to the wind of fashion. An object once much desired becomes passé, too obviously foreign in the turning tide of anti-Western sentiment. My own wife, now, she's a prime example of a fashion slave. One minute we are sitting

41

cross-legged on the floor eating with chopsticks, the next thing I know there's a brand new art deco dining table and I have to wear a bow-tie for dinner. Things change. Besides, a man needs to relax now and then, to be treated with the awe which his mother and sisters have led him to expect is his by right. If Theresa cannot adapt, surely she could show a bit more understanding?

Fariba Baniyazdi stepped over the huddled forms of her sleeping brothers. She gripped her chador between her teeth so that her hands were free to unbar the door. Chickens squawked into the dawn light slithering over frozen mud and slush. Fariba grasped the door frame for support. From neighbouring rooms, through layers of cardboard and sackcloth nailed over empty window frames, came the muffled murmur of waking voices.

Fariba skated along the wall of the compound towards the earth closet shared with five other families – about forty people in all. Already from the street came the sound of donkeys on their way to the bazaar.

'Mama.'

Aziz grunted and thrust aside her quilt as her daughter returned.

'She's sick again,' she said as Shahnaz fell from her nipple.

Fariba picked up her little sister then put her down quickly, sickened by the smell.

'Mama, you must take Shahnaz to the hospital.'

Her mother shrugged and pushed aside Hamid's arm as she sat up.

'Hameleh hastam,' she said wearily.

'Oh no, Mama. Oh no!' Fariba shivered and wept. 'What will we do, Mama? How will we feed another?'

Her mother didn't answer.

'You must take Shahnaz to the hospital, Mama. The

42

doctor at school said anyone can go. You don't have to pay.'

'She will die.'

'No, Mama. They will make her better.'

'It is the will of God.' Besides, Aziz knew people went to the hospital and only came out to be buried.

'Mama, I will come to the hospital and show you where to go. I know.'

'Faribaja, it is too far. What about the others?'

'They can stay with a neighbour. Please, Mama. Poor Shahnaz!'

Fariba's mother stood up, at knee level a small circle of pinched faces with enormous eyes.

'Come, we must light the fire, Fariba. Your father will wake soon.'

'Mama, there's no charcoal.'

'Go next door and borrow some.'

'I can't, Mama, I went there yesterday.'

'Go to Afshar's then. Quickly, before your father wants his tea.'

Fariba stared fearfully at the sleeping figure.

'Please, Mama, you go. I will look after Shahnaz.'

Fariba picked up her baby sister and began to rock her. Her mother wrapped a flimsy chador about her shoulders and slipped her bare feet into leather sandals. Fariba heard her cough as she stepped outside into the cold air, then the rap of her knuckles on the door opposite.

When Aziz returned her cupped hands full, she tipped the charcoal into the metal tin which served as cooker and heater, struck a match, and blew gently until a blue flame arose.

'Afshar will have her child today.' Aziz fanned the flame with her skirt. 'Her children will come here as soon as your father goes out.' Aziz placed the pan of frozen water over the fire. The children watched while the ice

43

shrank away from the metal rim then diminished in a slowly rotating circle. The water began to steam.

'Quick, Fariba, the tea-leaves.'

Fariba covered Shahnaz with a heap of old clothes and brought the tin tray of tea glasses, a screw of tea-leaves and a few sugar lumps.

As the warm and bitter smell of brewing tea filled the room, Hamid Baniyazdi sat up and scratched the stubble of his beard. The children retreated to the far side of the fire. On his haunches the man approached the warmth and sat cross-legged, feeling the glow on his inner thighs. The front of his pyjamas gaped open.

'Chai mikhaid Hamid?' Aziz held out the glass but did not look up. She had drawn the chador across her face until only her downcast eyes were visible. The children watched as their father sucked the brown liquid through a sugar lump held between his teeth. Another and another. Then Hamid stood up, stretched, yawned and scratched his groin.

Aziz poured the dregs of the pan into a glass and passed it round the six children.

Masoud Gabayan sat cross-legged in the tea room. He had only intended to peer through the window and wave to his friends. Now he sat, with glasses of tea lined up as his audience waited to hear each spine-chilling detail.

'You all know my wife, don't you?' The circle of listeners held their breath. 'She might not look much now but beneath her fading attractions lurks the true spirit of Islam. The true spirit of Islam. How many of you can say that much of your wives?' The listeners, abashed, thought of their wives at home in their kitchens. 'I will tell you about my wife. Four children she has borne me, though the third, may Allah have mercy on his soul, was not destined to live. My house is always clean and neat, my children clever, and she respects me as she should.'

44

Masoud paused for a sip of tea, a puff at the narghile.

'My Roya, Allah be praised, heeded the call of the Imam. She set aside her mops and dusters to lead a crowd of one million. My wife! As powerful as the Shah himself, may he be eternally damned. She walked and the people followed. The length of Shah Reza she walked with two million footsteps at her heels. Into the jaws of death without fear or hesitation. Up to the soldiers, the emissaries of Satan. She walked carrying flowers, bearing messages of peace. She walked until her shoes were worn through and the blood from her toes stained the snow. She offered roses and was given bullets in return.'

The listeners shuffled their feet, cleared their throats, and their beads clicked through their fingers.

'I have been truly blessed,' muttered Masoud, and bowed his head in prayer.

3

Shirin Khaksar wondered why she had bothered going into the office at all. She might as well go home again. Her floor of the Ministry seemed deserted, but there was a letter from her daughter. It had been worth coming just for that. She tried to imagine Central Park, filled with man-made snow. Jackie would have enjoyed the skiing in spite of the long queues to try out the course.

Shirin picked up the phone and dialled the drivers' extension. There was no answer. She looked through her appointments book, at the meetings that would not take place. Various items required attention, but was any of it worth the trouble, she wondered? Now that the Empress had gone, who would take an interest in the Social Services?

Out of the drawer, Shirin took her cigarette holder. She stood at the window, elegant in her black dress from Paris. She was irritated by the dust gathering on the window-sill and on the onyx ashtray. The waste-paper basket was brimming and the white carpet speckled with dirt. It would soon be ruined.

She crossed the room, removed her shoes, and balanced on one arm of the swivel chair to take down the photograph of the royal family. She gave them all a quick smile, the Shah, Empress Farah, the Crown Prince, then placed the picture face-down on top of the filing cabinet. The room felt suddenly empty. Shirin decided to look for a taxi. There was no point in staying any longer.

On the fifth and top floor of a block of flats in Shemiran, Fereydoun Homayoun sat miserably in a large black leather armchair. 'The Shah was too soft,' he said. 'He should have called out the troops in the first place. Liberalization. Look where it's got him.'

Theresa stood at the living room window. Today she could see as far as the minarets of South Tehran. It was an outlook as romantic as she could ever have imagined.

'The view has improved, hasn't it?' she remarked.

'No pollution, that's why. No oil. No industry. No traffic and no bloody work either.'

'Why doesn't the Prime Minister call out the troops?'

'He doesn't trust them, that's why. Look how they fight even among themselves. It's too late for that now.'

'But he's supposed to be in charge.' Theresa ran her fingers through her hair and walked backwards and forwards across the room. 'He never even said goodbye.'

'Who are you talking about now?'

'The Shah. He just left. They say he took a handful of soil in token of his love for his country.'

'Romantic nonsense.' Fereydoun snorted. He tilted his head against the back of the armchair and stared gloomily at the ceiling.

'Darling, what's the good of having servants if you can't organize them properly? You really should tell Muna to get the cobwebs off the chandelier.'

Masoud wound a thin scarf round his neck and beckoned to his son. Today, he felt, his son should be by his side. Hussein was sixteen now; he towered over his father in his tapered trousers and sheepskin jacket.

'You see, Hussein, we cannot be sure of the army. The army was trained by the Shah. From now on, we must make sure that its loyalty is to the people.'

Hands in pockets, Masoud headed north towards the Lavijan Barracks, home of the Imperial Guard. The Immortals, some called them. Hussein marched along by his father's side, flattered by the invitation. What a thing

47

to tell his friends! Boring old school, he hoped it would stay closed forever.

Nasty, noisy, smelly things, helicopters. Forgive me for subjecting you to this experience, but the opportunity seemed too good to miss. I have my contacts, you see, and have managed to attach myself to an aerial fact-finding tour of the city. Even the government has had to adopt a policy of stepping back from it all. They have lost control of the police and of the communications centres. Tehran is in a state of total chaos.

From up here though, you'll have to admit it is marvellous. Those millions on the move, converging by instinct on various points of strategic importance. Individual drops flowing into tributaries joining ever larger and larger streams. Streams swelling the rivers to become raging torrents that sweep away everything in their path.

The army barracks are in for it, of course, but first the people need to be armed. One of the north-bound currents diverges towards a machinegun factory, an instant arsenal for a people's army. If, of course, they know how to handle such weaponry.

From up here, unfortunately, we miss a lot of the atmosphere due to this infernal noise, and can only imagine the tinkle of glass, the crunch of splintering wood and then at last, ah, the exhilarating feel of smooth, cold metal.

And where are the Immortals? Not a sign of them. One soldier crosses the Parade Ground at a run, with a nervous glance in our direction. Do not accuse them of cowardice, the crème de la crème. They have been ordered not to fight, to remain in the barracks, seething and impotent like a tiger with drawn claws.

'Down with the Imperial Guard.' The very name evoked years of pent-up hatred.

'Look out, Dad!' Hussein grabbed his father's arm.

Masoud swung round to see the officer raise a pistol at the same moment as the crowd surged forward. Masoud and the officer fell to the ground, hopelessly entangled.

Hussein leapt into the fray, grabbing at his father's coat. Others, seeing the commotion, sprang on top. Underneath the pile of confused, scrabbling bodies, Masoud felt a bristling moustache against his face.

The pistol was jammed between Masoud and the officer by the weight of bodies. Masoud felt the shape hard against his stomach as he fought for air and light. He struggled like a panic-stricken swimmer, arms flailing, legs kicking towards the surface.

There was a bang and Masoud screamed. The bodies above him fell away as if by magic. Hussein was weeping. Masoud stood in triumph over the corpse of his adversary.

'Cut off his balls,' shouted a voice. Liberated by the spilling of blood, the men now laughed and cheered. Suddenly everyone was shaking hands, and congratulating Masoud. Shoulder-high, he entered the barracks.

In front of the concrete façade of the Parliament building the people halted. With their backs to the home of the teetering government stood the soldiers. Martyrdom was all very well, but each person hoped someone else would be chosen. There had been too many dead on the streets in the last few days.

Army and people studied one another warily. Only the khaki uniforms and healthy build distinguished one from the other, brothers and fathers from sisters, wives, mothers and children.

In both, the look of strain, the unspoken pleading. Don't push us! Don't make us! Please!

The minutes ticked by, the crowd a rifle's distance away. There would be no escape from the bullet in the stomach, the pain, the blood. In the front row. Or the next. Or the next.

Somewhere a clock struck. A child cried.

Outside the Majles the rifles were lowered. A soldier unfolded a banner and stepped forward.

'We are with the people.'

Theresa Homayoun stayed at home. Fereydoun said it was safer. She would be too conspicuous with her blonde hair and fur coat. The children were driving her mad. She told herself they were only bored, just as she was. They wanted to go to the park or play with friends. If Farah took out the train set, Reza wanted it. If Theresa distracted him with a story, Farah whined to sit on her knee.

Theresa called Muna to look after the children while she shut herself up in the bedroom with the newspaper.

In Morocco, she read, the Shah strolled with his family beneath the palm trees of a heavily guarded palace. The garbage in London, due to strike action, was amassing in such quantities that the health authorities were alarmed. Zulfikar Ali Bhutto was appealing against sentence of death in Pakistan and a smiling, well-groomed Patty Hearst in the States returned to the bosom of her family.

It was like the storming of the Bastille. Qasr Prison housed some eleven thousand prisoners. An enraged mob attacked the metal doors with clubs and sticks, crowbars and mallets.

The howls and bangs, the shriek of rending iron, echoed through the building. Guards fled and prisoners trembled at the disruption of their daily routine.

Screaming like banshees, the crowd swarmed through the courtyard towards the cell blocks, hoping against hope that those they sought might be somewhere inside. Others looted offices and dragged outside files, desks and chairs and photographs of the Shah, to make a huge bonfire.

50

Some prisoners were too terrified to leave their cells, others too physically disabled to leave even if they wanted to. Acrid smoke curled through the corridors. Liberty threatened to burn them alive.

Criminals slipped silently into the crowd, fearful of qissas, the law of retribution that could still be applied by their victim's family. For them the rule of Islam was to be feared more than the Shah's.

A bewildered woman stood empty-handed before the gate.

'Now I have lost everything,' she wept, while the press cameras flashed. 'Everything I have is in there.'

The crowd shook their heads. The poor woman was quite mad. Why, what more could she want? She was free!

From his perch on the shoulders of his comrades, Masoud Gabayan had a good view of what was going on at the barracks.

'Looks like they've caught somebody,' he reported.

'Who? Who is it?'

'I can't see, we're too far away. Over there!' His supporters surged in the direction he was pointing.

The million mirrors which had reflected the splendour of the Persian Empire since the days of Fath Ali Shah now reflected stubbled faces and the darkness of the chador. As recently as a few weeks ago this sparkling mosaic had fleetingly held in its lustre the royal levées of His Imperial Majesty Mohammed Reza Shah, King of Kings. Light of the Aryans, he who had said: 'I long ago promised myself that I would never be King over a people who were beggars or oppressed. But now that everyone is happy I allow my coronation to take place.'

The profane boots stormed up the marble steps towards the Peacock Throne. They desecrated the sulky glow of vast, hand-woven carpets. The shouts were of wonder now rather than of lust for destruction. Like tourists, even the oohs and aahs were suppressed, stifled by the profusion and richness of this Ali Baba's hide-out, a cave of riches chiselled from human misery.

In spite of his bird's-eye view, from two hundred yards off, Masoud Gabayan struggled to interpret the scene for his comrades.

'It's an old man,' called Masoud.

'They've still got hold of him. He looks very frail. He seems to be wounded. He's clutching a cloth to his neck and you should see the blood! It's pouring down his jacket.'

'Who is it?'

Masoud urged his bearers closer so that he could get a better look at the gaunt face, the bowed shoulders, the shuddering gait of one for whom every step is a mastery of mind over body.

'Allah be praised,' he cried at last, the fragments of memory and fear pieced together. 'It's General Nassiri.'

The General's captors became his protectors as they fought to get him into an armoured car. Frenzied men and women tore at the old man with their fingernails, screaming their anguish for loved ones missing, maimed or dead.

General Nassiri, former head of Savak, the Shah's secret police, whose name had once spread terror, was rushed away for medical treatment for the bayonet wound in his neck. He would not cheat the people by dying now. He would die, like the eighteen thousand who had passed through his hands, at a predetermined time.

Muna, the Homayouns' maid, listened to the two o'clock news while she cleared the lunch. The radio station was under the control of Khomeini's supporters.

52

'In the name of God, most gracious and merciful,' came the voice of the Ayatollah. Muna put down her dishcloth and stood respectfully, head bowed.

'Brave nation of Iran, sisters and brothers of Tehran, now that victory is near . . .'

Muna hardly heard the rest of the broadcast.

'Khanum,' she shouted rushing into the bedroom. 'The army has surrendered. The generals are all under arrest.'

Theresa was embarrassed, caught with skirt around her waist removing her laddered tights.

'How many times do I have to tell you to knock before you come into my bedroom?' she snapped.

Like a dusty black beetle, Mrs Emani scurried round the laboratory, back and forth between work bench and sink. From time to time she smiled as if carrying on a silent conversation with herself. Her grey silk headscarf slid gently over the crown of her head and settled around her neck. There was nothing she could do about it, her hands were full. When her glasses also slithered onto the tip of her nose she nudged them back into place with her forearm.

Into the rack went the test tubes, sparkling and dripping soap bubbles onto the draining board. In the dark room Mrs Emani moved almost invisibly about her work. Her black clothes blended well with the sombre surroundings, a colour she favoured not out of Moslem propriety, but like a nun.

As Mrs Emani walked along the boulevard towards the bus-stop she stopped to buy a paper and shook her head. Mrs Emani's thoughts didn't run on revolution and change. Life was as it was and you made the best of it. Perhaps if she had been younger . . .

She climbed the steps of the vehicle, out of the lashing cold. For Jamshid, life would be different. She was determined that Jamshid would go to Europe for his education. The bus moved slowly towards the north of the city through the wreckage of the day. A taxi would have been quicker but the bus was only half the price. Every rial mattered – for Jamshid.

Opposite the Catholic Mission on Shemiran Road, Mrs Emani got out. As she stepped onto the icy pavement she slipped and grabbed at the fellow passenger who had alighted with her. He brushed her impatiently aside and Mrs Emani fell heavily on the ice. Everyone in the bus laughed. Mrs Emani picked herself up and turned away along the road, testing each step with her toe before putting her full weight on it, like an old woman.

Inside the warm church it was heaven. She remained in the back row, fearful of making a mess as the slush dripped from her boots. Her glasses steamed up and she laid them on the shelf in front of her, hitched up her scarf, buried her face in her hands, and told God every detail of her day. She knew God would have far more important things on his mind, but she had no one else to talk to.

Prayers done, Mrs Emani headed for home via the corner shop.

On the threshold she was buffeted by the heavy shopping bags of a tall blonde lady who was coming in. Mrs Emani's eyes lit up. Vegetables and fruit?

'One kilo of rice, please.'

'Sorry, no rice.'

Funny, she could have sworn . . .

'Potatoes?'

'Potatoes nist.'

'Six eggs, please.'

'I could give you two.'

Mrs Emani accepted the two eggs gratefully; they would make a nice meal fried with some fresh bread.

At the baker's, the charcoal glowed red. Stripped to the waist, with sweat pouring down their backs, the men deftly flipped over the round, flat nan, using long-handled paddles. People gathered there for warmth rather than custom and were reluctant to be served. Mrs Emani was ushered to the front of the line.

She tucked the bread inside her coat, feeling it warm against her chest and stomach and the steam rising hot under her chin. She almost ran along the street in spite of the slush: she wanted to be home before Jamshid. A child should not return to an empty house.

Soraya Gabayan dropped her pile of books on the kitchen table and cupped her hands over the pan of boiling rice.

'I'm frozen,' she said.

'You're home early.'

'I was worried.'

'Worried? You?'

'Oh Mama. I couldn't work. The university is bedlam.'

'Oh? What's happening?' Her mother pulled out a chair and sat at the table.

'Our lot's been fighting with the Islamic students. What's for tea?'

'Estanbol-e-polo. Light the samovar, would you?'

'You got some kerosene! Did you have to wait long?'

'About an hour.'

'Poor Mama, you must have been frozen.' Soraya poured a small quantity of kerosene into the burner, adjusted the wick and struck a match.

'Are you going out tonight?' asked Roya.

'Yes. I don't know whether Peter will manage to get there though.'

Roya sat at the table, too weary to move. If Soraya was going out with Peter there could be a tin of tuna fish or even some caviare for tea tomorrow. A whole day without having to queue! She often thought about Peter, whether he treated Soraya like those men she read about in the books hidden behind the flour sack. Tall, dark and

55

handsome, wealthy and clever. Roya wondered what it must be like to be given flowers, to go out for a candlelit dinner. Perhaps a dance – dancing like she had seen on films, close together Western-style.

As Roya drained the rice, she leant heavily on the sink to take the weight off her aching legs. Her chilblains were agony too, now that the blood had returned to her swollen feet.

Mrs Emani hardly had time to pick up the clothes scattered about Jamshid's bedroom floor before the front door opened.

'Haminja, I'm here.' Her voice was muffled as she reached under the bed for one last dirty sock. She heard the thud of Jamshid's satchel on the kitchen floor.

'Jamshidja!' Mrs Emani hurried towards her son, arms out-stretched, with a smile of welcome.

'What's for tea?' Jamshid turned away before his mother reached him.

'Fried egg and nan.'

'God, is that all? I'm starving.'

Mrs Emani lit the paraffin heater and stood the frying pan on top.

'Did you have a good day?'

Jamshid grunted and took a book from his schoolbag. Mrs Emani put both eggs onto her son's plate. A growing boy needed so much sustenance. She dipped her own dry bread into a glass of tea.

Fariba Baniyazdi and her mother had made little progress along the street which led to the Jewish Hospital, carrying Shahnaz. The road and pavement were jammed with people. Horns blared and headlights blazed as some cars managed to forge a passage. Faces were pressed grotesquely against the windows, counting the wounded and the dead.

'Dochtaram mariz-e,' Aziz whined, pawing the shoulder in front of her.

'Ill? Our people are dying . . .'

'What's happening, Mama?' Fariba clutched her mother's chador.

'There's been fighting.' Aziz neither knew nor cared who was fighting whom, or why.

'Mama, I thought the revolution was over now.'

Shahnaz whinged. Aziz pushed forwards, half turning to protect the baby with her body. Then, totally exhausted, she remained where she was, pinned to the spot, tortured by the thought of Hamid returning hungry to the empty room.

'Have you seen today's paper, Khanum?' Shirin Khaksar's secretary smoothed the sheets on the desk then sat in her usual chair.

Shirin looked at the photograph on the front page. At the face she knew so well. So it had come to this. No carnation now in the famous buttonhole. No pipe. The cheeks sagged in lifeless jowls, but the patient, good-humoured expression remained.

As she read, Shirin was aware of her secretary's scrutiny. She must be careful not to over-react, not to betray her deep sorrow. Hoveyda could have chosen exile while he still had the choice, but he had remained loyal to his country.

'I take responsibility for my actions. I am not afraid because I believe in God.' Amir Abbas Hoveyda. What a man, she thought! What would life offer to an exiled Prime Minister anyway? A directorship or two. A powdering of honorary degrees. A few days' notoriety in the international press, then the dull life of a stateless has-been. Shirin could sympathize with his reasons for staying. She had done the same thing herself, and hoped she could face the future with equal fortitude.

Tight-lipped and expressionless, Shirin handed back the paper.

'What do we have on the agenda for today?'

Outside the restaurant, Soraya Gabayan waited for Peter as she always did on a Thursday night. She smoked one cigarette after another and stamped each one, half finished, into the snow. She fixed her eyes on the mounting pile of fag-ends to avoid the gaze of any passer-by. After an hour, her feet and heart numb, she gave up and went home.

4

Do not concern yourselves on account of the handkerchief. Look! If I hold it up it is spotlessly white. Do you know the old nursery rhyme 'Ring-a-ring o' roses'? Though it will be familiar to many, its origins may be obscure to some. And the analogy is important. Way back in the days of the plague it was the custom to hold a perfumed handkerchief before the face. Some believed in its power to ward off disease, but its real effect was much the same as the proverbial clothespeg to dull the sense of smell.

People nowadays are not so uncivilized as to leave their dead lying in the streets, but the mortuaries (and, I imagine, many of the corpses) are literally bursting at the seams. The little fracas with the army has not been bloodless but let us be grateful for frosty nights.

However, it is no doubt my health which is of the greatest interest to you. My nose-bleeds are still 'intermittent to prolonged' and I begin to question whether their origin may not be nervous. I have long been prey to an excessive turmoil of emotion when I visit my mother's country, though in truth she hated Tehran.

I defy anyone to take a taxi into the bazaar, tassels of gold braid dancing from the velvet cloth on the dashboard, the radio playing a haunting nasal whine that goes right to the gut. Through the window floods the tang of spices and sewage. Horns blare, tyres screech, copper and brass smiths cling and clang.

There, what did I tell you? That proves it. Altitude has nothing to do with it. Pardon me. I must sit quiet and pinch my nostrils.

* * *

On their second trip to the hospital with Shahnaz, Aziz and Fariba Baniyazdi found the crowds had thinned. Inside the hospital, the hall was packed but silent. Men sat cross-legged on the floor and prayed. Women with chadors outspread like mushrooms sheltered their fearful children.

'They are all Moslems, Fariba.' Aziz backed towards the door.

'Wait, Mama, I will find a nurse. Give me Shahnaz.'

Aziz shook her head and held Shahnaz before her pregnant belly like a shield.

Fariba returned with a nurse. So beautiful the lady was in her short white dress and shoes, her black hair glossy under the white cap. Yet the men spat after her.

'I will be a nurse when I grow up,' whispered Fariba. The nurse looked down and patted Fariba on the head.

'Khanumja,' she said to Aziz, a hand on each shoulder. 'Come back tomorrow. Today, there are too many wounded. We cannot treat our own people.'

Hamid Baniyazdi and his friend Houshang shouldered their shovels and wandered onto the empty patch beyond the gravestones decked out with photographs and ribbons. In his head, Hamid tried to work out how much he would earn, how he would impress Aziz. Five hundred dead divided by how many diggers? Perhaps fifty. Multiplied by, say, one toman. Surely they couldn't pay less than that.

'Mind you,' Hamid turned to Houshang, 'I feel more like lying in a grave than digging one.'

'They're only for Moslems,' Houshang laughed.

An overseer spaced out the men. One man's width then a gap of one shovel blade. There wasn't room for more. At a signal, the shovels clanged against the frosted snow and the chanting ceased. Hamid removed his jacket and bobble hat. Blisters erupted then burst in a watery trickle on the palms of his hands.

The more robust men now stood in the graves, tossing earth up and over their shoulders. Those like Hamid, faint with hunger, rested frequently, leaning on their spades, gasping for breath.

'Houshangja,' Hamid muttered, 'what if the thousand wounded die as well?'

The overseer moved the men onto another row. They shuffled into a straight line as if on military drill. Dig, scoop, swing, dig, scoop, swing until the exercise became mechanical, the pain in the back and hands forgotten and the tomans piling up as high as the mounds of soil.

Then sunset, and the spades gathered onto a lorry. Houshang and Hamid hung around hopefully, rattling their hands in their empty pockets, but the lorry simply drove away.

'Perhaps we will be paid tomorrow when the work is finished,' sighed Hamid. Empty-handed, with no food in their bellies, the men trudged weakly towards the south.

Any Christian wife would have suspected her husband of being drunk. Roya Gabayan lay in bed wondering whether Masoud had taken leave of his senses. His cheeks were flushed and his eyes glittered as he rampaged around the bedroom.

'You should have been there. It would have done you good.'

In his mind, Masoud still stood in the crowded maidan, outside the Alavieh School.

Roya closed her eyes wearily, already hearing in her head the early call of the alarm and worrying that perhaps there was not enough yoghurt left for breakfast.

'I've never seen such a crowd. Such atmosphere, like a football match only better.' Masoud thumped a clenched fist onto the counterpane and Roya flinched.

'You remember, wife, when the Shah left? How happy everyone was? Such a feeling of change and . . . hope.' A half turn brought him to the bed end, leaning forward over the rail.

'This evening, it was all so quiet at first. Then some figures appeared up on the roof, very high up and small. But one woman saw at once who it was. "There he is!" she shrieked. "That's him. That's Nassiri." You should have heard her. "Murderer. Devil. Satan." Soon you couldn't hear any words, just roars of hatred. Then the shots.'

Masoud held his arms like a machinegun, hands pointing. 'Ratatatatatatatatatat.' He swivelled on his feet, spraying the room with imaginary fire, like a small boy playing soldiers. Then he switched roles and became General Nassiri.

'They started firing at the feet, you know, to give those bastards from Savak a taste of their own medicine, to let them feel what it was like to be in our shoes in the days of the Shah. And their legs just seemed to crumple up. But slowly, it happened so slowly.'

Roya turned on her side and closed her eyes.

'First they were like this.' Masoud stood straight, tall and proud. 'Then they were like this.' His body jerked grotesquely and fell in a shuddering heap. 'Then they were out of sight. We couldn't see over the angle of the building but the guns went on firing.

'It went so still. So quiet. You couldn't believe so many people could be so quiet. Then someone shouted "Allah-o-Akbar" and the spell was broken. Everyone began chanting: "Allah-o-Akbar. God is great." They shouted for Khomeini, for Bakhtiar. There was cheering and yelling as if a great evil had been removed from the earth. We vowed that all the other Corrupt on Earth must be rooted out. Our country must be cleansed by the shedding of more blood.'

'You shouldn't have taken Hussein. It's too late for a child to be out,' Roya murmured, half asleep.

'Child? He's a man now.'

'Khanum! Khanum!'

Theresa Homayoun paused, just long enough for the man to catch up with her.

'Salaam aleikum.' She had often bought photographs of the royal family from him. The children loved them. Real princes and princesses for their scrapbooks! Did they wear crowns all day long and eat from golden plates?

'Pictures, especially for you, Khanum. I know you like my pictures!' He thrust a pile of black and white prints into her hand. Theresa removed her gloves and then dumped her shopping bag on the ground between her feet.

'For you, Khanum, only five toman each. You are my very good customer.'

Theresa thumbed through half a dozen prints before she realized what she was looking at. Sprawled figures with limbs at grotesque angles. The same figures turned over, re-arranged, close-up. Bloodstains on snow. Stripped bodies on slabs in the morgue. White flesh. Snow-white. The dark round bruise that was a bullet hole. And the faces. She knew them.

As she looked at each photo, Theresa carefully placed it at the bottom of the pile. General Nassiri stared sightless at the sky. No longer one of the silk shirt brigade. Impeccable suits. Parties. Nightclubs.

She knew she should hand the pictures back now, but reaching the beginning she began to look through for a second time. She had never been so close to death before. The cloying tang of the street vendor's cheap cigarettes made her feel sick.

'You like, eh?' He was nodding and grinning. 'You take. For you I make especial price. Only four toman!'

Theresa was scandalized. To pay for this obscenity? She shook her head. The vendor looked aghast. The Khanum had shown such interest.

'You take for three toman, for the children. The little boy.'

Theresa thrust the photographs back at him. The man stepped away. Theresa wanted to be rid of the pictures. She should never have looked at them. It was degrading. As if she had been caught looking at the pictures in Fereydoun's desk, the ones he thought she didn't know about.

For the children? For Reza? Theresa flung the bundle in the direction of the stall, picked up her bag and ran, hearing the man's curses long after she was out of earshot.

Soraya Gabayan got off the bus at the nearest stop to the barracks. She still faced a long walk to the American base. She had been once before by taxi and endured the knowing glances, the exorbitant fare and the driver's comments. 'American doll,' he had called her. Before, she had met Peter in town or at the university, but everything was different now. He was hardly ever allowed out. Soraya regretted that she had not told him earlier about the baby.

At the gate a soldier winked and grinned at her request to see Peter but would not let her in. He said he would try and pass on a message later. How many visitations of a similar kind there would be before his battalion was evacuated!

The area around the base resembled a bomb site. It was hard to tell whether the snow-covered constructions were half finished or in process of demolition. Here and there the glow of a fire indicated the presence of squatters.

In broad daylight, Soraya told herself, there was nothing to fear. She walked, eyes on the ground, through the wasteland. A passing lorry showered her with slush while its occupants whistled and jeered. She decided to hail the next taxi that passed. Only there were no taxis.

Masoud Gabayan had not told Roya what he planned to do that day. He had not told anyone. Instead of heading for the shop, he had quietly joined the queue outside the headquarters of the Shah's secret police, in compliance with an order he had heard on the radio. All former Savak employees had been told to register their innocence.

Even in his days there as teaboy, Masoud told himself, he had not been easy in his conscience, but a job was a job. There had been Roya and the babies to consider.

Masoud turned up his coat collar and pulled his woollen hat low over his eyes. The lower part of his face was hidden by a scarf.

'Salaam aleikum, Masoud. Chetowri?'

Masoud nodded and looked away. Perhaps if he were to grow a moustache or dye his hair? From where he stood, Masoud knew that there were still three sides of the building to shuffle round before he reached the front. Not that he'd ever been through the main entrance. That was reserved for the generals, VIPs, people like that.

He had always used the small back door marked 'Staff'. From there it had been a short corridor's length to the kitchen where he brewed pots of tea, washed glasses and prepared trays. Now he was hearing that Savak had killed eighteen thousand people. And such terrible stories of torture. The worst he had seen had been a lot of frightened people eternally waiting in the corridors, but torture? No. Never.

Backwards and forwards, upstairs and down, between kitchen and offices where men in shirtsleeves sweated through mountains of paper. They hadn't looked like torturers, any of them. His blood ran cold at the thought. They had looked just like anyone else. In fact, not much different from himself. Masoud Gabayan, erstwhile

65

teaboy, currently proprietor of the Oriental Carpet Emporium. But ask anyone, ask his wife, his children, the neighbours. He'd always been a good husband and father. He didn't hold with beating his wife, that sort of thing. A word or two kept her in her place. He even gave generously to the poor and attended mosque on Fridays, when convenient.

'You remember,' he muttered through his scarf to the man in front, the one who had recognized him. 'You remember those dogs that used to hang around the kitchens?'

The man shook his head.

'Starving they were. Always there and always starving. Sometimes I used to open the windows and throw out scraps. How they used to fight. I used to think they would tear one another apart. You remember?'

The man shook his head and turned away.

'You must remember.' Masoud grabbed the man's sleeve and spun him round until they were face to face. 'The dogs got to know me. They knew how kind I was. Not like some who kicked and yelled at them.'

The other man hunched his shoulders. His face was blank.

'Do I look like a torturer?' Masoud whined.

Fariba Baniyazdi could hear her teacher's voice before she reached the classroom door. She took a deep breath and turned the handle. In the silence forty heads turned to look at her.

'Well?'

'I'm sorry, Agha. I was at the hospital.'

'Someone is ill?'

'My sister.'

The Mo'alem indicated she should sit down. Fariba's frost-chapped cheeks glowed in the warmth of the paraffin stove. Her fingers stung as she took her seat at the brown desk. She took out her exercise book and a pencil, then sat like the other pupils, hands folded in her lap, eyes on the blackboard.

It was covered in a jumble of hieroglyphics. From this far away she couldn't tell whether it was Hebrew or French. She had missed lunch but at least maths was over. And Shahnaz was tucked up safely in that enormous white cot with the cold metal bars and the starched sheets. Poor little Shahnaz, too ill to know she had been left. Now there were only her brothers left at home, four of them. Mussa was alright. She liked Mussa.

'Fariba!' The schoolmaster stood over her. 'Fariba, I asked you to read out that sentence.'

Oh God, which one? She stumbled through one of many and the giggles from the rest of the class told her she was wrong.

'Fariba. Come here.'

'Hold out your hand.'

She bit her lip as the ruler cut into her palm.

'Now, remain at the front until the end of the lesson.'

Fariba wished the earth would swallow her up. Her face was burning. She stared fixedly at the board. It was so easy to see from here. From her seat near the back of the class the words seemed to swim in a mist.

'Fariba, what does this say?'

Such an easy word. She knew it well. If only he hadn't asked she could have told him straight away.

The Mo'alem rapped on his desk. Six long hours he had spent on the rostrum today, and then to find a child like Fariba who didn't even pay him the courtesy of her attention!

Fariba stared down at her feet. The snow had melted, leaving the canvas sodden. She felt the approach of the Mo'alem's boots, the creak on the rostrum amplified by the space beneath which acted like a sounding board. The crack between the floorboards widened as if to swallow her up. The dark space between became a yawning abyss as the footsteps sounded right next to her. With a thud, she fell face forwards onto the ground.

Soraya Gabayan never knew quite what happened next. She had been walking towards the bus-stop when she became aware of the men. Whether they had come out from a gateway or had been following her for some time, she didn't know. There were three, or perhaps four. She tried to run. She lashed to right and left with her handbag, kicked and bit and scratched, but they were too many.

On a heap of rubble behind the shelter of the wall, they raped her. One after the other. Then they just left. It was so quiet. As if nothing had happened. She had been used and discarded.

One thought formed itself in Soraya's mind. Home. She had to get home. Home to her mother. She mustn't just lie there. Mechanically she straightened her hair, smoothed her coat, felt for her handbag, checked that her purse was still in it, and then stepped into the street. And no one seemed to notice. No one even gave her a second glance. On the bus she kept her face towards the window, feeling the unpleasant stickiness between her legs seep into her skirt.

At home, Soraya's mother was knitting in front of the telly. She looked up briefly, sniffed and looked back at her stitches. Nothing very interesting. Only a news bulletin. Some peasant woman. She would have turned off the set only she couldn't be bothered to get up. And now there was a woman wailing and shrieking, bringing her grief right into Roya's living room.

'My son was not in the police. Never has he been to Shiraz. Always he has lived in Azerbaijan with his mother, his family. His uniform was not a police uniform, he was a factory inspector.'

Anyway, Roya could not believe mistakes were made under Islam. Under the Shah maybe, but not under the Holy Law. The woman was obviously protesting about her son's execution out of fear. These days anything was possible.

Roya looked up at the screen again. Ah, a spokesman for the administration, to erase all possible doubt. But what was he saying? Had she heard right? That mistakes were possible. That there was not time to try so many people properly.

The phone rang. Roya carefully slid the stitches to the back of the needles and hurried into the hall.

Her husband still stood in the queue. A silent queue, each man preoccupied with the problem of establishing his own innocence. After a whole day Masoud was no nearer a conclusion. Round another corner of the building; he was getting closer. What reason had he to fear? Some of these others now, you could see guilt written all over their faces.

As for himself, well, what had a pile of dirty tea glasses to do with torture and murder? Of course there had been rumours, though he hadn't taken them seriously. How could he have known for sure what was going on? Good jobs didn't just grow on trees. Life was full of rumours. Pay them too much attention and you would never get anywhere. There was absolutely no need, he told himself, as he saw the steps in front of him, absolutely no need to worry.

The tips had been generous too. Not just the odd shilling on the edge of a teatray, but the contacts he had made in that shady business world, which had first placed him on the upward track from near-penniless stall-holder to carpet merchant.

But so many people! Half the population of Tehran seemed to be here, which was a comfort. Now, if there were any way of comparing the number going in with the number coming out . . . He tried for a bit, clicking people in and out on his prayer beads as if through a turnstile. He gave up when his thumbs met on the opposite side of the circle. Besides, it was impossible to tell if the people coming out were the same as those he had counted going in, nor how long each individual had spent inside the building.

Now that old gaffer in the green hat, a murderer if ever he saw one. He must have been inside for hours. But what did that signify? Checking, cross-checking, questioning, or merely a long queue for the men's lavatories?

Masoud wondered how it would help him even if he were registered innocent. Take a false accusation in the street, for example. He had seen enough street arrests and examples of mob vengeance over the last few days. Who was going to listen to him, or pause for long enough to go checking files? His presence here might even work against him in the long run – he might be seen now and recognized later as a Savak employee.

Masoud shrank further down inside his clothes. Even the jacket might be enough to identify him. Standard bazaar grey, common enough, but he could never wear it again, not now. He would give it away on his way home, as an act of charity. And the hat and scarf. He cursed Roya and her endlessly clicking needles. Her singular choice of colour. She'd be the death of him yet.

Soraya Gabayan climbed the stairs to the flat like an old woman. She eased her weight from foot to foot, leaning heavily on the banisters. As she put her key in the lock, she heard her mother replace the receiver.

'Soraya, is that you? I didn't hear you coming. That was Peter. He rang to say goodbye, he's being flown home tomorrow. He says he'll write.'

70

Soraya was sick in the middle of the hall carpet, a violent retching protest of her whole body.

'Darling, what is the matter?'

Soraya clung to her mother and wept.

Hamid Baniyazdi wondered why Aziz couldn't have gone herself instead of sending him, not that she would have stood a chance of getting anything, not in that fray.

Free cloth? Too tempting to resist. Never mind the bullet holes, a bargain was a bargain. Having discarded the perforated lengths, the draper padlocked his shop and hurried away. Like a pack of animals these people, he thought.

One woman had even taken out scissors and talked of divide and share. Rubbish, thought Hamid, in this life it was every man for himself. Snarling viciously he plunged into the circle of women. Brandishing a bolt of cloth like a weapon, he forced them to retreat.

Head down, heels up, Hamid flew. He shook off the last of his adversaries like flies. Round a corner, wham into a group of strolling Pasdaran.

'Well, well, what do we have here?'

Hamid shrank away but was encircled by the Revolutionary Guards.

'A thief, eh?'

Hamid simpered and licked his lips.

'It's damaged,' he said. 'Completely ruined, look. Full of holes. No use at all. Because of the Revolution.'

'And what has the Revolution to do with a Jew like you? *We* are the Revolution.' The spokesman held out his arms. Hamid threw the material at him. No price was too great for freedom. As the Pasdar staggered under the weight of the material, Hamid turned and ran.

The Mullah Afsharzadeh stumbled around his mosque in total bewilderment. The House of God a store-room for weapons? He wrung his hands and prayed to God for forgiveness. What could he do? The order came from the Ayatollah himself. All weapons in the possession of the people to be handed in to the clergy, so perhaps it was alright. He thanked God there was still time before Friday to clear up the ungodly mess.

Still the weapons kept arriving, each one greeted with a nervous 'Thank you, my son' from the Mullah. He jumped as a mountain of machineguns avalanched onto the floor in the furthest corner. The Mullah hitched up his skirts, and ran to inspect the damage to God's holy floor.

This is your Captain speaking. Surprised to see me in uniform, were you? Well, it's my wife's birthday in a couple of weeks, and I thought what better to send her than a photograph of yours truly as I cannot be with her. I wanted it to be a picture to be proud of for the occasion. The cap adds that extra couple of inches to my height. And there's nothing like a uniform, I've noticed, to send women really dotty – must be the gold braid.

Behold me then, making my way down Takhte Tavous. Past the American Embassy. Quite a crowd here today. The students have had a lot of fun here since the United States became labelled Public Enemy Number One. Today, for example, they have strung up an effigy. A very striking likeness, may I say, of Jimmy Carter.

I once attended a bonfire party at the British Embassy to commemorate some affair in the history of the English Parliament, I forget quite what it was all about, except that the name of the man struck me because it didn't sound English at all. Guido Fawkes. More like Spanish. Portuguese maybe?

But it's rather fun to build a guy, isn't it? Stuffed with straw. Some suitable clothing. Legs dangling grotesquely.

And how it burns! A great whoosh and flare and that's the end of it.

However, I mustn't be late for my appointment. Let us cross over. Do you know what Takhte Tavous means in English? The Peacock Throne. The ancient coronation chair, encrusted with jewels. Must weigh a ton. Some say that this priceless relic is no longer in the country. But if you were fleeing for your life, would you bother to take a heavy, uncomfortable thing like that with you? I certainly wouldn't.

Do you know, this place I'm going to is right next to Fereydoun Homayoun's office block. Not as smart, let me hasten to add. This is one of the original city dwellings the developers haven't managed to get their hands on. Three floors, no lifts, none of your modern double- or triple-glazed windows. In fact with an icy draught whipping round the waiting room it's quite hellish in here. Too cold to sit down.

And I don't believe there's anyone in that studio, even though I can hear the photographer's voice. These people are so proud. He wants me to believe he has another client, that I must await my turn as if it were still the good old days . . .

What a view from here! I bet Fereydoun never gets any work done these days. The American Embassy's becoming a real star attraction. Jimmy Carter's gone out in a puff of smoke. And what now? There's some of them clambering over the walls.

I hope Fereydoun's watching. Perhaps if I bang on the wall? But no, his office will be higher up than this, not on the same level at all.

By Jove, gunfire! Better keep a low profile. But who are they? Communists? Kurds? Fedayin? Mujahidin? Savak? God only knows. And not a shot fired in return by the Americans! They're all meekly parading round the front

73

yard, hands on heads. Office workers. Diplomats. Dis-
armed soldiers. What a pathetic sight!

Now a bit of drama from the street. Outriders. Followed
by the presidential car. The President himself? No. I
thought not. His deputy. Perhaps if I open the window I'll
be able to hear what he's saying.

'Dear brothers and sisters, in the name of God and of
the Revolution . . .' Phew! That was close. I got a nasty
bump on the head diving under this chair. There's a right
old slanging match going on. The Deputy PM is asking
who the invaders are – the invaders are asking who the
hell the Deputy PM thinks he is. Absolute chaos. You see.
I was right. No authority.

Aha! I hear my friend the photographic artist showing
out his imaginary customer. Better comb my hair.
Straighten my tie. Hope the bruise won't show. Thank
you, Sir. So good of you to call, Sir. Please come back in
three days and collect the prints. He closes the studio door,
but what did I tell you? Not a footstep on the stairs.
Nothing. There was nobody there at all!

Soraya Gabayan lay full-length in the bath. Her hair
floated around her in the water, heavy and long.

'Shall I call a doctor?' asked her mother.

'No Mama, please.' She feared any further intrusion.

'But you're bleeding.'

Soraya shrank lower into the water. After the initial
sting and pain as she lowered herself into the bath, the
warmth was soothing. Soraya wondered whether the
bleeding was because she was torn or whether she would
miscarry.

'We shall have to tell your father. And what about the
police?'

'What police, Mother? Have you seen a policeman
lately?'

'But what if you should become pregnant?'

74

Soraya suddenly saw the answer to her problem, for the time being anyway, until the time discrepancy should strike anybody. She realized that Peter had been worse than the men who had raped her. They at least had made no pretence of loving her.

'Did Peter say anything else?' she asked.

'I don't know. My English is not so good.'

'But there must have been something. Something about me.'

'Perhaps. He said many things that I didn't understand.'

'Will he ring again?'

'I don't know.'

Soraya closed her eyes and pressed her hands against her stomach. Inside she felt a hollow thud and gasped.

'You have much pain?'

Soraya nodded, feeling tears sting the inside of her eyelids.

'It is always so, the first time. For you it was worse.'

Soraya reached over the edge of the bath, groping for her mother's hand, and squeezed it tightly.

Aziz Baniyazdi put on her chador and sandals before speaking to her daughter.

'Look after the children, Fariba. I'm going to the bazaar. I've heard there are free kebabs. Wouldn't your father be pleased?'

Fariba sat on a heap of bedding. Her brothers crowded around her. 'Tell us a story, Fariba. Please, tell us a story.'

When Aziz joined the queue she couldn't even smell kebabs. Round one corner shuffled the line, then the next, then at last the tang of charcoal, a whiff of spiced meat. Aziz swallowed hard to stop herself dribbling. She hadn't eaten all day. Free kebabs. To celebrate. Never mind what. Would they give her eight? One for each of them. If the worst came to the worst she prayed that one skewer might hold eight chunks of meat.

She looked around, wondering where so many people had come from. Not from this area: they were neither the Moslem traders she knew nor from her own community.

Aziz shivered in her nylon chador, aware of the soft pressure behind her from a large lady in a fur coat pressing eagerly forward. Numb and light-headed, Aziz shuffled painfully into the space in front of her. Twenty or perhaps thirty people to go and then it would be her turn. She chewed the inside of her cheeks, anticipating the feel of flesh between her teeth. Smoke from the grill now stung her eyes. Oh God, be merciful, do not let them run out now! Closer and closer. She rehearsed the words in her mind. Eight kebabs, please. Eight kebabs. The stall-keeper faced her, grey from smoke and exhaustion, trapped by his rash, patriotic offer. He held out one skewer.

Aziz shook her head and tried to say it. Eight kebabs. Her lips were so cold that no sound came. She shook her head at the proffered kebab and held out both hands. The man shook his head. The woman in the fur coat shoved. Aziz looked round and realized how many people she was holding up. She heard the buzz of angry voices. With one kebab in her hand Aziz found herself roughly pushed aside.

Chins wobbling, the lady in fur demanded more and more. She held her shopping bag wide open and shovelled in skewer after skewer, dripping with grease. Aziz spun round to protest. It wasn't fair. She twisted her ankle on a clod of ice and fell.

She felt the jar of the fall right at the centre of her womb. As if on the rebound, the baby thudded against her bladder, and Aziz felt a warm wet stream trickle between her thighs. She sat there, stunned, feeling her stomach, wondering if this meant early labour.

The shopkeeper roared with laughter as Aziz struggled on to all fours and lunged after her fallen kebab. Just then a mongrel darted out of the shadows and seized it.

Still chortling, the shopkeeper held out another kebab. Aziz fumbled her chador around her, fingers numb, hands smarting from their sharp contact with the ice. Too fearful to step forward, she shrank backwards into the anonymity of the crowd.

Masoud Gabayan arrived home late. What a day! He was exhausted. Now he feared for his precious stock of carpets. Why had Allah directed the thieves to the shop next to his? Then he remembered the merchant was a Jew, and the thought brought him comfort.

But what was Roya saying? His wife, to say such terrible things about her own daughter? Soraya? Masoud frothed at the mouth like a madman.

'Please,' begged Roya, 'Masoudja, please calm yourself. You'll wake the children.'

Soraya lay on the floor, knocked from her chair by a violent blow to the side of her head.

'You whore,' screamed her father. 'You bitch. Look at yourself. No woman with self-respect would go around dressed like that. It's asking for trouble.'

'Please,' begged Roya. 'The neighbours.'

Masoud turned on her then.

'You did this. You brought her up like that. Fancy Western notions indeed. All that education and see where it's got her. She should have been married years ago. She'd have so many children by now there would be no time to gallivant after any filthy foreigner.'

'But Baba, I didn't do anything. I walked down the street. In broad daylight.'

'That's just it. It's the way you walk. Not respectably, veiled from men's eyes, but all lah-di-dah and bare legs.'

Masoud looked as if he was going to kick the girl

where she lay on the floor. Roya rushed forward dragging at her husband's sleeve.

'Leave her alone.'

Masoud lashed out at his wife. Roya clasped her head in her hands and wept silently. Abruptly Masoud stopped. His rage turned to tears.

Roya and Soraya hurried to his side. One at each elbow they supported him to a chair. Soraya made tea while Roya rocked Masoud against her breast like a child.

They sat round the table now, not looking at each other, tracing patterns in the tea Soraya had slopped as she set the full cups on the table.

At last Masoud spoke.

'No one must know,' he said.

'You are right, husband. No one must know.'

They all bowed their heads, apparently absorbed in the whorls and runnels of tea on the patterned Formica.

'But how will I endure the shame of her wedding night?' wailed Masoud.

5

On a practical level you may well wonder what I am doing in this city so long after the apparent completion of my assignment. I was ordered to wait on the Ayatollah in case of the need for a quick getaway. By the time the old gent had decided he was here for good, I had checked the plane and discovered so many faults that to be quite honest it was a miracle we arrived in one piece.

Spares and technicians will eventually arrive. In the meantime the Captain remains with his aircraft, although not, let me add, for twenty-four hours a day. I stay in the utmost luxury – not in some multinational hotel, those are not my scene at all. Step into a Hilton and you could be anywhere in the world. I prefer a flavour of authentic 'foreignness' provided it is allied to the comforts to which I am accustomed.

Behold me then, in my new residence. Slightly larger than the one overlooking the cemetery, the Hotel Alexander the Great is a modest eighty-bedroomed affair with, I believe, a staff of about one hundred. Put yourself in my place as the only guest and imagine that I am in serious danger of being trampled underfoot if I so much as raise a finger to indicate some minor requirement.

The manager now, he's become a regular bugbear. I eat less and less frequently in the dining room because he materializes every time I sit down. He weeps into my cornflakes, kebabs or caviare until I feel engulfed in the avalanche of his woes. His basic problem is that he is not allowed to sack staff (by order of You Know Who), nor can he afford to pay them. My payments, which consist of odd dollars, pesetas, deutschmarks, francs and yen which

I shake from the bottom of my briefcase or dig out of some overcoat pocket, are the only currency he ever sees.

For that reason, this fine sunny morning with a touch of spring in the air, let us step forth into the streets and seek our breakfast elsewhere. My word, that's a fine new variation to the poster of the Empress, over there to your left. Ha, ha, ha! Those teeth, like a vampire. Really, such imagination these people have!

The Mullah Afsharzadeh minced through the slush. He held his long black robe around his waist with one hand while the other clutched at the wall for support. At his age, if there was one thing the Mullah hated more than the freeze it was the thaw, this treacly, treacherous quagmire of ice and snow.

The Mullah beckoned to two small boys. Awed by his robe and turban they stepped forward to be arranged, one under each armpit, a reluctant pair of human crutches.

To the yoghurt shop he tottered, always sure of a good bargain, a walking insurance policy for Paradise. For years he had presided over an empty mosque. He had prayed for the Shah and he had prayed for those whom the Shah had led astray with his Western ways. For God was with the Mullah and he was with God. The Mullah was as sure of that fact as he was of the sun in the sky and the two boys pinned beneath his elbows. His trade was with souls, regardless of material considerations.

Like a crow he hopped from shop to shop, his wants few and easily satisfied. He lived in two small rooms devoid of furniture. He slept on a blanket on the floor, said his prayers and partook meagrely of yoghurt and honey. Day and night he was attentive to the souls under his charge. He took on himself their spiritual cares and their practical problems. He listened, he passed judgement, but there could be no compromise where God was concerned. God spoke and man must be humble before

His infinite wisdom. The Mullah looked on the souls in his care as raw crystals to be polished until they reflected the Divine Light. If pain was part of the process, no matter, let God's will be done.

'Thank God for the sun,' thought the Jew, Hamid, as he stood in the queue. But these women took their time! When the door of the latrine opened next, Hamid pushed his way to the front and put the women in their place with the stallion-like splash of his urine.

Afterwards he lingered in the yard, arms outstretched, face tilted to receive the sun's blessing. His children clung around his knees. Baba was in a good mood, they could tell. No need to fear him now.

Aziz hastened to make tea, to prolong this moment of peace. The charcoal lit with the first match and soon tea-leaves danced on the bubbling water.

Hamid, perched on the window-sill, graciously accepted the amber glass. Surely better times were on their way? Yesterday's news of the ban on imported meat was surely good. To feel the knife in his hand once more, the last feeble flutterings of an upturned sheep as its life-blood drained into the gutter. Such power of life and death he had held in his slaughterer's hand. Chicken, sheep, goats, it was all the same to him.

Idly, Hamid grabbed at a chicken. He held it squawking by the legs and tickled its neck with the point of his knife.

'Baba no,' the children squealed. 'No! That is Mama's best hen. Mama, Mama, come quickly.'

'Hamidja,' begged Aziz, 'Hamidja, please no. That is my best layer.'

Hamid laughed and pressed the knife a little harder. A speck of blood trembled on the brown feathers. The chicken became still. Aziz closed her eyes. The children stared. Though his knife ached for the spurt of blood,

Hamid flung the bird away. It fell heavily, staggered to its feet and limped away in a ruffle of feathers.

Hamid clasped his hands across his belly and roared at his own joke. His gums gaped and the air was filled with the stench of his breath.

'I'm sorry, but with business as it is . . .' The architect Fereydoun Homayoun spread his fingers and dropped his hands heavily on the desk. He looked at the young man with what he hoped was an expression of regret, almost paternal. The young man looked at the carpet.

'Any other time, I would have been proud to have you among my staff.' Fereydoun began to drum with his fingers on the table, wondering how much longer he would have to go on like this. The lad's work had been terrible considering he was a qualified architect, but Fereydoun had been under pressure to give him a job. The boy's father had held an important post under the Shah. Now, of course, matters were different.

'Perhaps if things improve . . . as I'm sure they will . . .' continued Fereydoun.

The young man shuffled to his feet and straightened his tie.

'Perhaps I should keep in touch?'

'Of course. I hope you will.' Fereydoun stretched across the desk and held out his hand.

'A reference might come in handy.'

'Oh, a reference.' Fereydoun drew a sheet of headed notepaper in front of him and began to write.

The sun was shining full on the shop front of Masoud Gabayan as Mrs Emani crossed the road. Tomorrow, Ali had said to call about the carpet, and that was ten days ago. Her footsteps quickened in anticipation.

The sun had a warmth in it today that made her forget the slush underfoot and think forward to spring. And summer. And Jamshid getting older and still no arrangements made for his education abroad.

She paused before entering the shop, lost in thought and frowning at the grimy dullness of the brass doorknob. Then she went inside.

'Salaam aleikum, Ali,' she called.

Ali grunted but did not look up from his work.

'Xube?' she inquired.

Ali snorted as if the traditional inquiry after his health didn't deserve to be answered. How could he waste time on trivialities with the cares of the Carpet Emporium on his shoulders and the huge stack of carpets awaiting his attention?

'The sun is pleasant today.' Mrs Emani stood fidgeting at the handle of her shopping bag.

'The sun?'

'See how it shines through the keyhole.'

With a pained cry Ali got up and spread a newspaper over a fine Kashani rug to protect it from the brilliant sliver of light.

'The sun makes extra work,' he said.

Mrs Emani nodded her agreement. 'If you have a soft cloth I could give the doorknob a quick shine.'

'Doorknob? Hah!'

'I just noticed as I came in. The fingerprints.'

'Fingerprints, Khanum? Apart from Mr Gabayan and myself, you're the only person who leaves fingerprints.'

'Perhaps if I could save you the trouble . . . Only yesterday I polished the – ' She had been about to say church brass. It was one of her favourite tasks, to rub up the candlesticks and then see them gleaming back at her from the altar during mass. But it wouldn't do to admit to Christianity, not now, in front of Ali. 'Some candlesticks. At home,' she added and smiled lamely. 'Such a difference it makes . . .'

'You women,' said Ali. 'Always the same. Nothing's

ever good enough for you.' He took off his fez and flung it on the floor in exasperation.

'Khanum, rest assured that if the doorknob was sufficiently important, then it would have received my personal attention.'

'Oh yes. I can see that. I'm sorry.' Mrs Emani turned towards the door. It wouldn't do to ask for her rug now, not after she had upset Ali.

'I must do my shopping,' she murmured. 'Perhaps today there are tomatoes.'

'No tomatoes.'

Mrs Emani paused in the doorway.

'No tomatoes in the whole of Tehran,' Ali shouted.

As Mrs Emani closed the door of the carpet shop behind her, she gave the doorknob a tentative rub with the forefinger of her gloved hand.

Roya, the carpet dealer's wife, looked at the clock and sighed. For a few minutes she sat with the book open on her knee. Those women! So beautiful, so free and yet so feminine. They knew so much. Lived such interesting lives and yet in the end sacrificed everything to this thing called love.

She returned the book to the secret place in the pantry and chopped onions for tea. Love must be a powerful emotion she thought. But then the men were so wonderful, there was nothing like them in Iran. Masoud had never had the power to move her in that way.

She melted butter in the saucepan then tipped it until it was coated in a thick golden swirl. Little by little Roya added the rice. Her dream had been to see her daughters live the way people did in those books. To see Peter and Soraya discuss politics, the theatre, even their friends, had been a joy. To see the love and honesty between the two young people had brought home to her the inadequacy of her own marriage.

It was all the fault of the Shah. If he had stayed, there would have been no Revolution, no Islamic Republic. Peter would be safely in his barracks, Hussein at school, Masoud in his shop, the police on the streets and Soraya . . .

Roya felt ill at the thought of the rape. In her mind it had become linked with the body of that dead student at the demonstration. With rumours of a thousand dead in Mashad, perhaps Tehran had escaped lightly.

Her knife bit through the purple satin of an aubergine. Slice by slice, Roya added it to the mince with a shake of cinnamon. She spread a layer of meat over the layer of rice, topped the meat mixture with the remainder of the rice, a few dobs of butter, a thick cloth and finally the pan lid.

Still only ten to three. Time to finish her book. She knew what the end would be: Rosie would marry Charles. But life was so unpredictable these days that Roya needed the reassurance of a happy ending, to know for certain that Rosie and Charles would live happily ever after.

Romance! My wife's attitude is much the same, though her literary tastes tend to be slightly more up-market. The novels she reads have had reviews in the quality press, but the sentiments contained are similar. If no tall, dark, handsome lover waits around the corner, it is necessary to invent one. How else to explain the meteoric rise of the Ayatollah?

This morning he left Tehran for Qom, and I wish this holy city peace. Since early morning the women have bowed and stretched in the streets in attitudes of prayer most graceful to behold. From closer quarters we can see that upright, they press their hands to their aching backs. Bowed low before the Almighty, they have worn through to the stubble of their scrubbing brushes.

It seems that they now wear, these women, the garments

with which they have buffed the kerbstones. No matter,
each hole in each dusty garment will win its indulgence in
heaven.

Green flags hang limp from lamp-posts, the green of
spring, of hope, of fertility – colour of the Prophet.

'Allah-o-Akbar.' The crowds burst the cordon of local
militia with carnations in their rifle barrels.

'Be blessed the family of Mohammed. Our leader has
come.' He alights at the shrine of Fatima to pay homage.
Homage to a woman. Daughter of the Prophet. Homage
to all womankind. The women go wild, seduced by a
gesture – by the promises not only of Paradise but of free
water, free electricity, free buses, in short, heaven on earth.

But remember Soraya. She too listened to the voice of
the Serpent.

'Miss Gabayan, where is your essay?'

'I'm sorry, it's not quite finished.

'Look, my dear, Revolution or no Revolution, we have
exams in a couple of months. Aren't you concerned?
Hasn't it occurred to you that the repeal of the Family
Protection Act will affect you personally? Because in my
opinion it will set you women back a thousand years.'

The professor leaned back and fingered his beard.
Should he shave it off? He had been shaken by that taxi
driver who hissed 'Communist.' It had been his hope that
the combination of beard and three-piece suit would
appeal to the left-wing students and the right-wing staff
on whom his job depended. What the heck? What were a
few whiskers. Now this girl was the one who ought to be
concerned. The rights she stood to lose if the law was
repealed, why it would mean . . .

The professor laid down his pen and looked up.

'Miss Gabayan, whatever is the matter?'

* * *

'Of course you must give up your job now,' Fereydoun suddenly announced.

'Why?' Theresa waited for the same old arguments – it looks as if I can't support you, a wife's place is in the home, the children need you. She clung to her job as her very last symbol of independence.

'Because of the political implications,' said her husband.

'Political implications?' Theresa was at a loss. She simply took dictation and typed each day from eight-thirty to twelve-thirty and collected a cheque at the end of the month.

'Oh come on, darling, don't try and tell me you've never thought about it.'

'But I haven't,' protested Theresa.

'Don't be so naïve. You know what they say.'

'No, I don't.'

'That your firm of solicitors had close links with the royal family.'

'Well, so did you,' Theresa argued.

'Darling, please be reasonable. Your job could put me in a lot of trouble.'

'What about my car?' To lose her car was the thing Theresa dreaded most. With it she could go where she liked. Fereydoun didn't like her to use taxis. He said it wasn't safe. 'I *need* my car.'

'You managed without it before.'

'Fereydoun, please.' Theresa felt her voice break.

'Come, come, darling.' Fereydoun held out his arms to her. Though Theresa despised herself for doing it she sat on her husband's knee, her arms clasped around his neck. Fereydoun's head nestled against her breast and he stroked her thigh.

'You shall have your car, darling.'

'Thank you, darling,' Theresa murmured. 'I will resign today.'

'That's my girl,' whispered Fereydoun through her long blonde hair.

Here I am, back already to share this little joke with you. Promises made in Qom cause the poor old Prime Minister and his government sleepless nights. Whence cometh all this running water, electricity and the money for the free buses? Divine intervention? Eshallah!

But there is one introduction I have yet to make – the flower of the Gabayan family, a delicate rosebud, poised, tremulous on the brink of womanhood. In figure now surpassing, in beauty at least the equal of the tarnished Soraya. If it is Eastern Promise you seek, look no further, though how Masoud could have sired such loveliness defeats the imagination.

At the sound of Soheila's footsteps on the stairs, Roya dived into the pantry and read the last few sentences of her book among the sacks of rice and flour.

'Soheilaja! I was just tidying . . .' Roya's smile of welcome froze.

'Whatever's the matter, Mama? Why are you staring like that?'

'Soheila, take that off. Don't ever let me see you dressed like that again.'

'You mean a chador, Mama? Why? You always wear one.'

'That's different, Soheila, I was brought up to.'

'Then why shouldn't I wear one too?'

'Soheila, after all the time and trouble spent on your education, what do you think you're doing?'

'Mama, all my friends wear chadors now.'

'But haven't you a mind of your own?'

'That is exactly why I am wearing a chador, Mama. We want to be taken seriously, for people to see our minds not our bodies.'

'But Soheilaja, it's so ugly. Your beautiful hair, I can't see it. You haven't cut if off, have you?'

'Mama, I want you to see the real me, not my hair.'

'But I love all of you, you are my daughter.'

'I'm still the same person inside.'

'Soheila, it's not that your hair or your body have any effect on me. But you're a very beautiful girl. To me your body reflects your whole character and personality.'

'Why are you making such a fuss?' went on Soheila. 'I'm nearly thirteen now. Let me decide for myself.'

'All these years I have worked and hoped,' sighed Roya, leaning against the sink. 'Such dreams I have had for you.'

'But it's *my* life, Mama.'

Shirin Khaksar looked at her daughter's writing on the envelope and was tempted to save the letter until she went home. Then, unable to resist the temptation, she spread the thin sheets of air mail paper on the desk.

Dear Mum,

How are things with you? I saw Dariush last night and he sure is worried. The new Embassy staff here are on the look out for Savak agents, likely to be disguised, they say, as students who have plenty of money but cannot pass their exams. If that doesn't just describe my brother! Honestly Mum, Dad gives Dariush far more money than is good for him.

You've no idea how many awkward questions are being asked about the previous Iranian Ambassador to the US. All the money he spent financing demonstrations in favour of the Shah and why he paid the school fees for Haile Selassie's grandchildren.

The strike of school buses is a terrible drag. Sometimes Dad gives me a lift, when he doesn't I go by subway. But I'm planning to walk as soon as the weather gets warmer.

Mum, I do worry about you. Why can't you come and stay for a while?

Shirin turned over the pages. As she read Jacqueline's letter, she could happily have caught the next plane out.

But Shirin knew that she would not be allowed to go now: her name was on the list of proscribed persons.

Still irritated by the amount of time it had taken her to find a parking space, Theresa Homayoun knocked on her boss's door and entered the office. She had intended to hand in her notice without delay, but suddenly it seemed that the boot was on the other foot. Theresa was quite prepared to resign, but not to be sacked.

'Why me, why get rid of me?' she demanded.

'Look Mrs Homayoun, while we greatly appreciate your work, there is no longer sufficient business to justify a private secretary for each partner.'

Theresa thought of recent mornings, time passed pleasantly enough polishing her nails or on quick sorties into the streets to hunt for peanut butter. The children did miss their peanut butter and it was so much better for their teeth than jam.

'Perhaps in better times . . . ?' The partner stood up, leaning across his desk towards her, holding out his hand.

Theresa stood up and ignored the partner's hand. There had been a time when they would not have dared to do this to her, when the matter could have been put right by a quick phone call from her husband. Times being as they were, she turned and walked out.

The partner was relieved. Such a lot of people to get through and not all of them would take the news as calmly as Mrs Homayoun. He looked after her regretfully. The foreign staff were so much more efficient. Reliable. As well as adding a touch of glamour to the office. The lawyer foresaw his doom in the shape of the middle-aged women in chadors who now darkened his offices. As if anyone wanted a secretary simply for her typing. He watched Theresa's departing legs and sighed. Her habit of scratching her left ear as she took dictation, her left ear like a tiny sea shell. Why, given a couple more weeks . . .

A university professor was an unlikely candidate to be first recipient of the news of Soraya Gabayan's pregnancy. Soraya was surprised at herself afterwards, though the feeling of relief remained, that at last somebody knew.

Now she fully intended to follow his advice that she should confide in her mother. She had resigned herself to the fact that after twenty-two weeks of pregnancy, a miscarriage was extremely unlikely. Not even rape had served to dislodge Peter's baby.

She practiced on the bus what she would say to her mother. 'Mama, I think I'm pregnant.' No. There were no longer any grounds for the 'think'. 'Mama, I'm pregnant' sounded too bald. She did not yet look pregnant, though she had trouble fastening her clothes, especially her jeans. 'Mama, my period is late' sounded more innocent. Let her family blame the rapists. Her father would kill her if he found out about Peter.

Soraya got off the bus. It was not going to be easy. She'd have to catch her mother alone. Perhaps when Hussein and Soheila were in bed and her father out of the house. But that would mean feeding her resolve all through supper. She reached the block of flats.

With eyes red and swollen, Roya Gabayan looked up as the second shadow of the day crossed her threshold.

'God be merciful,' she cried. 'Not you too. Such lovely daughters did I have. But now they're transformed into hideous crows. All I have done for you and is this how you repay me?'

'Mama, it's only a piece of material, I'm the same person inside.' Soraya felt the lie as she spoke it. How could she explain while her mother was in this state that she was wearing a chador to hide her stomach?

Roya slumped at the kitchen table.

'Such hopes I had for my daughters.' she wailed. 'My beautiful daughters who would go free where I fear to tread. Who would study and be happy like those women in the magazines. Think of Jackie Kennedy! But what do the pair of you do? Throw it all back in my face, everything I've done for you. And will you be content with a life like mine?'

'Mama, stop making such a fuss. Everyone's wearing a chador nowadays, it doesn't mean a thing, it's just the fashion. It's simply a veil, like you always wear.'

'Yes. Like I always wear.'

6

March 11th 1979. International Women's Day! My Chinese wife, in a Norman Hartnell hat, will be singing Fijian hymns in Notre Dame. Not that my wife shows any political or feminist consciousness whatsoever. She knows that the farmhouse in Provence, private schools for the children in Switzerland, annual visits home, and her entire life of luxurious idleness depend entirely on me. No. She will not be there in the same spirit as my mother, whose heart bleeds for her fellow countrywomen (when she gives them a thought), but because of the champagne reception afterwards and the opportunity to boast about her new holiday home.

That however seems to be the nature of women. Let us eavesdrop a while on the women gathered in the Technical Faculty of the University of Tehran. Among a gaggle of schoolgirls I recognize the delectable Soheila Gabayan. Chador she may wear, whose black diagonals emphasize her perfect complexion, but does she comment to her neighbour in the borrowed terms of Marxist analysis on the current state of women in Iran? Alas, she is giggling about the dowdy attire of the thick-waisted women on the platform.

Theresa Homayoun, I see, is on the balcony, conspicuous as ever, oblivious to the cries of 'Sit down Missis.' Ah, she has found her friend Homa, but now there are not two seats available together. Further kerfuffle, excuse me's, back a row, forward two rows, shuffle sideways, but I was told you couldn't save seats, etc. Such a fuss. People gesture angrily, flap their arms, the speeches are about to begin.

At last, order. They have plonked themselves down in the gangway after the precaution of dusting the step. Theresa frowns at her muddy glove. Outside it is snowing heavily. Half-molten flakes cling to the ends of her coat hairs, a shower of pearls against the black fur.

Nothing unpredictable about the speeches, I'm afraid, but plenty of audience participation. I caught sight of Soraya Gabayan somewhere down there just now. Of course the Law Faculty will be here in force. They have a vested interest in the day's proceedings.

But what man in his right senses would be here? There are a few reporters to whom I can attach myself for safety. A government spokesman sits on the rostrum looking mildly amused. I bet his wife isn't here today though. That dear lady will be at home, afraid that this foul weather might ruin her hair.

Disappointing though it may seem to the feminists among you, you are of course fully aware by now of the following facts, that (a) God is a man, (b) these women are manipulating the spirit of Revolution in purely selfish terms and (c) whatever they may say to the contrary, those we have met so far have proved themselves totally incompetent in the daily management of their own lives.

Yes! I anticipate your howls of impotent rage, dear ladies, but may I just support my thesis with a quotation from none other than His Imperial Majesty the Shah, one-time King of Kings: 'In a man's life women count only if they are beautiful and graceful and know how to stay feminine . . . What do these feminists want? Equality you say. Indeed! I don't want to seem rude but . . . You may be equal in the eyes of the law but not, I beg your pardon for saying so, in ability.'

Exactly! There we have it! An Imperial Proclamation! I am not a monarchist but it appears that on this occasion our former King and I do share certain views. But please, do not let me spoil your pleasure in these admirable proceedings. Please, listen for yourselves and make your own judgement.

Sabotage, some said, when the loudspeaker system broke down and fifteen thousand women poured out of the building in a gesture of solidarity with their sisters who were standing outside. Gaining courage from their numbers, the ranks of marchers soon doubled as more and more women left the sidewalks to join them. Blinded by the thick surge of snowflakes they trudged defiantly onwards to plead their cause, like some army deploying for battle. Then the single column branched to form an arrowhead, three prongs to strike simultaneously.

Soheila Gabayan and her school friends were swept towards the modest house of one of the religious leaders responsible for education, to beg to be allowed to continue their studies.

Soraya Gabayan was just one of ten thousand bound for the Ministry of Justice, determined to be allowed to practise their chosen profession and to defend the Family Protection Act. Their struggles would soon be drowned in the total submersion of the legal system by the Sharia Courts of the Mullahs.

Theresa Homayoun and Homa, her friend, chanted as they walked: 'In the Spring of Freedom there is no freedom at all.' Bareheaded and proud, in spite of the snow, they walked towards the Prime Minister's office to show their total rejection of hejab, of all repression and sexual discrimination.

In her chauffeur-driven car, Shirin Khaksar was travelling towards the Ministry for Social Development.

'Will you please turn that noise off,' she snapped, annoyed by its intrusion into her thoughts.

There was a click and a sigh as the driver complied with her wishes.

'Khanum,' he remonstrated. 'That was the Ayatollah.'

'I'm sorry.' One had to be so careful nowadays. 'Do turn it on again, but quietly, please, I need to think.'

Shirin laid aside her notes for the morning's meeting and stared at the slogans on the walls they passed. 'Down with Fascist Shah.' 'The Shah must die.' The month of freedom had done nothing to enhance the beauty of the city.

At the traffic lights, Shirin wound down her window just enough to pass out twenty rials and receive a copy of the day's paper. As the lights changed to green and the car edged forward the paper boy spat after her car. A chauffeur-driven Mercedes smacked of the luxury of a bygone era, perhaps she ought to take taxis in future, though Shirin wondered where that would leave her driver. One job less, one more starving family.

But there would soon be no alternative. Shirin smoothed the paper on her knee. She couldn't believe it. She looked again and her breath now came in short gasps.

'Look, Khanum!' The chauffeur braked hard and laughed as two Revolutionary Guards dragged a prisoner across the road in front of the car.

'Another of the Shah's stooges.' He clapped and gave a thumbs-up out of the window in a gesture of solidarity. 'I wonder if they'll get him as far as the prison.'

'Why ever not?' asked Shirin.

The chauffeur laughed and squeezed his hands round his own neck.

'Drive on,' she said abruptly. 'We shall be late.'

Shirin returned to the paper, but her hands shook. A middle-aged woman of her own Bahai faith had returned home after a day in the fields. Preparing the evening meal at her stove she had been surprised by two revolutionaries. They had tied her up, dowsed her with petrol and set her alight. When the flames burned through her bonds she had run outside to find her husband dying in a ditch.

The picture showed the dead mother surrounded by her children, the illegitimate offspring of an adulteress, since a Bahai marriage was no longer recognized under Islamic law.

In the back seat Shirin closed her eyes and prayed for strength. The stench of burning hair filled her nostrils, the terror of the silent children drummed in her ears, but she knew that she must hide her feelings, that her survival depended on this.

'Women Against the Veil' Shirin read on a placard outside the Ministry of Justice, where the car was forced to stop by demonstrators. She shrank back into a corner. She had to preserve her anonymity. She was already endangered by her faith, her job – and the jealousy of the men in her department.

'Women,' shrugged the chauffeur. 'The Ayatollah will soon sort them out.'

'The Ayatollah has also said that he will not tolerate insults to women.'

The chauffeur shrugged. 'You should be at home, Khanum, with your children.' He leered at the women in Western dress.

Shirin knew that although the women's cause was her cause, through them she stood to lose all she had struggled for over the last twenty years. And publicity could be fatal. She looked at her watch.

'Will we get to the office by ten?'

'We might be here all morning.'

'Can't you go another way? Round the back perhaps?'

'Look behind us, Khanum.'

Shirin saw that the road behind the car was solid with people. To the right were the women, on the left the men.

'It might be easier on foot.'

As Shirin unlocked the door, it was dragged open by the women who now surrounded the car. She clung on to her briefcase as her arms were taken by women on both sides, who greeted her, rejoicing.

'Please, I must join my friends over there.' Shirin excused herself with a nod in the direction of the Ministry of Education. At that moment a press camera flashed inches away from her face.

She broke away and struggled through the crowd.

Inside the office labelled Khanum-e-Shirin Khaksar, the assembled men had become impatient. Lounging in the armchairs, they looked at their watches and flicked ash into the onyx ashtray.

Shirin's deputy looked down into the street.

'She'll never get here now,' he said with satisfaction. 'I suggest we begin the meeting. Women are not reliable. It is not in their nature.'

The other men looked faintly uneasy. Khanum-e-Khaksar kept tight control over her staff.

'The Ayatollah said so,' said the deputy. 'You will please record that I formally open the meeting in the absence of the Khanum and that no apology has been received for her non-attendance.'

It was only a matter of time, thought the deputy, before he stepped into her shoes. High-heeled shoes at that, and nice legs – he'd often noticed them through the kneehole of the desk. He thanked God that his own wife was safely at home with their five children clinging to her skirts.

The deputy ran his fingers proprietorially along the chrome edge of the desk. He straightened his tie and shuffled his bottom into the black leather chair. Just a bit too high for comfort, in need of a slight downward adjustment.

The door opened and the deputy leapt to his feet.

'Khanum-e-Khaksar.' He beamed and bowed as the power of the Ayatollah's pronouncements faded in the presence of his superior.

Roya Gabayan put on the shelf five envelopes, marked 'Electricity', 'Paraffin', 'Food', 'School Fees', and 'Clothing'. With the greatest care she calculated that the total amount would last them for five months.

'So, you have sold the motor bike,' she had commented when Masoud had handed over the money.

'A man does not need a motor bike to enter the kingdom of heaven,' came the curt reply.

Roya was afraid these days of the fanaticism that ruled her husband's actions. While Masoud pursued the pathway to Paradise, she foresaw only total ruin for herself and her children. Just one slip and they would all plunge into the ocean of poverty from which they had escaped.

'But what about the shop?' she asked.

'What about the shop?'

'When will you sell another carpet?'

'Today, we march against the women. Tomorrow who knows?' Masoud shrugged and sipped his tea.

'The women? You would march against your own daughters?'

'Against the women who sin, who refuse the veil and offend God. The Ayatollah says . . .'

Roya struggled to keep her temper. She wrapped her chador more closely about herself. In spite of her efforts at self-control, Roya's voice cracked.

'We cannot live without money.'

Masoud looked up at his wife, only her blazing eyes visible. She suddenly looked years younger, desirable. He stretched across the table and thrust a hand inside her chador to stroke her breast.

Roya was trembling.

'When you have destroyed everything, will God provide food? Will he give us a roof over our heads?'

The hand that reached out to caress became the instrument of God's vengeance. The blow on the side of her head knocked Roya from her chair. She lay, a plump, middle-aged woman like an overturned beetle, struggling to get up, while Masoud left the room.

Masoud walked fast, clicking his beads. It was not just his wife that he hated, radiating perfection and promise one minute, sin and blasphemy the next, but all women. Near the Ministry of Justice, he saw the road filled with them, shameless in their tight Western jeans and with their bare heads, their dark hair curled and gleaming, eyes lustrous with cosmetics. They excited him in the way his wife did when she exhibited a will of her own. He would have liked to reach out and touch them, but did not dare, not like some men that he knew.

He saw some of his friends on the other side of the road, sniggering and making obscene gestures at the women. Some were even exposing themselves. Grinning, Masoud struggled to reach them. Weaving among the throng, he brushed up against a tall blonde lady. Masoud cautiously slid his fingers over the rounded curve of her buttocks, then pinched hard.

He walked on with his hand burning, his heart glowing. He'd done it. He'd actually touched her. Not a Moslem woman of course, that would have been a sin – but these foreigners! It was disgusting how they invited such attentions in a public place.

'They're no better than prostitutes,' he said to his mates.

'Just look at that one!' His friend held one hand over his mouth and chortled with admiration.

'This was worth coming for, wasn't it?' said Masoud. His excitement increased. His beads flew between his fingers, but however fast he murmured the Holy Name he could not dull the throbbing in his groin.

Roya's decision to march had been taken at the moment she picked herself up off the floor and realized that it was not just a question of the veil. If her chadored daughters accepted hejab, they were also repudiating the gift of choice and freedom which she had thought she could offer them. Soheila, a mere child of twelve, was simply taken in by fashion. Soraya dressed up like that was another thing. Perhaps she was mourning for Peter?

Roya blinked through the heavy snowflakes and cursed the Revolution – for opportunities spoiled and lives turned topsy-turvy. Even her husband, her Masoud, had gone as mad as the rest of them. He, who had never set foot in the mosque if he could help it. Now it was all 'The Ayatollah said this' or 'The Ayatollah said that' until she wondered whether he had a thought of his own left in his head.

Today, Mrs Emani's shopping bag was not quite empty. It contained a few potatoes and a tin of lard. She planned to make chips. As she scuttered along she thought how pleased Jamshid would be.

She made a quick diversion to the carpet shop, just in case. Two months it had been. Two whole months of putting her bare toes on the bare floor while she groped under the bed for her slippers. She had come to blame the missing rug for the intense cold in the flat, although she knew in her heart this was not so. Some mornings required the recital of the whole Litany of the Saints to dull the anguish of getting up, but God, she knew, would be merciful in His own time. He simply required patience. If the rug was not ready, she must be in some way at fault.

The door of the carpet shop was shut. Mrs Emani

pushed gently on the handle. Then she knocked and called out, timidly.

'Ali.'

The door swung open.

'Oh, it's you,' said Ali.

Mrs Emani smiled and shrank into the darkness of the recessed entrance.

'My carpet?' she ventured.

'I see that you follow the wishes of the Ayatollah.'

Mrs Emani smiled and blinked.

'Hejab,' said Ali. 'The veil.'

'Oh, yes. I see.' Mrs Emani plucked nervously at the knot of her black silk headscarf.

'You're really into the new Moslem image, I see. You should have seen them earlier, all those women going past. Disgusting, exposing themselves like that. How do their husbands allow such an exhibition? Why, if my wife ever . . .' Ali stooped over Mrs Emani, only inches away from her, spitting in his excitement.

The women sat peacefully on the steps of the Ministry buildings, content to let their numbers add weight to the grievances submitted in writing. They had faced death in the front ranks of the Revolution in the mistaken belief that the soldiers would not fire on them. Now they waited for their share of the liberty that was being bandied around.

Masoud Gabayan stood in the front row of the chosen, sneering and jeering cheerfully enough with his friends until melting snow dripped inside his jacket collar and his fingers became numb. It was boring just standing. He idly picked up a Coke can from the gutter and tossed it into the crowd. His mates laughed. Suddenly they were all stooping and picking up whatever they could get hold of – rubbish or stones.

The sight of blood fired passions further. In the name

102

of Allah, Masoud allied himself with the age-old Islamic punishment for sexual offences. He atoned for his lewd thoughts and felt his spirit cleansed with every missile. The women panicked. Some fell, others tried to escape but were hemmed in by the men.

With his friends, Masoud followed those few that got away, up the sidestreets, through narrow alleyways and passages throwing whatever came to hand. When the women took refuge inside buildings they broke the windows and howled, until the novelty wore off and their blood lust was assuaged.

'I could do with a beer,' said Masoud. They turned back into the main streets to find the shops and cafés looted. There was not a glass of beer, chai or Seven-Up to be had for love nor money.

Little Fariba Baniyazdi and her brothers were playing in the alley outside their home when Aziz said she was going to the Social Work Office, to ask for food.

'I will come with you, Mama.' Fariba did not want her mother to go alone. There could be danger in the streets, or Mama might fall again on the hard-packed snow and hurt herself.

'Please let me come.'

'It is better that you look after the little ones.'

So Fariba stayed, but the joy went out of her game, and although they played for an hour, there was still no sign of Mama coming back.

As evening came and a bitter chill settled on the Jewish Quarter, Fariba took her brothers indoors. They shivered together, cheeks red and chapped, fingers purple with cold. And still no Mama.

Then footsteps came nearer. Fariba looked up, eyes brightening. Mama at last? Food or no food, it didn't matter. Only that Mama should be safely back.

But the figure that stepped into the dark room was too

large for Mama. The children recognized their father and shrank back against the wall.

'Aziz?' growled Hamid.

'Mama has gone to get food.'

'She has, has she?'

Fariba put an arm around her nearest brother.

'Why isn't she back yet?'

No one answered.

'I said, why isn't she back?'

Hamid walked towards Fariba. Fariba bowed her head, hunching her body over Mussa, to protect him.

'I am back.' The voice came out of the darkness beyond Hamid. Hamid spun round.

'What have you got?'

Aziz held out a small packet of rice.

'Good God, is that all? Is that what I have come home to?'

Hamid lashed out with his arm and knocked Aziz off balance. She fell heavily, banging her head against the wall, scattering the precious bag of rice. The boys began to cry. Hamid turned on them with a snarl and they whimpered into silence.

Aziz lay where she had fallen with her knees drawn up to protect her unborn child. Fariba closed her eyes, not wanting to see, but unable to shut out the terrible sound of her father's shoes thudding into her mother's flesh. And the soft tap-tapping noise of the chickens as they pecked up the grains of rice.

'Where d'you think they're taking us?' Theresa Homayoun asked her friend nervously. Homa peered out of the bus window.

'Well, it's not Qasr Prison anyway.' They both smiled with relief.

Theresa and Homa were among the numbers of women loaded on to buses by the Revolutionary Guards.

104

'Evin Prison then?'

'It's possible,' Homa shrugged. 'We're going in the right direction, I think.'

'Will they keep us for long?'

'Who knows! It'll give our husbands something to think about. Let them look after the children for a change.'

'But Homa, I didn't tell Fereydoun I was coming.'

'Why ever not?'

'He wouldn't approve, and now I've lost my job I'm terrified of doing anything that might annoy him. He might take away my car.'

'Really, Theresa, if you can't tell your own husband how you feel, how will we ever get our point of view across to complete outsiders?'

The excitement and speculation on board the bus came to an abrupt halt when it stopped and dumped the women in the city outskirts some five miles away from the demonstration.

Homa suggested that they share a taxi and go straight to the nursery to collect the children, but Theresa wanted to get her car first. Fereydoun would be annoyed if she left it in the centre of town for the night.

A taxi soon stopped for Theresa. The driver indicated that she should sit in the front seat next to him. Theresa ignored him and climbed into the back.

As the taxi headed east, she was relieved to see that the crowds had cleared and the streets had returned to normal.

'Amerikayi-e?' asked the driver.

'Nakhehr. Ingelisi-am.'

'Cheh kar midunid?' The formula never varied. Are you American? What are you doing here? What they really wanted to know was whether she was on her own in the city.

'Shoharam Iraniy-e.' To reply that her husband was

Iranian was like a mantle of protection, one that she despised even as she used it.

The driver offered Theresa a cigarette, which she refused. He lit up himself and turned into the narrow street where she had left her car. There was no sign of the pale-blue Hillman she had parked by the kerb.

'Where did you say you had left your car?'

'Haminja!' Theresa insisted.

The driver indicated a smouldering heap of twisted and blackened metal.

'I'm glad that's not my car,' he chortled.

Theresa felt suddenly sick. What was she going to say to her husband?

She continued her way by taxi to the end of the street where they lived. She took out her keys as she walked the last hundred yards, aware of the dark figures that followed her. She thought of running, then determined to keep going at her usual pace, since it was unlikely that she could outstrip them in any case.

As she put her key in the lock, they surrounded her. How she hated them, bringing their poverty right to the door of her home, filthy rags wrapped round their heads to keep out the cold, and cheap pointed shoes.

'Barf Khanum,' they chorused. 'Xeily barf-e.' Theresa wrenched at her key. It had been snowing heavily all day and she knew that the piled-up snow would have to be removed from the flat roof.

'Panj toman,' the men grinned.

Theresa clicked her tongue against her teeth.

'Chahar toman, Khanum?'

Four was still too much. She squeezed through the front door and made as if to close it.

'Seh toman.' The men were whining now as they saw the door closing.

'Doh toman,' said Theresa firmly through the last inch. 'Two toman.'

106

The snow clearers raised their hands to heaven and wailed about their starving children and sick mothers. Theresa could not bear it. She would have preferred to close the door and clear the snow herself. But perhaps they really did have starving children and sick mothers. Having made her point in bargaining, she could afford to be generous.

She opened the door and the men rushed past her. Up the stairs, through the sitting room, on to the verandah then up the small iron staircase to the roof.

The children were not yet back and there was no sign of Fereydoun, although she had seen his car parked outside. When she went into the bedroom to take off her coat she noticed his lower half sticking out from under the bed.

'What on earth are you doing, Fereydoun?' Theresa started to giggle. Fereydoun emerged angrily, and walked into the sitting room to pour himself a whisky.

'You shouldn't have let them in like that. You can't just open the door to anybody these days, you know. It could be dangerous. Someone looking for me . . . you never know.'

Theresa flung herself onto the settee and laughed.

'You're too fat to hide under the bed, lying there with your bottom sticking out. If you're going to be arrested, at least leave me with a memory I can be proud of.'

In the mirror over the mantelpiece Fereydoun was annoyed to see himself blushing.

'You haven't seen the paper today then?' he asked.

The front-page article of the daily paper was one that would bring terror into many homes.

'The Chief Prosecutor of the Revolution is asking all dear compatriots that, if they have any documents, papers, complaints against any of these individuals of the previous regime they should at the earliest time possible, submit these . . . to the office of the Prosecutor at the Old Shemiran Road before reaching the Qasr intersection.'

Masoud rubbed his hands together and thought hard. Could he be of service? Surely among his papers . . . he turned off the radio as Roya walked into the sitting room. She wore her chador proudly, like a queen's robe.

'Mama, where have you been?' asked Soraya and Soheila.

'At the demonstration.'

'But why were you demonstrating, Mama? Are you suddenly going to fling off your veil and join women's lib?' The two girls shrieked with laughter.

'For you,' said Roya quietly. She went into the kitchen, sat down at the table and wept.

Minutes later Soraya, peeping through the kitchen door, was surprised to see her mother, head bowed under her black shroud. Suddenly she realized how much her mother was suffering, and wanted to make it quite clear that in her battle against the chador, she was not alone.

'Mama,' she whispered. 'Don't think that I want to wear this stupid old rag any more than you want me to. It's just that none of my clothes will fasten properly any more.'

As the truth dawned on Roya she wept, for in spite of all her ambitions for her daughters she realized that there was nothing in the world she wanted more than this grandchild. Her protests and marches had simply been against a part of herself whose existence she had failed to acknowledge. But the failure had to be lived with. Life had to go on. She must pull herself together. Be practical. No tragedy, not even Soraya's pregnancy, could be worse than the blow to a lifetime's dreams.

Soraya put her arms round her mother.

'Well, what shall we do now?'

'Well.' Roya dried her eyes and blew her nose. 'It's no good crying over spilt milk. We'll have a cup of tea. Say nothing to your father. Tomorrow we will go to the doctor. Not to the hospital, that wouldn't do. Mrs Nosrat downstairs, she has a niece who nurses there. We will go to one of those private doctors in town and ask him what to do.'

'I think you could put it over there.' Mrs Emani pointed to a small table in the corner of the room.

'It won't reach the plug,' said the man.

'Oh dear. What about here then?' The television set would be a nuisance right in the middle of the room. Perhaps she could shift all the furniture around when the man had gone.

When she was alone, Mrs Emani looked nervously at the large box which seemed to fill the whole room. She looked at the clock. Only an hour until Jamshid came home. What a surprise for him! Now he would be happy to stay at home with her in the evenings, now that there was something to entertain him.

Mrs Emani reflected on her luck. She was not a person to whom luck came naturally. She had spotted the advertisement quite by chance. A slight hold-up in the traffic, and there it had been, right by the bus window. New, low-price, TV rentals! She murmured a quick thank you to God.

So lucky that the electricity was working tonight. Mrs Emani chopped up some meat and set it to boil. A good meal in a room warmed by the cooking and afterwards she would watch television with Jamshid. It would be so good for his English and he would translate the bits she couldn't understand.

'Little House on the Prairie' would be on tonight. She had heard people at work chatting about it, something to do with a family in Canada. That would be nice for Jamshid. Give him an idea of how other people lived, other families, in other countries. She felt more and more

109

these days that Jamshid could do with a father, although heaven forbid that it should be her former husband. Jamshid was so obviously his father's son. It wasn't the blue eyes or fair curly hair that bothered her – she was very proud of the looks and colouring that proclaimed him an Isfahani – but in terms of character she felt vaguely uneasy.

'Jamshidja!' Mrs Emani was so excited as she heard him open the front door that she felt almost ill.

'Well, what do you think of that? Aren't you going to turn it on?' Mrs Emani wiped her hands on her apron.

Jamshid grunted and flung his satchel in the direction of a chair. It missed, and crashed onto the floor scattering books, pens and papers.

'Jamshidja, what's wrong? I would turn it on for you, only I don't know how.'

Jamshid put his hands in his pockets and stared at the set.

'There's no point, Mother.'

'No point?' Mrs Emani repacked the satchel on her hands and knees . . .

'Well, alright. I'll turn it on if you like.'

Mrs Emani served the stew. Such a lovely smell of meat and cinnamon. Such a treat! It must be adolescence that was making Jamshid behave like this. Perhaps he was too embarrassed to show her how pleased he really was.

'It's the Ayatollah.' Mrs Emani pushed her glasses back into place and peered at the clock. 'He's running late. Perhaps they don't like to interrupt him.'

Jamshid snorted. They finished their first course in silence. Mrs Emani stacked the dirty plates in the sink, then carried the fruit bowl over to her son.

'A pomegranate?' she asked. She turned the sound of the television right down. They ate their fruit. Mrs Emani washed up and made some tea. The silently mouthing

110

Ayatollah was lost in a fog as steam from the kettle clouded her spectacles.

'Do you think he's going to go on talking forever?'

'Oh Mother, you're hopeless. Don't you know anything about what's going on?'

Mrs Emani took off her glasses and wiped away the steam with the corner of a tea towel.

'I didn't buy a paper today.'

'It's not just today, Mother, it's all the time. Don't you know that nowadays there is nothing on television except the Ayatollah? Why else would a telly be going cheap except that no one else wants it?'

The thought of the car nagged away at the back of Theresa's mind all through tea, while she put the children to bed and during the evening while Fereydoun popped out for a drink.

'Never mind, darling,' he said in bed, stroking her hair. 'When things have settled down, I'm sure you'll find another job.'

'It's not the job, Fereydoun, it's the car.'

'Don't worry so much about the car. In fact, I've decided that we won't use mine any more, it's too conspicuous. We'll share yours instead.'

Theresa sat up, hugging her arms about her knees.

'But that's just it, Fereydoun, my car is . . .'

Fereydoun pulled Theresa back down beside him.

'Let's not talk about cars now,' he said.

7

*This is your Captain speaking in the name of God etc. etc.
Let us not slip into the trap of becoming parochial or
narrow-minded. The man before us, erstwhile Prime Minister, is not the only Premier in the world at this moment
battling for his life, in the face of Islam. In Pakistan at this
moment Zulfikar Ali Bhutto lies in a stripped cell, the only
furnishings a straw mattress and a bucket. Some say that
the latter is in fact a kindness, since he is said to be too
weak to walk as far as the toilets.*

*Now, Amir Abbas Hoveyda. Consider him carefully.
As Shirin said, the man has lost weight, but are prisons to
provide caviare and champagne as part of the regular diet?
No suit and no buttonhole, only a somewhat over-large
leather jacket. But times are hard for everyone. Improve-
ment, they say, is in sight. Why, only the other day the
Minister of the Interior pressed a button at Kharg Island to
resume the flow of oil to the nation. The fact that nothing
happened beyond a few faces turning red was merely a
technical hitch. There are indications of better things to
come.*

*As usual I digress. Revenons à nos moutons! Though
the foreign press is banned, local reporters are here in
abundance. The courtroom is a classroom, much like those
in which Hussein, Soheila and Fariba sit every day. It is
badly lit, with not a picture on the walls save, of course,
His Holiness. There are rows of wooden desks and chairs.
The defendant will sit in the front row. The judge will
stand in for the Mo'alem on the rostrum.*

*Enter, supported by two guards, the defendant, mum-
bling his objections. The time, forty-five minutes after*

midnight. The man is only sixty but seems positively senile. He should take a leaf from the book of the Ayatollah.

If I lean closer, I can catch the odd phrases – wasn't told of the charges, was promised an afternoon session, has taken sleeping medication, think of his old mother. What a spectacle! Thank God for a judge who doesn't slur his syllables.

'This is a Twenty-Four Hour Revolutionary Court.'

Such zeal, such devotion to duty! I see my friend Masoud Gabayan up there in the back row, snoring loudly. It's all this fresh air and marching, there's nothing like it for giving a man a good night's sleep. That, and being at peace with his Maker. Mashallah, but the Islamification of that man is something to wonder over! Only today, he handed over some documents relating to Fereydoun Homayoun, something to do with profiteering and corruption.

The old man's coming to life now. You can see his French connections every time he speaks – that fluidity of gesture. They say he speaks better French than Farsi. What a picture for the papers! He's really putting up a good fight for his life now.

What's that? An adjournment? The fact that this is the first trial ever to go into a second day does him credit. Or are they waiting to see what their near neighbours will do in Pakistan, looking perhaps for a precedent under Islam?

Spring brought to the Mahalleh a sea of mud.

'I wouldn't have recognized her,' laughed the women around the tap. For baby Shahnaz Baniyazdi was back home. They clucked and pinched the dimpled legs and ran their dirty fingers through the soft curls. Shahnaz laughed, clinging to the tap for balance, jigging up and down in a little dance. She blew bubbles through her lips and the women clapped.

'Aieeee, but she's a beauty!'

113

'To think that we thought her dead.'

Their own thin babies were nothing in comparison.

Away from the prison of her sterile cot, Shahnaz was beginning to explore. She picked up a handful of chicken droppings, laughing to feel them ooze between her clenched fingers. Then she stuffed her fist into her mouth.

Fariba came running. She had only left Shahnaz for a few minutes to go to the toilet. She stooped and hooked the mess from her little sister's mouth with her forefinger.

'Mama, you should keep Shahnaz indoors, away from the dirt.'

'How can I, Fariba, with the little ones running in and out and the door always open? She is fat now and healthy, you worry too much.'

Perhaps she was right, thought Fariba. Her little sister sat in the mud, like an angel warm in the sunshine. She picked Shahnaz up and ran into the kucheh, a child with a new doll to show off.

Masoud Gabayan and his son Hussein sauntered down the main street. Nothing much was happening today, nothing exciting. People strolled through air honey-coloured by exhaust fumes. The traffic snarled bumper to bumper.

'It's quicker on foot,' the father remarked.

'What shall we do, Dad?'

Masoud shrugged.

'I suppose we could call in at the shop, see how things are going.' Masoud was wondering how long it was reasonable to keep carpets repaired and unclaimed, letters and bills unanswered, before he could claim ownership. He should perhaps seek legal advice, only from whom? Who were the legal authorities in such matters these days?

'Look, Dad.' Hussein was tugging at his sleeve. 'Can I have a go?'

'How much?'

They pushed their way through the crowd towards the sounds of rifle fire.

'What do you have to do?' asked Hussein, anxious for the feel of a gun.

'How much?' Masoud called out.

'Shoot-a-Shah, one rial.'

A penny. Seemed reasonable, but Masoud wasn't one to let money slip through his fingers.

'A rial eh?' He thrust his hands into his pockets, rocking backwards and forwards, squinting in the direction of the target.

'Any prizes?' he asked.

The stall-holder shook his head.

'Please, Dad, I want to have a go.'

Masoud dug into his pocket for a rial, clattering the loose coins one against the other. He searched through the handful of cash before extracting one penny.

'I'd better show you how to do it first, Son.'

Masoud raised the rifle to his shoulder and looked professionally along the barrel. He shuffled forwards.

'Ten paces, Agha, is here!' The stall-holder indicated with his toe that Masoud should step backwards.

Masoud squinted at the colour photograph. They were all there, the Shah, the Empress, Crown Prince Ali and the other children. Which one should he aim for? He eased the barrel this way and that. A slight variation in angle and he would miss the target altogether.

'Hurry up, Dad, I want a go.'

Masoud fired, missed the board and hit the wall of the American Embassy compound.

'I could have done it if you hadn't rushed me,' he said.

Hussein took the gun, nonchalantly flung himself on one knee, and fired from the hip.

The crowd roared and rushed to inspect the photograph. A bull – right through the Imperial Brain. Masoud slapped him on the back. Kissed him on both cheeks. The boy was a genius – his son!

Fereydoun Homayoun wondered how much longer he dared go on using the white Mercedes. It seemed ostentatious even when he drove it himself.

'I thought it would be nice if there were just the two of us,' he said.

Goli turned and smiled. Once she would have leaned across and kissed him. Now, as he parked the car outside the airport, she only wished he would hurry up and unload the luggage.

'There's plenty of time, darling,' he murmured, leaning towards her.

'Someone might see.' Goli shrank back nervously against the passenger door.

'You still have the address of my parents' flat in Paris? I shall be over some time when all this is settled.'

Not that Fereydoun intended to live in Paris. The family apartment in New York was more his style. But it was nice to think of Goli in Paris and available during the occasional holiday.

Goli nodded. Fereydoun already seemed part of her past.

'Thank you for the ticket.'

'I'll miss you.' Fereydoun's hand stroked Goli's knee. She pushed it away.

'Just look at the time,' she said.

'Goli, I don't know what I shall do without you!'

'Theresa will be glad to see the back of me.'

Fereydoun got out of the car and unlocked the boot. The car was besieged by porters. There was more work to be had at the airport than in the bazaar.

'Perhaps I should come too.'

Goli was alarmed. Her dreams of the West did not include Fereydoun. Since he had insisted on staying at

116

her flat instead of going out for their evenings together, she had begun to feel as if they were married. Besides, she knew that one of the reasons he had bought her a plane ticket was to avoid further payments on her flat.

'What about the children?' Goli's smile was so sweet that Fereydoun threw all caution to the winds and embraced her.

'The children,' he murmured, his voice thick with emotion.

Goli's passage through the airport was paved with banknotes. Fereydoun, fearing that otherwise she would despise him, had tucked money inside her passport, her customs declaration and her ticket. As a final gesture, he bought a hideously large bottle of perfume.

'Darling,' she whispered, and was swallowed up by the endless corridors.

Fereydoun returned to his car to find it surrounded by people. Probably just looking, but . . . He began walking quickly towards town. He could send his driver to collect the car, tomorrow perhaps, when it had ceased to attract so much interest. He would give him some money, tell him to keep quiet about Goli. Not that he could afford a driver any more, but the driver was one person whom he could not afford to sack. He knew too much, not just about Goli but also about Fereydoun's shadier contacts in the building world. Another one of his trained staff would have to go instead.

Fariba Baniyazdi was teaching her brothers to play hop-scotch. She held her chador under her chin with one hand as she traced a line in the mud with her fingers. Yek, doh, seh, chahar, in the slime.

'Me first, me first, Fariba,' begged Mussa.

'You must watch me, see how it's done.' Fariba hopped the length of the pitch. Her chador flew out behind her like wings. She hopped barefoot, her toes splayed for

117

balance. Shoes were put away except for school. Her legs were splattered with mud. Hop, hop, to the turn at the end of the pitch where her foot slid sideways and Fariba fell full-length in the mire. Her brothers shrieked with laughter. Fariba ran home to her mother, in the court-yard, surrounded by a gaggle of women.

'I fell over, Mama,' she wailed.

The doctor's hands measured the height of the fundus. He measured rib-cage to pelvis, then transversely across Soraya Gabayan's stomach. Next he held a microphone against the stomach wall and the baby's heartbeat echoed through the room, thud-thud, thud-thud. For the first time, Soraya was aware of the separate life that awaited the end of her pregnancy and not just the shame of her expanding stomach.

At the sound, Roya shrank into her chador. This was the final proof, if she had needed one beyond her daughter's bulging stomach and strangely beautiful look these days – the skin drawn tight, almost transparent over her cheekbones. The heartbeat also called to some deeper emotion in Roya. It was her grandchild calling for the love and protection that she would have to deny it for Soraya's sake. Inwardly, she wept.

The doctor turned away from his patient.

'When did you say the rape took place?'

'February the seventeenth.'

'I think we had better discuss details of the confinement.'

'Already?' murmured Roya. 'Surely there is plenty of time for that later.'

The doctor led the way through to his consulting room. His nurse escorted Soraya into the waiting room. Soraya sat engulfed in canned music, mesmerized by goldfish swimming heavy and languid round and round a tank. Her feet sank into the soft pile of the carpet and her heart sank into her feet. How could her mother afford all this?

Opposite Soraya sat a woman nearing the end of her pregnancy. Soraya looked away, appalled by the ugliness, the distortion. Though there were moments when she felt a certain tenderness towards her child, and relished the gentle swimming movements inside her, she could not bear the thought of looking like that. She walked over to the desk.

The nurse looked up.

'Can I help you?'

'Yes. I would like an abortion.'

'I beg your pardon?'

'I said, an abortion.' Soraya kept her back to the pregnant woman on the bench and fingered her mother's wedding ring. She twisted and turned the gold band, angry now that she had agreed to wear it. 'I'm not married,' she explained.

'I'm sorry, an abortion is not possible. It is too late for you to consider an abortion, the risks . . .'

'But I don't want it.' Soraya bent closer, whispering.

'But the baby is almost viable.'

'Viable?'

'It might have a chance of survival, with good care.'

'And without care?'

'I'm sorry, we can't help you.'

Soraya returned to her seat blushing and guilty, resting her text book on her stomach. *The Family Protection Act – Implications for the Future.* Not that it looked as though she had a future. She tried to concentrate. 'The major achievement of this act was in divorce. It removed the unconditional right of a man to divorce and made divorce subject to approval by the Family Protection Court so that . . .' Beyond the page Soraya could hear her mother's voice. She felt like a small child whose parents had been summoned to the headmaster's office on account of some

119

misdemeanour. When her mother emerged, the whole truth would be out.

Roya was red-eyed when she left the doctor's consulting room. In silence, without a glance at her daughter, she crossed the waiting room. Soraya followed into the street. She had almost to run to keep up with her mother's pace. The baby in her womb bounced up and down, landing each time with a thud against her bladder.

'Mama,' Soraya gasped, clutching her hands to her stomach, her pelvic muscles contracting to stop the leak of urine. 'Mama!'

Roya turned, as if aware of her daughter for the first time. Two black figures, in mourning for something lost. Roya reached out her hand from among the black folds, across the gulf which divided them.

'I wanted so much for you, my daughter. I wanted you to feel that the whole world lay at your feet. That your whole life would be governed by choice. Now I see that for women there is no freedom, we are simply slaves – if not to others, then to our own emotions.'

Roya walked on more calmly now, majestic in her sorrow. Soraya followed like a dark shadow.

'Sorayaja, it is difficult for me, but I am trying to understand.'

Soraya was at a loss. She had expected anger.

'Sorayaja, when you were born I was younger than you are now. My family married me to a man I had never met and I bore his children. I expected no more from life. But you, could you not have done something better?' Roya paused, fumbling in her handbag for a handkerchief, suddenly again the mother Soraya knew.

'But Sorayaja, at least you loved him.'

'Love!' Soraya stalked off in the direction of the bus-stop, leaving her mother to follow as best she could through her tears.

* * *

120

Aziz Baniyazdi's pregnancy blossomed, while she herself shrivelled and withered like an over-ripe seed case. She felt no joy when Hamid's seed took life of its own. There was simply a dreary inevitability about this baby and the next and the next.

'Your pills, Mama.' Fariba held out her hand, two red tablets, one brown every day after school. Otherwise, Mama never remembered. Fariba was not sure what the pills did, but since the hospital had saved Shahnaz, she knew they could save her mother as well.

Fariba was frightened. Her mother neither spoke nor sang these days. She scarcely bothered washing or cleaning, but dragged herself heavily about the room or the compound, to collapse in a weary heap in one place or another.

'Mama, do you know what I heard in school today?' Aziz looked up from the tray of rice. Chickens cackled around her mother's legs waiting for discarded husks.

'I heard that in the Niavaran Palace there is a special switch that will blow up the whole of Tehran.'

Aziz, alerted by the tap-tap of beaks on the tin tray, lifted the rice above her head away from the hens.

'But you don't need to worry, Mama, now the soldiers have taken over the Palace. They haven't found the switch yet, but they soon will.'

Aziz shooed the chickens away and resumed her task.

'Mama, why would the Shah want to blow us all up?' She squatted down in front of her mother, squinting at the tiny white grains. Her mother shrugged. Such things were beyond her understanding.

'I had an eye test in school today,' Fariba chatted on. 'The doctor says that if I had eye glasses I would see more clearly.'

'Don't tell your father. He would be mad.'

Fariba picked at the grains of rice.

'Leave that.' Her mother's voice was sharp with anger. 'I don't know how many grains you've thrown away. Go and see if Shahnaz is awake.'

'But this is absurd,' said Shirin Khaksar into the telephone. 'Of course women should be allowed to state their case. You should ring up that new controller of television, what's his name?' During the slight pause, Shirin shifted the receiver to the other hand. 'Yes, that's the one, ring him and demand time on the air.'

'But Khanum-e-Shirin, the decisions are no longer made by the controller.'

'Look, Anna, it seems as though we are heading for victory. They have already backed down on making the chador compulsory. I've never seen a chador inside the Ministry, apart from on the cleaning women. Modest dress is all that is required. Now, we should press the point home. How dare they dictate to us on matters of dress!'

'Khanumja, they say that our fashion is based on decadent Western models and that any plan for women's lib is simply a plot by Western cosmetic companies.'

'I would say that such a comment is so contemptible it is hardly worth answering.'

Shirin ended the conversation with a feeling of utter helplessness and futility. It was not so much that the dictates of the governing Mullahs were preposterous, but that there was no room for debate or protest. The forthcoming referendum gave some hope, but before then, the more people that made their views known the better. The women had marched in the forefront of the Revolution. The nurses had come out on strike in support of their right to wear uniform. Shirin rang for her secretary.

'To the Editor, *Kayhan International*. On behalf of all

women in my country . . .' she began. Her secretary shrank back into her chair as if she were trying to make herself invisible below the level of the desk, to hide her chador from Shirin's eyes.

8

The Vernal Equinox approaches. Such lovely words, such a lovely opportunity for celebration. The Iranian New Year! Not some chilly night at the end of December for people already jaded by the festivities of Christmas, but a time full of the promise of spring, when day and night are of equal length and the long winter darkness is over. Of course, the Iranian New Year no longer really counts in the Islamic calendar, but old habits die hard. The spirit of tradition reasserts itself confidently and defiantly. It is interesting, isn't it, to observe these customs from a sociological point of view?

I am not, you see, entirely ignorant of the methods of scientific research. The people I have introduced to you have been selected not according to a personal whim, but on the basis of rigorous sampling techniques.

You in the West might feel that any discussion of social class is old hat. In this city we could talk about geographical area if you prefer – the divisions of contour line have much the same effect as those of education or income.

Hence, behold Shirin Khaksar, at the top of the social scale and only slightly below the dizzying heights of the southernmost tip of the Royal Gardens.

Marginally downhill in every respect live our friends the Homayouns. Their unfinished house, which they would have moved into by now were it not for the Revolution, hangs like a castle in the air, clinging to the perilous slope below Shirin's septic tank.

Descending a few contour lines nearer to sea level brings us to the good woman Khanum-e-Emani, who poddles

through life in a state of such unawareness that it is only
possible to place her geographically. The term decayed
gentlewoman somehow springs to mind as we see her
shuffling through the comfortless interior of a once noble
house.

Next we come to Masoud Gabayan and family, solidly
middle in every respect – middle-class, middle of the city,
middling good, middling bad.

At the bottom of the heap, be it on grounds of income
or altitude, where the effluvia from the north ooze to the
surface, sucking the feet into a treacherous quagmire of
poverty, live, or almost live, the Baniyazdis.

Thus it is my hope that this sample will provide the basis
for informed anthropological discussion on the habits of a
Middle Eastern community.

Theresa continued sewing. Though there had in the past
been occasions when she had entertained Goli in her own
home, there were limits. She had reached a reluctant
acceptance of the status quo for the sake of peace. She
could even try to accept that it was normal for Fereydoun
to keep a mistress. But in her own home? It was asking
too much.

'I said what about a party?' Fereydoun was pacing up
and down the room. 'There are so many people we ought
to have round. We haven't invited anyone for weeks.'

'Shopping is not easy these days.'

'The servants could see to that, if you'd only let them.'

Theresa swore as her needle slipped and dug into her
thumb.

'You could tell the servants to do the mending for you
as well.'

'I prefer to mend my own underwear.'

'Well, I've made a list of the people we will invite,'
said Fereydoun. 'Not a sit-down meal, I think. A buffet
would do.'

'A buffet is a lot more work. It's so fiddly.'

'Then tell Mohammed to do it.'

The guest list lay on the coffee table between them.

'Anyone you want to add?' asked Fereydoun.

'I haven't time to read it now, I'm late. I'm meeting Homa at half past ten. Anyway, I don't really feel like a party at the moment. Not while things are so unsettled, darling.'

'Nonsense, darling, it would do you good. Take you out of yourself. Give you something to do. You've been letting yourself go a bit since you stopped work.'

'Have I?'

'Well look at you – still in a dressing gown, and you haven't touched your hair this morning.'

Theresa looked at Fereydoun's increasing girth but said nothing. She had noticed that lately he left the top button of his shirt undone, underneath his tie.

'Why don't we have a game of tennis one day?' she asked.

As soon as Fereydoun had gone to work, Theresa took Farah and Reza to the nursery. Farah stood in the back of the car, just behind her mother's seat, her fingers twined round her neck.

'You're choking me, Farah,' Theresa protested, loving the feel of her daughter's small arms. She dreaded the parting at the nursery gate. Reza ran off as usual without looking back. Farah clung and wept and had to be peeled from her mother by one of the nursery assistants. Theresa enjoyed this display of emotion.

'I'll see you at lunchtime,' she said.

'You've no idea how bored I get,' Theresa told Homa as they sat drinking coffee.

Homa nodded sympathetically.

'For a while it was lovely not to have to go to work. I enjoyed the feeling of being on holiday.'

126

'Let's have a cake. I'm starving.' Homa called a waiter to wheel over the cake trolley. Since the one decent patisserie had closed down, it was only the international hotels that provided good cakes. Theresa selected a large cream-filled meringue that exploded inside her mouth in a puff of sugar.

'What's the time?' she asked as she wiped the last crumbs from her chin.

'Still half an hour to go.'

'Fereydoun wants us to give a Now Ruz party.'

'That would be lovely.'

'But he's sure to invite Goli. I don't want her in my house any more.'

'Goli? Didn't you know she's left Iran?'

'Left?' Theresa was astonished.

'Fereydoun took her to the airport on Tuesday. I think all of our husbands have had to tighten their belts.'

Homa laughed, and for the first time Theresa found herself able to laugh too.

'Doesn't it bother you though, that your husband sees other women?'

'I think you expect too much,' said Homa. 'You expect romance to last forever. We just accept that men are like that. The first time might be hard, but then you realize that you are so much freer to get on with your own life.'

Now the threat of competition was gone, Theresa found this philosophy easy to accept.

Roya felt nervous as she spring-cleaned Hussein's bedroom, but every corner of the flat had to be spotless for the New Year. On her hands and knees she peeped over the edge of the bed at the opposite wall. The poster of the Ayatollah stared grimly back, six feet by four. The massive head seemed to fill the whole room. The gaze was unflinching. This was the man who had called her to

127

march and defeat the enemy. She wondered whether she would heed the call today.

In the foreground of the poster was a figure, stretching from the Ayatollah's chin to the bridge of his nose. Legs half bent, rifle cocked, squinting along a barrel aimed directly at Roya's breast. Her Hussein, posed and photographed with the Ayatollah himself!

To think that this man was her son. The bronzed chuckling cherub who had once followed her about the house with dustpan and brush, copying everything she did. Roya felt a stab of excitement as she looked at him now, stern and threatening. How could this be the same person?

Hussein was surprised when the bell rang for the end of school. He checked his watch. He had no memory at all of the afternoon's lessons.

'Are you coming with us?'

Hussein looked up and shook his head. He was a good bit taller than anyone else in his class. Just a bunch of kids, they were, whereas he . . .

'I have to get home,' he said. He bundled his books together. He longed to be home, not to see his family or do anything special. It was the thought of the poster. It dominated his thinking just as it dominated his small room. He'd been surprised when his father had agreed, just like that, for him to pose for a photograph. He didn't usually part so easily with any money, let alone five hundred rials. Perhaps he was still dazzled by the spectacle Hussein had made at the Shoot-a-Shah competition? He still went on about it to all his friends. And for Dad to have bought two posters! The other one was to put in the shop, he'd said. Hussein tried to imagine his picture towering over the dusty carpets. Hussein the Magnificent. The Intrepid. The Instant Urban Guerrilla.

'Out of the way, boy.'

Hussein jumped aside as the garbage cart rattled past. Boy? Did they know who they were talking to? He bounded up the stairs praying that his mother would be out. Not that she ever was.

'Is that you, Hussein-ja?'

Hussein locked his bedroom door behind him. Why, the picture was even better than he had imagined. He flung his satchel onto the bed, and then his coat, his eyes riveted to the gun barrel. He stood, legs straddled, admiring himself, and felt a tightening in his groin. This was life. He was a man. Under the stern unseeing gaze of the Ayatollah, Hussein masturbated.

Jamshid Emani left the classroom and wandered listlessly across the courtyard. How was he going to get through the evening? What the hell was there to do? No ice-rink. No coffee bars. No discos. Just another evening of his mother with the Ayatollah yakking away on the television. She wasn't like other mothers. How could he invite his friends home? The first time she had come to school, his friends had asked if she was his granny. He'd made sure she hadn't been near the school since.

Certainly never to meet him after school. No one else was ever collected, not on foot anyway. A car was alright, chauffeur-driven, very acceptable. It was a year now since Jamshid had caught a bus right outside the school. He walked to a further stop, so that no one would see him in the queue. He had suffered a couple of unpleasant incidents when he had been approached by men, but those were easier to endure than the taunts of his classmates.

Holding the satchel in front of him by one strap (how he would have loved one of those smart attaché cases), Jamshid savagely kicked it at each step. It was somehow satisfying. Then he remembered that note about the school concert. He knelt down and rummaged through his books. He had to destroy the note before he went home.

From an upstairs window, the college principal watched Jamshid. He was concerned about the boy. Such a nice youth, and his mother was a saint, as far as he knew, the only Iranian Catholic on their books. And she didn't seem the type to have endured so much for conversion – the plane ride to India, a secret ceremony, and then the return to raise her son single-handed. The boy and his mother deserved more help than he had given them in the past.

The forthcoming theatricals. There was a way to bring Jamshid out of himself a bit and give his mother something to be proud of. It would help his English too, to speak the language in public. He tried to imagine Mrs Emani's pride, sitting in the front row, all in black. The principal opened the window.

'Hey, Emani! Come up to my study for a minute.'

The presents were all wrapped and the table laid according to custom. Theresa wondered if the children would ever be able to sleep for excitement. On the table were the four candles, one for each member of the family. The requisite goldfish swam monotonously round and round its glass bowl.

'Darling, you can't sack Mo after the party.'

'Darling, I have to.'

'But he's worked so hard. Have you seen all the food he's prepared. It's magnificent.'

'He will have to go, darling. We can't afford so many servants. Can't you understand that?'

'No, I can't. He says it's because you've never liked him.'

'Rubbish! He's no worse than any other cook.'

'But Fereydoun, he's got eight children.'

130

'Darling, I have sacked thirty of my office staff this month. His eight children are his own lookout.'

'But I told him I would talk to you.'

'Darling, please keep out of things you don't understand.'

Fereydoun had stamped off then, into the bedroom to change, while Theresa checked her list. The seven items beginning with 's'. Sib. She rubbed the red apple on her skirt until it shone. Seer, a garlic clove. Not a very good specimen, somewhat dry and shrivelled up, but the best she'd been able to find. Serké, a small cut-glass decanter of vinegar.

'Mmmm. I love sumac.' Soheila Gabayan held the bowl of spice under her nose and sniffed. 'Have you made the kebabs, Mama?'

Roya nodded, happy to be in the kitchen with her daughters. She loved the little celebrations that enriched the texture of family life.

'I wonder whether I could find any caviare,' she said.

'Mama!' Soraya laughed at her mother. 'We know your success at shopping is nothing short of a miracle, but even you must admit that some things are impossible.'

'Peter would have got me some,' Roya said wistfully, then wished she hadn't mentioned him. 'I'm sorry, Soraya, I didn't mean to upset you.'

'It's alright, Mama.' Soraya closed her book.

Roya missed Peter. Hussein had been at home more in those days, drawn into the kitchen by Peter's presence. He liked trying on Peter's army cap. Now Hussein would be out with his father. Not at the shop, but doing what Masoud called 'man's work'. Attending demonstrations, tribunals or executions, or sitting in the mosque with the Mullah, soaking up the passionate rhetoric.

'Senjed,' said Roya, placing the bowl of dried fruit on the table. The three picked at it in silence.

131

'Why don't you girls take off your chadors in the kitchen – just for tonight,' suggested Roya, trying to recapture their earlier joy. 'I promise not to look at your bodies, only at your minds.' The girls laughed.

Then Masoud burst into the kitchen and flung a copy of the newspaper onto the table in front of Soraya.

'Look,' he gloated, jabbing with his finger at the centre column. 'Read that. Young couple flogged for making love. That's what you deserve, isn't it?'

'Masoudja, making love can hardly be equated with rape.' Roya spoke with little conviction, even though the remark was true as far as her husband was concerned.

'Oh?' Masoud turned on Roya. 'Oh, it's all very well, the way she dresses now, all modesty and veils. Like bolting the stable door after the horse has gone. Inviting trouble the way she did, begging for it. Now she thinks a chador will hide the shame underneath, but it won't fool anyone for much longer. Soon her sin will have grown so large that all the world will see.'

'Masoudja, please, more quietly.'

Hussein stood sneering by the door, a carbon copy of his father. The womenfolk still sat at the table, heads bowed, waiting for Masoud's rage to burn itself out.

'And what's this?' Masoud seized the scrap of paper that was his wife's list for the New Year Celebrations. 'We are to keep pagan festivals nowadays, are we? Those of God are not enough, eh?'

'There's a concert at school for Now Ruz,' Jamshid Emani told his mother.

'That's nice, dear. Can I come?'

'Oh no.' Jamshid stared into his mother's eyes. 'Parents aren't invited.' She would never find out. She didn't mix with other parents. He almost relented as he watched her, sitting there so tired and dusty, wrestling with her knitting. But it was unthinkable to have her there among the Mercedes and the pearls, toting the inevitable shopping bag and twitching at her headscarf.

'What will you do, Mama?' he asked, feeling guilty.

'Don't worry about me. I shall probably go to mass, then have an early night. The New Year will still be there in the morning.

Jamshid reached into his pocket and took out a rather crumpled paper bag of sweets.

'For you, Mama. Happy New Year.'

Mrs Emani peeped into one corner of the bag.

'Samanu!' she said in amazement. One of the s's for the New Year's table. There were tears in her eyes.

'Look, Jamshidja.' Mrs Emani held up her knitting. 'This is your present. Only a few more rows to go. I managed to find some wool, so many places I had to go to. But you will need a smart jumper when you go to Europe.'

Jamshid looked at the shapeless mass and thought he would die rather than wear such a garment. Especially in Europe, where he would smoke and drink and dance. But she was his mother and he had deceived her. He swallowed hard.

'It's lovely,' he said.

Mrs Emani beamed. She held out the bag of sweets made from wheat shoots.

'Have one.'

'Look, Mama!' Young Fariba Gabayan proudly held out her Hebrew book. 'Look, it's a picture of Israel. The teacher said it was very good. Look at the green grass and the fruit trees, and the blue sea.'

While her mother looked at the book, Fariba went outside to the tap. Then she put the pan of water on the charcoal burner.

'In Israel, Mama, there is work for everyone. Even for Baba there would be work. We would live in a flat and have two taps – one for hot water, one for cold. We would drive about in a car.'

Aziz was absorbed in the picture. Fariba dragged her brothers away from the fire. They were too close, it was dangerous.

'Mama, all you have to do is go to the Social Work Office with Baba and say we want to go to Israel. Israel is like . . .' Fariba stopped, at a loss for words to describe the wonders of Israel – the schools, the hospitals, the abundance of food – where her Mama would be well and happy. At last she found the right word. 'Israel is like heaven, Mama.'

At last Aziz looked up, clutching at the vision that lit her daughter's face.

'Like heaven, Fariba?'

Fariba nodded as she shook rice into the boiling water.

'But not for us, Faribaja. Not for us.' Aziz closed the school-book, and Fariba felt her slipping away again behind a wall of fatigue.

'Mussa, go and see if the hen has laid an egg.' Fariba sent her little brother into the yard, while she took a mirror off the wall. An egg on a mirror, part of the New Year's rituals. But there was no egg today.

'Never mind,' said Fariba. 'We will find something else. We will go and look for sabzi for the table.' Sabzi, the seventh and most humble of the s's. Grass. Somewhere in the Mahalleh, surely she would find a blade of grass?

New Year's Eve. From her sitting room window Shirin Khaksar could see all over town the glow of bonfires as she waited for the phone call from New York that would wish her a Happy New Year.

Around each fire, a group of people, each drawn irresistibly towards it.

> 'My blackness to you
> Your whiteness to me,'

chanted children and adults as they leapt over the flames, consigning their sins to the fires of hell, emerging on the other side, innocent and renewed, like a phoenix from the ashes. New life. New hope.

Soraya looked into the heart of the fire and dreamt of innocence while Roya dreamt of a new life for her daughters and herself.

Fariba jumped over the fire, laughing, and tried to get her mother to jump too, for she still believed in its power. But Aziz wouldn't jump. She hadn't the strength.

Arm in arm with his friends, Jamshid jumped time and time again, thinking of Europe and girls, while alone, at home, Mrs Emani prayed, then slept.

Theresa moved radiantly among her guests. Fereydoun was proud of her. He loved her. From the balcony, wine glasses in hand, they chuckled over the antics of the street urchins, daring them to build the fires higher and higher. The urchins waited for the shower of pennies, pennies from heaven, and jumped as they had never jumped before.

Masoud, Hussein and the Mullah prayed, seeing in the flames the spirit of Islam, fierce in its purifying heat.

All night the revels lasted, until the first streak of dawn appeared in the sky. The trials were suspended. Elections drew near. The Ayatollah was with his people. As if emerging from a long dark tunnel, the New Year was ushered in with a chorus of hope, the traditional greeting of the dawn –

'See light!'

9

*These days when I leave my hotel, I step into a street
festooned with posters about the forthcoming referendum.
Now, you folks abroad will no doubt have heard about
this referendum since it has become a matter of some
interest both nationally and internationally, and no little
cause for dispute. The old man has put it as simply as he
can. Do you want a return of the monarchy or do you
want an Islamic Republic?*

*He really has done his best to reduce the issue to
essentials, and put it in a way that the majority of the
people will understand. I mean, what else can you do with
a population that is eighty per cent illiterate?*

*Of course there are problems. No register of electors.
How to contact nomadic tribes? The intellectuals nit-
picking. The students acting outrageously as usual. Some
people are being real dogs in the manger and refusing to
vote at all, because they say there is nothing to vote about.
Some tribes like the Kurds and the Baluchis are demanding
autonomy.*

*Green is the colour you must remember. It's quite easy
really – the colour of spring, of life, of rebirth. The colour
of the Prophet. The colour of the 'yes' vote. The campaign,
as I have said, is well under way, in the streets and on
television. You cannot escape the message. Even old Roya
is glued to the telly these days. In spite of her prowess at
shopping, she hasn't been able to find a single romantic
novel in the whole city that she hasn't read.*

Roya had attended a rowzeh earlier in the day. Prayers
plus tea and biscuits. Good biscuits they were too. She

would have to ask the Khanum for the favour of her recipe. Roya's eyes were still red with weeping. She had no idea that the Mullah could be so passionate a reader. It all went to show that you shouldn't judge by appearances. A lump returned to her throat at the thought. Just the right quaver in his voice, tear in his eye, slight tremble of the hand as he held the sacred book, and there she had been, blubbering like the rest of the women.

Now this. As if she hadn't suffered enough for one day. Roya's knitting fell onto the carpet as she groped for her handkerchief. On the TV screen a hand rose from a grave clutching a green slip of paper. At the same time a voice rang out from Heaven: 'The Martyrs of the Revolution will be watching you.'

Oh, the sonless mothers, the daughterless mothers, the widows! Roya howled into her hanky.

Powerful stuff, eh? The Ayatollah obviously believes in a strong man at the helm and the Shah would have agreed wholeheartedly. So would any Prime Minister, but Prime Ministers are hard to keep track of these days.

Record turnouts are expected. Everyone will vote, from the shores of the Caspian Sea to the Persian Gulf. And all you have to remember is, put the red slips for the return of the monarchy, blood-letting, sin, etc into the rubbish bin and the green – remember, green for Mohammed – into the voting box.

Each mosque has become a polling station, where people like our good friend the Mullah Afsharzadeh watch the faithful vote for God and Islam. He sees the green slips slither into the boxes and offers thanks to his maker.

Enter Hamid and Aziz Baniyazdi and their numerous bacchi.

At the doorway, Hamid and Aziz hung back. Though Fariba had assured them that it was quite safe to enter the mosque, they had said so at school, they were still fearful. But it was their right to vote. Their duty to vote. And the Ayatollah had promised his protection to all Jews and minority groups.

'But in a mosque, Hamid?' Aziz was terrified. The family stood in a frightened bunch until nudged by the rifles of the Pasdaran in the direction of a long table. Hamid tried to look nonchalant, and even managed a whistle until silenced by a look from an official.

Hamid showed his identity card. With a rifle at his back he took the two green slips of paper handed to him. He passed one to Aziz. The official obliged by putting the red slips into the rubbish bin himself.

'Soraya, this is the last time I am telling you. Put on your coat and come.' Masoud Gabayan stood in the doorway of the flat breathing fast.

'Baba, I'm not voting.'

'Sorayaja, please do as your father wishes.' Roya hovered between her husband and her daughter.

'Mama, it is a complete farce. I am not voting.'

'How can you utter such blasphemy? Who can gainsay an Islamic Republic? Have you no shame?' Masoud stepped towards his daughter, fists clenched.

'Oh come on, Father.' Hussein took Masoud by the sleeve. 'Who cares what she thinks anyway?'

Hussein on one side, Roya on the other, Masoud was escorted into the street.

'Would you have voted, Soheila, if you'd been old enough?' Soraya asked her sister when they were alone.

'No. There is no choice.'

'If you won't come with me, I shan't go.'

'Oh, alright then, I'll come.' Theresa Homayoun had never been inside a mosque, and the opportunity was perhaps too good to miss. 'I shan't vote though.'

'Well I will,' answered Fereydoun. 'And, I shall jolly well vote for the Shah.'

'Good for you.' Theresa fastened the top button of her dress and followed her husband.

The driver was waiting outside in his own car. Fereydoun had come to the arrangement of hiring his driver's car until it was safe to use the Mercedes again.

'You see,' Fereydoun turned aggressively towards Theresa as soon as they were seated, 'I refuse to be bullied. I shall vote for the Shah if I feel like it. If he wants us to vote, and offers a choice, he should expect people to speak their minds.'

'It's not me you need to convince. Go ahead. Vote how you like. I mean, that's the whole purpose of the exercise.' Theresa settled back in her seat, determined to enjoy the outing.

When they arrived at the mosque, the driver opened the door for Fereydoun and he got out briskly.

'Wait for me,' called Theresa, opening her own door and hurrying through the gate after him. The courtyard was even more beautiful than she had imagined. A place of peace. God's garden. In the centre of the yard was a large pond, which she knew from photographs would be covered with lilies later in the year. There were shrubs showing tightly wrapped bundles of green at the tip of each branch. At the far end of the stretch of water yawned the enormous tiled arch leading into the mosque. Above it glowed the dome, turquoise against a cloudless sky.

Fereydoun marched up to the voting table and produced his identity card. The official handed him the green slip. Fereydoun shook his head and continued holding out his hand. The official thrust the green card forward again. Fereydoun drew back his hand, refusing to take it. The men at the table conferred, in some agitation. Two Pasdaran strolled over to see what the fuss was about.

139

Theresa looked round and wondered what Fereydoun was doing. She hurried over.

'The other card please,' he insisted, politely but determined. At the same time, Theresa saw him swallow nervously. He was being pig-headed again.

One of the officials was bent over double, rummaging in a metal waste-paper bin. When he stood up, his face was as red as the slips of paper for the Shah's return. He shook his head.

'I'm sorry, Agha. I cannot find the right one.' He gestured apologetically. 'Perhaps the gentleman would like this one instead?' He again held out the green card.

'No. I would not.' Fereydoun was shouting now. It was obviously quite the wrong behaviour for a mosque. Theresa stared at the opposite wall, at the posters of the Ayatollah waving a green card, smiling. Even with her limited Farsi, she could sense that Fereydoun had got hold of the wrong end of the stick. It would be so much better if he just did as he was told.

'How dare you,' shouted Fereydoun. The officials shrank back into their chairs. Some of the waiting voters giggled. The Mullah strolled over.

'I think,' he said, 'that the gentleman has a perfect right to vote as he wishes. The Ayatollah would not like to think that pressure had been put on anyone to vote against their will.'

'What are you going to do about it then?' Fereydoun sneered.

Theresa feared the situation was getting out of hand.

'Oh come on, darling. As if one little card will make any difference anyway.'

Leaning over the table, Theresa picked up the green card that was causing all the trouble and popped it into the 'yes' box. Then she grabbed Fereydoun by the arm and led him away.

* * *

140

Shirin Khaksar, like most of her friends had stayed at home. She knew that there could only be one outcome to the referendum. It was a waste of effort to pretend otherwise. She sat and juggled with budget figures for the coming year, knowing that this exercise too was merely hypothetical. It was, she told herself, an exercise to preserve her sanity, to convince herself that life would carry on as normal. The tragedy of the situation was that the fate of so many people hung upon her plans for the coming year. So much suffering that could have been avoided if the administration had not chosen to ignore her Ministry completely.

'Thank you for coming with me, Jamshid.' Mrs Emani smiled nervously at her son. 'I was worried about coming on my own. It's years since I've been inside a mosque.'

Jamshid scowled and looked the other way.

'I'll wait here,' he muttered, leaning on the gate post, whistling, pretending he was not really with her.

'But where do I go?'

Jamshid jerked his head in the direction of the queue, then looked the other way again.

Mrs Emani crossed the courtyard, expecting martyrdom at every step. Under her scarf, her right hand gripped the medal of Mary and the child Jesus. 'Holy Mary, Mother of God,' she prayed as she stumbled over the uneven cobbles, 'pray for us sinners.' She stepped on the heel of the man in front of her. He turned and spat.

Mrs Emani doubled her 'Hail Mary's'. She said a prayer for herself. Another for the Shah and his family. Poor things! Even a holiday in the Bahamas would not be much fun, what with all the worry. And an 'Our Father' for the princes, such dear little boys.

There she was, at the front of the queue. 'Help me Jesus.' And there was a basket full of red slips on her right. Just imagine, she thought to herself, so many people hoping for the return of God's anointed King. Mrs Emani placed her card reverently on top of the pile.

'But what do I do with this one?' she asked the official, waving the green card.

'Put it in there,' he said.

Mrs Emani walked over to the ballot box he indicated, and posted the green slip. How kind of them, to avoid hurting the Ayatollah's feelings like that, putting the rejections in an enclosed box so that nobody could see.

Happy that she had done her duty, Mrs Emani turned back in search of her son.

10

Spring is in the air – in the cloudless blue of the sky and in the cherry blossom beneath my window. Pigeons coo in the gutters and young lovers stroll arm in arm . . . but no, my vision plays me false. That was another time, another place. Here there are no young lovers, or if there are, they have more sense than to wander through the streets together.

Let us forget for a moment that three hundred and fifty people have been executed in the last two months, for today the sun shines kindly. I feel its warmth on my forearms as I lean on the window-sill. Let us close our eyes and imagine – what? Breathe in the sounds and smells from the streets, and find ourselves – where?

In some far-off Eastern land where sun and snow bite with equal savagery, where fountains play and children starve, and women glide by like ghosts beneath their veils. Tall grows the poppy, blood-red in the sunshine, stirred by the wind to whisper of dreams. Fair is the blossom of the almond in spring and in late summer a peach blushes in the heat.

Deep within this land there is a house, within the house a maze of courtyards, within the courtyards, corridors and walled gardens. In the centre of the maze, where droplets of water tinkle into a marble basin with the softness of a dulcimer and the perfume of roses hangs heavy, the women lived.

In the andarun, the passage of days is marked by the itinerant shade of a cypress tree, moving like some giant phallus in a clockwise direction across their lives.

But soft, what disturbance is this? Ah, the motor car.

The air already hazy with exhaust. So many cars, so many people per car! It is impossible to count the heads, among the carpets, saucepans and samovars piled deep on the back seat. For today is the Sizdah Now Ruz – thirteenth day of the New Year, National Picnic Day.

The day to leave one's house, doors and windows open wide, to let out the spirits of the old year and let in the new. A day to have faith in the old traditions and overlook the malevolent tendency of certain contemporary spirits to leave, laden with the best carpets and silver.

The Spring of Freedom, this has been called. The Ayatollah has been affirmed in his position by the unanimous support of a record turnout of voters. Here comes our old friend the Mullah, like a spring chicken – a new lightness in his step and his beard glowing white in the sunshine. Let us too wander awhile and bask in the gentle warmth of the sun before its ferocity overwhelms us in the coming months.

'Oh the sun shines bright in my old Kentucky home, it's spring and de darkies . . .' But I forget myself in the temporary insanity of the season. There can be no singing in public, by the unanimous consent, etc. etc. etc.

'What a lovely day!' Roya stood at the bedroom window. Masoud grunted, rolled over and went back to sleep. Roya hurried into the kitchen to check the picnic. Large pan for the chelo. The other pan – full of meat – to take out of the fridge. She tied the lid on with some string so that no gravy would slop out. Tomatoes in a paper bag. A chopping board and a knife. Sabzi, for the salad. A chinking bag full of bottles, Coca Cola and lemonade. A few shirini to munch in the indolent heat of the afternoon. Temperatures were forecast to reach seventy degrees. If only the children would get up!

'I don't know why you go to so much trouble, Mama,'

said Soraya, yawning as she came into the kitchen in her nightdress. 'It's all superstition anyway.'

'It's the one day in the year when we all go out together. Besides I like the old customs.' Roya rolled up a carpet and added it to the pile for packing.

'I think it's all a ridiculous fuss about nothing.'

Theresa Homayoun was buttering bread. The bread was old and gritty.

'Darling, you should remember that your children are Iranian and they must get to know our customs.'

'Not all customs are worth keeping. Anyway, I hate picnics.' Theresa opened a tin of sardines. Sardine and egg sandwiches was the best she could do. There had been no tinned ham, spam or luncheon meat left in the shops, no peanut butter and no cheese. The sandwiches looked as grey and unexciting as they would taste. She had been pleased to find some biscuits.

'Home-made,' said the man from the local supermarket, proudly. They looked it. Theresa thought back to the glories of the Austrian patisserie. She knew that like all local biscuits, however appetizing they looked with their sprinkling of cinnamon, they would dissolve into a dry powder that clung around the mouth and teeth.

And there was some turkish delight that Muna had made. Would it be safe to let the children eat it, or not? Thank God for the oranges!

'Would you like coffee or tea?' Theresa asked Fereydoun.

'We can buy some Coke when we get there.'

'Will it be cold?'

'Darling, how would they make it cold out there?'

'Well I'm not drinking warm Coke. Anyway, it's bad for the children's teeth.'

'It wouldn't hurt them for once.'

Theresa filled a bottle with juice and a thermos with

tea. There seemed so much to take for one day out. The picnic fitted into one small bag, but the extra clothes, the flannels and towels, the dry pants, books and toys would more than fill the boot.

The Gabayans drove for an hour and a half into the country. Roya sang for much of the way. From time to time she looked back at her three children and smiled. There was not a cloud in the sky. Masoud stopped by a river lined with trees whose leaf buds just showed green.

'What a beautiful spot,' Roya sighed.

Masoud grunted, got out of the car, spread the rug, lay down on it, and closed his eyes. Hussein wandered along the riverbank kicking loose pebbles into the water, with a bored frown on his face.

Roya and the girls humped all the paraphernalia out of the boot. Seated cross-legged on the ground, Roya lit the burner.

'The rice always tastes better cooked in river water,' she said to Soheila. Soheila sat on the rug near her mother. She pulled strands of hair over her face then plaited them, humming, aware of the cold gurgle of the river and the warmth of the sun on the top of her head.

Soraya sat on a large grey stone further along the river bank. A legal textbook lay open on her knee. She dipped one hand into the icy water and gasped at the cold. On the mountainside beyond, the gullies were streaks of white, packed with snow. It was an idyllic spot. Soraya would have liked to lie back and feel the warm sun on her growing stomach. To give up all this subterfuge and pretence.

Instead she sat huddled with her chador close about her, while her eyes stared unseeing at the open book. Soon she was to leave for Isfahan. She was being sent away, to bear her baby out of sight, among relatives she hardly knew.

146

Roya sang as she cooked. She shook the pearly grains of rice into the boiling water. Through the steam she could see grass, and hear birdsong and the sounds of the river. Beyond that she refused to think. She let the perfection of the day envelop her, shrinking within the small cocoon of happiness and wishing that it might last forever.

'But this is awful. We can't stop here.' Theresa Homayoun looked out of the car window at the bare earth, the litter, the crowds.

'But it's beautiful, darling. Trees, river and grass, what more could you want?' Her husband turned off the engine and climbed out. He stood, stretching his arms high above his head. The sun fell warm on the white flesh between his trousers and his shirt. 'Come on. It's lovely. It's spring!'

Theresa undid her safety-belt and let the children out of their car seats.

'They'll get filthy,' she said. Fereydoun shrugged. He took Farah by one hand, Reza by the other and ran towards the river.

'Be careful,' called Theresa, following with the picnic. If she looked carefully enough at her feet, she could see that there were a few straggly blades of grass and the river was pretty enough dancing in the sunlight. But where could she sit?

All around, other people sat on enormous rugs. Pots of rice boiled. Samovars steamed. Theresa felt ashamed of her sardine sandwiches, of the way everyone looked at her. Trust Fereydoun to choose somewhere like this! She began to realize that he had not come for the peace, but as usual, to a place where he would be seen and noticed.

Theresa dusted a stone with her handkerchief and perched on it. She was wearing her white trousers. She put on sunglasses, anticipating a headache. Someone would have to unpack the car at the end of the day, cook a meal and put the children to bed. And that would be her.

Fereydoun, Reza and Farah teetered on a rock in the river, squealing and laughing as the water lapped against it.

'Be careful,' called Theresa. Wet shoes would be the last straw. She hurried down the bank. Distracted, her family looked up and lost concentration. Backwards and forwards they swayed as Fereydoun yanked the children's arms high into the air.

'Look out, Reza's got one foot in the water,' shouted Theresa. 'I haven't brought any spare shoes. Really Fereydoun, you are the limit.'

The courtyards of the Mahalleh oozed mud, but the sun was warm. The inhabitants emerged cautiously, sitting on their doorsteps, or perched on window-sills above the filth, letting the warmth dispel months of cold and inactivity.

Fariba removed the sacking from the window. She wedged open the door so that the accumulated foulness of winter was carried away by the gentle breeze. She draped the bedclothes over the wall in the sun. She swept the floor.

The women chatted around the tap while they did their washing. Fariba was pleased to see her mother join them. Perhaps she had been worrying unnecessarily.

'Well, well, Aziz!' clucked the women, nudging one another, looking at her growing stomach. 'Another son, eh?' Aziz laughed self-consciously.

'My Esther will be married this spring. She's a woman now.' The neighbour proudly held up the bloodstained rags that indicated womanhood. 'What about your Fariba?'

'Oh no, not yet,' Aziz protested. 'She's only a child.'

148

'She's a big girl though. Can't be much younger than my Esther. Must be ten now?'

The women squeezed and dipped, squeezed and dipped the colourless rags in and out of the stone trough.

'What about this Revolution?' someone asked.

'Just an excuse for the men not to work if you ask me.'

Revolutions seemed alien to a day of early spring. There could be no danger in the sunshine.

'Now we are all free, that's what *he* keeps telling me,' screeched another woman. She pointed to Aziz's stomach and her ribs rattled as she laughed, like a shower of dead leaves in autumn.

Shirin Khaksar picnicked on her balcony, with a sandwich and a cup of tea. For her the day was filled with memories. Days by the river when the children were small, playing ducks and drakes, paddling until their little feet were wrinkled and blue with cold. More recently, there had been invitations to ski, to share the restaurant reserved for the royal family. The sheen of sunlight on snow through steamed-up windows. Those days were nothing compared with the earlier ones, rich with children's voices.

From the street below came the sounds of happy families. Under every tree, on every patch of grass. Everywhere pots of water steamed while children romped and squealed and took unwonted liberties with their prostrate fathers.

Mrs Emani picked her way among the groups. She wished Jamshid were with her, but he had been invited out with a friend for the day. In her bag she had a roll of flat bread containing goat's cheese, but alone she lacked the courage to sit down and eat it.

She looked this way and that, beaming on the children,

envying the plump capable women who doled out food. Perhaps somewhere there might be someone she knew?

Mrs Emani began to feel hungry, even a little faint. She mumbled a prayer of acceptance to Jesus. It was obviously not her fate to be part of a large family. She had been an only child, given by her parents in sigheh, a temporary marriage which had left her as a single parent with a young baby. No. Her family, her reward, awaited her in heaven, but there were times when she suffered the pangs of mortal longing.

'Hey! Khanum-e-Emani!'

She turned, screwing up her eyes in the direction of the voice. Someone she knew? The voice was familiar but she couldn't quite place it. Still, he knew her name and she followed the direction of the call. A tall man stood there, waving a napkin.

'Ali!' she said. She had never seen him standing up before.

'Please you are my guest.'

Ali bowed. Mrs Emani inclined her head in silent thanks.

'My wife.' Ali waved a kebab in the direction of the short stout woman, who held out a steaming plateful of rice for their visitor. Mrs Emani sank onto the carpet, beautifully darned as she would have expected.

'Your own work?' she asked. Ali laughed delightedly. Mrs Emani sat and smiled happily, the sun seemed brighter and warmer than before.

11

'Three hundred and fifty dead, Royaja.' Masoud stabbed at the newsprint as if it was his personal enemy. 'And that is without counting these.'

Roya stared at the handwritten list fluttering in front of her. Her stomach lurched as she looked at the writing.

'Amir Taheri, Fereydoun Homayoun, Ali Motazery. What is this list, Masoud?'

'The Revolutionary Prosecutor has asked. I am the humble servant of Allah. These people must be brought to justice.'

'Masoudja, how have these people harmed you that you should bring such disaster on them? Let bygones be bygones.'

'You speak with a forked tongue, wife. These people corrupt the very air they breathe. They pollute our country.'

'Corrupt upon Earth, Mama.' Hussein's voice grated from bass to soprano. He put his arms round his throat and made strangled noises.

Roya took out her knitting and took a deep breath before speaking.

'Masoudja, trials have been suspended. There are to be no more executions. Let it remain that way. Let there be no more bloodshed . . . We have an Islamic Republic. What more do you want?'

'I shall not rest until my country has been purged and purified.' Masoud stood up, hands raised, eyes fixed on the mountains, the glow of the sunrise on his face. 'You women, you cannot understand, you are weak and sentimental by nature. You always look for hope, but

151

where a tree is rotten the only answer is to cut it down lest it damage some passer-by. There must be more trials, more executions. We demand it.'

'And the list, Masoud, who else is on the list?'

'Aha! Now you're talking.' Masoud leaned across the table and pushed the sheet of paper closer, so that Roya could read it.

'But Masoud, these people have only disagreed with you. That is not corruption . . .'

'I knew you wouldn't understand. Stick to your dishes.' He snatched the list away. 'Mind your daughters. God only knows, they need help. Leave these matters to people who know what they are doing.'

Masoud jammed a small fez on top of his head.

'Come, Hussein.' The two flounced towards the door. 'You'll see. That bastard Hoveyda, and everyone like him. We'll get them in the end.'

Masoud and Hussein stomped out of the flat, leaving all the doors open. Wearily Roya clambered to her feet. How her legs ached these days of endless queues, but at least it was spring and her chilblains no longer troubled her.

'Hussein,' she called down the stairway. 'What about school? What about your education?' The outside door slammed and she was left with the echo of her own voice.

'Please, let's go to Qom, Dad,' Hussein begged as they walked along the street. Masoud hesitated. How long was it since he'd been to the shop? Really, he ought . . . but the air was crisp in the early morning. A day in the country? He twisted his beads around his fingers, undecided. He put a hand into his pocket for a handkerchief and instead felt the crackle of paper. His list. His own little pogrom. It seemed as if Allah was pointing the way.

152

'Mashallah, thanks be to God.' Ushering his son before him, Masoud changed direction for the bus station.

In the south of Tehran the dust had begun to rise, and would stalk the city on its daily grind. Sand-coloured upper storeys hovered foundationless on a sea of sand. The squat, flat rooftops were punctuated here and there by the bulbous dome of a mosque. And everywhere were the people. They scurried to and from the bazaar, the heart of the capital.

Masoud thought lovingly of his stall. It was the stall that mattered most to him, not the shop which earned all those dollars of foreign exchange. Nearer to his heart lay the dusty recess deep within the bazaar where his carpets gleamed in the solid golden pillars of sunlight streaming through the vaulting.

'It will all be yours some day,' murmured Masoud as they sat on the bus, and he gave his son's knee a squeeze.

Hussein coughed and looked out of the window. He saw a beggar drag himself to the edge of the jube to urinate. Hussein stared. The man had no legs, yet he could perform just like anyone else. Hussein wound down the window and flung out a few rials. The man scrabbled for the coins in the dust.

'Of course, they are all millionaires,' said Masoud, but he was proud of his son.

On in a southerly direction the coach travelled, criss-crossing the railway line through miles of makeshift dwellings, then on to the highway to Qom. The tarmac was a dazzle of heat and light. Hussein slept, his head lolling against his father's shoulder. Masoud put an arm round the boy to steady him. He seemed younger, more vulnerable, when he was asleep. More in need of a father's care.

The countryside rolled by – flat, barren and monotonous. Then on the floating horizon, suspended on a shimmering sea of dust and light, appeared the golden dome of Qom.

'Husseinja, Hussein, wake up.' Masoud shook his son and pointed at the vast onion of shimmering metal. Masoud's beads flicked through his fingers as if totalling some vast reckoning on his abacus at the end of a day. His lips moved in a blur of prayer that escaped like a faint moan.

'Shit,' said Theresa.

'Darling, please don't make a scene.'

'I am not making a scene, I simply want a game of tennis.'

'Darling, please be reasonable. It's not that man's fault. The Ayatollah has said that women's sports must be stopped.'

'If he's worried about my virginity, he's too late.'

'Darling, please.'

'Well, what the hell am I supposed to do with my life? I can't work, I can't drink. I've lost my car and my friends have left the country. What can I do?'

'Darling, please! People are looking.'

'Let them look. I am taking off my tracksuit and playing tennis as we arranged.'

'Please, Theresa, don't. You must keep your legs covered.'

'What's wrong with my legs? I always thought you liked them.'

'Darling, please, keep your trousers on.' Fereydoun grabbed hold of the elasticated waist band and pulled while Theresa pushed. The chief attendant of the courts looked on impassively.

'Ferangi!' he muttered contemptuously, clicking his tongue against the roof of his mouth, head tilted back.

'And tell that man to stop staring at me.'

'He won't stare if you will keep your trousers on and go away quietly, like a good girl.'

'And what will you do?'

'Go into the clubhouse and see if there is anyone there who will give me a game.'

'But won't you even complain?'

'I can't, darling.'

'Stop calling me darling. I can't stand it.'

'Sorry, darling.'

'If you really loved me you'd go in there and tell them you'll never come here again.'

'Darling, please just get into the car and go home.'

'Not with him driving.'

The driver stared straight ahead as if he hadn't noticed what was going on.

'Take her home,' Fereydoun snapped.

'How dare you tell me where to go. What is there to do at home anyway?'

The driver looked at Fereydoun, wondering whom he should obey.

'Very well,' he said. 'Go where you like.'

Fariba Baniyazdi ran all the way home. Though her brothers called 'Wait for us' and her friends shouted after her 'Fariba ku? Where are you?' she soon outstripped them all. Across the dusty maidan, in and out of alleyways, the perfume of spices, the stink of dung, through the zebra patterns of the slanting sun.

Underneath her chador, her treasure was safe. Safe to show Mama. Mama would be so amazed, so proud of her daughter. Round a sharp corner, the sun in her eyes, bump, into a donkey. The donkey swayed, bracing its pitiful legs against the heavy panniers of salt. Fariba rebounded off the coarse sacks and fell, hitting her head.

The donkey driver paused only to spit down at Fariba, cursing her and all womankind in the name of Allah.

Fariba walked on more slowly now. There was a gaping split in her chador, but Mama would put everything right. She pushed open the door. Where was Mama? Not among the group of women around the tap. Not gathering in the day's washing from the mud walls. Not on the doorstep picking over rice for tea. Fariba's heart contracted with fear. She ran across the yard into their room.

'Mama!' Fariba wailed, blinded by the sudden blackness.

'Mama,' she called more desperately. Only Shahnaz sat up, startled out of sleep.

'It's alright, Shahnaz. I'm here. Fariba's here.' She picked up her little sister. 'Hush now.'

Then in a corner, something stirred.

'Mama?'

Fariba stumbled through the bedding and fell on her knees beside her mother.

'Mama, I couldn't find you. I was frightened.'

Her mother reached out an arm and pulled the child towards her.

'I'm better now you're back,' said Aziz. 'I'll get up. Tidy. Cook. Baba will be angry.'

Fariba hid her treasure in her bedroll and folded it away, waiting for another opportunity. Some time when she was alone with Mama. The thought of the small parcel gave her a warm feeling while she helped. Mama would be so pleased. No more scoldings at school, all her work perfect from now on. Her life would be totally different.

In spite of her mother's illness, Fariba sang as she swept. Why, she felt so strong she could even make her Mama better. Her mother looked up from the doorstep, picking the tiny husks and stones out of the rice. She sneezed, dazzled by the gleam of the white grains and the glint of metal where the paint had worn off the tin tray.

Aziz began to hum Fariba's tune. Lulled by the sound,

Shahnaz snuggled against her. Fariba, singing in duet now, felt that her heart would break with happiness.

Theresa was happy. Fereydoun needed her. He loved her. She spent hours each day shopping, seeking out little extras to make the evening meal an occasion. She showered, washed her hair and changed each afternoon. She encouraged the children to run to their father when he came home from work, to show him their paintings and cardboard models from nursery school. Fereydoun was the perfect father.

Theresa went into the bedroom where the children lay, drowsy with sleep.

'Goodnight, Farah.' Theresa bent and kissed the child's forehead. She loved Farah so much at this hour of the day, so clean and soft and vulnerable.

'Stay with me, Mummy.' Farah wrapped her arms round Theresa and held on to her tightly.

Very softly Theresa sang 'Mary, Mary, quite contrary' until the grip loosened. By the time she turned to Reza he was already asleep.

Fereydoun stood in the doorway, watching. He loved to see Theresa with the children. At such moments marriage fulfilled his deepest dreams – Goli's company was nothing by comparison.

Theresa jumped when she realized he was there, watching her.

'Darling,' he whispered, pulling Theresa towards him. With his foot he closed the nursery door.

'What about dinner?' Theresa asked. 'The servants will be putting it on the table.'

'Never mind the servants.'

'See this!' Masoud Gabayan thrust the newspaper under Roya's nose. 'See what the Ayatollah says – nothing namby-pamby about him! "We try these people according to documents, but our objection is that they should not be tried. They should be killed."'

Roya stared at her husband. One trip to Qom had completely unhinged him.

'Of course,' Masoud continued, 'it's all because we went to see him.'

Perhaps, thought Roya, he was trying to occupy himself so as to leave no time for thinking about Soraya's pregnancy. And if such diversion relieved the pressure on her daughter, perhaps it should be encouraged. There had been mornings when he had wept and prayed that this nightmare should not happen to him.

'You remember, Roya,' he had said on one of these occasions, 'how we didn't let her run and play with the other children. We were so worried that any sudden jolt might break the hymen. Now look at her, shaped like a spice vat!'

'You always were old-fashioned in your views, Masoud. People don't think like that any more.'

'But they do, Roya, they do. The shame of it if any of my friends ever found out.'

'Masoudja, how many women do you think bleed on their wedding night?'

'All of them.'

'That is not true. I've read about it in the magazines. It only happens to forty-four per cent of virgins.'

He had been so angry then that she had been frightened.

'Then they are not virgins. They are not as they should be. You, wife, you talk with the tongue of the devil.'

And Roya had to hear once again the catalogue of her failures until she began to doubt herself. Perhaps she really was to blame for Soraya's downfall.

Bedtime. And still young Fariba Baniyazdi had found no opportunity to show her mother her secret. Fariba took the bedrolls down from the shelf. Out fell the small red case with a clonk on the concrete floor.

'What's that?' Her brothers pounced.

'Stop. Those are my spectacles.'

Her mother turned round.

'Mama, please stop them. They will break them.'

Aziz waddled into the fray and seized the glasses.

'Mama, see, they've bent them.' The glasses hung lopsided on Fariba's face so that one eye looked through a lens and the other peered over the top of the frame.

'Where did you get those, Fariba?'

'The doctor gave them to me, Mama. So that I can see the letters on the blackboard.'

'Mashallah! That is good, Fariba, if it helps with your work.'

'Doesn't she look funny.' Mussa capered up and down in front of his sister making faces. The others followed suit, mimicking the idiot boy who lumbered from the neighbouring room each morning.

'Look Baba, doesn't she look silly?'

'Shut up,' said Fariba. 'Lots of people wear glasses. Look at the papers and the magazines. Even the Empress used to wear glasses sometimes.'

Now Hamid stood up. He walked over and snatched the spectacles from his daughter's nose.

'No daughter of mine will go around looking like that.' He flung them against the wall as hard as he could. The lenses shattered and the boys grabbed the frames.

Fariba said nothing.

Aziz spoke up. 'Hamid, you shouldn't have done that.'

'No daughter of mine is going around looking like that.'

'Hamidja, it is only for school.'

'Why does she need to go to school anyway?'

'Nowadays it is important that a girl should read and write.'

159

'You can't.'

'But for Fariba it is necessary. Things are changing.'

'For Fariba only marriage is necessary. And who will marry her if they know there is something wrong with her?'

Fariba sat, dazed.

'Tell me who has seen you looking like that?' Her father rounded on her.

'Only the children in my class.'

'Only the children in your class,' he mimicked. 'And they will tell their families. Oh God, how will I ever live this down?' Hamid buried his face in his hands and wept at the shame of having an unmarriageable daughter.

12

Blood flows again – not just executions but also these
interminable nose-bleeds. I sometimes fear that this fre-
quent loss of blood may begin to affect my health. Ice
packs and pinchings are so frequently applied that my skin
feels excessively tender. One doctor suggested cauteriz-
ation, but I dislike anything painful, and the thought of
singeing flesh turns my stomach.

However, enough of my health for the time being. Let
me escort you to a veritable spectacle, a son et lumière.
Most of Tehran is there, although they would be warmer
at home and have a better view on the telly. But it is the
atmosphere which makes these occasions. You have to
have atmosphere. The common feeling that unites individ-
uals and creates that homogeneous entity, the crowd. What
is a football match, without the brass bands and the packed
stands and the feeling of being all for the home team?

Here one group of friends, there another, one in thought
and outlook, excitement, anticipation. They'll never dare,
yes they will, no they won't, aah, ooh. Salaam aleikum,
halé shoma, handshakes all round.

'It's a fine night, Hamid.' Houshang stamped his feet and
slapped his hands together. Hamid Baniyazdi grinned,
looking up at the clear skies.

'Could be a frost.'

'Aré. But sunshine tomorrow, eh?'

The air was so clear that the stars seemed to dance, in
flashes of brilliant green and blue.

'There's a good crowd.'

'Oh yes, a good turnout. You'd expect that though.'

'We might even get our pictures in the newspaper.'

Hamid laughed. He couldn't afford a newspaper, but it was nice to think of himself in print, for all to see.

'Of course, there's nothing like an execution to draw the crowds nowadays.' Houshang cupped his hands over his mouth and blew into them.

'People like a bit of blood. Remember, Houshang, eh? How they used to gather round while we worked. The women and children were the worst. How they squealed!'

'Oh yes. A quick chop chop and the blood spurting into the gutter . . . We worked well together, didn't we?'

'Mashallah! Those were the days, Houshang.' Hamid sighed and shook his head. His family had not lacked in those days. There was always the odd scrap here and there. Not so much that anyone ever noticed. Just a few marrow bones for the kiddies to suck. A sliver of meat shaved off here and there – enough for a stew. The odd hen for special occasions. Yes, those were the days.

'What's the time?' Masoud Gabayan turned to his son, Hussein. He didn't have a watch himself. He could barely tell the time. He knew when to open and close the shop, and his mealtimes. But Hussein. There was a clever lad. Always one for gadgets. He liked to know how they worked too.

'Not time yet, Baba.'

'It's chilly.'

The boy nodded.

'There'll be a touch of frost tonight. Good crowd though.'

Masoud edged his way forwards, nearer to the centre of the square. It was warmer there, where the crowd was thickest. Masoud was cross that he hadn't brought a coat. While the days were so warm it was easy to forget how cold the nights could be. Because of the altitude and the mountains, Hussein said. He was probably right. Masoud

162

didn't know. The weather was as it was. As it always had been. Just that he forgot.

Outside the Alavieh School, a few loudspeakers clung forlornly to telegraph poles. Like the hiss of a dragon came the call for silence. The Ayatollah would speak. Not directly, of course. On tape.

The crowd was tense, straining to hear. A verdict was expected today. They could yet be disappointed, find they had turned out in vain. Hoveyda's trial had become a matter of international concern. There had been telegrams from abroad. Foreign intervention it was called. Interference, in Masoud's opinion.

'We try these people according to documents,' came the voice of the Ayatollah, 'but our objection is that criminals should not be tried, they should be killed!'

The rest of his speech was drowned by a roar of approval.

Shirin Khaksar sat next to her radio. She was listening to the news on the BBC World Service. Pleas for clemency had been sent by the heads of state of most European countries.

She glanced at the newspaper, at the photograph of the former Prime Minister. He seemed shrunken inside large folds empty of flesh. He wore a cheap leather jacket, though she knew he would never have possessed such a thing. She mourned the loss of the cigar and the carnation whose perpetual freshness had been almost legendary.

How much, Shirin wondered, had her own decision to remain in the country been influenced by Hoveyda's presence. Was she in some way trying to emulate him? If so, she could well finish up the same way. She shivered and began pacing up and down the room. Was her work really that important? What Revolutionary Tribunal would value the strides taken in social welfare? They would be seen simply as another paternalistic plot to repress the peoples of Iran.

Shirin lit a cigarette and turned off the radio. Looking south over the city, she felt suddenly afraid. What was she now but an unveiled woman, and a Bahai at that? Everything was stacked against her survival. She should have packed her bags and scampered in the wake of her royal patrons. But there was also Manuchehr. She felt sometimes that the shadow of her former husband hung poised, waiting, just waiting for her to set foot across the border. She feared Islam less.

Yet, cheated of their real quarry, the Shah, she had watched the people's lust for blood become insatiable. Now, she was deprived of the immunity of a government employee. Bahai'ism had been denounced as a heretical sect. She was on the list of persons forbidden to leave the country without special permission. There was only one possible outcome.

Shirin sat down and wrote a letter of resignation. She left the letter for her secretary to deliver to the Prime Minister.

For their sakes, it was better not to contact anyone she knew. With sufficient money, she hoped, for some months' living expenses, and a couple of suitcases (one of clothes, the other packed with papers and books), Shirin set off for the nearest bus-stop.

'Why don't you go to youth club tonight, Jamshid?' Mrs Emani was worried about her son. What was there for a teenager to do in the evenings nowadays?

'Because there isn't any bloody youth club, that's why.'

'Have you got a nice book to read?'

'Books, I'm sick of books.'

'I could get some of those old books out of the attic.'

'Who wants to read stuff like that?'

164

'What sort of books do you like then?' Mrs Emani put the kettle on to boil.

'American books. English books. You know – paperbacks.'

His mother nodded. She had seen books like that lying around in Jamshid's room. Some of the covers worried her, but the teachers said it was good for Jamshid to read English. Such a clever boy he was – such thick books some of them. They confused her, all this left to right business.

'Let's have a cup of tea then,' she suggested, pulling up her headscarf, nervously tightening the knot under her chin.

Jamshid flung his school book on the floor and flounced out of the room.

'Where are you going, Jamshidja?'

'Out.'

Mrs Emani sighed and picked up the book. Ferdowsi. Selected works. Such a lovely poet, she had enjoyed reading his poems at school. But the young people nowadays, all they wanted was entertainment. Ice-skating. Parties. Discos. And of course there was nothing like that any more.

'Darling, I shall be working late tonight.'

So it had happened at last, thought Theresa. Fereydoun had met somebody else. She stood quite still, staring at the white telephone.

'Darling, are you still there?'

'Well,' said Theresa, slowly, 'I'll see you later then.' She put down the receiver.

As she ate dinner alone, Theresa thought that she might as well resume her Farsi classes. She would just be in time if she hurried. Asking Muna to look after the children, she went into the bedroom to change. Trousers to go into town. It would be better to have her legs

165

covered. She drew the line at a headscarf, but decided on a blue knitted hat. It would keep her ears warm on a chilly night.

Theresa drove into town and parked the Mercedes down a sidestreet where she hoped it would go unnoticed. Then she walked round the corner to the British Council building. Although only a minute early for the class, she was surprised to find herself the first to arrive. She sat and thumbed through her textbook. A chapter on etiquette.

'After you.'

'No, please, after you.'

'But please excuse my back.'

'A flower has no back.'

Theresa tried to imagine having such a conversation with Fereydoun. In the morning, perhaps, when they collided in the corridor leading to the bathroom?

At eight o'clock, Theresa went to look for the janitor. He was in the entrance hall as usual.

'What has happened to the Farsi classes?'

The man shrugged.

'Farsi classes,' she repeated loudly. 'Kojast?'

The man smiled and nodded. Theresa was annoyed that after three terms of lessons she couldn't even ask where the classes were being held.

She felt badly disappointed. Not that the classes were very exciting, but she had enjoyed the company of other expatriates struggling to learn the language, and the visit to a café afterwards. She looked down the sidestreet where she had left her car. It was surrounded by men – thieves or Revolutionary Guards, she couldn't tell. They were looking through the car windows. Now they tried the doors. Theresa had tested them only from the inside, forgetting the child safety locks.

She watched as the men removed her library books from the front seat. They ripped out their pages before

166

piling them up in the middle of the road. On top, they placed Farah's knitted Piglet. One of the men took Theresa's spare powder compact from the glove compartment and ground it to bits with his heel.

Then, obviously pleased with themselves, they set fire to the small heap of belongings. Theresa ran back inside the British Council and pretended to read the notice boards until they had gone.

Fereydoun Homayoun had, for once, told Theresa the truth. He was working late, with a fearful speed. Fereydoun was scared. He sifted through the filing cabinets, removing letters and plans which might be compromising. 'His Imperial Majesty requests that . . .' Into the bin it went. A receipt from the Pahlavi Foundation. That query about additional toilets for an orphanage once under royal patronage . . .

Fereydoun now devoted all his working hours to this task. There was nothing else to do. Construction sites stood idle. Gangs of erstwhile labourers roamed the town and camped in unfinished buildings.

When the rest of the staff had gone, Fereydoun went into the office basement, where the shredder and incinerator worked overtime. He consigned his dreams of fame and fortune to the flames, working in a frenzy while the vengeance of Islam descended from Prime Minister to Major-General, from Major-General to Private, from the aristocrat to the man in the street, seeking ever less spectacular victims to feed its fires.

Outside the Alavieh School, the crowd became restive, waiting for the verdict. Thousands of cold feet stamped to keep warm, the sound rippling like an ancient army on the move. The tramp of feet drowned even the exhortations of the Ayatollah. All eyes were trained on the school roof, waiting for a fresh sacrifice upon the altar of

Mohammed. Those nearest the school building pressed backwards, unable to see over the parapet of the roof.

'God, Houshang, I shall get a crick in my neck if they are much longer,' muttered Hamid Baniyazdi through chattering teeth.

'It won't be long now, Hamid. Just be patient.'

'Perhaps we came too late?'

'Well,' said Masoud Gabayan, 'that's one of the penalties of coming early. We've been pushed to the front and shan't see a thing.'

'Oh Baba, can't we go further back then?'

'Not a chance.'

From within the building came a muffled shot. The crowd leaned forward, listening. Was it . . . ? Then another, unmistakable this time in the sudden silence. Two shots? Masoud looked at his son, puzzled. Then a voice over the loudspeaker. No one could make out the words, but they had only one possible meaning.

'Hell,' said Hamid. 'They didn't even let us see.' His friend's reply was drowned in the frenzy of cheering and dancing which followed.

'Never mind, son.' Masoud patted Hussein on the shoulder. 'I'll buy you the photographs in the morning.'

Roya Gabayan tuned in to the Tehran Home Service, still hoping against hope. After all, he was an old man. But Hoveyda was dead. Executed by a Mullah. The first shot, fired through the shoulder, had failed to kill him. A second shot was fired through the neck.

Shirin Khaksar got off the southbound bus on Shemiran Road, opposite the Catholic Mission. She waited until the other passengers had dispersed before she picked up her suitcases and set off for the house where her cousin had found lodgings during her university studies.

168

Shirin was not sure of the address, nor of the name of her cousin's landlady, but knew she would recognize the house when she got there. She stumbled up the uneven dirt road, the suitcases banging against her shins, shoulders and arms aching. Then she recognized the shabby grey doorway in a low grey building. She stepped quickly into the recess and hammered with her knuckles at the wood.

Mrs Emani opened the door and stared at the stranger.

'Salaam aleikum, Khanum.'

'Please, may I come in?' Shirin was anxious not to be seen.

'My house is yours.' Mrs Emani held open the door and stood back to allow the stranger inside.

'I am looking for somewhere to stay,' Shirin explained. She kept her face averted, her headscarf pulled forward to hide her face.

Mrs Emani was trying to place her. Where was it that she had seen her before?

'My cousin lodged with you two years ago. She was studying French at the university. Parvin, her name was.'

'Ah. What is she doing now? I never heard.'

'Teaching, in the States.'

'You used to visit her here?'

'Not as often as I should.'

'My home is not very comfortable. A hotel would suit you better.' Mrs Emani glanced at the cut of the coat, the imported shoes, the leather suitcases.

'I have reasons for wanting more privacy.'

'You are married? Your husband? You see I am alone, except for my son. I don't want any trouble.'

'We are separated.'

'You need time to think things over?' There had been a time when Mrs Emani could have done with breathing space.

'Do you have a room? I would look after myself, not

169

be any trouble. If not . . .' Shirin moved to pick up her cases.

'There is a small flat, but it is neither cleaned nor aired.'

Shirin turned back.

'I can do all that myself.'

'Please, follow me.'

Later that night, the Mullah Afsharzadeh heard a knock on his door. He unrolled himself from his blanket on the floor and stumbled towards the door.

'Well, well. Agha Gabayan. At this hour!'

Masoud stood on the doorstep, not knowing what to say.

'My home is yours in the name of God.' The Mullah opened the door wide, beckoning the man inside.

The two seated themselves cross-legged on the carpet, facing one another.

'God is ready day or night, to extend his mercy to us,' intoned the Mullah. 'Let us pray together.'

Masoud had become completely tongue-tied. He did not know where to begin. His eyes wandered over the pattern of the rug. A fine wine-red. Kashan probably. Hand-made, a hundred years old at least. Probably worth thousands. It was hard to find such craftsmanship nowadays.

The Mullah's voice flowed on, soothing, monotonous, crooning. Like a child listening to his mother's lullaby, Masoud felt at peace.

The Mullah's voice ceased. Between the two men a single candle flickered in a saucer. The flame cast grotesque shadows under the Mullah's chin, illuminating his nostrils and burying his eyes in dark caverns. His eyes were closed. Only the slight click of prayer beads and a faint movement of his lips indicated that the Mullah was awake.

Masoud slipped into the high-pitched whine of a bazaar beggar, humble before the spiritual bounty of God. A cringing abject wail of denunciation lest he too be incriminated. His tirade became ever more vicious, against his wife, his daughter, the evils of Westernization and then against the snares of materialism which threatened his own soul.

He prayed for God's help and forgiveness, and the Mullah listened.

13

Good morning! Another lovely day and a letter from my wife on the breakfast tray. Postmarked Provence. Another holiday? And you will be saying to yourselves: 'Did she like the photograph?' Let me satisfy your curiosity at once. It's all here in the first paragraph. The picture arrived safely, not through the post but delivered by hand – another pilot's, actually, who offered to deliver it to her in person.

In fact, I had really gone to town and bought an exquisite frame to set off the photograph. Have you ever seen one of those frames used for Persian miniatures? No? Well, let me describe it to you.

The Persians are masters in the ancient art of inlay – delicate gleaming confections of varnished wood and stone. Indeed, it is often the frame rather than the picture which attracts the eye. The one I chose, in purple, emerald and green, cost a small fortune and many hours in the bazaar plying my wits against the locals.

The frame measures some four feet by two. Extremely eye-catching, it leads the eye gradually to the centrepiece of my humble self, standard postcard sized, in full regalia.

My wife writes that she was so delighted with the present that she took it down to the farmhouse. In Paris, she says, she is surrounded by little reminders of my existence, but in the farmhouse (where I have never been) she finds it easy to forget me completely.

Unfortunately, when she tried to hang the picture, the weight was too great for the ancient walls, and she now awaits the arrival of a local plasterer to repair the damage.

In the meantime, she has returned the picture to its

wrapping paper and slipped it down behind the wardrobe for safety. She will not, she says, entrust anything so precious to locally bought nails again but will look for some good quality picture hooks on her return to the capital. Personally, I am delighted by her good sense. I sometimes fear a slapdash, impulsive tendency in my wife and it is gratifying to see, on this occasion, just how much time and energy she is expending on her husband's portrait.

And I really looked my best, though I say it myself. Not like, yes, here it is, front page as usual . . . our former Prime Minister under the Shah. No English papers being printed now, only Farsi, not that I ever let on to the staff here that I cannot read the half of it. Now, I have always made it my business only to be photographed at my best. But excuse me for a moment, my coffee will be getting cold.

Well, what's the old gentleman been up to? Still putting on a good show, I hope. Acquitted and halfway to Europe with a bit of luck. I wish I was in his shoes. I could slip down to Provence and give my wife a real surprise. Sometimes I wonder if I will ever get away . . .

'Waiter! You've forgotten the sugar again!' He really ought to remember by now that I always take sugar in my coffee, first thing in the morning only. I have a theory that it sweetens the breath.

Where was I? Yes. Hoveyda. More pictures on page two. That much I can understand. What do you mean, bang bang, Sir? Cash only, Sir? Twenty-five rials, Sir? Oh my God! One of your most famous politicians dead and all you can think about is money? *This is beyond a joke.*

'Take them away, Hussein. I don't want to see them.' Roya Gabayan thrust the pictures back into her son's hands. 'If ever you bring them in here again I'll burn them, do you hear?'

'What's the matter with you, Mama? They're only

173

photos. Baba bought them for me. Everyone's buying them. There's no need to make such a fuss. Look at this one! That's him sitting in the chair after the first shot. Then there's this one, after the second shot. He really looks dead now, doesn't he! Then this one's taken in the mortuary . . .'

Roya put her hands over her ears and left the room.

Masoud Gabayan sat in his stall in the bazaar. He felt justified in the extravagance of having bought two sets of pictures by the number of people they had attracted. He sipped his tea, balanced on a small wooden stool, and wished that everyone crowding round for a look had come to buy carpets.

'Well, Hamid, could you have done a neater job yourself?'

Hamid Baniyazdi laughed, showing his toothless gums. He stared at the trickles of blood, black on the white flesh. It was a pity that the Agha hadn't bought coloured photos, but then he always was mean.

'Houshangja, if it were me, I never strike twice.'

The two men sat on a rolled up carpet and laughed until the tears ran. Masoud joined in, gratified to be the source of such merriment.

'Be reasonable, darling. One servant is plenty for us – it's only a small flat. Muna can clean, help with the children, and still have time left over for cooking.'

'Muna has never even boiled an egg in her life.'

'Of course she has, for her family.'

'But not for mine.'

'Well, I'm sorry, darling. Business is not doing well at the moment. We have to be careful what we spend.'

'But darling, today is Muna's day off.'

Fereydoun shrugged and went off to the office.

Theresa went into the kitchen to make a start on the

174

breakfast dishes. She was horrified by the thick grease on every surface. She put on an apron and rubber gloves and began scraping fat off the cooker top. It was then that she saw the cockroach walking across the kitchen floor. Five inches long, antennae waving.

It was too big to step on. Theresa felt sick at the thought. She found the fly spray and sprayed until the vapour tickled the inside of her nostrils. The cockroach now moved as if demented, darting this way and that. Theresa took refuge on one of the kitchen cupboards until the maniacal zigzags ceased and the cockroach rolled over on its back.

An hour later it was still there, legs waving in the air. Theresa rang Homa.

'Pour oil down the drains so that they can't climb up,' advised her friend.

For the rest of the day Theresa trod warily round the dead insect and was unable to settle to anything. Fereydoun would deal with it in the evening.

Fereydoun had hailed a taxi to get to work.

'Takhte Tavous,' he said as he climbed in.

The driver grinned. Too familiar by half, thought Fereydoun.

'Look Agha!' All the way to town the driver kept pointing out the new signs painted on walls, swerving perilously close to the oncoming traffic. The walls of the American Embassy sported 'Death to America', 'Death to the Shah', graffiti in blood.

Fereydoun fumbled in his pocket for change.

'And you heard about last night?' chortled the taxi driver. 'First bullet, no good. These Mullahs don't know how to handle a gun. Second bullet in the neck. You want pictures? You buy them over at that stall. That is a very good friend of mine, give you good discount. Tell him you are my friend.' The driver held a finger to his shoulder. Bang. He held a finger to his neck. Bang. And slumped over the steering wheel.

With an acute pain in his stomach, Fereydoun dashed into the office and upstairs to the toilet.

Shirin Khaksar looked through the pile of papers on the table. The overall impression they made was not to establish her innocence but to sound like whining excuses. She had written most of them during the night, in a panic following the news of Hoveyda's death.

Now she saw that they would not do. She piled the papers in the grate and set fire to them, then seated once more at the table in her overcoat, she looked at the blank sheet of paper in front of her.

Outside the window, under the mulberry bush in the small courtyard, brown birds hopped leaving footprints like arrowheads in the frost. Shirin sat back and lit a cigarette, peering through the smoke at the misty outline of twigs and branches. Then she remembered her hands. She must use the cigarette holder which was in her handbag. She flipped through the contents, powder, lipstick, comb. Her bus ticket from last night. A photograph of the children taken many years ago. Little faces almost forgotten, yet she could relate to them more easily than to the teenagers they had become. Notebook and diary. Out of curiosity she turned to the date. April 12th. Meeting with the architect in the morning to discuss plans for a new hospital at Rezaieh. In the evening a talk to the American Women's League, 'Women under Islam'. Probably her absence was the most eloquent gesture she could make.

The possibility crossed her mind of going to the meeting at the Embassy and seeking political asylum. But then, there must be so many people like herself, of little interest to the outside world. Why should anyone bother to help her?

Shirin sighed and looked back at the piece of paper on the table. Never look at a blank sheet during an examination, write something, even if it's only your name and the question. That's what her teacher always said.

Shirin Khaksar. Date of birth: October 15th 1939. Address. Which address? The old or the new? Whatever street name she put would probably have been changed by now anyway. But an address always followed next. She wrote resolutely, Khiabun-e-Shah. The Street of the King.

Then how to continue? A little biographical data perhaps? A sort of c.v. Parents, brothers and sisters. Religion? She left that blank; perhaps she would fill it in later.

Education?

In France and England.

Further education?

A degree in economics at London University and postgraduate studies in politics at the University of California.

How did you obtain your first post in the Ministry of Social Services?

I applied through the usual channels (in triplicate), stating qualifications, experience and . . .

And perhaps the fact that the late Prime Minister had close ties with your family?

I was not aware of any preferential treatment. I had worked hard. I was well qualified for the post.

And you consider these qualifications rendered you capable of returning to impose Western ideology on a Moslem people?

Man's basic needs are irrespective of race or creed. Everyone needs food and shelter, education, treatment if they are sick . . .

Ah, but what sort of sickness? The sickness of Western imperialism?

177

I would have hoped to have avoided some of those evils by learning from their mistakes as well as their progress.

And you continued, through your work, to send young people abroad to study so that they would return in the thrall of capitalist . . .

I sent them abroad to receive an education that was not available in this country.

You sent them abroad, including your own, and how many have returned?

Shirin was grateful for the knock at the door that distracted her from her thoughts.

Mrs Emani had looked at the newspaper photograph for a long time. Then she had been to church and prayed. The face looked up at her. So beautiful. So poised. Sacked for misappropriation of government funds? Corrupt upon Earth? Mrs Emani didn't believe a word of it. And yet, the woman had deceived her, coming to her house like that, using her home as a hiding place. She prayed that God would tell her what to do.

Shirin went to open the door. Before she got there, the newspaper was shoved underneath. Her own face looked up from the mat. Shirin flung open the door, wanting to explain, trying to imagine how her landlady must feel.

'Mrs Emani!' she called. 'Mrs Emani!' but the small black figure scuttled round the bend in the corridor without a backward glance.

Masoud Gabayan plonked the gold-plated telephone on the kitchen table.

'Compliments of the Shah,' he said.

Roya walked round it suspiciously. Once. Then again. She bent forward and sniffed it. Then she reached out and touched the gleaming curve of the receiver. It felt

178

cold. When she withdrew her hand she could see the dull semi-circles left by her fingertips. She wrapped her chador round her hand and rubbed away the blemish.

'You'd need an army of servants with telephones like that.' She laughed nervously. 'From the Shah's desk?'

Masoud nodded, grinning widely.

'Lift that up and you might get the President of the United States himself.' He roared at his own joke, clasping his hands across his stomach.

Roya looked at the telephone with awe. She stepped back, wrapping her chador closely around herself, as if President Carter himself might appear in the room at any moment.

'How much did it cost?' she asked. This was something she could relate to. When Masoud didn't answer, she knew it must have been a lot.

'A telephone always comes in handy,' he said.

'Of course.'

Hussein grabbed the receiver, and began speaking into it. 'Hello, hello. This is the Shah. Get me Moscow.' With his free hand he made a gesture of slitting his throat, and added: 'Make it fast or else . . .'

'Of course,' Roya said, then paused, waiting for the hilarity to subside, 'it will be impossible to find a telephone engineer these days – but it might look nice on the sitting room cupboard.' She turned the telephone round as she spoke, holding it at arm's length. She knew she would never be able to hold it so intimately as to speak into it.

'I can probably connect it myself.' Masoud picked up the instrument and walked towards the hall.

'No Masoudja, please . . . !' Roya ran after him, clinging to his arm. Her chador slipped from her head. 'If it doesn't work then what will we do?'

'I will tell all my friends to ring me,' said her husband.

'Masoudja, if it doesn't work think of all the business we might lose.'

Masoud hesitated. Then he looked at the old black telephone. After a moment's thought he placed the gold one next to it.

'I wonder if it will make my voice sound different?'

'I expect it will have a much richer tone,' said Soraya, who had watched silently up till then.

Shirin Khaksar sat again at her table, pen in hand, but she did not write. Not any more. As soon as she had sat down, the voice of the Examiner had been there. Accusing. Questioning. Doubting. Leaving her scarcely enough time to deal with one problem before he was on to the next.

'That case now of Dariush Nizanpour.'

'The sacked bus driver?'

'Ah! So it made an impression on you.'

'Of course. It was in all the papers. The individual cases remain in one's mind long after the statistics are forgotten.'

'You feel guilty then?'

'It was a difficult case. There were many others of a similar nature which the press ignored.'

'What do you know about Savak?'

'We all lived in the shadow of the Secret Police.'

'In connection with this particular case?'

'Their involvement was possible.' Shirin shrugged and lit a cigarette.

'I would put it more strongly than that.'

'That I cannot say. Only that Mr Nizanpour disappeared at the height of his notoriety.'

'Because he defended his rights? Because he asked for compensation? Because he demanded his pension?'

'Mr Nizanpour was sacked for endangering lives by

being drunk on duty. He ignored warnings though the penalties were spelled out.'

'Under the Working Man's Compensation Act . . .'

'Now you are asking me about a legal decision. That is a matter for the judiciary.'

'But his family! What did you do about them? He had twelve children, you know. They lost everything – home, income, father, security.'

'If, in my position, I had considered every individual case, the whole machinery of the Social Services would have ground to a halt.'

'What else is the Social Services Department for, if not to help individuals?'

'You are confusing the role of social worker with my role in the administration. Look at the literacy rates,' Shirin begged, walking up and down the room now, rubbing her arms to keep warm. 'Look at the number of girls receiving education. The health facilities in the villages. The hospitals and orphanages. The pension schemes, National Insurance, Maternity Care, Infant Welfare, Town Planning!'

But the Examiner was no longer listening. She could tell by the silence in the room as she ceased speaking. She stamped her feet. The small paraffin heater was inadequate for the draughty room.

Then she had an inspiration. She would make a korsi. Over the table she spread the eiderdown from her bed. Underneath the table she put the paraffin heater. Then she sat at the table, drawing the eiderdown over her shoulders, tucking it in over her back and legs. Slowly, the warmth seeped through her whole body, starting from her feet.

She laughed to think of herself, Shirin Khaksar, like any old peasant woman, keeping warm by korsi. Warm as in the days of her childhood on family holidays. Warm in the heart of a family. She closed her eyes and dreamt of those happy days.

Theresa Homayoun sat at home alone in the evenings since her relationship with Fereydoun had resumed its usual footing. Not that they ever quarrelled openly. Theresa wished that they did. Fereydoun snapped at the children and was abrupt with Muna. Theresa, he always called darling, with icy politeness.

She didn't like to go out in the evenings any more. The incident outside the British Council had upset her. At home there was not even any television worth watching. She was sick of reading. Bored and lonely.

Her expatriate friends had left. Her Iranian friends were busy with their families. She preferred not to be dependent on her in-laws. Like her mother, Theresa was an only child. If there were any relatives, they had never been in touch. There had only been Theresa, her mother, and her father, a retired factory worker who had died some years earlier. In houses very like the one Theresa was brought up in, her schoolfriends now raised their families. Two up two down terraced houses and an outing to the pub on Saturday nights. On reflection, her present life was better.

She wrote to her mother. 'Dear Mum, The children are well.' She always started like that. Her mother feared the worst when a letter arrived. 'No news is good news,' she used to say. Then she was stuck. What else was there to write?

Theresa doodled on the blotting paper, stared about the room, then for once in her life letting her feelings take over, turned instinctively to her mother.

14

'I'm sorry.' Mrs Emani tightened her headscarf and stood in the shop doorway bobbing up and down apologetically. Like a farmyard hen, thought Masoud Gabayan. She set his teeth on edge.

'Look, Khanum, why not just buy a new rug? There's not much life in that old one. I could even offer you a few rials discount in part exchange on a new one, though it would cripple me financially.'

'I'm so sorry, but it's precious to me. It's been in the family for a long time.'

'It won't do much to keep your toes warm in winter. Now, a nice thick, new wool rug perhaps, machine-made but with a good thick pile. Just the job.' The old prayer rug would fetch a handsome profit on the export market. Americans really went for them like that, wafer thin, on their last legs. Antiques they called them.

Mrs Emani shook her head.

'Well, we'll do our best. I can't promise anything, mind you, eh, Ali? One needle through those old threads and the whole thing might fall apart.'

'Oh dear, I didn't realize . . . I could just take it away then, I didn't mean to cause so much bother.'

'Never disappoint a customer, that's my motto. You asked for it to be mended, and mended it will be. Of course, I can't accept responsibility, Khanum, but we'll do our best. Now, good morning to you.'

Masoud turned and hurried away before there could be any further argument. Silly old bag. Had no idea of the true value of things. It was lucky his own wife had a man to look after her. She'd let herself be cheated right, left and centre.

As he walked, Masoud took the list out of his pocket and read it again. Not that he didn't know the opening instructions by heart: 'The Revolutionary Prosecutor asks all dear compatriots . . .' And here he was, obeying the call. Documentary evidence, now there was the stumbling block. There must be something on that architect fellow though. A real bastard. Trying to pull wool over the eyes of a bazaar trader! No, he'd known at once, as soon as the man landed a contract with the royal family, that his own house would never get built. Masoud spat in the dust.

To be told it was because Roya didn't like the plans! She could have said so herself, couldn't she? How could she not be pleased? Upward mobility, Soraya had called it, moving from one room in the south to a flat in the centre and finally to an architect-designed house in the north. He'd even promised Roya fitted carpets. What woman could possibly resist such an offer?

He knew women better than that. That Homayoun had been putting him off, currying favour with the Pahlavis. And now, who knew when he would ever be able to afford such a venture? Masoud Gabayan had missed the chance of a lifetime, and he would teach that architect fellow a lesson he wouldn't forget.

'Where are you going, Soheila?' Roya Gabayan watched her younger daughter standing by the sink with a cup of tea in her hand.

'Demonstration.' Soheila blew on her tea to cool it. 'And I'm going to be late.'

'What time does it start?'

'Nine-thirty.'

'You've plenty of time yet.' Roya sat wearily at the kitchen table, scratching a mosquito bite on her leg.

'Yes but I'm meeting Farideh and Parvin first.'

Soraya stumbled into the kitchen, just awake. She leaned on the door frame for support, adapting herself to the bulk of her stomach.

'You shouldn't go round in just a nightie,' said Roya.

Soraya ignored her mother. 'What's the demonstration for this time?' she asked her sister.

'Fatima, it's her anniversary.'

'Soheila, you're too young for such things.' Roya got up and poured tea for Soraya, who took it absent-mindedly.

'It's a good thing I can't demonstrate any more, little sister.' She patted her stomach. 'Or we'd find ourselves on opposite sides.' The two girls laughed.

Soheila moved closer to her sister.

'Is it moving? Let me feel.' Soheila rested her hand over the bulge in her sister's nightdress. 'Ooh. She kicked me! Her own auntie!'

Roya frowned nervously and closed the door.

'Really, girls! If your father found out how you two carry on. You're not even supposed to know anything about it, Soheila.'

'Oh Mama, I'm not that dumb.' Soheila looked thoughtfully into her steaming cup. 'Besides, I'm looking forward to being an auntie.'

'Never let me hear you talking like that again. We'll none of us ever even see the child.'

'I've got it all planned out, Mama. Peter will come back and marry Soraya, and they'll go to the States with their baby and live happily ever after.'

'The way you talk, Soheila. A lot of romantic nonsense.' Roya was taken aback to hear her daughter utter her deepest wish. 'It's not right, all this Fatima business, a girl of your age rampaging the streets. You'll end up like your sister.'

'I'd be proud to.' Soheila put her arms round Soraya, who was weeping, and kissed her on the forehead.

'Back soon,' she called out cheerfully and swung out of the door, chador flying. 'Fatima' clap, clap, clap, 'Fatima' clap, clap, clap echoed across the hall, then was dulled by the slamming of the front door.

Roya turned to her elder daughter.

'Have you done your packing yet?'

Soraya shook her head. Roya poured more tea. She handed a glass to Soraya then began fiddling with the knobs of the radio. The voice of the Mullah intoned the Koran. She switched it off again.

'Mama, I'll miss you.' The two women groped for each other through their tears.

'It's a good hospital they say.' Roya sniffed. Blew her nose. 'The doctors are European. They will understand.'

'But Mama – my baby.'

'Sorayaja, you'll soon forget. Once it is all over.' Both of them knew this was a lie. 'Have you written to Peter?'

Soraya shook her head.

'If he wanted to marry me, he'd write. I don't want him to feel any obligation.'

'But for the child's sake?'

'Mama. You keep telling me it will find a good home.'

'But it's my grandchild.'

'If I'd married Peter you'd have lost both of us.'

'No. I'd think about you. You'd send photographs. And Baba is rich. I'd visit you.'

'Not any more, Mama. When did he last sell a carpet?'

Soheila galloped round the corner, 'Fatima' run, run, run. 'Fatima' run, run, run, round the next corner, a tricky one this, ninety degrees, a blind turn, always a risk. Crash!

'Bebakhshid,' she gasped, not looking up, to avoid a

direct glance. She tightened her chador around her face, sidestepped, regained her balance.

'Why Soheila! In such a hurry too!'

Soheila's gaze travelled upward from the dusty black hem dragging in the dust, up over the bulging coal-black belly, along the tangle of grey-white beard, the thin-lipped smiling mouth. Then lowered her eyes again.

'Mullah. I'm so sorry. I was in a hurry.'

'And why such haste in one so young?' As he spoke, the Mullah Afsharzadeh reached out and laid his hand on the girl's head in benediction.

'It's Fatima's birthday.' She looked up now, directly into the Mullah's face. 'Today we march for Fatima, that all young women may take her as their model.'

'Ah yes, my child, I commend your sentiments. For was not Fatima the perfect wife? The perfect mother? The perfect daughter?' His gaze travelled up as he spoke to the angle of squat roofs black against the sky. Sparrows twittering in the gutters, building their nests. As his eyes journeyed down again, Soheila lowered her eyelids demurely. Her chador stopped short at ankles crossed by slender patent-leather straps, fastened by tiny gold buckles to the outside of her shoe. So delicate, so ridiculous, thought the Mullah.

'And yet,' he intoned, 'Fatima was not helpless. She fought for her own people against injustice and tyranny. Daughter of the Prophet, she followed the advice of her father Mohammed. She was his closest companion. On his advice she married Ali and bore him children, Hussein and . . .'

'Father, please, I am late.'

'Go with God's blessing,' murmured the Mullah. Why should a young girl listen to an old man's sermons on such a glorious morning? He laughed at himself and withdrew his hand from the girl's head, feeling still the

187

surprising softness. Why, the child must have a mass of curls tucked away under that veil.

'Fatima' run, run, run, 'Fatima' run, run, run. Soheila jumped as someone grabbed her arm and spun her round.

'Where are you going, little sister, all on your own?'

'Oh, it's you, Hussein.' Soheila relaxed. 'I'm going to the demonstration. It's Fatima's birthday.'

'I might as well come with you.'

'You should be at school.'

'And what about you?'

Keeping one hand under his sister's elbow, Hussein walked on. Men in the street now gave her a wide berth, for which she was grateful.

'But you can't demonstrate, Hussein, it's only for women.'

'Who cares about Fatima?' he laughed. 'I just want you to introduce me to that friend of yours. What's her name, the one with big breasts?'

Soheila blushed.

'Zeinab, you mean. I won't introduce you to her. You never introduce me to your friends.'

'That's different. It wouldn't be right.'

'Zeinab's very clever, Hussein. She wants to go to university. She works very hard.'

'Soheilaja, I'm not interested in her studies, it's her breasts that interest me.'

'Hussein, you shouldn't say such things. Please leave me alone. Go away.'

But Hussein maintained his grip on her elbow.

'What does her father do?'

'He's got a factory. Shoes, I think.'

'If you introduced me, perhaps she'd come out with me one night.'

'Her parents would never allow it. They'd kill you if they found you hanging around their daughter.'

'What rubbish you talk, little sister. With a figure like that they should expect trouble.'

Soheila regretted her own lack of breasts. There was a small swelling around each nipple, but if she were honest, she had to admit that no one else would notice.

'Do I have a nice figure, Hussein?'

'You? You're just a kid.'

'I'm nearly thirteen.' Soheila sighed and wished that someone loved her. One of her brother's friends. Abdul Hassan perhaps. He was so good-looking. Tall and slim. But he never seemed to notice her at all.

'Hussein, what would you do if one of your friends asked me out dancing?'

'I'd kill him,' said Hussein cheerfully.

Soraya was packing. Not much. A couple of old cotton dresses of her mother's that would accommodate her bulge. A sponge bag, nightclothes and something for the return journey.

'I'll take this.' She held up a full cotton skirt, tight-waisted, that swung as she walked. 'It's always been my favourite.'

'It'll be a long time before you're slim enough for that. You won't just go back to normal overnight. Besides you should cover your legs for the journey – perhaps you could wear trousers underneath.'

'In July, Mother? I'd die of heat.'

'Haven't you got something long and loose?'

Soraya slid her dresses one by one along the wardrobe rail.

'This red one perhaps?'

'A bit bright. It'll be alright though under a chador.'

'Under a chador? You must be joking, Mother. I won't wear a chador ever again.'

Roya left the room. The last thing she wanted was to quarrel on her daughter's last morning at home.

* * *

189

Mrs Smith's reaction to Theresa's letter had been immediate and decisive. She had taken off her apron and headscarf, removed her curlers, combed her hair and set off for the nearest travel agent.

Now she sat in the white Mercedes with Theresa on their way from the airport. Already Theresa's joy in her mother's arrival was wearing thin, and she was beginning to dread the next six weeks.

'Do you know, Theresa, 'e said to me, that airport chappie: "Ee luv, I do like your 'at" and I said never mind me 'at, where's me bloody suitcase? It's a nice 'at though, isn't it? I bought it specially. Didn't want to let you down.'

Mrs Smith paused only to light a cigarette.

'Now then, what's all this Ayatollah business? Pictures all over the place, aren't there? Look at that! Don't 'alf look fierce. It's them eyebrows what does it. Don't smile much either.'

'Mother, please!' Theresa tapped her mother on the knee and indicated Fereydoun's chauffeur.

'I've always believed in speaking my mind, as you very well know, Theresa.' Mrs Smith leaned forward and tapped the driver on the shoulder.

'Well young man, and what do you think of all this revolution business?'

'The Ayatollah is a very good man, Khanum.'

'Well, I'm not so sure about that. All these deaths we keep hearing about. It's not right, you know. And what's all this about candles. Candles in our day and age! I've got them though. In me suitcase. Where is me suitcase?'

'In the boot, Mum.'

'Oh yes. I've got your Tampax too, luv. Had a struggle with those in customs, I can tell you. Same man as liked me 'at. "What's these?" he said. Well, I was that embarrassed I didn't know what to say. Then he pulled two out of the box, stuck one in each ear and said

190

"Radio?" I didn't know where to put myself. And books, 'e wanted to know if I'd got any dirty books. Well, I said to 'im, just who do you think you're speaking to, young man? And he patted me on the arm and waved me through.'

By now, they had arrived at the flat. Theresa led the way upstairs. The chauffeur followed with the bags.

'And where's that 'usband of yours?'

'He's at work, Mum.'

'A fine way to greet his mother-in-law, I must say.'

'Let me take your coat.' Theresa hung the coat in the hall cupboard. 'A new coat as well, Mum?'

'Didn't want to let you down, luv.'

'You should have cut off the label.'

Mrs Smith turned and tripped on the corner of one of the handwoven rugs scattered on the polished floor.

'Now what's wrong with a good nylon fitted carpet, I'd like to know? I've read about all those people making carpets. Little children some of them. It's not right. Doesn't your husband earn enough to buy a decent carpet? All that building for Princess this and Princess that.'

'It's best not to talk like that, Mum. People here don't like the royal family any more.'

They went into the living room, where Muna appeared with a tray of tea.

'Eee, Muna luv, it's good to see you again. Remember me, eh? Theresa's mum, that's right. And do you remember how to make a good strong cuppa, eh? That's right, luv, in a nice cup and saucer, with milk and sugar. Glasses for tea. I don't know! And 'ow's yer 'usband? And the children? Theresa tells me you 'ave a new baby. I've brought something for each of them, you know. I'll just get my suitcase.'

'Mum, just sit down for a minute, you must be tired.'

'Yer right, luv. I get that excited. And Reza and Farah? Oh, the little loves! What time do they get home?'

Theresa thought she should have known that sending the children to nursery as usual so that she could have a cosy tête-à-tête with her mother was a forlorn hope.

'And 'ow's that 'usband of yours?' Mrs Smith suddenly remembered the purpose of her mission – to sort out her Theresa's marriage.

'He has got a name, Mum.'

'Ee, luv, I never could pronounce it, could I?' Mrs Smith chuckled, took off her shoes (but not her hat), leaned back and supped her tea.

Mothers! And where would we be without them? Someone to grumble and moan about, but always there to pick up the pieces. Though I still remember school sports days, and Mother straight from Paris making everyone else look positively anaemic. But was I proud of her? Not a bit! All I wanted was for her to be inconspicuous, like, say, Mrs Emani.

But Mother adored me. Always made sure I was provided with interesting companions and excursions during the holidays, and she never failed to greet me at the airport, or come to wave me off.

She's been just as conscientious since my marriage. Our reception, you know, was the talk of Paris – based on the two thousand five hundredth anniversary of the monarchy celebrations at Persepolis. Silk pavilions, handwoven carpets, fountains and roses everywhere. And imported belly dancers. Why, people would have given their souls for an invitation.

Yes. Blood is definitely thicker than water. And it seems the lot of mothers to suffer for their children. My mother has suffered the gravest concern over my health. She even wrote to recommend a certain specialist, an old friend of her family. I am not one to fuss on account of my health,

*as you well know, but I felt it incumbent on me to call on
this gentleman, if only to pass on my mother's regards.*

*I called at his house in Niavaran. A house did I say?
Palace would be more accurate. But he had been dead for
years. The family's gone now as well and the place taken
over by Pasdaran. It grieves me, you know, to see rifles
carelessly flung about marble floors. Some people just
don't know how to behave in a civilized manner.*

*Anyway, I wrote to Mother that my nose-bleeds become
less troublesome the longer I am here. To reassure her of
the state of my health, I went back to the photographer in
Takhte Tavous and ordered another print of my portrait.
So that she can see for herself.*

Fereydoun arrived home when Mrs Smith was on her
third cup, and Theresa's mind was a fog of the doings of
people she hardly remembered.

'Ee, luv.' Mrs Smith was on her stockinged feet in an
instant. 'You look proper poorly. Been overdoing it, have
you? It doesn't do, all these late nights, burning the
candle at both ends.' Mrs Smith patted her son-in-law on
the shoulder from a safe distance. She'd never been able
to bring herself to kiss him. She'd never really taken to
foreigners, even when her Theresa took to marrying one.
But it had been a good match. A classy girl, her Theresa.
She had style. She deserved something like this.

'Well, it's good to see you, luv.' Mrs Smith retreated
behind the coffee table.

Theresa looked at Fereydoun for the first time in some
weeks, and was shocked. There were heavy pouches
under his eyes. His skin was grey. He hadn't bothered
with a tie.

'You need more fresh air and exercise,' remarked
Theresa. 'And more sleep.'

'I just called in to see you, Mother. To welcome you.'

193

Fereydoun poured himself a cup of tea, took one sip and put the cup down again.

'I've had a good idea,' said Mrs Smith. 'What you two need is a holiday. Leave the kiddies with me for a few days. I can manage with Muna to help me.'

'No, Mum. You're not here for long.' Theresa wasn't sure which prospect appalled her most: to stay with her mother or go away with her husband.

'That would be nice, Mother. In a while. I have a few things left to clear up in town first.' Fereydoun stirred his tea.

'And who do you have to clear up first?' Theresa sat down abruptly opposite him, daring him to admit it openly. Fereydoun leaned across the table, wanting to diminish the distance between them. As he reached out his hand, he knocked over the milk jug.

In the ensuing confusion, Fereydoun left. He walked down the road feeling utterly alone, wondering who would care in the least if anything were to happen to him. Theresa? The children? They would quickly forget. His mother? Perhaps.

It was time, he decided, to reopen the communications which he'd severed out of loyalty to Theresa, to protect her from his fiercely disapproving mother. To give her time to establish herself in his country and the freedom to bring up her children as she wanted to.

But now he needed his family. If anything were to happen, and it could any day, he would need all the help he could get. He would ring his mother as soon as he got to the office, perhaps arrange a visit at the weekend. Mrs Smith's presence could be relied on to smooth over any minor difficulties.

'Would you like me to leave?' Shirin Khaksar sat in Mrs Emani's kitchen, drinking tea.

Mrs Emani shook her head. She had spent the day in thought and prayer.

'It wouldn't be safe for you to go round now, looking for somewhere to stay. But please, you must go soon. I have my son to think about.'

'As soon as I'm ready.' It would not take her long, Shirin thought, to complete her preparations.

'More tea?'

She nodded. Any excuse to stay and talk. She watched Mrs Emani stand up and walk over to the draining board, pour out the tea and walk back. It was a long time since she had watched anyone do anything so straightforward and it was somehow comforting.

'We haven't agreed on the rent yet.'

Mrs Emani was embarrassed. She wanted money for Jamshid's journey, but felt it wrong to take any under the circumstances.

'You are a Christian?'

Shirin's last words threw Mrs Emani into a panic. If her visitor was a woman with a secret, so was she. The pictures of Mary, small and discreet but nevertheless there. A crucifix over the mantelpiece. Her missal left carelessly on the chest of drawers. Mrs Emani's hand flew to the knot of her headscarf, worrying it as she struggled for words.

'I am a Bahai,' said Shirin.

Mrs Emani's fear at the sudden depth of their involvement was aggravated by an unexpected knock at the door.

'You must go to your room,' she whispered.

Shirin wrapped her coat around her and tiptoed down the long corridor, as Mrs Emani opened the front door. It was only a neighbour wanting to use the phone, but as soon as she'd gone, Mrs Emani knew what she had to do. God would understand. She bundled her religious artefacts into a shoe box which she hid in the broom cupboard behind her dusters. She thought of the early Christians taking refuge in the catacombs and prayed that God would not expect too much from her in the way of physical courage. Her rosary she tucked round her neck, beneath the collar of her blouse, gasping at the coldness of the metal links against her skin.

As the taxi drew up outside the bus station in the south of the city, Hamid Baniyazdi rushed forward and grabbed Soraya's suitcase. This was a new venture for him, something he had thought up with his friend Houshang.

'I can manage myself thank you.' Soraya insisted.

'Rubbish,' said her mother. 'It's far too heavy. It's all those books.'

'I'll need something to pass the time.'

'You could try knitting.'

Hamid followed the two women, sweating, and wondering how much they would give him.

'Khanum-e-Gabayan, isn't it?' he asked.

Roya nodded.

'And your daughter? The elder Miss Gabayan, isn't it? I didn't know you had a married daughter.'

Roya's heart went cold. Soraya was trying to read the destination plates on the front of each bus through the dust and the people. She held a small bag in each hand and her chador between her teeth. It had flapped open revealing her obviously pregnant stomach.

'Soraya,' hissed Roya, 'you're forgetting yourself.'

Soraya looked down, saw her stomach like a sandbank exposed by the receding tide, and blushed.

Roya couldn't remember having seen the man before. She took five toman from her purse.

'You don't know me?' asked Hamid. 'Sometimes the Agha gives me work in the bazaar. The Agha is a munificent man. Very kind. Always very kind. Only sometimes there is no work and I have children, Khanum.

You will understand that, being a mother yourself. And soon to be a grand . . .'

Roya cut him short, handing over the five toman and turning her back.

'In you get, Soraya, quickly before anyone else recognizes us.'

'But Mama, there's still twenty minutes to go. The bus will be like an oven in the sun.'

'Soraya, please do as I say.'

Soraya embraced her mother over the bump of her baby. 'Mama,' she whispered, suddenly frightened. Roya hugged her daughter and grandchild as if she would never let them go. Then she pushed Soraya away and up the steps.

'I'll pray for you.'

'You want taxi, Khanum?' Roya turned away from Hamid's voice. So close. Too close.

'I can manage perfectly well myself, thank you,' she answered with a glittering smile.

Hamid could hardly believe the weight of coins in his hand. Only midday too. There was no point in doing any more work today, not with so much money in his pocket. So, Mr Gabayan had a pregnant daughter. Funny he'd never mentioned it. His Aziz was pregnant too. Perhaps he would take something back for her. A pretty scarf? A bracelet?

He ran his fingers through the money, feeling its comfortable jingle cold against his thigh.

'What're you doing, Hamid? That's the Shiraz bus arriving.' Houshang tugged at his friend's sleeve.

Hamid did not answer, not in words. Silently he took his hand from his pocket and held it out, palm upwards, so that the coins glinted in the sunlight. Houshang whistled and shook his head in admiration.

'Someone dropped it?'

197

Hamid shook his head. Houshang leaned closer.

'You stole it?'

Hamid looked offended.

'Mr Gabayan's wife gave it me. You wouldn't expect that, would you, such a tight-fisted old bugger he is.'

Houshang shook his head, torn between joy for his friend and regret that the money wasn't his.

'We won't work any more today,' said Hamid. He put his arm round his friend's shoulders. They picked their way through the sheep and goats, laughing at the peasants squatting among their livestock.

'I thought of buying something for Aziz first. Mr Gabayan's daughter has a belly like this. It reminded me of my wife.'

Houshang nodded.

'I don't know,' Hamid continued. 'Aziz has just let herself go lately. She's not the girl I married at all.'

'But the sons, Hamid. Four sons. That's a blessing.'

Hamid hugged Houshang in silent sympathy. They meandered on.

'Never mind, Houshang. Five daughters is something. Think of the bride price.'

The two stopped, and sniffed. The smell of meat cooking over charcoal made their mouths water.

'A kebab?' Hamid led the way, following his nose towards the source of the wonderful smell – a small metal burner in the gutter, a man flapping a sheet of newspaper, the smoke billowing.

Hamid and Houshang sat on the kerb, teeth tearing into the charred flesh, until their stomachs were heavy with unaccustomed meat. Then they sat back feeling the sun warm, warm and languorous, watching the girls go by.

'What about the Ghaleh, Houshang?'

'Can't afford it, Hamidja.'

'Look, I'll treat you. We might not be able to afford

198

the best, but there'll be someone who'll do it for our price.'

'You're a real friend, Hamid. I'll . . . I'll do the same for you one day, just you wait and see.'

Arms linked, they crossed the southern quarter towards the walled red-light district. Hamid led the way. He'd been once before. He ushered his friend along, boasting of his exploits. Houshang listened hungrily, almost dribbling. Hamid remembered Aziz.

'Perhaps a ribbon?'

'Oh yes,' Houshang nodded wisely. 'Women like things like that. Pretty things.'

The narrow streets were crowded. There were girls on the street corners, girls on the doorsteps, pictures in the windows. Tempting. But always at the last minute Hamid lost courage. After all, he had never actually . . .

'What about a pipe first?' he suggested.

'Do we have enough?' Even here, thought Houshang, opium would not be cheap.

Hamid felt in his pocket. He could only reckon in concrete terms, laying aside one coin for this, another for that. He felt in one pocket. Then in the other.

'Oh come on, Hamid.' Houshang was becoming impatient, watching the women who passed by as if each one might be the last.

Hamid couldn't believe it. A hole in his pocket perhaps? He would beat Aziz when he got home. There was no hole. He removed his woollen hat from his head and scratched his scalp in bewilderment.

'Houshangja,' he muttered hoarsely, 'I've been robbed.'

So! It's all been said before, you know. Think not of your bodies but of your souls. Earthly treasures rust away but set your store in heaven, where moth and rust will not consume.

So, if material freedom is lacking, how about a touch of spiritual consolation?

'Lift thine eyes, oh lift thine eyes, to-oo the mountains, whence cometh . . . whence co-ometh . . . whence co-ometh . . .'

But soft, here cometh the Mullah.

The Mullah continued his visitations, pondering the return of the Imam as he went. He offered thanks daily to God for preserving him to see such a time.

He took no active part in the Revolution himself, but sat back and waited for God to tell him what to do next, either through the voice of the Imam, to whose exhortations he listened avidly over the loudspeakers, or more directly, through the voice of God in his meditations.

He no longer wrote his own sermons, but relayed the Ayatollah's. And his congregation swelled and his heart lifted at the sight of the rapt upturned faces where before there had been bare marble floor.

'God is merciful,' he mumbled, seeing even old Hassan Ali, the stolen car dealer, among the faithful.

Another man much in his thoughts was Masoud-e-Gabayan. He thanked God that Masoud had turned to God in the hour of his need. For Masoud epitomized the crisis at the centre of contemporary life. The conflict between East and West, between Islam and the godless.

He, the Mullah, had often seen the eldest girl, may God have mercy upon her, shameless in tight jeans and tight jumpers, revealing what had best been hidden, talking when she should have kept silence. And now she was paying the price.

The younger girl though, poised on the threshold of womanhood, may God protect her. For her soul he would struggle with the Devil.

Over the days, as the Mullah pondered the problems

of the Gabayan household, he ceased to see the haggard features of Masoud on his midnight visit, or the hostile face of Roya as she reluctantly opened the door, or even the rounded figure of Soraya, now mercifully departed.

Instead he saw the younger daughter, Soheila, her does' eyes large and trusting through the dark triangle of her chador. The exquisite nostrils. The first flowerings of a young soul. A soul in need of guidance, a rough stone he would burnish to a glowing crystal that would please its Maker.

15

Isn't this a wonderful idea? I mean, what's the good of having palaces empty of people but bursting with treasures, when their realization in cash terms could do so much good? The Revolution benefits and there's many a small fortune to be made on the side. Masoud Gabayan might not let on, but one of the reasons ready money is so short in that household (and I have this on good authority) is that a certain warehouse at the airport is simply stuffed with carpets worn by the feet of royalty and eunuchs. Mark my words, that man will be a millionaire one day.

But for now! Larger artefacts having been disposed of, we move on to personal items. The Royal Wardrobe. Fancy yourself dressed as a king or queen? Then look no further. Forgive me if I seem unnecessarily flippant today, but the post brought a letter from my mother which is causing me the gravest concern.

You will remember the saga of my photograph. Well, my mother writes that my colleague and supposed friend who undertook to deliver it carried duty to such excess that he not only delivered it to my Paris address, but insisted on personally taking it down to Provence. And, writes Mother, three weeks later, he is still there! Now, I'm pretty broad-minded. I mean, I believe in the modern marriage. But, I was shocked.

Let's look at this another way. Imagine yourself a young mother alone with two small children for three months. Nannies and servants just aren't the same as having Father around. And let's face it, she's so lovely that it would be sacrilege to try and describe her to you. I believe categorically and absolutely in a wife's devotion, fidelity and innocence. She has been led astray. She has been indiscreet. And tongues will wag.

What are you going to do about it? asks Mother. Sometimes you know she can be really Persian – positively pre-Sassanid. She obviously expects me to leap on a plane, surprise them at dawn and avenge the family honour. For one thing, I am still under contract to remain here. For another, I have always viewed physical action with distaste. It is not appropriate to modern, civilized, cerebral man.

No. If my wife feels unloved, I must prove otherwise. Hence, behold me at this sale. For what could please my wife more, I ask myself, than genuine Paris fashion at a give-away price? A dress to make her look and feel like a princess. I know that women love these little attentions, and my wife is the *most feminine little thing.*

Theresa Homayoun gasped as the dress was held up. She would have given anything to possess it. The material shimmered softly like the glow of candlelight on water. She knew before the bidding started that she would never be able to afford it and sank back in her chair with a sigh.

Next to her, Homa shrugged. From behind, came giggles. Theresa turned round frowning and saw eyes brimming with laughter before they retreated behind their chadors.

'Whenever would you wear it?' asked Homa.

'I don't know, but it would be nice just to think of it hanging in my wardrobe.'

'It wouldn't look right on you. Don't forget the Princess has different colouring.'

In the back row, Hussein Gabayan guffawed among a group of friends. The Pasdar held the dress (all profits to the Revolution) in front of him. He curtseyed and the audience cheered. He simpered, then minced from one side of the room to the other and the audience went wild.

The Princess's clothes exceeded their wildest expectations.

Hussein leaned weakly against his friend, drained by laughter. They'd given school a miss for the occasion. He lit another cigarette and gestured whereabouts on the female anatomy the dress would hang.

The auctioneer called for silence. He lowered the starting price for suddenly there were no bids. Down, down it plummeted, a give-away now. He raised his gavel. Theresa put up her hand. Everyone turned to stare. A foreigner? That explained it.

'And the next item' evoked more wolf whistles while the Pasdar handed Theresa her purchase. She fingered the dress as it lay on her lap. Away from the light, like a fish out of water, it faded to a dull grey.

Outside the auction room, Soheila and her classmates were feeling bored. They put down their placards and sat on a patch of grass in the sunshine.

'I can't think who'd be seen dead in her clothes anyway,' said Soheila. 'I mean, we used to see her picture in the paper every day, but nobody dresses like that now.'

'We must take every opportunity to denounce Western imperialist dress,' stated Zeinab, the intellectual of the group, admired by Hussein.

'Hussein only went inside to see what was being auctioned.' Soheila felt bound to defend her brother.

'Did he? I don't think he takes our cause seriously. My brother's in there too.'

'I saw him.' Soheila blushed. She had been in love with Zeinab's brother for a whole week now. 'It's different for men,' she said, to hide her confusion.

'Do you think there are just dresses or . . . other things as well?'

The girls giggled and thought of the underwear they had seen in hidden copies of Western magazines.

'I saw one ferangi go in – with blonde hair. No one else would dare wear them.'

The girls lay back on the grass, letting their chadors fall open, luxuriating in the sun's warmth.

'Zeinab,' asked Soheila at last, 'why do some women feel they have to dress up like that?'

'Ignorance. They don't know any better. They don't realize that men will only value them as objects.' And Zeinab must know. Zeinab with her well developed body and stock of magazines on which they poured such scorn. The only one who had 'started'. Who knew about these things.

'Why don't men have to cover themselves?'

'Because women can control themselves but men can't.'

'Why not?'

'It's their sex hormones,' said Zeinab knowledgeably.

'But don't women have sex hormones? Don't they ever want a man?' Soheila thought of Zeinab's brother. Of the way her body went all hot when he was near her. All a matter of self-control. She was embarrassed by her failing.

'No,' said Zeinab. 'Not real women.'

Also watching the auction was Roya Gabayan, horrified to realize that her son was sitting in the back row.

'Hey,' she whispered to her neighbour, 'that's my Hussein behind us.' Her neighbour stared resolutely ahead.

'Nothing to be ashamed of,' she muttered, blushing. 'Why shouldn't we come out for a bit of fun? It's not as if we meant to buy anything.'

Roya thought of the money in her handbag. Not that she was going to spend it. She had simply brought it in case of emergency. To catch a taxi home if the auction finished late, or perhaps buy some delicacy for Masoud's tea.

'Of course,' said her friend, 'now if there was a bargain that was really too good to miss . . .'

Roya looked at her neighbour with admiration. Put like that, there was nothing at all to feel guilty about. She would enjoy herself and forget about Hussein.

'Look at that,' she murmured as another dress was held up. The material alone must have been worth a thousand toman. She liked to imagine the royal family in the palace, all dressed up, lovely clothes, jewels, crowns, like something out of a fairy tale. She missed the pictures in the papers. Nowadays it was all demonstrations, Mullahs and dead bodies. In those days you could open the paper and dream.

'Hey look! It's that blonde woman again. It's alright for her, I suppose.'

Roya looked up as her friend dug her in the ribs.

'I know her,' she said. 'She's married to that architect.'

'Hamedani? He's in prison.'

'No, Homayoun. The one that designed that house for us. Fereydoun. That's his name. Masoud's really got it in for him. He's on his list.' Roya took another look at Theresa.

Masoud Gabayan carried his list with him everywhere. At odd moments during the day, he would take it out of his pocket, scribble a comment here, amend, add, cross off. It cheered him up to be doing something positive when the hours passed and no customer crossed his threshold.

'Time to shut up shop, Ali,' he said, standing up. He moved to close the door.

'Bebakhshid, Agha.'

Masoud swore. There she was again. That dreary mouse of a woman about her wretched rug.

'Salaam aleikum, Khanum.' In spite of the greeting,

Masoud only held the door open a crack, just enough to speak through.

'I'm so sorry, am I too late?'

Masoud looked at his watch with exaggerated care.

'Sa'at-e-panj o nim-e.'

'I'm so very sorry. It's about my rug.'

'Khanum, it is late. I am tired. I have carpets worth millions of toman and you keep asking about one trifling rug.'

There was no answer from the other side. Mrs Emani had turned and fled.

When the doorbell rang, Roya Gabayan shoved her novel into its hiding place, turned down the rice, smoothed her hair and adjusted her chador. Then she opened the door.

'Why, Father! Please to come in. My house is yours.'

The Mullah inclined his head and stepped inside.

'Please, sit down.'

He perched uncomfortably on the edge of the black plastic settee and glanced at the clock.

'My husband is unlikely to be home for some time,' murmured Roya, hoping he would go away.

'My other visits finished earlier than expected.' The Mullah had hardly been able to restrain himself from coming earlier, to be in time for . . .

Roya was grateful for the footsteps on the stairs. Hussein and Soheila home, chattering, laughing. Then came their sudden silence as they looked in the sitting room.

'Please, children. The Mullah.'

'Good afternoon, Father.' Soheila hoisted up her chador, which had slipped to trail over her shoulders like a cloak as she ran. But not before the Mullah had noticed the long, slender throat, the skimpy school jumper . . .

'Soheila-ja, bring tea for the Mullah.'

'I have homework to do,' muttered Hussein and left the room.

'Father, I apologize for my son.'

'It is good that a young man should take his studies seriously.' The Mullah sat back, waiting for Soheila's return, for the moment when she would place the teatray on the table and momentarily release the grip on her chador. Perhaps he would ask for something else, something not on the tray, to see again the swirl of material as she turned towards the kitchen, the ankles in their demure black stockings. God forgive him.

'The weather is becoming hot,' he remarked.

Roya nodded. Stared at the pattern on the carpet.

'It is a sign of God's approval, this bounteous sunshine.'

Roya nodded again. Soheila served the tea perfectly. She merited each approving glance bestowed on her by the Mullah.

'Soheila too will go to the university,' said her mother. 'She is a clever girl.'

'Not too clever. God willing.'

Soheila left the room as quickly as she could, before she could be caught up in the boring conversation.

Theresa felt guilty about going out without her mother earlier in the day, but she enjoyed getting away for a bit. To make up for the desertion, she and Homa took Mrs Smith out for tea.

'Eee, luv, I don't know if I could manage another.' Mrs Smith clasped her hands across her stomach and stared regretfully at the plate of cakes. 'Well, I just might,' she said. 'One of those small ones perhaps. One with chocolate on the top.'

'More coffee?' Homa beckoned to the waiter.

'Yes I will. Eee this is grand, luv.'

Theresa looked up and smiled.

'You'll go home like a balloon, Mum.'

'No luv, not me. A few days back at work will soon see me right. There's nothing like a bit of polishing.'

'Go on, Mrs Smith. Have another.' Homa held out the cake plate again.

Theresa sat back, relieved not to have to bear the brunt of her mother's conversation. She enjoyed sitting in that seat in that particular hotel with its uninterrupted view of the mountains. And the shops in the hotel arcade, she enjoyed those too. It was such a change to wander in Western surroundings and browse without fear of losing her purse or having her bottom pinched.

Though she had given up many things in an effort to economize, the weekly outing with Homa remained sacrosanct. It was not coffee and cakes she was paying for, but an atmosphere in which she could relax and feel at home.

'There's no more milk,' her mother said, holding the jug upside-down, letting the last drops drain into her cup. Homa raised her hand, an almost imperceptible signal, yet it always brought a response.

Today the response was exaggerated – a gang of armed men burst through the door.

'We are taking over this establishment in the name of the Revolution,' said one.

'What's that, luv? What's 'e saying?'

'That they're taking the hotel over in the name of the Revolution.'

'My, how clever you are to understand all that.'

'On your feet,' yelled one of the Pasdaran.

'Stand up, Mother,' muttered Theresa.

'I'll have you know, young man, that I'm in the middle of my coffee.' Mrs Smith remained in her seat and sipped on. The men were pointing and shouting at the two younger women.

'Hejab!'

'Heads,' whispered Homa. 'He wants us to cover our

heads.' She pulled a silk headscarf from her handbag.
'It's best not to argue.'

Theresa looked in her bag but only found a
handkerchief.

'Have this,' said her mother, and produced a plastic
rain-mate.

'I can't wear that,' Theresa protested but Homa knotted
it firmly under her friend's chin. 'It's only for a while,'
she said.

A man came and stood next to them.

'He wants to know what you've got on your head, Mrs
Smith,' Homa translated.

'What I've got on my head?' Mrs Smith stood up at
that point and walked steadily towards the man. 'You
want to know what I've got on my head? It's me bloody
'at, and what's more, young man, it's good enough for
Buckingham Palace so it bloody well ought to be good
enough for you.'

The might of Islam retreated hastily, rifles clattering as
they squeezed through the swing doors.

On a bench in one of the many corridors of Qasr Prison
sat Mrs Emani. Through her black jumper she fingered
the rosary beads around her neck, pressing them hard
against her collar bone. She wondered whether they
would torture her.

The guards responsible for her arrest sat smoking and
laughing. Just boys, thought Mrs Emani. Only boys like
her Jamshid. She smiled and they smiled back.

'Why am I here?' she asked. And they laughed. 'They
will miss me at work. If I could just use the telephone?'
They seemed to find this funnier than ever.

Mrs Emani was worried, but she would never confess.
She would never betray the woman she had taken into
her home. She didn't want to spend the rest of her life
with blood on her hands. But Jamshid? Her work? She

had only popped out for a bit of shopping in her lunch hour. She had found a few tomatoes, such a treat for Jamshid's supper.

After two hours of doing nothing, Mrs Emani felt hungry. She took the tomatoes from her shopping bag and passed them round. Nice tomatoes. Juicy. The Pasdaran bit into them and giggled as the juice dribbled red down their chins. They licked their fingers and nodded their thanks.

Jamshid wouldn't be worried. Not yet. She was sometimes not home until after him. At church though? They might wonder at church why she had missed mass. There might be no one at all there tonight, to receive Christ's blessing.

At eight o'clock, the guards announced it was too late to do anything more. The Prosecutor was still tied up in court. And they all had families, wives, girlfriends to go home to. Mrs Emani was locked in a cell.

Fereydoun felt his world closing in. From one minute to the next there was no obvious difference, but he could feel it happening all the time. Prime Ministers, Cabinet Ministers, down through the ranks of the Civil Service, First Secretaries, Second Secretaries, down through the administrative to the clerical, then a sidestep into the professions. The tentacles of Islam were reaching further every day, grabbing almost at random.

He looked round his office and hoped that his papers were now in order. There was nothing more he could do. He looked at the telephone. Today he hadn't even bothered to check whether it was working or not.

His secretary had her instructions. The sealed envelope which she was to deliver straight into the hands of his mother if . . . and there she would receive a substantial cash payment. That was his lifeline. Otherwise, on whom could he rely?

211

Fereydoun had considered and dismissed the idea of flight. In a few years' time, it would have been different. By then he would have amassed sufficient funds abroad. Business had been booming, and it had all come to this.

A holiday was what he needed. A bit of peace and quiet. Relaxation. It would be good to get away with Theresa. He hadn't seen much of her lately. It would be good for both of them.

While Mrs Emani said her prayers and went to sleep, Shirin Khaksar was pacing up and down her small bed-sitting room. Jamshid sat at the table, watching her anxiously, waiting for her to say something.

'If anything has happened,' she said to the boy, 'if she has been arrested, they will quickly discover it is a mistake.' Jamshid was enchanted by her company. He asked whether she would like to watch the news on television. Shirin felt it was better to stay in her own quarters. There might be a raid.

After Jamshid had gone to bed, Shirin couldn't sleep. She would rather face her prosecutors fully alert and dressed. She packed her suitcases, so that she would be ready. As time went by her admiration for Mrs Emani increased and she began to feel more hopeful. The pile of cigarette ends in the grate mounted. When the cigarettes were finished, Shirin chewed her fingers. Dawn broke. And still there was no knock on the door. No footsteps, no clatter of rifles against the stone walls. Nothing.

Mrs Emani woke suddenly, fearful of having overslept and missed early morning mass. She groped to her left for her glasses. Her fingers touched cold concrete. Then she remembered.

She felt under her pillow. There was only her shopping bag, empty now that the tomatoes were finished. She sat up and saw the locked door.

'Dear Saint Anthony of Padua,' she prayed to the patron saint of lost causes, 'help me to find my glasses.' She felt along the length of the bed, shook her coat that had served as an extra blanket, and waited for the comfortable plop of her spectacles falling onto the mattress.

She tied the grey silk headscarf under her chin, put on and buttoned her coat against the early morning chill and went about the room on all fours. She felt along the rough edge between wall and floor, along the gap where a cold draught swept under the door, and finally found herself back where she had started.

'Dear God, Saint Anthony, the Blessed Virgin Mary, all you angels and saints help me,' she wept, her chest tight and her breath coming in short gasps. Perhaps they had taken them away in the night? Perhaps this was to be her torture.

Mrs Emani knelt and prayed. She prayed until the sun rose and she heard footsteps in the corridor. She felt in her pocket for a handkerchief, and her fingers closed on the cold round oval of a spectacle lens.

Smiling now and calm, shabby and bespectacled, Mrs Emani went to meet her doom.

Before the sun rose too high in the sky, Aziz and Fariba Baniyazdi set off for the hospital. Fariba carried Shahnaz, her hip thrust out to one side to bear the younger child's weight. She stopped frequently, humping her sister into place and staggering as she settled back again. Fariba's chador slipped from her head and trailed behind her in the dust. Other pedestrians trampled on the hem from time to time, jerking her to a sudden halt.

Shahnaz no longer waved her dimpled arms. She lay weakly against her sister's body and grizzled. Her face was caked with a sticky slime, and a crust had formed over her eyelids.

Aziz trailed behind her daughters, dragging her feet through the dust, clutching a small boy in each hand. Fariba glanced back occasionally, to make sure that they were still following. She caught sight of Mussa diving now and then for some piece of litter that had attracted his attention. The little group formed an island forcing the main current of people to divide and rejoin on the other side.

Such a lovely day! I've been to the post office to send off that dress for my wife. Formidable queues there were. Queue one. Customs declaration. Queue two. Contents passed. Queue three. Weighing and purchase of stamp. On second thoughts, I didn't post it after all. Thought of an alternative way. Took back the parcel, endured the pitying look of the clerk, finger tapping at his temple. Mad, indeed! I'd have been mad to have left it with him.

Never mind. I'm sending it home a safer way. Not a pilot this time. Oh no! A burnt child fears the fire as my mother used to say. I shall go to the Intercontinental Hotel and chat up one of the air hostesses. With a bit of luck, Giselle will be there – she's always had a soft spot for me. It'll probably cost me a drink, perhaps even a meal, but in delightful company and no worries about my wife's fidelity at the end of it.

But who have we here, coming towards me? Hussein Gabayan, Pasdar Extraordinaire. Servant of the Revolution. Schoolbooks a thing of the past. A man. Rifle slung over one shoulder. Straight back. Slight swagger.

Know what it reminds me of? Please feel free to join in. You know the song of course:

     'So grand and official with his nose in the air.
     Well I gave him a look sort of sideways, and I . . .'

Were you speaking to me, young man?
What was I singing?

A hymn? Of course it was a hymn. You'd like a translation perhaps? A cigarette? Aré. Good French tobacco – as smoked by the Ayatollah's bodyguards whilst in exile. My pleasure entirely. Good day. God be with you. Phew! A lucky escape that. I can feel perspiration trickling down under my fringe. Just remember, you oaf (pardon me, I am of course referring to myself) – NO SINGING IN PUBLIC. BY ORDER. Catchy tune though, you must remember it. Top of the Pops. 1962. 'So grand and official . . .' Whoops. Nearly did it again. Steady on. A few deep breaths. Then, off to find Giselle.

Fariba held her sister close, waiting for her mother to catch up, swaying softly from side to side, singing gently.

Hussein tapped her on the shoulder.

Fariba turned. Her ten-year-old gaze met the buckle of his leather belt, travelled up, over the Che Guevara jacket, then the neckscarf and on to the beak of his nose.

'Don't you know there is to be no singing in public places?'

'I was only singing to the baby.'

'A woman's voice should not be heard on the streets.'

Hussein leaned against the wall, gun under arm, thumbs thrust through his leather belt, cap on one side, chewing gum.

Aziz caught up with Fariba and was stunned into silence, seeing no further than the uniform, the gun. Other people gathered round. Then more. Hussein no longer slouched. He drew himself up. Tall and straight.

'What is your name?'

Fariba shrank away from him, back against the wall of people who pushed her forwards again. She tried to pull up her chador with one arm. To answer. But the sound stuck in her throat.

'I said, what's your name?' Hussein bent over Fariba, his face so close that she could smell the gum on his

215

breath. The people at her back nudged her. 'Answer him,' they said. 'Go on. Answer him.'

Fariba licked her lips. At last she managed just one word: 'Mama!'

Aziz pushed her way through the crowd.

'My daughter. My daughter!' Aziz was weeping. She lost hold of Mussa and Sadeq as she forced her way to her daughter's side. Fariba could hear them screaming somewhere behind the wall of bodies. But Mama was there, next to her. Mama would make everything alright.

'My apologies, Agha. My apologies. She is only a child. Thoughtless as are all children.'

'She was singing.'

'Singing?' Aziz was puzzled.

'Bare-headed and singing in a public place.'

Aziz turned to Fariba.

'Mama, Shahnaz was crying and I sang to her.'

'They're Jews,' shouted someone in the crowd. The cry was taken up with gathering force and volume like a whirlwind. Jews. Jews. Fariba could hardly breathe.

'Mama?' She buried her face in her mother's chador. The warm familiar smell of kerosene and rice. The familiar blackness of her own family.

Aziz's voice became a high-pitched whine as she cringed before the young soldier. 'Beh bimarestan raftim . . . We were on our way to hospital. The child is sick. Only look. See how sick she is. Her legs are like . . .'

The shouts of the crowd were now so loud that they drowned the voice of Aziz and her lost and frightened sons. The people pressed forward. Hussein looked around uneasily. Things were getting out of control. All he'd wanted was a bit of fun. To tease the girl a bit.

He waved his gun in the air.

'Stand back all of you. Stand back.' He meant no harm to the child. Or her mother. Jews or Moslems, it was all the same to him.

216

'Stand back,' he yelled. But nobody could hear him. He would fire a few shots into the air. To make them take notice.

Hussein pointed his gun at the sky and fired. The crowd evaporated as if by magic. Fariba and her mother crouched on the pavement, sheltering Shahnaz with the bridge of their bodies. When they looked up, everything was quiet. The street deserted except for Mussa and Sadeq, hands over their ears, shrieking with fear.

'And no more singing,' said Hussein sternly. He sauntered off, hands in pockets, gun over his shoulder, whistling at the sun.

16

'What are you reading?'

When she heard the disembodied voice of her ex-husband, Shirin Khaksar put down her book and sighed. She always read when she couldn't sleep. Now it appeared she couldn't even read in peace. The accusing voices seemed to be everywhere, attacking every move she made.

'It's a book by Flaubert. *Madame Bovary*. You won't know it.' Shirin despised herself even as she answered. Why was she replying to questions from someone who wasn't there?

'Some dirty French book, eh?' Her husband's voice tonight had a sneering, lustful edge. Perhaps if she talked to him, reasoned with him, he might prove more reasonable in return. Shirin laid her glasses and book on the bedside table.

'It's not a dirty book,' she explained to the voice, as patiently as if talking to a child. It was a tone she had practised for years before admitting that her marriage was a failure. 'It's a very beautiful book – about a French doctor and his wife.'

'All French books are dirty.'

Shirin ignored the statement, grateful that the voice could not offer physical violence.

'I said, all French books are dirty.' The voice was slurred now. Shirin drew the bedclothes around herself as if there really were someone there.

'I am not interested in dirty books. Not like you.' She was annoyed with herself for retaliating but she couldn't stop herself. 'Don't tell me you're leading a blameless life in New York, because I won't believe you,' she heard herself say. 'Who is it now? I hope for your sake that she's rich.'

'What a dirty mind you have, Shirin. You have never understood a man's feelings.'

'I tried to understand you for years.'

She turned out the light and lay with her head under the pillow. That was another trick she had acquired during her marriage, to shut out his taunts, to protect her head as he lunged at her. She lay waiting . . . but of course there was no one there, she told herself. Though the voice went on and on.

'Why can't you leave me alone?' she wailed into the dark room.

'You wheedled your way into a man's world and now you must take the consequences. Any other woman would have been content with looking after her children and her husband.'

'And her husband's mistresses? And paying for his cars, his clothes, his drinks and his gambling debts? No thank you. There is more to life than that.'

'Quite so. There's always death.'

At that, Shirin sat up and switched on the light again. She re-arranged her pillows, picked up her glasses and her book.

'I said, there's always death.'

Shirin had thought a lot about death lately. She flicked through her book, trying to remember where she had got to. Not that it mattered, she knew it almost by heart. She read out loud now, rolling the French cadences around her tongue, making the room echo with the sound until her husband's sneers gradually faded into silence.

On the morning after Mrs Emani's disappearance, Shirin went into the kitchen and cut herself a slice of bread. It was stale. Opening the window she crumbled it on the sill, then waited for the birds to find it. One by one they arrived, small brown sparrows, quite undisturbed by the loudness of the voice only Shirin could hear.

'It's your fault, you know. She's probably been arrested. The only decent thing you can do is to give yourself up before you harm any more innocent people.'

'Very well, I will. Not now though. After lunch perhaps. First I must wash my hair, dress, pack. There is so much to do.'

Shirin knew as she spoke that she did not have the courage to give herself up. Not yet. After all, would anyone hurt a woman like Mrs Emani? As soon as the thought entered her mind, Shirin decided that it was only too likely. Mrs Emani was a born victim.

When Mrs Emani entered the room, everyone stood up, even the Prosecutor. She stood clutching her empty shopping bag, looking nervously over her shoulder to see whether someone of importance was following her.

'Please sit down.'

Mrs Emani sat down quickly on the chair in front of her, hoping to be less conspicuous. Her arrival had caused considerable consternation.

'Nist.' 'Nist.' The word was hissed from person to person. 'Nist?' queried the man behind the desk. 'Nist?' the word whispered its way back along the row until it reached the last man, who had no one to pass the message on to. He shrugged, shook his head and swallowed nervously.

'Khanum,' intoned the Prosecutor, 'you are brought here on the charge . . .'

Mrs Emani bowed her head and prayed to God to give her strength.

'Of being Her Royal Highness, the Princess . . .'

Mrs Emani looked up and began to take notice again.

'. . . but since that charge is patently ridiculous, I must apologize on behalf of everyone here.'

The rest of his words were drowned by the laughter in which Mrs Emani joined. Her glasses twinkled, her eyes watered. Tea and shirini were ordered. Mrs Emani cleaned her spectacles, sipped the hot sweet liquid and apologized time and time again for taking up so much of everyone's time.

A car stopping outside the house was enough to make Shirin Khaksar hurry to the window. She peered through the shutters which she kept permanently closed on the street side. She saw the black car, the uniformed occupants, the armed guards. Well, she was ready, anxious to get it over with. She put on her coat, picked up her cases and walked along the corridor towards the front door.

Mrs Emani closed it behind her. There was the sound of car tyres screeching on gravel.

'I'm home,' called Mrs Emani. 'I'm back. Just imagine, they thought I was the Shah's auntie!' She chuckled at the memory.

The Shah's auntie! Well, I ask you – Mrs Emani! Could anything be less likely? Still, it was just a touch of misguided zeal. It's all ended happily and no harm done. A bit of amusement all round – and really, laughs are hard to come by these days.

I've never told you about my evening with Giselle. Did I say it would cost me a beer or a meal to get my parcel delivered? Well, the answer was both! Such an evening we had of it. Drinks at the hotel in her bedroom – nothing improper, believe me, but a hotel bedroom is about the only place to obtain alcohol these days. Then, on to a restaurant – the Xanadu – tables in the courtyard, a slight chill to the air, flowers, candles, really quite Parisian. The food was good, given the limitations we have to accept at present, and as my mother says, presentation, chéri, presentation is the key.

Giselle really is most attractive company. Tall, fair and willowy. Quite like my wife really, if you imagine her stretched and bleached. Quite stunning. She used to be a dancer you know, Giselle. I suppose she was destined for the ballet with a name like that. But she never quite made it to the top, she confided to me over the omelette aux fines herbes, and didn't want to stay in the back row of the corps de ballet for ever.

Really, I found the whole evening most stimulating. In fact it was all too much for me – Giselle hanging misty-eyed onto my every pronouncement – and I was thrown into a state of such emotional agitation that, as the dessert was served, it was as if the floodgates of heaven were opened. Blood everywhere!

Waiters rushed round with buckets of ice. Napkins. Giselle was immediately at my side, calm and confident, like a vision from Paradise. Leaning over me, pinching my nostrils, cradling my head to her bosom in a most delightful way. I must confess to malingering longer than was necessary in the strictest medical sense. Why, she even insisted on escorting me to my hotel and seeing me safely into bed, and only left with the greatest reluctance on hearing my protestations that I would be perfectly alright.

But when she'd gone, I felt acutely depressed. I even contacted the Ayatollah's office and requested permission to leave. The answer was No. Then I had the idea of sending for my wife to show her a bit of my mother's country. At once, I wrote a letter to that effect. I think that a few days' holiday, unencumbered with children or relatives, a second honeymoon if you like, can only have the most beneficial effect on a marriage. I anticipate her reply with the keenest of pleasure.

* * *

It was late afternoon when Theresa and Fereydoun Homayoun, on their holiday, stood at the side of the road, which continued north to the Caspian Sea. Their destination lay to the east, along a dirt track. The Mercedes was safely locked up in the garage, Mrs Smith had gone with Farah and Reza to stay with Fereydoun's mother in Golak, the most northerly suburb of Tehran.

A lorry pulled up and the driver ordered his passengers into the back, among the sacks of flour and charcoal, leaving the cab free for Fereydoun and Theresa. The cab was festooned with fairy lights. Dolls danced on pieces of elastic from the roof. Small figures perched on the dashboard on a fringed velvet cloth.

It was cold, so cold that Theresa shrank close to her husband and he responded by putting an arm round her.

'You ski?' asked the driver.

Fereydoun clicked his tongue and tossed his head.

'Is no ski now. Hoteli is empty. Very bad.'

The lorry lurched and rattled through the sea of mud, formed from melting snow. There was a sickening lurch as the wheels lost their grip and the driver laughed and pressed down the accelerator.

After some fifteen miles they arrived at the final stage of their journey. Fereydoun stood below the cab, holding out both hands. Theresa jumped with the sudden feeling that she would, after all, enjoy this holiday.

They continued their way by donkey. One for the luggage, one for Theresa, while Fereydoun walked by her side.

After a bit, Theresa got off, her feet and hands numb with cold. She felt safer on the ground, with the huge drop down to the river gorge on one side. She clung to Fereydoun's arm as they slithered along the track.

All thirty villagers turned out to see the arrival of Fereydoun and his foreign wife. Men, women and babies stood in the doorways. The children were bolder, running

223

after them up the slope to their holiday cottage, tweaking at the hem of Theresa's coat.

'Aren't they beautiful, Fereydoun?' Theresa felt a pang of regret for her own children. 'I must bring some of the children's clothes next time we come.'

They arrived at the log cottage in the last glow of sunset, which for a time kept the acute cold at bay. They stood on the small terrace looking down on the village, at the centre of a spider's web of tracks. Purple shadows gathered in the valleys and mountain peaks glowed blue under their covering of snow.

'We could do with a few sheep and goats to warm the place up,' said Fereydoun later, as they sat indoors in overcoats and gloves watching the meagre fire which their guide assured them was all the fuel he could spare. The flames sent flickering patterns over the rafters and whitewashed walls, but though they sat almost within the fireplace, their breath formed clouds of vapour.

The next morning Theresa lay in bed until she heard a woman from the village arrive and put a bowl of milk on the kitchen cupboard. Theresa pulled her jeans over her pyjamas, then put on all her jumpers, and finally her down-filled anorak. Like someone in a straitjacket she clumped through the jumble of last night's love-making. The cigarettes stubbed out on the concrete floor. The empty half-bottle of whisky. The overturned glasses.

She wondered whether she might be pregnant, though she hadn't told Fereydoun she wanted another baby. She wanted it to be a surprise.

Theresa skimmed ash and hay off the milk, then put it on the cooker to boil. She took a tray from the cupboard and set two glasses and the tin bowl of sheep's yoghurt. She knew Fereydoun would be pleased; he'd always wanted more children.

224

When the milk boiled, Theresa scattered in one gloved handful of oats and stirred.

That morning, for the first time in his life, the Mullah Afsharzadeh found himself unable to pray. Each time he turned to face Mecca, he saw not his Maker, but Soheila Gabayan. For sixty years he had offered his soul to God at the prescribed times, and now a single profane image threatened its lustre.

He was a worried man. And as worry crept into one aspect of his existence, so it sneaked into other avenues of his daily life. At the time when his soul should have rejoiced at the turn of his fortunes – the filled mosque, God's kingdom established on earth, the new reverence accorded him in the street, and even the letter which he now carried in his pocket – that rejoicing was as nothing beside the face of a thirteen-year-old girl.

The Mullah felt his soul teetering on the brink of an abyss. At any moment it might plummet into the black depths of sin. Yet God was merciful. Even today He had offered inspiration, which the Mullah had considered carefully, with reference and cross-reference to the Koran and the holy teachings of the Shia Moslems.

The letter put the final seal of approval on his plans. He had been summoned before the Ayatollah himself. He, Qorban Afsharzadeh, child of a simple peasant, was to head one of the Revolutionary Tribunals as the interpreter of Islamic Law. He trembled at the prospect. God was good, God had shown His servant His favour. The Mullah was now bound for the Oriental Carpet Emporium of Masoud Gabayan. Pinioned beneath his right arm, as had become his custom, was a small boy.

'Your Holiness,' exclaimed Masoud, in the process of removing the iron bars which protected his property. 'Your Holiness, what an honour.'

The Mullah searched his pockets for a coin for the boy who hovered expectantly between the two men.

'Do not expect earthly rewards in the service of God,' snapped Masoud. 'Be off.'

Masoud drew back the last bolts and held the shop door wide open.

'Come in, Your Holiness, come in. Ali, a chair for the Mullah, be quick about it.' Masoud took out his pocket handkerchief and dusted the chair before the Mullah sat down. Then he took some loose change from his pocket.

'Ali, a glass of chai for the Mullah!' On second thoughts, Masoud pocketed the rials. The tea shop would hardly expect payment for a holy man's tea.

In silence, the Mullah groped beneath the folds of his robe and produced his letter. Masoud was duly impressed by the official language and obvious importance of the document.

'And so you see, Agha Gabayan, I am summoned to serve the Islamic Republic.'

'Congratulations, Father. The Republic could have no finer servant.' Masoud bowed and smiled as he spoke.

'I am to be a judge!' The Mullah shook his head in amazement.

'A judge,' echoed Masoud. 'My daughter too studies the law.'

'You are forgetting, if you will pardon me for saying so, that a woman cannot hold legal office under Islam.'

'Of course, Father. In any case I doubt the wisdom of her continuing her studies. They have brought enough trouble already.'

He stopped speaking as Ali returned with the Mullah's tea. The Mullah drank it nervously, then scrubbed vigorously at his beard with the black cuff of his robe. Afterwards, he sat for a while, preening the long grey hairs which drooped from his chin, down over his chest.

'Please,' he said, 'I wish to speak in confidence.'

With a nod the Mullah indicated Ali, who was polishing the brass doorknob with a look of ferocious concentration. News of his appointment could spread through the bazaar, he would be glad if it did, but as for the other matter which lay so near to his heart . . .

'Ali, you will take your lunch hour now,' said Masoud.

Ali looked at his watch. It was only ten o'clock. He left the shop, slamming the door behind him.

'Your daughters, Agha,' began the Mullah when the dust had settled again. 'Your daughters need help. I fear for the younger as I did for the elder. Too much learning is dangerous in a woman.'

Masoud hung his head in shame.

'What can I do, Father? If I suggest Soheila stays at home, well, my wife would not hear of it.'

'With the example of her sister before her, we must take special care. She is in need of spiritual guidance. How old is she?'

'Thirteen next month.'

'You are thinking already of a husband, now that the marriage age has been lowered?'

Masoud shook his head.

'My wife wouldn't hear of it.'

'She is ripe for marriage. Take note of her sister's downfall!' The Mullah thought of the tiny feet, the softly developing curves of Soheila's body. He mopped a last dribble of tea from the corner of his mouth.

'But who will marry her now, Father? If she marries and the sins of her sister become known it will be said that I have brought dishonour on her husband's family. If I confess beforehand, then who will marry her?'

'If someone would take her regardless of contamination and dishonour?' The Mullah leaned forward eagerly.

'Then, I would indeed praise God.'

'Masoudja, my son. My appointment weighs heavy upon me. It places new burdens, new cares on my shoulders which will be hard to bear alone. I need to be relieved of the worry of domestic affairs. In return I would offer eternal salvation through my expert guidance. I would willingly undertake the redemption of your younger daughter's soul if you will entrust her to me as my wife.'

Masoud was still speechless when the Mullah left. Ali returned to find him sitting in front of an open ledger, staring into space.

'Are you alright, Agha?'

'Of course I'm alright,' snapped Masoud Gabayan, father-in-law-elect to a Mullah, and no ordinary Mullah at that. It all went to show that he was right and Roya was wrong. Just where had all her fancy notions of education got his daughters? The Mullah's offer proved that the traditional avenue of advancement by marriage simply couldn't be beaten. Father-in-law of a Mullah! Masoud almost chuckled out loud. He stifled the sound by shouting at Ali.

'Get on with your work.'

Ali picked up the duster and continued buffing the doorknob until his distorted image shone back at him. He dreamed back to the day when those foreign devils came into the shop with their short skirts and bare legs. Sometimes, leaning over to take another rug from the pile, he would brush against a cool white arm. There had been little time for doorknobs in those days. Instead, the constant bargaining, the touch of painted nails on his forearm. The crackle of notes stuffed into his shirtsleeve before he entered the official cash sale in the register.

He was sometimes left in such a state of excitement by these encounters that he would retire to the toilet in the back yard and . . .

'How many times are you going to polish that doorknob?' growled Masoud. 'Have you nothing better to do with your time? I don't pay you for doing nothing.'

Ali sighed, picked up the broom and swept the Mullah's holy footprints from the shop floor.

Masoud could not keep the excitement to himself for long. He left early for lunch, hurrying along to the chai khuneh where, as luck would have it, he found a group of friends smoking together.

'Seen the paper?' muttered one, thrusting a much thumbed copy under Masoud's nose.

Masoud felt little sympathy for the defendant in the case. This was an Islamic Republic – traders who over-charged deserved punishment. Let them be flogged or fined or beaten on the soles of their feet. Such temptations were behind him now that business was at a standstill. Besides, he had more important news.

'Today I received a proposal of marriage for my younger daughter.'

'I'd suggest whoever it is takes the older one, she's getting a bit long in the tooth.' His friends laughed and Masoud retreated into an offended silence.

'I even heard,' said one with a long look, 'though it's only bazaar gossip of course, that your daughter . . .' He stopped at the expression on Masoud's face.

'She is studying to become a lawyer. She has gone to Isfahan to prepare for her finals, away from the distractions of the Revolution.' Masoud had to protect his honour but he also wanted to defend his daughter. He had been proud of her, once.

'Well, Masoud, tell us your news. There's not much good news nowadays.'

'Well. Today the Mullah called at my shop . . .'

Masoud left the tea shop cheered by the enthusiasm of his friends. They all thought as he did. The same way as his old mother. Dear old lady. Even though she lived down in Shiraz, he really ought to make an effort to see more of her – she would be one hundred per cent behind him now. Poor old lady. Not up to much physically any more, but mentally just as good as ever. She'd said all along, only he'd never listened, that Roya wasn't right for him. There'd always been this wilful streak in her. That was what had attracted him in the first place. But now her unorthodox views were threatening. She could cause him a lot of trouble. He had to hand it to his old mother. She'd been right all along.

'Mama, why don't you visit Shahnaz?' Fariba Baniyazdi sat on the doorstep in the sun.

'It's too far.'

'She would like to see you.'

'I'm too tired.'

'I will stay with the little ones.'

'But I can't go there without you, Fariba.'

Fariba feared going alone. Not that she was afraid of the hospital, like her mother was. Fariba loved the nurses in their white dresses, Shahnaz's wide, gummy grin through the bars of her cot. Since the incident with the soldier, it was the journey that frightened her. She slunk through the streets, a small black shadow trying to be invisible, to give no one cause for offence.

'Mama, you should go. You wouldn't recognize Shahnaz now. She has a face like this,' and Fariba blew out her skinny cheeks, patting them to make them red. 'And her arms! She has dimples, here, just above her elbow. Mama, she is so beautiful that I think they will soon send her home again.'

Aziz sat with her hands clasped round a small glass of lukewarm tea.

'Say something, Mama, aren't you pleased?'

'She is better in hospital. How can I look after her so well?'

Fariba looked at her mother and was frightened. She seemed to have shrivelled like some of the beggar women

230

in the streets, skin parchment thin over her bones. She saw each day how her mother was left with only the scrapings of the saucepan while her father and brothers devoured as much as they could.

She hated her father. The way he sat closest to the stove, guzzling like an animal. She hated the nightly ritual of her mother's feeble protests and her father's frenzied jigging under the bedclothes, doing something terrible to her mother before he fell asleep.

Occasionally Hamid Baniyazdi picked up a bit of work. That day at the bus, he had been lucky. More often he was in the bazaar, carrying a bale of material from lorry to stall, a sack of rice from here to there. Sometimes he was unlucky, his pockets still empty at the end of the day.

A tap on the shoulder. Hamid spun round.

'Houshangja, Salaam aleikum.'

'How about a pipe, Hamid!' The clatter of small change in Houshang's pocket. His arm round Hamid's shoulder. This was friendship, the close touch of hands, the understanding. Sharing the good times and bad . . .

Fariba watched her mother. The once frightening, witchlike boniness of her fingers was a thing of the past. They were now monstrous slugs, puffy and swollen, as she listlessly swilled the washing in a bowl of grey water.

'Mama, you must go to the hospital,' Fariba whispered. Her heart almost stopped then at the fear in her mother's eyes.

'Fariba, people only go there to die.'

'That's not true, Mama. It's not true at all.' But suddenly looking at her Mama, it seemed perfectly possible. Her Mama! If that happened, Fariba wanted to die too.

Fariba leapt to her feet.

231

'Stop that,' she screamed at the boys. 'Stop making that awful noise.' She fell upon them, scratching and hitting, tears pouring down her face, until the boys ran away, frightened.

Then Fariba sat down again next to her mother.

'Mama, we will go to Israel. Everything will be different there.'

The other women were gathering in the courtyard, preparing the evening meal.

'Israel did you say, Fariba?' called one.

'Haven't you heard then? It is best not even to talk about Israel.' The woman plonked her heavy pan of rice on the edge of the stone trough.

'The first Jew was executed today. For sending money to Israel.'

Aziz turned to her daughter.

'Fariba, you must never mention Israel to me again.'

17

Shirin Khaksar sat up straight and pressed her hands
against the small of her back. She realized now that
everyone carried some measure of guilt. For things they
had done, or might have done. It was all simply a question
of decisions taken in the light of information available at
the time. Yet now she'd finished writing to her daughter,
Shirin knew that the accusations would begin again.

She was grateful for the short respite while she concen-
trated on her letter. Her relationship with Jackie appeared
the only blameless thing in her life. Yet even that, she
told herself, was questionable.

Although it was one o'clock, Shirin didn't feel hungry,
but she decided to eat something. She would feel better
later – perhaps even go for a walk at dusk. She pushed
back her chair, stood up, and went into the kitchen.

'What are you doing?' came the voice.

So. It was back. But she would not answer. Not this
time, even though the voice bore an uncanny resemblance
to her old schoolmaster. The Mo'alem! She could still see
him sitting on the rostrum, emphasizing this point or that
by tapping his ruler against the edge of the desk. The
ruler that in moments of wrath became a weapon.

'I said, what are you doing?' It was louder this time.

Shirin took a loaf from the cupboard and removed two
slices. She was no longer a seven-year-old, to be bullied
in her own home.

'I asked a question. You are wasting my time.'

Shirin heard a chair grate, the stump of boots on a
wooden floor, and she gave in.

'I'm making a sandwich.'

'With that?' The voice was contemptuous.

'It keeps better than unleavened bread.'

'In my day there was no choice. We ate what we had always eaten, not some Western importation. Now what are you doing?'

'I'm opening a tin of cheese.'

'Cheese, in a tin. Let me see the label.'

Shirin began to turn the tin over, then quickly slammed it back on the cupboard. But she knew from his exclamation that he had already seen 'Produce of France' stamped on the bottom.

'Sandwiches, eh? The sandwich,' he intoned, 'is named after John Montagu, Fourth Earl of Sandwich. Owing to the hours he spent at the gaming table, his beef was brought to him between two slices of bread. As such, the sandwich is not only a habit of foreign extraction but also of corrupt origin, a symbol of Western decadence. I would advise you to eat no more of these "sandwiches" for the good of your soul. Have we not been told:

> "Intoxicants and gambling
> Are an abomination
> Of Satan's handiwork;
> Eschew such evil
> That ye may prosper."'

Shirin carried her sandwich back into the sitting room and sat at the table.

'Can't you let me eat my lunch in peace?'

'Peace is the prerogative of the righteous.'

Shirin looked out of the window, into the small courtyard where Mrs Emani was scuttering back and forth, sweeping the flagstones. Mrs Emani puffed like a dragon, clearing a narrow path that led nowhere.

She looked up as she walked back towards her own part of the house. She saw Shirin watching from the window and smiled apologetically.

Shirin rose to her feet, one hand on the latch, to call out to her, offer a cup of tea, desperate for someone, anyone, to converse with, to keep the schoolmaster at bay. But Mrs Emani had gone, leaving no trace of her presence except the small path that led in a circle round the tiny courtyard. A puff of wind, and all was as it had been before.

'I suppose you know about her?'

Shirin refused to answer. She was well aware of the tell-tale statuary about the house and of Mrs Emani's frequent visits to the Catholic church.

'If you went to the shops, you could get some decent bread. Some Iranian nan. Warm, crisp and wholesome.'

'I don't like to go into the shops.'

'Aha. Then you admit you have reason to hide?'

'I admit nothing. It was a statement.'

'Why do you always talk as if you were defending yourself?'

'Because of the way you question me. I do go out. I take a walk each day, but nowhere where I might be recognized.'

'That implies you have something to hide. Some feeling of guilt?'

'You made me feel guilty even as a child, when I'd nothing to feel guilty about.'

'But now! What about religion for a start?'

'My religion has nothing to do with my actions, which have always been for the good of the Iranian people.'

'How can we leave out religion? You belong to a heretical sect.'

'I believe in the one true God and in his prophet, Mohammed.'

'And the Imam? What about the Twelfth Imam?'

'Let's change the subject, shall we? My personal beliefs in no way affect my allegiance to my country.'

Shirin left the sitting room, slamming the door behind

her. To keep her teacher out. To concentrate on the hum of the kettle, louder and louder until the water bubbled and the lid rattled up and down. She turned it off at the plug.

'You know what they did to Hoveyda?' The voice had followed her. 'He was a Bahai.'

'You're wrong. That was his father.'

'But you saw what they did to him – the papers, the photographs, the reports. Two bullets it took.'

'Go away, please go away.' Shirin had known even as a child that there was no compassion in the Mo'alem. She rested her head on her forearms on the kitchen cupboard and wept.

Until there was a knock on the door.

Mrs Emani stood humbly in the corridor, clutching her shopping bag.

'I would have called earlier, only I heard you speaking,' she said. 'Do you want anything from the shops?'

There was nothing Shirin wanted, except company, some pretext to invite her landlady in.

'You look tired. You work too hard. I saw your light on so late last night.'

'Please, won't you come in? Have a cup of tea?'

Mrs Emani began to back away down the corridor.

'A biscuit perhaps? Or a sandwich?' As if she were bribing a child. Shirin felt she had to get a real person inside the flat, to prove that there really was no one else there. So that she could say to the voices: 'You are part of my imagination, I can dismiss you at will.'

'Well, if there's nothing I can get . . .' Mrs Emani's voice trailed around the bend in the corridor.

'Yes, yes please, there is something . . .'

Shirin was thinking desperately, what could she ask for, just to ensure that Mrs Emani returned. To know there would be a knock on the door later.

'Please, some nan. Wait, I'll get my purse.' Shirin ran back into her living room, searching for her bag. Into the bathroom. The kitchen. Back again to the front door, to tell Mrs Emani that she would pay later.

As she closed the door, she saw the bag hanging on the hook behind it. At the same time, she heard a mocking laugh.

'Nan, eh?'

'You! You hid it, didn't you? I never put my bag there.' Her voice rose to a wail as she looked around the empty flat.

I have decided that what this revolution is all about is really Men's Lib. *Not a fashionable term and I'm sure a lot of you women will be up in arms, but please hear me out. No interruptions, no jumping up because the milk's boiling over, no screaming and clawing, above all, no tears. OK?*

The position of the male in Iranian society under the Shah was being slowly and consistently eroded. Look at the statistics if you don't believe me. Education for women. Jobs for women. Family planning for women. Everything conspired to give women more, and men, in consequence, less.

Until the men couldn't take any more. They'd seen what lay ahead by looking at the West. I can see it by giving the example of my wife. I gave her a boy and a girl. A flat in Paris. A country house. A standard of living way above anything she could have expected, given her intellectual abilities. And how does she repay me?

No wonder that the men here rose up to defend their rights. A bit of emotional appeal, a bit of flattery, soon won the women over. 'The blood of each martyr is a bell which will awake a thousand of the living.' He soon persuaded them to fight against their own interests and depose the Shah. All that claptrap about freedom! They fell for it alright. And they still haven't woken up to the fact.

Oh it just shows – men are infinitely the superior sex. Larger brains too. And that's an indisputable fact. They've got the women to ensnare themselves, like rabbits. The more they struggle the more the noose tightens. And like rabbits they haven't the brains to see any way out of their predicament.

All this Fatima business! Fatima the glorious. The pure. The virtuous. And yet my friend the Ayatollah put it in a nutshell: If Fatima had been a man she would have been as great as Mohammed. *But she wasn't.*

'I think it's an insult, Mama.' Soheila and her mother were watching the news on television. 'To say "If Fatima were a man she would be as great as Mohammed" misses the whole point. She is our model because she was a woman.'

Roya knitted on through the demonstrations in Qom, the chants of the masses that she knew by heart. 'The only party is the party of God. The only leader is Khomeini.'

'What are you knitting?' Soheila fingered the soft pink wool.

'A bonnet.'

'Mama!'

'It's my grandchild. I can still knit for it.' Since Soraya left, Roya had knitted two matinée jackets, with matching bootees. She had now moved on to a larger size for the following winter.

'No grandchild of mine goes to strangers empty-handed.'

'Mama, what nonsense you talk.' Soheila bent and kissed her mother. 'I'm going to do my homework.'

The television camera moved from random shots of the crowds to focus on a Mullah, holding up a tiny baby. A lost baby. Roya wondered who could lose a baby that way. It must have been deliberate.

Minutes later, when she glanced up from her pattern at the screen, there was the baby again. Why did no one claim it? Why did no one out of all those thousands of people admit that . . . unless . . . what if . . .

Roya heard footsteps on the stairs, banished thoughts of Soraya, and hid her knitting in a plastic carrier bag underneath the settee.

'Why, Masoud, you're early!' There was no welcome in her voice, only surprise. She hurried into the kitchen. He must be fed.

Masoud was glowing with enthusiasm and energy.

'We finished early today.' To hear him talk, you'd think he was the judge and not just one of the audience. 'Yes, First-Class Corrupt upon Earth. First-Class Corrupt!' Masoud chuckled at the memory.

'He has been executed, Masoud?'

Her husband nodded.

'What had he done?'

'Disgusting, that's what he was.' Masoud licked his lips. 'Quite disgusting. He imported Indonesian prostitutes, hundreds of them, you know, small-boned, delicate . . . a millionaire he was too. Mind you, he couldn't read or write. He was an ignorant man.'

Roya held the heavy rice pan under the cold tap.

'And d'you know what else? He threw his enemies to the lions in the amusement park.'

'I don't believe it, Masoud.' Roya laughed at her husband's naïvety. She struck a match and held it to the gas.

'But everyone knows it's true. Everyone has heard about it.'

'Gossip!' said his wife.

What Masoud really wanted to talk about was the Mullah's proposal, but what had seemed such an easy

239

thing to do while he sat in the chai khuneh now seemed a different proposition. He sat tongue-tied through the evening meal. Perhaps it would be easier to talk later, when the children were in bed?

He looked at his daughter, chatting happily about her friends and school, and wondered whether the marriage was such a good idea after all.

Hussein was taken with the idea of that free trip to Mecca, offered to anyone who would kill the Shah.

'After all, Dad, it's quite legal. Killing him. He's been condemned by a Revolutionary Tribunal. The only problem is, how am I to get to South America?'

Masoud sighed. It all boiled down to money. And he couldn't spare any. But he felt that his son was again pointing the way, focusing his mind on the essentials of the Revolution. There was no room for sentimental thoughts. Islam was the important thing. Islam!

'That picture will have to go,' he said suddenly. Startled, Roya looked up. She had always liked that picture. A girl, with her back to the artist, sat looking at a vast panorama of forests and mountains. Such a lovely view! It seemed to mirror her own longings for something beyond her own domestic horizons.

'I like it,' she said.

Masoud got up and took the picture off the wall. It might fetch a few toman in the bazaar. The frame wasn't bad.

Roya ate steadily, but her knife and fork trembled.

'Mummy likes that picture, Dad,' put in Soheila.

'What's wrong with it anyway?' asked Roya.

'The girl is unveiled.'

'Oh Daddy, you're so old-fashioned. Art is different from everyday life.'

'That will do, Soheila.' Roya knew that any argument would only make her husband more stubborn. With a bit

240

of luck he would have forgotten about the picture by the time supper was over.

Masoud was agreeably surprised by his wife's support. Why then did he suffer from this inability to speak about the matter that weighed so heavily upon his mind? It was the flat. The whole flat was wrong. The furniture, the ornaments, all smacked of the West. It made Islam seem like an alien way of life.

'The furniture will have to go too.'

'The furniture?'

'Yes, the furniture. Are you deaf?'

Roya looked round in disbelief.

'All of it?'

Masoud nodded.

'The tables and chairs?'

'We must return to the true spirit of Islam.'

'The beds?'

Masoud nodded again.

Hussein and Soheila were trying not to giggle. By comparison with this assault on her life-style, the loss of the picture was nothing. Over twenty years she had built up her home, her only achievement in life. And now . . .

'Are you going out tonight?'

The would-be model of Islam nodded. 'I have a meeting to attend. Jalasseh daram.' He rolled the syllables round his mouth. He had never attended a meeting in his life before the Revolution. And tonight was no ordinary meeting. Tonight he was invited to accompany the Mullah, his future son-in-law, to the abode of the Imam. Not to see the great man himself: no, he would wait outside. But he would walk where the Ayatollah had walked, breathe the same air, see those who had spoken with the man.

As soon as Masoud left, Roya called Soheila and Hussein to help her arrange the flat according to Islamic principles.

241

'But where shall we put all the furniture?' Soheila was amused, but thought the idea impractical.

'It can all go into Soraya's bedroom.'

'But where will Soraya go?'

'We'll worry about that when the time comes.'

Hussein and Soheila carried tables and chairs into their sister's empty bedroom. Then Roya's precious settee and the coffee tables with thin, brass-capped legs. When they'd finished, the sitting room looked twice its usual size, a vast expanse of orange, nylon, fitted carpet.

From their parents' bedroom, Hussein and Soheila removed everything except the storage cupboards. Roya wondered how she'd ever get up off the floor in the morning now the bed had gone, but was determined to see her husband's silliness through to its logical conclusion.

When the living room, kitchen and bedroom had been stripped of furniture, Roya lowered herself cross-legged onto the carpet and opened the newspaper. She was in the middle of a report on the restrictions of sunbathing and mixed swimming, when Masoud opened the front door.

He crossed the hall, his mind aglow with revolutionary fervour. Counter-revolutionaries must be hunted down to clear the way for the true Islamic Republic which he, Masoud Gabayan, would serve as layman on the same tribunal as his friend the Mullah.

He stopped as he opened the sitting room door. His first thought was that he had been robbed. Justice would be meted out, a hand for a chair, an eye for a table. But there was his wife, sitting calmly in the middle of the floor, her chador a wide dark circle on the carpet.

Roya, aware of the children hovering in the corridor, looked up briefly to say 'Good evening, husband' before she lowered her eyes again, afraid that she too might laugh.

Masoud leant against the doorframe. He had been

looking forward to a quiet half hour reading in his favourite armchair before bed.

'I'm thirsty,' he bleated.

Roya scrambled onto her knees and then her feet, suppressing the grunts and groans she would have given way to if alone. In the kitchen she made tea, then returned and spread a small white cloth on the floor in front of her husband.

'Your tea, Masoud.'

'Where's yours?'

'I'll have mine in the kitchen. It isn't right that I should eat and drink with you.'

But she didn't leave the room at once, not until she had had the satisfaction of seeing Masoud lower himself uncomfortably to the floor level to take his refreshments. She smiled as she closed the sitting room door behind her.

Theresa Homayoun stood at the cottage window, high in the Elburz Mountains. Over her anorak she had draped a thick blanket which trailed behind her. Her chador, she called it. It was bitterly cold.

'What are they doing?' she asked Fereydoun.

Below in the valley, small figures circled round the village carrying lighted torches. She could hear voices and drums.

'They're frightening away wild boar.' Fereydoun came and stood next to his wife. He put an arm round her shoulders.

'Does it work?' Theresa's eyes followed the procession of lights, weaving among the network of paths.

'They think it does.'

'But how do they survive the winter?'

Fereydoun shrugged. 'It's a real challenge. But it's fun, isn't it?'

Theresa wondered how she was going to survive the week.

Later on in the evening, Fereydoun took Theresa into the village. They slithered down the hill and followed the general drift of people into one of the mud houses. At the door stood their host of the evening, beaming and bowing, flattered by their attendance.

Fereydoun sat amongst the men round the dung fire. Theresa joined the women at the other end of the hut, next to the animals' enclosure. She would have sat on the carpet with the others, but a chair was produced and she perched on it awkwardly, feeling exposed.

'Sard-e,' she remarked, trying to bridge the terrible gap between them. 'It's cold.' The women seemed to find this remark excruciatingly funny. The small girls giggled, rocking backwards and forwards with their hands over their mouths. Young women hugged one another until their bracelets tinkled. Grandmothers cackled like crows. Even the men turned and grinned.

Theresa slid off her chair into the circle of women. They plucked at the sleeves of her velour jumper and clicked their tongues in admiration. How fine. How soft. The children stroked her long hair and twined it round their fingers, marvelling at the colour.

'Make-up?' asked one hopefully.

Theresa opened her bag.

'Would you like to try some?' She passed the powder, mirror and lipstick to the girl on her left, who giggled but made no move to accept them.

'Shall I do it for you?' Theresa applied red to the girl's lips, eyeshadow, mascara, powder. She took the top off her perfume bottle and passed it round. The women sniffed suspiciously. Then they became bolder. Cosmetics passed from hand to hand. Theresa sat back and watched.

Behind her she could hear the goats. Someone threw

more fuel on the fire. The men were playing a game with dice. Theresa counted thirty-two people in the hut, the entire village.

She told the women where she came from. That she had no brothers or sisters. That her father was dead. She tried to describe her own children, and her flat in the city, where water flowed from a tap and everyone had a car and a radio.

'You take my daughter Zahra back with you,' said one woman. 'She is a good girl. She will work and save money for her dowry.'

Theresa looked at the girl in her pretty lengths of brightly coloured cloth and tried to imagine her in Tehran. She tried to explain that the Shah had gone. They all nodded. The Ayatollah had returned. There was trouble in the city, fighting and discontent. It was hard to find food. Her husband had no work, no money.

They raised their calloused, weather-beaten faces and laughed in polite disbelief.

'But no one will hurt you, Khanum. My daughter is safe with you.'

Next morning Zahra and her mother were waiting on the doorstep when Theresa got up.

'My daughter is yours,' said the woman.

Theresa didn't invite them in but they followed, into the kitchen, from stove to pan cupboard, back to the stove, over to the water jar, the mother's voice a shrill whine.

Then Fereydoun appeared, bleary-eyed. The girl stood silently by the door, a scarlet-fringed shawl wrapped around her head.

'How old is your daughter?' he demanded abruptly.

The mother shrugged.

'She's only a child,' said Theresa. 'Tell her to go away.'

'Darling, please let me handle this. You have to be

careful not to give offence, not to upset people.' He turned back to the woman. Theresa could not keep up with the speed at which he talked, but the woman seemed pleased. She left, leaving the girl standing by the door.

'Fereydoun, what is going on?'

'The girl will stay and help while we're here.'

'But I don't need any help.'

'She can wash up and sweep the floors.'

'But sweeping the floors is the only thing that keeps me warm.'

Theresa tried to read, migrating after the patch of sunshine as it moved across the room. When she got up to make coffee, the girl was there to do it for her. When she picked up the bucket to go to the stream for water, the girl smiled and took the pail out of her hand.

Theresa watched Fereydoun watching the girl. She knew exactly what her husband was thinking. Her holiday was ruined. The girl was pretty; large eyes, tanned and slim. She kept in the background like a shadow, but like a shadow, she was always there.

'Why don't you go for a walk, if you've nothing to do?' Fereydoun suggested.

'If you'll come with me.'

The girl was now bent over the dustpan, like a peasant in the fields, straight legs, straight back bent at the hips, rounded buttocks in the air. Theresa had no intention of leaving them alone together.

'I tell you frankly, Khanum, I was terrified. I have never seen so many women gathered together before, all in black.'

Mrs Emani shook her head in wonder.

Sitting in a small beam of sunshine that illuminated his fingers like a spotlight, Ali continued with his work.

'The Ayatollah said that if Fatima had been a man, she might have been as great as Mohammed.'

Mrs Emani put down her shopping bag and sat on the window-ledge, glad to be out of the sun for a while.

'Your wife and family are well?'

Ali nodded gravely. He squinted at the light through the needle's eye, threaded and knotted another length of wool.

'I wonder . . .' Mrs Emani faltered, head buried in her large bag groping among the contents, 'if I may offer you some things for the children, some warm clothes for the winter?' She did not like to say that she had knitted the jumpers specially. Even she had to admit that they didn't look particularly new after the hours spent unpicking and knitting up Jamshid's old sweaters. She put them on the floor discreetly wrapped in brown paper.

Ali did not look at them.

Mrs Emani took off her glasses and wiped them on the corner of her jacket.

'I hear there are pomegranates in the bazaar,' said Ali.

Mrs Emani nodded gratefully. It was his way of accepting the gifts. The day was too hot to go traipsing all the way to the bazaar, but it was nice to imagine the hard-cased fruit stacked in glowing piles on the fruit stalls. She stood up to take her leave.

'Perhaps I should call next week about the rug?'

'Perhaps.' Ali did not look up as she went out. Such a busy man. Mrs Emani hoped she had not disturbed him.

18

'Fariba, you must take my place.'

The child nodded dumbly. She knew she should be happy that Mama was going to the hospital to be made well by the doctors and nurses. Like Shahnaz.

'Will you see Shahnaz in hospital?' Fariba asked.

'I don't know.'

Fariba buried her face against her mother's side.

'I shall miss you, Mama,' she wept.

'It won't be for long, Fariba.'

Fariba helped her mother to her feet.

'Perhaps I won't go after all. I will be better soon.'

'Mama, you must go. I am going to take you.'

'But your father, what about your father?'

'The nurses explained to him, Mama.'

'But he will be angry.'

'Don't worry, Mama.' Fariba shepherded the younger children to a neighbour's room, while her mother shuffled to the door on her swollen feet.

'Lean on me, Mama.' Fariba was just the right height for her mother to lean on.

They moved slowly through the maze of the Mahalleh. The night air dampened down many of the smells, and was chilly after the heat of the day. Fariba had chosen to go at night when the streets would be deserted, when flies no longer swarmed over the stacks of cows' heads and rotting vegetables on the pavements. Even so, she placed her mother between herself and the wall, ready to protect her with all the strength of her ten years.

About the long dark walk back, on her own, she did not like to think.

'You were very rude to my mother,' said Fereydoun Homayoun.

'Was I?' Theresa was surprised. She sat in the taxi with both children on her knee, hugging them close and wondering how she could ever have left them.

'She had tea all prepared, you know.'

'But I just wanted to get home.'

'Think of all the trouble she had gone to. Quite apart from having the children and your mother for the week.'

'Oh come on, Fereydoun. She doesn't do anything herself. She just gives orders to the servants.'

'I still think we should have stayed.'

'But Mum is already at the flat, getting organized.'

'*Your* mother, yes.'

'Fereydoun, that's very childish. Besides, when do you ever give your mother a thought?'

'How do you know what I've been thinking?'

'I've had a very good idea what you've been thinking over the last few days. I've been watching you. That poor little girl.'

At the corner of the street Fereydoun stopped the taxi and got out to buy a newspaper.

'Don't wait for me,' he said.

Reza cried as the taxi drove off.

'Want to go with Daddy,' he wept.

As soon as Theresa opened the flat door, Farah and Reza dashed inside to find their toys. The flat felt cold and musty. Theresa kept her coat on and went into the living room.

'Eee luv, I'm that sorry,' came her mother's voice. Mrs Smith looked up from the chaos. Papers. Books. Letters. Bills. Magazines. 'You'd best ring the police now you've come.'

Theresa sat down heavily on the settee.

'We'll wait and see what Fereydoun says. Where's Muna?'

'Gone if you ask me, luv. Look at this!' Mrs Smith pointed to the slides scattered about the room, deliberately trampled on, photograph albums ripped apart and pictures of the children torn from their frames.

'They're that bonny, aren't they?' She held up a photo of Theresa, Fereydoun and the children. A studio portrait.

Theresa had never liked the picture. It had been taken to please Fereydoun's mother, who liked pictures like that.

The sight of herself and Fereydoun posed stiffly together, smiling to order, his arm round her shoulder, had always sickened Theresa. And she could hardly recognize the children, coerced into those artificial smiles with the promise of an icecream and a trip in a rowing boat afterwards. And then, on the way to the park, Fereydoun had suddenly announced that he couldn't go with them. He had another engagement. For Theresa, this was the first indication that the gossip she'd heard might possibly be true.

Fereydoun had liked the photograph. He ordered an extra copy to stand on his desk in the office. It showed the family exactly as he wished them to be. Poised. Confident. Respectable. Theresa began to cry.

'Now don't you take on so, luv. You just sit there and I'll make a nice pot of tea.'

Theresa sat. This was no ordinary break-in which would have left the flat stripped bare, right down to the curtain rails and the last teaspoon. She thought of trying to restore order quickly so that Fereydoun need never know. Perhaps, after all, his fears were justified – but then so were her suspicions of his 'late nights at the office'. He had given her sufficient cause to cry wolf.

When she saw her husband standing, stunned, in the doorway she felt only anger.

'Did you buy a paper?' was all she said.

And yet, Theresa liked to think that her child was conceived that night, in the darkness broken by the pattern of headlights on the bedroom ceiling. A night when Fereydoun made obvious his need for her.

Shirin Khaksar read and re-read the letter from her daughter. It was a welcome change from the arguments that raged inside her own mind.

She was touched by the letter. By her daughter's concern that what she had to say might hurt her mother. Shirin was hurt, yet she agreed wholeheartedly with the Bahai belief that a child must be free to choose her own religion at the age of fifteen. If Jackie had chosen to embrace the revivalist Christianity of her friends, it was understandable.

'Of course, it's all your fault.' The voice startled her. Manuchehr! She might have known that her husband would want to be involved.

'Is it?' she asked wearily. 'I think it's a perfectly natural reaction for any teenager. At her age it doesn't necessarily mean anything.'

'Thank God that at least she hasn't chosen your religion.'

Shirin realized that Manuchehr was really out to wound her this time.

'Your remark only shows how little you have ever understood "my religion" as you call it.' Shirin got up and walked over to the window. It was time to end the conversation, to dismiss him from her mind. But he wouldn't go. She pressed her forehead against the cold pane of glass. The light from her window just reached as

far as the mulberry tree, the fat buds bursting into leaf.
Soon now, there would be blossom.

'She's becoming a whore. Just like you.'

'That is one thing that you could never accuse me of.'

'You should see her now – short skirts, long hair,
make-up, a different boy each night.'

'While Dariush, I suppose, sits at home doing his
homework?'

'It's different for a boy.'

'He takes after his father then?'

'You're lucky I acknowledge that I am his father.'

'You know that, at least, is true.'

'Ah, but in the eyes of the law the children are
illegitimate. Our marriage, following the rites of your
religion, is neither legal nor valid. And you are nothing
more than a prostitute.'

'Manuchehr, there are some things which are unalter-
able in spite of "the law". We were in love, we married,
and you cared nothing for your religion – hence we
followed mine.'

'I married you because it was the only way to get you
into bed with me.'

'Ah, so you did love me.' Shirin lit a cigarette and
paced up and down the room.

'My dear Shirin, you are so naïve. You still confuse
love and lust.'

'You loved me and I loved you. You can't take that
memory away no matter what you say now. You remember Isfahan? How happy we were then.'

'Happy, yes. But love? No.'

The voice had stopped now, but the uncertainties it
had raised in her mind lingered on. The whys . . . What
ifs . . . Hows . . . And still the pages of her defence lay
untouched on the desk, gradually turning yellow in the
warm spring sunshine.

* * *

In the bazaar, Hamid Baniyazdi was hawking himself unsuccessfully from stall to stall with his friend Houshang.

'Heard the news?' asked Houshang.

Hamid grunted, thinking as he went of his motherless, penniless family. He picked his way carefully through the bazaar, barefoot, having laid up his shoes for the summer.

'The Ayatollah says everyone shall have a hundred kilowatts free.'

'A hundred kilowatts?'

'Yes. It is to help the poor.'

'Where can we collect them?'

'I don't know, but my wife says I must find out today in case there are none left.'

'You sure it was a hundred?'

'Aré. A neighbour's friend heard it on the radio.'

Hamid stopped.

'We shouldn't be wasting our time here looking for work. Let's go to the social workers now.'

Houshang nodded. They turned and made their way towards one of the exits.

'A hundred what's?' muttered Houshang.

'Well, a kilo can be this big.' Hamid outlined a vast towering shape as high and as wide as a house.

'Or this!' Houshang gestured a more modest-sized package. Hamid nodded and lashed out with his right foot at a group of hens.

'So a hundred could be, well, as big as a mosque.'

'Or like the weight of a good Isfahan carpet.' Hamid's eyes shone. Carpets – now there was something he could understand.

'Porter!' came a bellow from a nearby stall. Hamid and Houshang looked pityingly at the ragged men scampering in the direction of the shout. They obviously hadn't heard about the hundred kilowatts.

* * *

Hamid and Houshang found the usual queue of women and children outside the Social Work Office. As the sun's benevolent early morning face became a scorching demon, the line transferred itself from the sunny to the shady side of the street. The women shrank back against the wall, covering their faces, as the men approached, walked to the front of the queue and up to the desk.

'We've come about the hundred kilowatts.'

'What?' The social worker looked up from the endless reports, receipts and referrals.

'We heard about them on the radio.' Hamid tightened his pyjama cord nervously.

The social worker began to laugh as she realized what they had come about.

'Salim,' she gasped, 'give them their hundred kilowatts.'

Hamid and Houshang shuffled nervously. Salim put down the tray of tea he was carrying and roared with laughter. At the same time he pointed to his head. Houshang and Hamid looked down at their feet.

'I'm sorry.' The social worker mopped her eyes. 'A kilowatt is a measure of electricity. Look, you see the bulb in the ceiling. Turn it on, Salim! The amount of electricity it uses is added up in kilowatts. The Ayatollah wants everyone to have free light, but there is no electricity in the Mahalleh.'

'So we can't have our hundred?'

'No. You have no wires in the Mahalleh.'

Hamid looked up at the light bulb. With the sun so bright outside, he could hardly see that it was on. It looked a poor bargain. Just another dream trampled in the dust. Like the Ayatollah's offer of housing loans. Fifty per cent free, if he could have raised the rest.

'In Israel?' he inquired. 'Does every house in Israel have kilowatts?'

The social worker nodded.

'Very well, I shall go to Israel.'

254

'Is there any skill which you can offer?'

'I can slaughter according to the law. And I have many sons.'

The social worker shrugged and turned to the next client.

'Darling, please don't burn that piece of paper.'

Theresa Homayoun struck a match and held it under the corner of the page.

'Darling please! That could mean life or death to me.'

'And why should I care if it does?'

'You don't understand, darling. It's all perfectly legal. You are living in Iran now, you know.'

Theresa was finding the scene satisfying. She had never seen Fereydoun so panic-stricken before.

'Very well, Fereydoun. Let us be Iranian then. You married the girl on a temporary basis according to Iranian law. As your first wife I object, and demand that you divorce her according to the same law.'

'Darling, please don't talk so loudly, someone might hear.' Fereydoun glanced anxiously towards the office door.

'Shahla might come in at any moment. What do you mean bursting in here like this anyway, and going through my papers?'

'It was a good thing I did. I won't let you ruin that child's life. You will send her back to her village.'

'Who translated it for you?'

'I can read a bit of Farsi myself, you know, and Shahla did the rest for me.'

'Oh God.' Fereydoun sat down and licked his lips.

'Fereydoun, I am waiting. Come on, say it after me. "I divorce thee, I divorce thee, I . . ."'

'It wouldn't be valid. You've been reading too many novels. We'd have to have the girl here, and witnesses.'

'All right. Get her here.'

'Darling, it's all a fuss about nothing.'

'Is it?'

'Yes. It won't affect our relationship at all.'

'Oh? And that poor child? Fun for a few weeks and then what? Who'll want her second-hand?'

'Theresa, you know nothing of such matters.'

'I'm learning all the time, Fereydoun.'

'Darling, just be reasonable for a minute, please.'

'Fereydoun, I am not a complete idiot. I know perfectly well that when you have finished with her, there will be only one life open to her – that of a prostitute.'

'But all that has changed. Under Islam there can be no prostitution.'

'Hah!'

'Darling, you know that you're the only one I love. You know that I'll never leave you, don't you.'

Theresa applied the match to the certificate of temporary marriage.

'And to prove just how much you love me, I will expect you to divorce her by tonight.'

Sigheh marriages! Are not temporary unions every man's dream? How much trouble would be saved in the divorce courts. Everyone would be happy except the lawyers. And how many people go into marriage with any notion of it being permanent?

As far as I can see, the only awkwardness in serial marriage is the children, and even that is taken care of under The Law. The length of the marriage is specified in the contract. A fixed sum of money is paid. The women create problems for themselves. It all boils down to this yearning for babies. And look at the trouble it gets them into – Roya, Soraya, Aziz. Freedom and choice? They chuck it all in for the sake of romance and babies. Even Shirin Khaksar fell for it, once.

But Sigheh – where was I? Ah yes! I have to reveal to

you the most unlikely candidate of all. Mrs Emani. You start in disbelief! But look at her now. In the face of this revelation I defy you to show me a woman who is completely without vanity, who cannot be seduced by a token.

She removes her glasses and peers into the mirror, searching for the beauty that attracted Jamshid's father eighteen years ago. She thinks that she is simply too short-sighted these days to see it.

And you see, she seized at the chance. Love! She was bowled over by it! Six months of heaven on earth, and every day hoping that he would change his mind, that the six months would become a lifetime. But he'd paid his money. The six months passed and he was gone. And Jamshid on the way.

Of course, there was still the length of oddeh before all hope died. Two menstrual periods in which he was legally entitled to change his mind. Twice the moon waxed and waned. Twice she failed to bleed. Oh yes, the child was definitely his. But was he impressed? No. It's only women who get all emotional about babies.

Not just two months has she waited, but for seventeen years. And the dream is still there, behind the misted eyes and greying hair. And if earthly love lets you down, sublimate! Turn to a heavenly lover who will never let you down. So Mrs Emani found God. He loved her for what she was. And she loved Him passionately in return.

The girl stood uncertainly in the doorway of the kitchen. She still wore her red-fringed shawl wrapped around her head. Roya looked at her doubtfully.

'She's just what we need. You've been looking tired lately.'

'But Masoud, I don't need any help in the house. I manage perfectly well on my own.' Masoud's sudden concern for her aroused Roya's suspicions.

'It's all settled, wife. She can have Soraya's room and give you a hand. Think of all those queues for food and fuel. It will save your legs.'

'A country girl like that would be cheated at every turn.'

'She'd learn.'

Roya thought of her quiet days alone. She didn't want anyone else around. And an illiterate country girl would be no substitute for her Soraya.

'How old are you?' she asked.

'Chaharda.' The girl smiled. Such a lovely open smile. Fourteen, yet so well-developed, so mature compared with her Soheila. But those clothes . . . already she wondered how she might help the child.

'Masoudja, where did you find her?'

'Ali brought her to the shop. He's a cousin of some sort. She came to Tehran to work for a European woman who then turned her away.'

'Well, well, Masoud, give her the bus fare and send her back to her mother.'

But Masoud wasn't prepared to give the girl up so easily.

'Perhaps she could help Ali in the shop? She has strong hands, she might even learn to mend carpets.'

'I'm sure that would be better.' Roya walked across the hall and opened the front door so that they could both leave.

'Ferdowsi! Hafez! What rubbish are you reading now?'

'They are two of our greatest poets.' Shirin took off her glasses and put them down on the mantelshelf.

'Imperialist rubbish.'

'I distinctly remember you praising them – having us learn page after page by heart. And we did learn it. Because we were so frightened of you. At the time I hated it, but not any more.'

258

'My ignorance appals me. Let us be grateful that I have now seen the light.'

'That's a fine way to talk. You've been dead for years.'

'Let us call it, retired . . .'

Although the book lay open on her knee, Shirin recited more lines from memory.

'The sacred duty of the teacher is to protect the sanctity of schools against the inroads which anti-Islamic forces may make into your hearts and minds,' continued the Mo'alem.

'As far as that is concerned you have failed. I have such love for our old poets and classical literature that I fear I am beyond redemption.'

'The time will come, Shirinja, when all our ideas of literature will have to be revised. Imagine! No more of this grovelling sentimentality by poets trying to earn a living.'

'Twenty-five years ago, you said that the expressions of Hafez were the truly felt adoration of a humble subject towards his all-powerful monarch.'

'Time can prove us all wrong. Think of something modern and relevant. What about this:

> O Khomeini, you are the light of God
> Saviour of Oppressed People.

How's that?'

'And you criticized my choice!'

'But this speaks the truth, Shirinja.'

'Just as Hafez's verses spoke the truth at the time. And still do. Come on, Baba! You've been too long underground. Your thinking is becoming clouded. Listen to this:

> They say the Lion and the Lizard keep
> Their Courts where Jamshyd gloried and drank deep.

That is poetry.'

'Oh the ancient palaces! Persepolis! Have they suffered much?'

'I spent my honeymoon in Isfahan, you know. The hotel in the middle of town, arches round a green courtyard and in the centre a floodlit pool. But we didn't care what lay beyond the window. Do you know, I even gave up my job to please Manuchehr. Had two babies in quick succession and then phut! It was all over.'

'Of course, you were wrong all along, setting your store by earthly treasure. But tell me about the old town.'

'It's funny, isn't it, I still can't see it clearly. In spite of official tours, schools, hospitals, orphanages, co-operatives, if anyone ever says Isfahan, all I see are the arches and the lily-pool.'

'But what about the mosques?'

'Baba, why do you keep asking? What are buildings? It is people that matter. In Shiraz last week a woman was dragged from her home and beheaded – a Jew she was. Mothers have been shot in front of their children. Graveyards desecrated. And you ask about buildings?'

The Mo'alem nodded.

'OK then. The mosques are intact. Fuller than they have ever been before. People go there in their thousands, not to hear messages from God, but political propaganda relayed over loud-speakers. For additional entertainment, there might be something really exciting, a few army officers fighting for their lives before the Tribunals.'

'I'm sorry, Shirin. Some of these things are beyond an old man's understanding.'

'Then why taunt me with all that "Saviour of the People" business?'

'Ah, Shirinja, but the true Islam! Listen to this: "Give the good tidings to my devotees who listen to different voices, then choose the best." '

'Baba, who will listen to you now?'

But he was gone. He never had been able to take criticism, and as children they would not have dared offer any. Shirin wished he had stayed. In such a gentle mood even his company was better than none.

She opened her book but her enjoyment was gone. Perhaps even the book might condemn her? She could burn it, but what was the use? It was not concrete evidence that she feared.

Night was drawing in. Shirin put on her coat and made some tea. Then she tied on her headscarf and walked briskly down the hill towards the gardens. She kept to the shaded areas under the trees, glad of the lack of street lighting. Any danger which might attend a well-dressed woman, still good-looking, walking alone at twilight, was insignificant beside the fate she imagined for herself.

To Hamid Baniyazdi, the days of poverty under the Shah had acquired a rosy glow. Life had been predictable. His income meagre but reliable. The children attended school and had hot dinners. There was always the Social Work Office to fall back on in time of need.

Now there was only fear and uncertainty. Fear of sudden noises, of crowds, of heavy boots stamping through the slime of the Mahalleh proclaiming the advent of a God who was not his God.

Hamid sat on the doorstep, pyjama'd legs stretched before him, squinting at the sun. What else was there to do? There was no prospect of work now or in the future, not in his profession. Only Moslems were allowed to slaughter, and he had no other skill to offer. And now, not even a wife on whom to vent his frustration and bewilderment.

But there were the children – he was good at begetting children. Boy children. Not like poor Houshang, who had only daughters. Cheered by the thought, Hamid hurried out to find his friend.

Meanwhile, Aziz lay in the high white bed. She lay on her back, her stomach a mound under the white sheet, fearful of moving. The bed was so high, the gleaming floor such a long way down.

And she had already caused so much trouble. Aie, it was wonderful the hamum, the sparkling tub of water, the chrome taps reflecting her face.

She fingered the Viyella nightie. A miracle it was, soft and warm to the touch, high under her chin, loose and comfortable over her stomach. Even her hair felt different, soft and shining with that shampoo. Such lovely hair it had been, when she had married. Thick and black like a chador . . .

Aziz wrapped her chador around her and lay, sterilized and shining, clean as the sheets, the walls, the floor, stiff as the starched linen, and wept for Fariba and home.

'Sleep there.'

Fariba obeyed her father, and moved into the space usually occupied by her mother – between him and the little children. It would make it easier for her if one of the younger ones woke in the night.

She was not happy though, so close to Baba, his breathing hot and loud in her ear. But Mama had said, take my place, so perhaps she had meant it like that as well. But what if she turned over in the night and bumped into her father? She was more afraid of that than of his anger.

Now the rattling intake of Hamid's breath was very close. She lay rigid under her mother's blankets. Then he breathed out, fluttering hair across her cheeks. She brushed it aside and wept silently. She wanted her Mama. She could cook and sweep as well as any girl of ten. She could love and care for her little brothers. She could do all these things, but only if Mama was there in the background.

'What right have you to enter my office like this?' Fereydoun Homayoun demanded. He sat on the edge of his desk while the men ransacked the filing cabinets. 'You can only do this sort of thing with the proper authority. Show me your permit.'

'There is no authority but God.'

Fereydoun lit a cigarette and tried to look calmer than he felt. He was almost grateful that at last something was happening, something to end the terrible weeks of waiting and wondering. Now there was nothing more he could do. He strolled over to the window and glanced down into the street. On the opposite pavement he saw his secretary hailing a taxi. Part One of the plan was in operation. She looked quickly upwards as she climbed into the vehicle, but gave no other sign. Nor did he.

As the taxi drove off, Fereydoun turned back into the room and flicked ash onto the carpet. It suddenly didn't matter any more. He doubted whether he would ever see his office again.

Fereydoun marched the length of Takhte Tavous surrounded by his escort. He turned up his collar in spite of the sun. He still had his pride. A few people stared, but another arrest provoked little reaction nowadays. He walked stiffly, made awkward by the extra layers of clothing he always wore nowadays, to be prepared. He'd heard that he'd be glad of them at night, where he was going.

Afterwards, Fereydoun remembered that walk in extraordinary detail. The pattern of flat roofs against the blue sky. Sparrows perched on the gutters. Women with

263

shopping bags. An empty cigarette packet underfoot. The graffiti.

'With what am I being charged?' he demanded at the prison gate, determined not to be cowed by the immensity of the grey building.

'It is not necessary for you to know.'

'I demand to know. It is my right and I wish to contact my lawyer.'

'People like you do not need a lawyer. You are a criminal and deserve to be treated as such.'

'But what have I done?'

In Shemiran Mrs Homayoun, Fereydoun's mother, handed over five thousand rials and dismissed the secretary. Then she made a phone call to the Law Society, who said there was little they could do. They received too many similar phone calls every week. She took a taxi to Fereydoun's flat.

'Oh, it's you, Mother.' Theresa stood back. Her mother-in-law swept past her, across the hall and into the living room.

Mrs Smith sat on the floor, her hair in curlers, a mug of tea in one hand, doing a jigsaw puzzle with Farah and Reza.

'Eee, I didn't expect company. How are you?' Mrs Smith got to her feet, and pumped Mrs Homayoun's hand up and down while the mug of tea in the other hand slopped onto the carpet.

'Mind the carpet, Mum,' said Theresa. 'I'll get a cloth.'

'Theresa, you really should leave such things to the servants,' reproved her mother-in-law.

'I am the servants,' Theresa said.

Mrs Homayoun smoothed her dress. She said nothing to her grandchildren, who likewise ignored her. Theresa returned with a floorcloth.

'My dear, I'm sorry to tell you, Fereydoun has been

arrested.' Mrs Homayoun took a step towards Theresa, who backed away from her outstretched hands with their manicured fingers and diamond rings.

'Why didn't I hear first?'

'My dear, these are troubled times. I promised Fereydoun that I would look after you. You can come and live with me.'

'Thank you. I'd rather stay here.' He should have discussed it with her, she was his wife. 'It's very kind of you, Mother, but I couldn't leave. This is our home.' A familiar battle this, one Theresa could understand.

'It is what Fereydoun decided.'

'He should not have made the decision without consulting me.'

'He didn't want to worry you.'

'I'm his wife. I have a right to be worried.'

'This flat is not safe any more. It will be watched and probably searched. Think of the children.'

'Come on, luv.' Mrs Smith now entered the argument. 'Perhaps it's for the best.' She had put a headscarf over her curlers, her 'hejab' as she called it.

'I may follow later,' said Theresa. 'I need time to think about it.' She wondered how long it would take her mother's hair to dry.

'I will take the children with me now. The taxi is waiting.'

'No, the children stay with me.'

'Now don't be silly, luv. I'm sure Mrs Homayoun knows what's best.'

For the first time since she entered the room, Mrs Homayoun took notice of the children. She bent down, all smiles, and took some sweets from her handbag.

'You would like to come to Granny's, wouldn't you?' she said.

Farah and Reza looked up doubtfully.

'We can finish our puzzle later,' said Mrs Smith,

bundling the pieces into their box. 'Here, Reza, you carry this.'

'Well, we'll expect you later,' said Mrs Homayoun, leading the way to the door. Mrs Smith followed, ushering the children before her.

Theresa could hear their voices all the way down the stairs. Yet still she made no move to prevent their departure. She was too shocked, not so much by Fereydoun's arrest as by his betrayal of her. The implication that he couldn't trust her, and that she wouldn't be able to manage on her own. She stood at the window watching the children climb into the car, hoping that they might look up and wave. But the car door slammed and they were gone without an upward glance.

Mrs Smith came and stood next to her at the window, breathing heavily after climbing the stairs. In her headscarf and curlers. How often had Theresa told her not to go around like that in case anyone called. There was a hairdryer in the bathroom. When she felt her mother's arm around her shoulders, Theresa brushed it off angrily.

'Eee luv. I'm that sorry, I don't know what to say.' Theresa took a step away. 'That nice husband of yours wouldn't harm a flea, would he?'

'He has got a name, Mother.'

Her mother stood in helpless silence.

'Go on, Mother, say it. Say his name.'

Theresa could see the struggle that was going on inside her mother and almost felt pity.

'Go on, Mother, say his name. Just once. Say it.' Theresa felt a terrible desire to get her own back on someone, for the horrible dreariness of her childhood, for the sham of the marriage she had imagined would be an escape into something better.

'Say it, Mother. Go on, say it.' For her mother's simple acceptance of everything at its face value.

'I'm waiting, Mother.' For wearing curlers when her

266

mother-in-law came to call. Theresa's voice was getting louder and shriller.

'Mother! Will you say his name. Just once. Say it.' Theresa was screaming now. Frightened. Wondering what would become of her, of Fereydoun.

She watched her mother rub her forehead, looking suddenly old and frail and bewildered. And she momentarily hated her for being so powerless.

'I'm waiting, Mother.'

She saw tears ooze down the furrows of her mother's cheeks. The red spots where the curler pins dug into her scalp. And realized that there was nobody she could turn to.

Mrs Smith blew her nose. 'I'll go and make a nice cup of tea, luv, and then we'll do our packing.'

Theresa leant her forehead against the cold pane of glass and wept.

Fereydoun sat bolt-upright, avoiding the eyes of everyone else in the room. Anyone could see that they were all criminals. Shifty-looking types. He, personally, wouldn't trust them with an inch, whereas he, well, he had done nothing. They couldn't prove a thing. He had nothing to fear. He was clean-shaven, respectable, wore a decent suit. From London actually. Given a fair trial and a good lawyer – well, his mother would see to all that. She'd look after Theresa and the kids too, so he didn't need to worry about them.

He clutched on his knee what he laughingly referred to as his 'prison bag'. Clean shirt, change of socks and underpants. A few books. His favourite chocolates and a few packets of cigarettes. Not so much to smoke himself but to use on the guards. A quantity of small change for the same purpose.

After the initial shock of his arrest, Fereydoun was feeling quietly confident. After all, he was a decent chap and most of the officials seemed decent chaps too. He would have trusted them with driving his car or cleaning the office any day of the week. They would soon all come to their senses once this Ayatollah business died down. That man, now, who'd taken down his particulars. He wrote a neat hand. One had to be always on the lookout for people like that if one were to run a successful business.

'Excuse me,' Fereydoun called to a passing official. He stood up to attract attention.

'Sit down!' The guard jerked his gun in Fereydoun's direction.

'I'm so sorry,' said Fereydoun walking towards the man. Man to man. The gun aimed at his navel.

'I said sit down.' The safety catch clicked. Fereydoun sat down hastily.

'The toilet?' he whispered to the man on his left, who shrank away, wanting nothing to do with him. Smart gent, city suit, another one for the chop.

'Excuse me.' Fereydoun turned to the man on his right. 'Where is the toilet?'

The guard looked up angrily. In spite of the congestion in the small room, a space appeared on each side of Fereydoun. He regretted the large, rich lunch at the Intercontinental. He didn't usually indulge himself in the middle of the day. And he'd had the good luck to obtain a couple of bottles of beer . . .

Of course, he should have asked at the desk while they were filling in his forms. Only he hadn't liked to. Probably it was just nerves. A bit of self-control and the feeling would pass. He rocked backwards and forwards on the bench, crossing and re-crossing his legs. The other men were all staring at him now. He smiled an idiotic smile. This was worse than anything he had anticipated.

19

I have had a letter from my wife. A few days ago actually. I was just unable to share the news until I had recovered my usual emotional equilibrium. I have suffered nose-bleeds and headaches of a hideous intensity and my general state of nervous debility will more than adequately explain the dark hollows around my eyes. Indeed, I went out and bought myself this large pair of dark glasses which have unfortunately led on occasion to my being mistaken for an American. However, I pause often to study my reflection in shop windows and have decided that there are no grounds whatsoever for such an accusation.

In between shop windows, I stop at each roadside stall to purchase pomegranate juice. A waiter in my hotel suggested that I may be suffering from anaemia due to loss of blood. He recommended pomegranate juice on account of its high iron content.

An unfortunate side-effect of the juice is, pardon me ladies, constipation. Forced to resort to a chemist's shop, I invested in some senna pods which I scrupulously swallow every morning after my cup of black coffee. After a laborious half hour in the bathroom, enlivened by the daily paper, I fling open the window and am ready to face the day.

However, I digress from my original point, the pain caused me by my wife's letter. Is it the dress, you ask? Does it not fit? Could it not be altered in some way? The dress, dear friends, is the least of my woes. Suffice it to say that it has been donated to the dressing-up cupboard of the children's nursery school. My wife cannot, she says, afford to be seen dead in it. In Tehran it might cause a *sensation. But for Paris, alas, it has arrived some years too late.*

No. It is not the dress whose coils tighten around my neck until I gasp for air. It is – Giselle! Having carefully avoided the pitfall of another pilot (for what a handsome, dashing lot we are!), my wife now writes that she has fallen madly in love with Giselle. And her feelings are reciprocated.

They have both moved into the farmhouse, and like Marie Antoinette are playing at life à la paysanne. Strawberries and cream. Picnics sur l'herbe. They even dress in calico smocks. All harmless pranks that winter will soon enough nip in the bud. But worse is to come . . .

The plasterer has repaired the bedroom wall damaged by the weight of my picture. A decorator provided the final touches. And I now hang there in all my glory. Watched by my wife and Giselle as they lie in bed together, thinking of me fondly, she assures me.

And was I flattered by this last intelligence? You know well how broad-minded I am. I even swallowed, let us call it, the sigheh of my wife and that pilot. But even I must confess to being stunned by this. My wife! Mother of my children. Lying in my bed, indulging in who knows what obscene practices. However, I can scarcely rush down with a shotgun to blast Giselle off the face of the earth, nor carry out the recommended Islamic practice of flogging, though they both deserve it. I have written to my mother to ask her advice. In my shoes, what would you do?

But now, excuse me. Just the effort of talking about such a painful subject is exhausting. No. My wife will not be joining me for a holiday. She says she cannot leave her lover. For my part, I will go and lie down on my lonely bed.

'Salaam aleikum.' Mrs Emani closed the door of the Oriental Carpet Emporium noiselessly behind her. She stood for a moment peering into the gloom, surprised to see a girl there, among the piles of carpets.

'My cousin Zahra,' explained Ali.

The girl was sweeping energetically. The bristles rasped on the concrete floor and catapulted dust into the air. Zahra coughed from time to time. So did Ali.

'Perhaps if I open the door?' Mrs Emani reached out for the handle.

'No.' Ali scrambled to his feet. 'The sun! Think of the carpets.'

'My carpet?' she inquired.

'Ah!' Ali pointed to the heap of rugs. He lifted up the corners nearest to him, a glimpse of autumn as he leafed through. 'See, Khanum, only ten to go, and then it will be your turn.'

Mrs Emani smiled happily. Though there seemed little difference in her rug's position from last week, she was impressed to find some method to Ali's work.

'Perhaps next month?' Secretly she hoped next week, but if the worst came to the worst she had already survived one winter and could easily manage another.

'Chai mikhaid?'

Mrs Emani was taken aback. A cup of tea for her? Such hospitality.

'Merci.' She sat on the corner of a heap of carpets and placed her shopping bag between her feet. She began to take off her shoes, then she remembered where she was.

'Zahra! Tea for the Khanum,' shouted Ali. The girl vanished into the small room behind the shop.

'She is from the country?'

Ali nodded.

'She must be a help to you around the shop.'

'She cleans and makes tea. I am teaching her the art of carpet mending but . . .' Ali shook his head. 'She is a peasant. She is used to reaping and sowing. Her hands are large and clumsy. But the boss likes her.'

271

'He is well, Mr Gabayan?'

'He is well. We see more of him since she arrived.' Ali jerked his head towards the kitchen. 'Otherwise, he is busy. He sits on a tribunal. He is a very important man. He pays me now in dollars, but my wife cannot buy food with dollars.' Ali sighed.

'Ah food, shopping.' Mrs Emani shook her head in sympathy. 'Today I have bought oranges, such lovely golden oranges. But what a price!' She prodded the bulges in her shopping bag with her heel. 'Please, I ask you to accept some oranges – for your family.'

Ali said nothing. Mrs Emani leaned forward and piled the fruit in a small pyramid by his feet.

Zahra brought tea on a small tin tray with fragments of the Shah in enamel just visible underneath the glasses. Mrs Emani nodded and smiled her thanks. Zahra placed Ali's glass on the floor next to him then stood staring at the oranges.

'You would like one?' Mrs Emani held one out.

'Have you no work to do?' Ali asked his cousin. The girl took the orange and left.

'There is something wrong?' asked Mrs Emani. There had been a definite progression in her relationship with Ali since the picnic.

'I do not approve of sigheh.'

'She is so young. It is not right.' Mrs Emani sipped her tea thoughtfully.

'Temporary marriage is all very well. The parents think only of the dowry, but they will not want her back afterwards, probably pregnant. And who else is there but me.' He frowned, holding his needle up to the light. 'The only relative in town. And what can I do with a girl who is no longer a virgin? The Agha pays now while he wants her, but later? There will be extra mouths to feed on the pittance he pays me.'

Mrs Emani clicked her tongue and shook her head, flattered by the confidence.

'My house is large,' she said, spreading her hands expansively.

'Masoudja.' Roya Gabayan started to speak, but her husband raised his hand for silence.

'Wife! I have news of a very high honour. Very high indeed. The Mullah wishes to marry our daughter.'

'I don't think Soraya will think much of that.' Roya laughed at the thought.

'Not Soraya – Soheila.' Masoud sucked his coffee noisily.

'She's only a child.' Roya laughed again. Such a preposterous suggestion! The Mullah – older than her own husband, and Soheila not quite thirteen!

'Roya, it is a great honour. He knows about our elder daughter, and yet will marry the younger as an act of charity.'

'Dear God,' thought Roya, 'he's taking it seriously.'

'No, Masoud. I will never allow it.'

'*You* will never allow it? What is it to do with you?'

'I am her mother.'

'The prophet said: "Do not consult with women since their brain is like their body; weak and delicate!"' Masoud snorted, choking on his coffee.

Roya became worried. She was used to verbal abuse and even physical violence, but not this quiet resolution. She was not sure how to tackle it.

'Let me fetch you some more coffee, Masoud.' Roya stood up with a smile, her back to her husband, time to think while she heated the small copper pan over the gas.

'Why so much coffee?' he asked. 'What are we celebrating?'

'Masoudja, I have been thinking of visiting Soraya.'

'Ah.' He blew noisily at the thick, hot, black drink.

'Masoud, I must go to her.'

'Why? Is she sick?'

'No. She is my daughter and I want to be with her when her time comes.'

'She must suffer alone and atone for her sin.'

'Masoudja, to be raped is not a sin.' As soon as the words were out, Roya knew she shouldn't have said them.

He hurled the cup across the kitchen.

'The day the Mullah marries Soheila, you can go and visit your other precious daughter.'

'I'm so sorry, Mrs Homayoun, for the inconvenience it may cause you, but I have to close down the nursery.'

Theresa was speechless with dismay at the thought of long days in her mother-in-law's flat trying to keep the children happy and quiet. Mrs Homayoun liked children to be seen infrequently, and heard not at all. Of course, things would not be so bad while Mrs Smith was still there. She loved spending time with the children. But when she left, Theresa didn't know what she was going to do.

'You see, apart from the problems with heating and food, there is also security.'

'Security?' Theresa stood, clinging on to the children in the middle of the path, to stop them rushing into their classroom.

'The nursery could become a target.'

Theresa tried to imagine who could possibly harm a bunch of little children.

'And it's hard to find trained staff nowadays.'

Theresa turned back to the car where her mother was waiting.

'What's up, luv?'

'The nursery's closing down. We can't go shopping today.'

'I want to go to school,' screamed Reza, digging in his heels, tugging at his mother's hand.

'Look, Reza, Gran's got a nice sweetie for you.' Mrs Smith held a sweet over the back seat. Reza clambered in after it.

'You shouldn't do that, Mother. It's not right to bribe. And think of his teeth.' Theresa started the engine and accelerated viciously.

'It worked though, didn't it?' Mrs Smith smugly popped a sweet into her own mouth as well. 'You want one?' She held out the bag.

So many days had passed with no news of Fereydoun, that Mrs Homayoun decided to call at the prison.

'But not you, my dear,' she said to Theresa. 'You would only get him into more trouble. They don't like foreigners.'

'Will you take a letter for me?' Theresa was fairly certain that she was pregnant – all but a test. That would have required a trip to her doctor which was impossible at the moment with her mother-in-law controlling the purse strings, watching every move.

She knew the real reason for her mother-in-law's visit to Fereydoun. She couldn't wait to get rid of her and the children. The way she had leapt at Mrs Smith's suggestion that Theresa and the children return to Manchester together! Not that Theresa could leave now. She wouldn't abandon Fereydoun whatever happened. But for the children to go – well, that seemed sensible. And her mother would love having them. The only obstacle to their departure was that Fereydoun's written permission was required before they could leave the country. It was this, Theresa knew, that had prompted Mrs Homayoun's sudden burst of maternal concern.

But Mrs Homayoun's attempt to see Fereydoun failed. Visitors were not allowed. She must wait until she was sent for. She returned home in a black mood. On the way she read Theresa's letter, then tore it into tiny shreds and scattered them out of the window, wondering whatever Theresa could have been thinking of to get herself pregnant just then.

Should she tell Mama or not, little Fariba wondered. She sat beside her mother's hospital bed and they held hands, looking at one another. Fariba did not like to spoil it all by talking about her father. His frenzied, iron-hard rubbing against her during the night had no place here.

'Look who I've brought!' said a nurse, smiling. And there was Shahnaz, weeping resentfully in front of these two strangers, holding up her arms to the nurse who had carried her.

Fariba forgot her own problems.

'Mama, look at Shahnaz. She is as fat as you!' But Aziz did not seem to notice.

'How are the boys?'

'They're alright.'

'And you, are you getting on alright at school?'

Fariba frowned. How could she tell Mama that after the sleepless nights and the housework she sometimes fell asleep at her desk? But she was not in trouble, for no one ever noticed. Teachers were short, classes doubled in size.

'It was better when I had my glasses.'

Her mother nodded.

'If I had glasses but hid them from Baba?'

'That would be wrong.'

Fariba had thought of keeping her glasses a secret from everyone at home if she got another pair. But they would find out. Someone in class would tell.

'Your father says no one will marry you, with glasses.'

'But Mama, lots of people wear them. My teacher!'

'She has a husband?'

276

'No.'

Fariba watched Shahnaz toddle laughing from patient to patient, cramming biscuits and sweets into her mouth with dimpled fingers, thoroughly at home. Fariba thought it would be the most wonderful thing in the world to have a baby like Shahnaz of her very own. But of course she would have to have a husband too.

Still, if that was all Mama had to put up with every night it would be worth it. As far as she was concerned her father could rub himself against her as much as he pleased. She didn't mind that so much as the stench of his breath. But she couldn't talk to Mama about it, not here with so many people around.

'Masoudja, Hussein should be at school.' Roya stood, barring the kitchen door.

'Hussein is a man. If he wants to serve the Revolution, I will not stand in his way.'

'Revolutions don't last forever, and then what will he do?'

'He will serve the Islamic Republic.'

'As what?' Roya took a step towards her husband. Hussein slipped through the door. 'As a tea-boy?'

'Why not?'

'He is a clever boy. His education has been good and expensive. I had hoped . . .'

Hussein did not hear what his mother hoped. He was down the stairs, onto the street, away from his mother's fussing. He had his father's blessing in what he was doing, so why worry? He was just the sort of chap they needed, good officer material he fancied . . .

Down the street, off to join his mates. A demonstration to keep an eye on today. Might be a bit of fun. All those women! He knew the type – smart, middle-class, posh accents, demanding the release of their sons. But they wouldn't get anywhere. Only last night he'd heard someone saying on the radio that they should all have been killed on the first day instead of being held in prison, because they weren't even worthy of contempt.

In front of the mirror, Mrs Homayoun applied a little face powder and lipstick. Not enough to be obvious, but she wanted to look her best. It was her first demonstration.

'But *you* can't come, dear,' she said to Theresa, who stood watching her. 'It wouldn't be appropriate. This is for mothers, not wives.'

'But, Mother, I want to feel I'm doing something for Fereydoun.'

'In that case, the best thing you can do is to leave the country as soon as possible.' Mrs Homayoun turned and smiled. 'How do I look?'

Theresa turned to go into her bedroom, but her mother was sitting on the bed, reading to Farah and Reza. Instead she went into the bathroom and slammed the door.

Mrs Homayoun arranged her shaped headscarf. Almost a hat, really, a bit more flattering than a plain silk square. As she stepped back to take a final look at the overall effect, she heard a car horn.

She felt a flutter of excitement. She'd seen so many demonstrations on television. And here she was now, crammed into a small orange taxi with five other women all giggling like schoolgirls. It was quite reassuring. After all, what could they possibly do to so many?

From the far end of the street Hussein saw the women, a black-veiled army, chanting in the sunshine. 'Khomeini we fought for you. We gave you the fruit of our wombs.'

Hussein stood among the two hundred or so Pasdaran blocking the way. He realized with mounting horror that most of the women were not as he had imagined. They were mostly, well, like his own mother.

'Give us back our sons.' He could see their faces now, faces lined with grief. He wished he hadn't come, that he was back in school with his books. The reassuring drone of the teacher. He stood there not knowing what to do.

Then bottles and stones were flying and he was pushed forward into the mêlée. The thud of sticks on flesh. Screaming. Weeping.

And suddenly it was over.

'They're running away,' shouted his friend, brandishing a chador and a clump of hair.

Hussein's hands were shaking. He grabbed the chador and wrapped it round his shoulders, fluttering his eyelids, hands outstretched beseeching. 'Give me back my son.'

Roya leant on the banisters, shifting her weight from one foot to the other.

'You can have no idea,' her friend was saying, 'of the strain of a daughter having her first. I can't sleep at nights. I feel positively haggard. I jump every time the phone rings.'

Roya could imagine it all very well, only she was denied the pleasure of sharing it. She plonked her shopping bag on the top stair and listened enviously. Potatoes and carrots were all she had for her trouble today. No meat, no eggs.

'My daughter is so fat,' went on the neighbour, 'that she can't sleep, poor child. Or eat. She can't come round here any more, she says the stairs make her ankles swell. Poor lamb. It seems only a short while ago she was only this high, and now . . . well it will soon be over, all that pain and suffering. Then she can forget it. You do, don't you? It's soon forgotten.'

Roya couldn't imagine her own beautiful Soraya ever getting like that. In fact pregnancy had made her lovelier than ever, her skin transparent and accentuating her high cheekbones. Whereas Mrs Nosrat's daughter had never been much of a . . .

'Of course, I shall be sharing her room in hospital. I've told my husband he'll just have to manage as best he can. A daughter needs her mother at such a time, don't you think?'

Roya nodded, every word a knife in her heart. She would go to Isfahan, she decided. The very next day. Masoud could not possibly exact such a monstrous price as Soheila's marriage.

'The telephone,' shrieked her neighbour, turning and running up the stairs. Roya let herself into her own flat and closed the door behind her, thankful to have made her escape.

It was closing time before Masoud Gabayan went to the shop. He waited for Ali to leave before he acknowledged Zahra's presence. Today he had brought her a copper bracelet, only a few rials from the bazaar, easily worth it to see the joy on her face.

There had been a time when his daughters had looked at him like this, when their love could be bought with a cheap trinket. But not for years now. They were so clever, his daughters, they made him feel small and ignorant – whereas this child who knew nothing, who had nothing . . .

He was surprised at the strength of his feelings as he dragged her behind the mound of carpets.

He was less pleased when she wept as he turned to leave her.

'Please,' she whispered. 'I am frightened here alone.'

Then Masoud was angry. What did she want from him? He couldn't take her home. Roya had already refused to have her, and he needed Roya. He pushed Zahra back inside the shop and locked the door.

* * *

Roya's hands were trembling as she peeled potatoes. She despised herself for her weakness. She'd been weak all along. No good would come of it. The lies, the deceit, the shame and guilt piling up inside her.

Night after night, week after week, she had lain in bed listening while Masoud's voice droned on and on, cataloguing her failures as wife and mother, until she felt responsible for the shame of the entire family.

And it could all have been so easily avoided by being honest from the start. Accidents happened even in the best families. And the baby, her grandchild, the little voice that would never call her Granny. She had forfeited all this out of cowardice. Out of being afraid to face a bit of scandal that would have been unpleasant, but would soon have blown over.

Roya put on the potatoes and opened the pantry door. Down behind the rice sack she no longer kept romantic novels, but knitting patterns and tiny garments, finished and unfinished. She could fit in just a few rows before Soheila came in.

20

In the stinking earth closet, Fariba Baniyazdi looked with horror at her blood-stained pants and wondered whether her time had come to sit around the tap with the other women every month, washing away the stains. She shrank from the thought of the coarse laughter. Whom could she ask? Perhaps her friend Mina on the way to school.

Grey with the pain between her legs, Fariba struggled to keep up. Perhaps she was going to die. Then who would look after her brothers?

'Mina,' she asked at last, 'Mina, do you bleed yet?'

Mina laughed and shook her head.

'But my sister does. She's twelve.'

Fariba perched on the edge of her chair, knees up on the desk rail to avoid any pressure on her bruised and swollen vulva. She scarcely heard the lessons. She wanted to see Mama, but knew she couldn't walk that far. Besides, Mama would not be expecting her, she would be alarmed to see her before Friday and wonder what was wrong.

Hamid, her father, did not return home that night, or the next. Fariba's bruising and swelling abated. When he did return she lay quietly and let him do what he liked with her. It was easier that way.

As time passed the pain lessened. Fariba assumed that it all had to do with taking her mother's place. It was simply part of being a woman.

Theresa was beside herself with worry. Her mother was due to leave that afternoon. Tickets had been bought for

the children. Two days ago there had been an announce-
ment on the radio that prison visits would recommence.
Relatives were asked not to call until invited.

The radio in Mrs Homayoun's flat had been on ever
since. Theresa had not moved out of earshot. The lists of
permitted visitors went on and on, but no Homayoun
among them. Not until that very morning, soon after
breakfast.

Theresa had never known her mother-in-law to get
dressed quite so quickly. Then she was off to the prison,
quite forgetting the bag that Theresa had carefully packed
for Fereydoun. The sweets, biscuits and clean clothes.
But she had taken the bundle of notes to ease her way
into the prison, and the pen and paper that would ensure
her grandchildren's departure.

Now Theresa and her mother stood at the living room
window, anxiously looking down the street, watching for
Mrs Homayoun's return. The suitcases were packed. Mrs
Smith added two more pins to her hat.

'It's so draughty there, luv, what with all that tar and
those great engines.'

Any more pins and her mother would look like a
hedgehog. Theresa chewed her nails. She looked at her
watch again.

'Won't you come too, luv?' asked her mother.

'No. Not while Fereydoun is in prison.'

Mrs Smith sighed. According to Mrs Homayoun, he
might be inside for years – if he came out at all. She
didn't dare say such a thing to Theresa. There was her
journey with the grandchildren ahead of her too. That
made her nervous: eight hours in the plane, and how was
she going to manage when she got home?

She opened her hand luggage and flicked through the
contents; books, paper, pencils, teddy bears (packed by
Theresa) and sweets (packed by herself). Nothing like a
few sweets to keep children happy in her opinion.

'Will you be alright, Mum?'

'Don't worry about me. I hope that husband of yours will be alright.' She smiled with more confidence than she felt. 'You will write, won't you?'

Theresa stood stiffly while her mother hugged her.

'Here she comes,' she called out, relieved to see Mrs Homayoun's taxi speeding along the avenue of plane trees.

Mrs Homayoun got out of the taxi waving a sheet of paper like a semaphore. Her mother-in-law had done it. She'd got Fereydoun's permission. Theresa picked up the bags and hurried downstairs, through the front door, across the garden, calling Farah and Reza as she went.

Roya Gabayan strained the potatoes. She wouldn't tell Masoud that she'd decided to visit Soraya until he'd had something to eat. He was unpredictable these days. Before, he'd been a man of passionate outbursts and prolonged silences. Now, he seemed reinforced with steel, inflexible in thought and action, governed entirely by Islam.

Roya was determined that Soheila should stay at school. She couldn't care less whether the Prophet's younger wife was thirteen or even nine. The fact had no relevance at all to her Soheila. Her Soheila was still a child.

Meals were now silent affairs, seated round the cloth on the floor. Uncomfortable stretches of time in which Soheila kept her eyes on her plate, Hussein ate fast and left as soon as possible, and the only sound was Masoud's stolid munching, his eyes fixed on a point somewhere between the wall and the ceiling as if on some higher vision.

Tonight he was in a good mood though, Roya could tell. There was an inward smirk detectable in the lift of his shoulders and the slight upward tilt at the corners of

284

his mouth. But she wouldn't say anything now, not while the children were there.

Hussein left soon enough. 'Soheila, your homework,' she whispered as she cleared away the plates.

'Let me help you, Mama.'

Roya shook her head. Poured the thick Turkish coffee and placed a small tray of cakes in front of her husband. Then she hovered anxiously, waiting to begin, picking up a few crumbs, wringing out the dishcloth.

'Stop fussing about, wife,' growled Masoud through a mouthful. And Roya lost heart. How could she talk to a man who guzzled like that? She sat meekly opposite him, eyes on the floor, and knew that she would never visit Soraya.

'Don't do it, please don't go . . . no trouble at all . . . stay as long as you like,' Mrs Emani had protested. But Shirin had insisted on leaving, going to the nearest guard post, where with greatest difficulty she persuaded them who she was, and only after several hours, found herself under arrest.

Mrs Emani was lonely when Shirin went. She missed the shared pot of tea, having someone to talk to in the evenings when Jamshid was out rehearsing for his play. All the little events of her day had taken on a new significance while there was someone at home to tell them to.

In the Evin Prison, Shirin felt more at peace than she had for a long time. No more worries about being recognized. No fears of the unexpected visitor. And best of all, no voices to torment her. Their absence, she concluded, was due to the continual activity around her. The mother in the opposite bed changing her baby's nappy. A young girl unrolling her prayer mat in a small space between the bunks. Toddlers lisping political slogans, and always talk, sometimes political, sometimes religious, or just family gossip.

285

Shirin suddenly realized how much she had lost touch with ordinary people over the years and how much she had missed out on family life.

Her days were reassuringly tedious and restful. Eat, clean, read, eat, read, eat, read, sleep. The women kept the prison spotless. Shirin's hands and knees became calloused, but her mind was strangely liberated by the physical labour. She found time to look back calmly over her life and to realize that her plans for an elaborate defence were a waste of time.

She still did not know what charges would be brought, but judging by past trials and statements, it was not she who would be on trial but the regime for which she had worked. Her personal life concerned her more. She watched the women with their children. She would have liked to join them in planting tomatoes in the small courtyard, but they kept themselves apart from her and called her 'Taqih' – aristocrat – and wanted nothing to do with her.

Since the departure of her mother and children, Theresa Homayoun found that regular long outings were necessary for her sanity if she were to continue living with her mother-in-law. By mid-June the weather was tempting enough to lure her to the swimming pool of the Intercontinental Hotel. Hours for Ladies' Swimming one to one-thirty, new Islamic regulations. Afternoons – men only.

In the changing room, she looked regretfully at her figure and knew that she wouldn't be able to get away with wearing a bikini for much longer.

Pulling her stomach muscles as taut as she could, Theresa stepped onto the warm flagstones and out into the sunshine. She swam a few lengths – good exercise in pregnancy, she had read – ordered a long, cool drink, then stretched back on her towel.

The sun had a delicious glow. Drops of water trickled

down her body and evaporated. She felt her skin tauten and burn. Her eyelids closed and she lay pinned to the ground by the weight of heat.

She was woken abruptly as her glass toppled over, and splintered. Fragments of glass glittered dangerously in the sticky pool of lemonade. An empty Coke tin rattled on the flagstones. Theresa sat up. Another can hit her on the shoulder. Then one on the knee. Startled, rather than hurt, she cried out, looked round, then up. There she saw them, the hotel domestics, their missiles lined along the balcony walls, ready to launch a second salvo.

She grabbed her towel, bag, sunglasses and book and ran for the shelter of the changing room, weeping with shock. What had she done to upset them?

The manager traced on his own body the skimpy outlines of Theresa's bikini. He did not smile openly, but Theresa could see the look in his eyes. Any minute now would come the invitation . . . her anger would be futile. She turned and left the hotel as fast as she could.

Theresa walked north towards her mother-in-law's home, in no hurry to get there. By midday she had reached the tree-lined Shemiran Road. Tired and sweating, she stopped at the Catholic church. She was not sure what made her go inside; perhaps the shade, perhaps some appreciation of the old notion of sanctuary, perhaps she just needed a place where she could sit quietly and think. And she needed to think clearly, for time was running out.

Her mother-in-law took it for granted that Theresa would leave the country with her. Not, hopefully, to live with the Homayouns in New York, but with her own mother and the children in Manchester. Even Homa said there was no point in staying on.

Theresa slid into the back bench of the church. It was cool and dark. Peaceful. She knelt and peered through

287

her clasped fingers, through the haze of pink flesh to the light on the altar. She knew she was right to stay. Fereydoun (in absentia) was her whole life, her love, father of her child. She would stay as near to him as she could.

It was then that she felt the kick against her stomach wall, resonant as a drum beat. She gasped, pressing her hands against the small swelling that was her baby.

Mrs Emani, fingers dripping with holy water, crossed herself and stepped inside the church. She recoiled in surprise. Someone was there. In her place. She put down her shopping bag, genuflected and crossed herself again.

'Mary, Mother of God, where shall I sit?' For ten years she had sat in that very place. It didn't matter that the rest of the church was deserted, row upon row of empty benches.

She skirted round the back of the church, stopped, genuflected at the centre aisle, and scurried to the opposite back corner. It was not a place she liked, next to the hymn books and the poor box.

Kneeling now, Mrs Emani peered sideways at the person in her place. Fair hair. Unusual. Must be foreign. She pressed her knuckles into her eyes and tried to pray. Looked up and over again at the foreigner. Saw her jump, hands clasped over her stomach. Ill perhaps? In need of help?

Mrs Emani stumbled the length of the pew, one foot up on the kneeler, the other on the floor. Up down, up down, across the aisle, no time now for genuflexion or sign of the cross, she hobbled into the opposite bench.

'You are alright?'

Theresa looked up, glowing.

'My baby moved.'

Mrs Emani smiled. 'Is good.' She plumped down next to Theresa. 'You come here before?'

Theresa shook her head.

'Is very lovely, this church.'

'I must go,' said Theresa. 'I must be getting home.' But she didn't move, didn't really care when she got back.

'There is something wrong? The baby?'

'No.'

'Why don't you come to my home, have some tea?'

This idea appealed to Theresa. She was hungry and thirsty. She followed Mrs Emani, a little breathless, teetering in her high heels over the rough track.

'Where are you from?' Mrs Emani asked, trotting by her side.

'England.'

'You have family there?'

Theresa nodded. They were now in a part of the city she did not know. She wondered whether she had been wise to accept the invitation.

'Is it much further?' she asked, nervous about returning along these backstreets alone, with no chance of a taxi until the main road.

'We are here.' Mrs Emani stopped abruptly and began to rummage through her handbag. Her glasses slipped down her nose. She knelt on the pavement, feeling deep down inside the bag.

'Is here somewhere,' she smiled. She began emptying the bag. Purse. Rosary. Scraps of paper. Bus tickets. A spectacle case. Comb. An onion and a bar of chocolate.

'You would like?' asked Mrs Emani, breaking off a piece of chocolate, holding it out. 'Is good?' She watched as Theresa reluctantly ate the sticky mess. Such a treat, chocolate, these days. So pleased to have been able to offer some to this nice girl. She would save the rest for Jamshid. She wasn't worried about the key. This happened every day. At last the bag was empty and there it was, gleaming against the dark lining at the bottom. She held it up, unlocked the front door and ushered Theresa inside.

Such shattering news I received today! I can, you note, still laugh at my adversities. I have not altogether lost my sense of humour. What has in fact shattered, finally and irrevocably, is my portrait.

In spite of the new plaster and the imported Sheffield steel picture hooks, my portrait hung on the wall – note this – for three days and three nights. On the morning of the fourth day, as my wife set foot out of bed, the thing simply tumbled from the wall.

I had always thought my wife such a fine and delicate creature. Have I been misled? Has she feet of clay like the rest of us?

The damage to the wall has been repaired again. But the portrait is in ruins – the frame reduced to a mere jigsaw and my own image pierced by a thousand daggers of glass.

Now what, I ask myself, caused such vibrations? Merely my wife's foot? Or the lingering vibrations of sexual passion? The sudden movement of Giselle reaching out towards her lover, to keep her by her side? My wife doesn't mention these things, but I can feel them through the very paper she writes on. They haunt me. Torture me. Allow me no rest by day or night.

And what is more, between them, those women have killed me. And this I can prove, absolutely. When I went into the bathroom to shave this morning, I looked in the mirror. As we all do. We men. And I saw nothing. I was not there any more.

21

Since I am no longer here, I decided to call at the Ayatollah's offices and ask if I may leave. What further use can I possibly be, I reasoned. But the funny thing is that nobody else has the slightest difficulty in seeing me. What they cannot see is that I have been murdered. Annihilated. By my wife's sins.

I saw such a delightful chap. A Mullah. He said she'd be lucky to escape with her life here. Even stoning would be too good for her. He sympathized with the strain I am living under. Appreciated the depths of my homesickness. Reminded me that we are all called at one time or another in our lives to serve a higher ideal, and that perhaps this opportunity was what was being offered to me. This last comment has given me much food for thought. I have been guilty of forgetting who I am, of losing spiritual direction in the morass of my own affairs.

He was surprised that I was so upset about my wife. I should simply divorce her and marry another. He suggested that I embrace Islam. The Prophet has said that all women are the same. With a new wife 'it would be the same as with the other one.'

I told him I would have to consult my mother about this. But he quoted the Prophet again. 'As far as you can, do not consult with women since their brain is like their body, weak and delicate.' Really, this Mohammed seems to have been an astute sort of fellow.

'What the hell do you mean, I can't have a lawyer?' Fereydoun Homayoun took a step forward and leaned on the official's desk, breathing heavily.

'You are being tried as a criminal, not as an accused.'

At the sound of the raised voices, a guard came in from the corridor. Fereydoun looked at the gun and stepped back.

'I'm sorry, Comrade, it's my nerves. I don't sleep well. Perhaps under the Islamic Republic there are no lawyers?'

There was a packet of cigarettes on the table. Fereydoun's hands were shaking. He would have liked to ask for one. The official held out the indictment. The Pasdar took the paper, put a hand under Fereydoun's elbow and led him away.

Corridor, door, more corridors, more doors, stairs down, and finally Fereydoun stood at the steps outside the prison gates. He looked over the city, feeling the sun burn the top of his head. Down the steps towards the mini-bus, drinking in every detail, the blue sky, the buildings, the graffiti, the smell of kebab from a roadside stall, the whisper of a breath of wind. He sat with the indictment unopened on his knee, savouring every second of his journey to the court.

Theresa was on her way to visit Mrs Emani. They met every day at the church. Sometimes they talked. Sometimes they just sat together in silence. Theresa almost thought she believed in God, for something had surely led her into the church at the particular time when they had met.

Mrs Emani hurried through her days illuminated by a new sense of joy. Soon, it was all settled. Her Jamshid would go to England on Theresa's ticket. She had written to confirm his school place. In the holidays he would stay in Manchester with Theresa's mother. As for herself, she had acquired a beautiful daughter, for Theresa would come and live with her. Mrs Emani would cook and clean and be Theresa's willing slave. When her time came, she would deliver the baby herself.

Theresa sang as she sorted her belongings. Her mother-in-law sighed with relief. No more arguments. The girl had come to her senses. She booked the plane tickets for two days' time. Her own flight to New York being slightly earlier than Theresa's to London, they could share a taxi to the airport. It all fitted in very well. Mrs Homayoun would be glad to be gone. There was nothing she could do to help her son, and it was too risky to await the outcome of any trial.

The Mullah Afsharzadeh put his papers on the desk, wrapped his robe around him, and from the teacher's rostrum nodded down at the assembled people, men on his right, a black sea of women to his left.

At his right hand, Masoud Gabayan (layman, friend of the Mullah, chosen by the people in their righteousness for his knowledge of Islamic requirements and revolutionary principles) – seated himself and studied the criminals in the front row. Hah! That architect fellow, the one who'd cheated him out of his new house. Glad to see him looking slightly less sure of himself. Masoud took the crumpled list from his pocket and crossed off the name of Homayoun.

The Mullah looked at Masoud, thought briefly of Soheila, then bowed his head in prayer, mindful of his brief from the Almighty to save the people from sin, corruption and earthly desires.

Fereydoun peered nervously round the court to see whether there was anyone he knew. His mother, surely? Theresa – he hoped not. Brothers, sisters, friends? No one he recognized except his driver and secretary. If they were to turn against him, there was no hope.

'In the name of God, the Merciful and Compassionate,' intoned the Clerk. Fereydoun sat up straight in his crumpled shirt and trousers, hanging on to every word as the charges against him were read.

'First charge: Friendship with the enemies of God, hostility towards the friends of God.' A gentle reminder from the Mullah that they were there to suggest punishment with reference to Islamic Law:

> 'The punishment of those
> Who wage war against God
> And his apostle and strive with might and main
> For mischief throughout the land
> Is execution . . .'

Fereydoun was on his feet, clutching his trousers, cursing Theresa mentally for letting them out.

'May it please the court to note that never in any instance have I been guilty of hostility towards the Imam or the Islamic Republic. My very presence here, when I could have left the country as so many others have done, proves that . . .'

He was interrupted by cries of 'Sit down' and a gesture from the Mullah that he should remain seated.

'The evidence?' queried the Mullah.

At this point, Fereydoun looked round again and saw to his horror, leaning against the wall, several more of his former employees.

Unaware that her husband was fighting for his life, Theresa was playing bridge. She had taken up the game to pass the long empty days with neither children nor home to care for.

'What do I do,' she asked, 'if I have thirteen points but no five-card suit?'

'That depends,' said Homa, looking very professional, cards in one hand, cigarette dangling from the side of her mouth. 'If you have a good four-card suit bid that.'

Theresa looked at her hand in despair. She always hoped for a hand with so few points that she wouldn't have to bid. The highest card in her four-card suit was a ten. 'Can I bid one no trump?' she asked her partner.

The two other women sighed and put their hands down on the table just a bit too loudly. Leaning back, they began talking about the weather. Of course, they were lucky to scrape a four together at all these days. You couldn't afford to be choosy. Their husbands found the same thing at the sports club, hard to get a decent game of squash.

'Look,' said Homa, 'just bid one club.'

'But I haven't got any clubs.'

'It's a convention.'

'One club,' said Theresa, having no idea what a convention was.

'Two no trump,' said Homa.

Their opponents spread out the newspaper.

'Look at that. Disgusting waste.' One of them jabbed a finger at the picture. 'A hundred and fifty-six thousand pounds worth of alcohol poured away. Champagne, wine, whisky . . .'

'They say that people living nearby complained of the fumes,' chuckled Homa.

'Court order, it says here.'

Theresa sat staring at her hand, wishing that the ground would open and swallow her up.

'Second charge,' read the Clerk. 'Participating in activities to bolster the former hated regime, bribery and association with the former Shah's court.'

Fereydoun felt fairly confident on this one. They couldn't prove anything, not after his careful destruction of papers in the office. He flicked further through the indictment. Oh, there was something he'd forgotten – all those newspaper snippets. The photograph of himself arriving at a party at the Golestan Palace . . .

* * *

Mrs Homayoun had kept the news of Fereydoun's trial from Theresa. After all, what good would it do her to know? She would only worry.

'Third charge,' read the Clerk. 'Drinking alcohol and gambling.'

'Oh ye who believe,' quoted the Mullah:

> 'Intoxicants and gambling
> Are an abomination
> Of Satan's handiwork.'

Should be home and dry on that one, thought Fereydoun.

'Drinking,' the Mullah reminded the court, 'must have been done voluntarily. Has there been a confession?' He removed his glasses and peered down at Fereydoun, who shook his head.

'Were there two witnesses present?' asked the Mullah.

The court sat silent.

'I must remind you,' continued the Mullah, 'that drunken behaviour or vomiting is not sufficient evidence. The act of drinking must have been seen.'

The trial of Fereydoun Homayoun was unusual in that it was prolonged. At the end of the first day, Masoud called in at his shop. He suspected that Ali was not being completely honest with him. Zahra's needs were becoming increasingly expensive. Masoud was sure that not all the demands made upon him by Ali were on her behalf. He was being blackmailed in a mild sort of way. His temporary marriage certificate was perfectly legal, signed by two Mullahs, quite in order. But he didn't want his family to know. Roya would certainly be jealous. How could a woman of her age compare with a girl the age of his younger daughter? He was simply respecting his wife's feelings in wanting to keep the marriage quiet.

'Tonight you go and buy chelo kebab,' said Masoud, handing over some money. While Zahra was gone, he took out the cash book. It was a short and depressing business checking the figures. No sales at all. Some slight expense in mending materials for Ali, tea and sugar. More tea and sugar. A huge increase. And candles. Did the girl think he was a millionaire to pay for her sitting up half the night drinking tea and burning candles?

He heard the rustle of Zahra's petticoats against the door before she turned the handle and stepped in out of the dark, her scarlet-fringed shawl wrapped around her head, the shining tray heaped with rice and meat balanced on her head. He closed the book and hurried across the shop towards her.

An Ayatollah had been murdered in the kucheh just outside his home. Hussein and his friends, relieved from their spell of guard duty at the prison, made a slight detour on their way home so as to pass the place of the assassination. It was easy to tell the exact spot from the crowds gathered there.

People stood aside to let them pass, wary of the military-style clothes. As their view of the scene opened up, Hussein could see the bloodstained cloth lying on the ground. Next to it, the white turban of the Mullah and a pair of black-rimmed spectacles.

On an impulse, Hussein took from his pocket a pencil stub and a scrap of paper. He wrote: 'Teacher, we congratulate you on your martyrdom', tucked a corner of the paper under a fold in the turban, stood up and stepped back. His friends murmured their approval.

The next morning, Mrs Homayoun senior was wandering round her house, trying to decide just how many more things she could manage to take with her.

'Perhaps just a few more paintings,' she said, turning

to Theresa. 'Really, if I took them out of their frames, they would take very little space.'

'But Mother, you have far too much luggage already.'

'Perhaps just that small one then, it's so valuable. They're all originals, you know.'

'Imagine having to leave one of your suitcases behind, just because of a painting.'

Her mother-in-law hesitated. Stood cracking her knuckles before she spoke again. 'Theresa, I don't know if I can leave after all. I'll never find such a lovely house.'

'I'm sure you will. There are beautiful apartments in New York.' Theresa was terrified that her mother-in-law might decide to stay after all. 'Think of the lovely shops!'

'Ah yes, the shops. Only I shall be so poor.'

'Rubbish, Mother, you'll be very well off.' Then another thought occurred to Theresa. 'Don't forget my allowance, will you. Have you got my mother's address?'

'Oh yes dear, it's here in my bag.'

Fereydoun sat in court, listening to the fourth charge against him; the dissemination of poisonous ideas and sexy magazines.

Now he knew why Muna was there, hand raised, ready to support the indictment. He hadn't before given a thought to the magazines which had gone from his bedside cupboard. They'd seemed of no significance beside the other accusations which could have been levelled against him.

The Mullah Afsharzadeh, on his rostrum, opened a magazine from the pile, then shut it again quickly. He passed them on to Masoud, who took slightly longer before handing them to the Clerk. The magazines were passed around the room, making slow progress from row to row, men leaning impatiently over one another's shoulders for a glimpse as they passed along the row in front. They were all, thought Fereydoun, considerably more dog-eared than when he had owned them.

Fariba Baniyazdi walked along the ward towards her mother's bed.

'Mama, will you come home soon?'

Fariba pulled up a chair and sat, knees under the bed, leaning forward.

'When the baby is born.' Aziz stroked her stomach complacently, contemplating the days of peace still remaining to her.

'How long is that?'

Going home didn't bear thinking about.

'Not yet. Next month perhaps. I don't know.'

'Mama, we need you.'

Aziz looked carefully at Fariba for the first time. In the face of her daughter, she saw all the despair and weariness that had formerly been hers. What right had Fariba to come and worry her just when she was enjoying a bit of comfort for the first time in her life?

'The doctors say I need rest. I must not be worried,' she whined. Surely she had earned it? Then she stretched out her arms and pulled the girl towards her. What could she do? She hugged Fariba tightly against the lump of her unborn child, and breathed in the charcoal and staleness of home. Fariba struggled to be free from the arms which were rounded and soft, smelling of soap and talcum powder, not like Mama at all.

Charge five: adultery. The atmosphere in court was thick in the midday heat. Masoud had long since removed his jacket and tie and unbuttoned his shirt. He slumped back in his chair, doodling on a piece of paper.

Fereydoun ran his fingers round the back of his collar, easing the sticky material away from his neck. He uncrossed his legs and planted his feet firmly apart.

299

In the centre of the ceiling a heavy wooden fan revolved slowly, causing barely a movement of air. A few blue-bottles hummed against the windows.

At the word adultery, most of the spectators brightened and began to take notice again. The Mullah read quietly:

> The woman and the man
> Guilty of adultery or fornication,
> Flog each of them . . .'

Fereydoun jumped up. This was something he knew about. Something he and his friends had sniggered about as teenagers. His chauffeur too was on his feet, giving details of trips to Goli's flat.

'Under Islamic law,' Fereydoun said, 'four witnesses to penetration are required. Four men or eight women or two men and four women.'

'I think, my friend, that you can leave the arithmetical calculations to the court,' said the Mullah. 'However, regardless of our comrade's evidence, giving details of Mr Homayoun's visits to his so-called mistress's flat, if there are no witnesses to the actual misdemeanour, we can only put a kindly construction on these episodes.'

Mrs Emani and Jamshid sat on a bus on their way to the airport. Jamshid looked steadily out of the window, dreaming of Europe.

Mrs Emani was wondering what to give Theresa for lunch. Tomatoes and cucumbers? Very refreshing in this heat. A bowl of cool yoghurt? She took out her knitting. No longer the thick heavy garments so tiring to her fingers and wrists, but a small, white matinee jacket.

And as she knitted, she prayed. One Our Father for the plain rows, a Hail Mary for the purls, a Glory be to the Father for every dropped stitch, and there were many as the bus stopped and started.

* * *

300

Theresa and her mother-in-law drove to the airport in silence. Theresa could feel damp patches under her arms and along her spine and kept looking at her watch.

'You will write and let me know how you are?' said Theresa, worried about the banker's drafts. She had to keep her side of the bargain with Mrs Emani: there had to be enough money to look after Jamshid in the holidays as well as to care for Farah and Reza. Mrs Homayoun gave no sign of having heard.

'You will write, won't you, Mother?'

Mrs Homayoun nodded in an abstracted way. 'I do hope they remember to meet me at the airport,' she said.

'If ever you're in England, Mother, you must visit your grandchildren.' Theresa spoke without any hope of this ever happening.

'It would be so much easier if they came to New York.'

The traffic moved slowly. Not a breath of wind stirred the mustard-coloured air. The sky was a lurid blue. Theresa wound down her window. A man on a motor bike reached through and pinched her on the breast.

'Shut the window, Theresa,' said Mrs Homayoun.

Theresa left the window open. She wasn't a child to be told what to do. Another jam and the hand was back again.

'Theresa, will you please shut the window!'

Hot and embarrassed, Theresa complied.

'He shouldn't be allowed to get away with it.'

'And who's to stop him?' Mrs Homayoun looked at her watch.

'The Ayatollah says that everyone who doesn't show proper respect to women . . .'

Mrs Homayoun leaned forward and tapped the driver on the shoulder.

'Agha, we have a plane to catch.'

'My taxi is old. It would be expensive.' The driver turned and grinned. Mrs Homayoun shrugged.

'A hundred toman,' he said.

Mrs Homayoun clicked her tongue against the roof of her mouth.

'Fifty?'

Mrs Homayoun ignored him.

'Twenty-five! Last price!'

Mrs Homayoun fingered her pearls and looked out of the window.

'Yes, twenty-five,' said Theresa.

The driver turned hard right and the car careered onto the wide pavement scattering pedestrians and donkeys.

'Will you never learn?' Mrs Homayoun glared at Theresa.

Theresa sat forward on the edge of her seat, easing the material of her dress away from her back. They continued their journey in silence.

At the airport, Theresa scarcely felt the cool lips of her mother-in-law brush her cheek before she was gone through the barrier without a backward glance.

Then Theresa went over to the British Airways counter. Mrs Emani and Jamshid were already there. Only three other people were left in the queue. Theresa handed over the ticket, suddenly anxious about what she was doing. In twelve hours she could have been safely home in Manchester with her children.

'It is so kind, what you are doing,' mumbled Mrs Emani. 'So kind.'

Jamshid stood aloof from the scene, whistling to hide his nervousness and hoping that the plane would not make him sick.

'Goodbye, my son.' He realized that his mother was going to kiss him. In front of all these people!

'Goodbye,' he grunted and set off as fast as he could, following the battered suitcases along the conveyor belt.

'Jamshid, aren't you going to thank Mrs Homayoun?'

called his mother. She could still see his curly head over the top of the partition.

'It doesn't matter,' said Theresa.

'So rude.' Mrs Emani shook her head and picked up Theresa's suitcases.

Theresa watched Jamshid until it was too late to call him back, to say that she would, after all, go home to her mother and children.

Mrs Emani plonked down the suitcases and took Theresa in her arms. 'I am your mother now,' she said.

The charges and evidence against Fereydoun Homayoun, Architect, had all been presented. The Clerk made recommendations to the court for suitable punishment.

'Taking into account the charges and applying the verses of the Holy Koran, it is requested that the defendant be sentenced to death and his property and that of his family be confiscated.'

The man next to Fereydoun offered him a cigarette. He sucked at it greedily.

Mrs Emani and Theresa arrived home as the phone rang.

'Theresa, how pleased you must be with the way Fereydoun's trial is going!' It was her friend Homa.

'Trial?' Theresa sat down heavily on a chair.

'Yes, didn't you know?'

Theresa couldn't answer.

'Theresa? Are you there?'

'Yes.'

'Your mother-in-law knew. Didn't she tell you? I thought you were keeping away deliberately.'

Theresa now understood the real reason behind her mother-in-law's hasty departure.

Fereydoun too understood why she had gone. If only he had been more far-sighted himself, he too would have left the country long ago. He had failed to read the signs clearly, assuming that life would settle down and continue in the same old way after the initial upheavals.

He heard the verdicts of guilty on the charges of bribery and association with the Shah's court, the dissemination of poisonous ideas and sexy magazines, and hostility towards the friends of God. His wealth and that of his next of kin were to be confiscated.

'Owing to lack of evidence for the other charges, and because of the defendant's architectural expertise,' read the Mullah, 'Fereydoun Homayoun is sentenced to life imprisonment, and his services will be used in prison in accordance with government plans.'

As he was led out, Fereydoun saw Theresa, sitting at the back of the court, all in black among the black-clad women. He walked on, not wanting to draw attention to her, touched by her presence when the rest of his family had gone.

Theresa pushed forward through the people and the guards, reaching out, trying to catch his hand.

The Pasdar moved him on. The crowd swirled thickly about this man who had so narrowly escaped death, to whom such unwonted leniency had been shown. The news gave hope to many people.

Theresa fought her way to the school door, just in time to see the mini-bus drive away, and Fereydoun's face a blur in the back window.

'Come,' said Mrs Emani, struggling to her side. 'Let us go home and celebrate.'

22

Behold me, like a thief in the night, creeping up the narrow metal staircase on to the roof. In one hand, my nightshirt and toothbrush, in the other, papers, pen and a torch. My faithful valet de chambre staggers after me, half hidden under a roll of bedding and a mattress.

As was the custom in far-off Galilee, so is it here quite common to take to the rooftops in time of excessive heat. There are of course those who prefer to stick by their air-conditioning – but for me, well, nothing can beat an elevated situation.

And the magnificance has to be seen to be believed! Imagine, the sharpest sliver of a crescent moon shimmering in a dark-blue velvet sky. The jagged pinnacles of mountain peaks aspiring higher and higher like the ghostly spires of some monstrous cathedral. The gentle sheen of the stars in the Milky Way. Oh yes! It is good to be nearer the heavens. Nearer to my home, my dwelling place.

I will now put on my nightshirt. Excuse me. Modesty demands that I retire for a moment behind this chimney stack. So cool is the nightshirt, allowing the current of air to circulate around the thighs and the . . . but pardon me. The ladies!

How I gleam now, white in the darkness. Transparent. Translucent. See! I raise my hands, like Christ at his Ascension. But no. Nothing happens. My feet remain on the rough concrete. For a moment I thought we had lift-off. Just a hint. A faint billowing of material in a sudden flurry of air. But it is obviously not the time. My mission is not yet accomplished.

Instead, I shall compose myself. And wait for Divine

*Inspiration to fall with the kiss of starlight upon my brow
. . . Pray forget those recent passionate outbursts against
my wife. For a while, human emotion threatened to distract
me from the task for which I was intended. Life is not easy
for God-Made-Man. The weaknesses of the flesh are
almost beyond endurance. However, let what I have written
stand. A warning to you all. Be on your guard. You know
not the day or the hour.*

*As part of this programme of disciplining the flesh, I
have decided to forgo physical sustenance. I stoked up on
a good lunch. More courses than is my wont. Since then I
have taken nothing but a few sips of water. Already I feel
earthly desires drain away as I prepare for the moment
when my soul takes flight and leaves its leaden prison.*

*'I will not stir from this place until I have completed my
writings. For I intend to leave behind a testament that is
truly universal. That will encompass all creeds and all
nations. Yea. Wherein you will find the answer you
seek . . .*

The Gabayan family was sitting down to supper when
Masoud suddenly spoke.

'Mother's coming to stay,' he said.

Roya felt as if someone was strangling her. She put
down her fork.

'Why?' she asked.

Masoud replied in a shower of rice and gravy: 'I am
her son. Isn't that enough?'

'We haven't seen Granny for a long time.' Soheila was
anxious to prevent a quarrel.

'God!' said Hussein, scraping up the rest of his rice.
He flung down his plate and left the room.

'She can have Soraya's room.' Roya was already planning for the visit. It gave her a face-saving way of restoring
all the furniture to daily use. A comfortable bed at last.

'When will she arrive?'

306

'Tomorrow. She needs medical treatment.'

'Oh?' Roya thought with despair of her dwindling funds. 'And who will pay?'

'I'll ask the Mullah.'

Roya feared being obliged to the Mullah. With Soheila's thirteenth birthday in a few days' time.

That night she lay awake, worrying about this and that, Soheila's education, how Soraya was getting on in Isfahan, what she would do after the baby was born, and money, money, money.

Every day Masoud was off to his precious tribunal and every night he came home bursting with importance and with tales of fresh horrors. Even his gait had changed. He no longer walked, so much as strutted down the street. Roya shivered for those on whom his displeasure fell.

And how could Masoud sleep with so much on his conscience? Such nice people some of them had been. She had to be careful nowadays what she said. Talking with him was like treading a minefield. If she mentioned the price of oranges he threatened the shopkeeper with prosecution.

Yet it seemed that crimes were no longer crimes. She had even read that ordinary criminals were no longer to be arrested. The prisons were full.

Where would it all end? Her Masoud was as bad as the rest, a tiger of Islam with an insatiable appetite for blood. He'd been so solidly respectable before, not that he hadn't always had a temper. He was easily roused.

In spite of all his hard work, the Tribunal brought in no salary. And she was expected to feed everyone on air apparently, but there was no way his mother would understand that.

'Masoudja,' she asked timidly, shaking his shoulder, 'Masoud, I need money to go shopping. I have nothing to feed your old mother with.'

Masoud was in mellow mood and feeling mildly guilty after an evening with Zahra.

'Money eh?' He reached under his pillow and took out a handful of coins. 'Expenses,' he explained.

Roya looked at the money and felt uneasy. But after all, she had to feed her family, and it wasn't as if she could put a name to any of the victims. Perhaps they were guilty after all, in the eyes of God. Who was she to judge?

'Thank you.' She took the money and slid it under her pillow. 'Masoudja, how did it go tonight?'

'Didn't you hear the shots? Perhaps you couldn't from here. Six of them. Hiraba. Corrupt on Earth.'

'But what had they done, Masoud, to deserve death?'

'They were members of the Imperial Guard.'

Roya could feel the hard lumps of the coins under her cheek. She vowed she would not touch them. She would rather starve. That they all starved. She would give the money to the first beggar she met. Blood money, that's what it was.

Theresa wrote to her children once a week. She tried to think of little things that might amuse them, to draw pictures, to send photographs to keep her image alive in their minds.

In return she received hasty notes from her mother in between cleaning jobs and collecting the children from nursery. Theresa, on the contrary, had time on her hands. Mrs Emani did all the housework and shopping as well as her job.

'You must rest,' insisted Mrs Emani, laying her hand on her own plump stomach and pointing to Theresa's bulge.

And Theresa rested, in the shade of the mulberry tree in the garden. She dozed, swelling with love as she thought of her family. Her children seemed perfect, the sleepless nights and temper tantrums forgotten. She carried their photographs everywhere with her and looked at them at odd moments.

Over a cup of tea before bed they looked at the pictures together. Mrs Emani would become quite speechless with admiration once she had exhausted her limited English. Once, Mrs Smith sent a photo of Jamshid and the little ones in the garden, playing football. The two women were overjoyed.

Mrs Emani took one whole day a week off work for her prison visiting. She took the dispensing of little comforts very seriously, almost religiously. Her visits to Shirin and Fereydoun were also motivated by affection. Though Mrs Emani never met Fereydoun, she had come to see him through Theresa's own rose-coloured spectacles.

Her love and admiration for Shirin buoyed her up during the long, tedious bus journey to Evin Prison. A small, plump, insignificant woman, she never had any trouble gaining admission. She could have been anyone's mother.

'You are very kind,' said Shirin. 'You really take too much trouble.'

'No trouble, no trouble at all,' protested Mrs Emani. And she meant it. She felt well repaid for the hours of searching and queuing as she laid the fresh fruit and vegetables on the bed. And a dress from Shirin's suitcase (still in Mrs Emani's pantry), freshly laundered.

'The pens,' asked Shirin. 'Have you brought the pens and paper?'

Mrs Emani produced them last from the flat bottom of the basket with an imprint of cane from the weight of the oranges.

'Thank you, you are very kind.'

Mrs Emani smiled as she watched the children playing tig around the bunk beds. Really it didn't seem like a prison at all. More like a hospital. And like a typical visitor she often couldn't think of anything to say. Not until it was time to go. Then there was so much left unsaid.

'Is there anything you need next week?'

Shirin shook her head.

'I pray for you. Every evening when I go to church.' Mrs Emani took Shirin's hand and clasped it between her own. 'I haven't heard from Jamshid yet.'

Shirin put both arms round Mrs Emani and hugged her.

'I expect he's busy. My children are the same. I keep writing to them. To my daughter anyway.'

'No news yet of your trial?'

Shirin shook her head. The warden stood impatiently by the door. 'Thank you for coming.'

Mrs Emani turned in the doorway and waved.

'I'll see you next week.'

A visit to Qasr Prison was less pleasant. Mrs Emani talked her way in each week and left her gifts in a small cardboard box with an official. Whether they reached Fereydoun she did not know, but she continued to call. Theresa received no acknowledgement, but then perhaps Fereydoun was not allowed to write letters.

His cell was small, stuffy by night and even worse during the heat of the day. He dreamed of an ice-cold lager and of air-conditioning. He also thought of Goli. Theresa seemed more distant, though he was flattered by the fact that she had stayed near him. The thought that she might bear him a son in spite of his physical absence excited him.

He started letters to her that he never finished, little anecdotes of his tedious days which might amuse her. 'Did you know,' he asked, 'that under Islam a toilet may not face Mecca from either the front or the back sides?'

310

Fereydoun was in solitary confinement. From the calls from the minarets on Fridays, he worked out that his parcels arrived on Wednesdays. On Thursdays he washed his shirts with the hard green soap packed by Mrs Emani. He draped them over the one chair to dry. Eczema had run riot under the whiskers sprouting from his chin since the confiscation of his razor. He became obsessed by the idea that he smelt, as did his cell and the corridor outside. But no one seemed to notice. Perhaps they all stank together. Except for one. The tall, slim youth who obviously had a mother to take care of him. His shirts were always clean and crisp, his skin smooth, hair soft and shining, faintly perfumed by shampoo. Fereydoun hovered by the small window in his cell door, waiting to catch a glimpse of Hussein Gabayan as he passed.

Outside in the corridor, Hussein of the smooth skin and shining hair hoped that it would not be long before he was drafted out of this stinking hole.

The initial satisfaction of seeing enemies of the faith under lock and key had been replaced by boredom and disgust. It was better than being in school but not quite the life he had imagined for a Pasdar.

While he patrolled the grey corridors Hussein nurtured his secret ambition of becoming an officer in the elite corps of the Army of Islam. Then he would challenge the Infidel, like some Crusader of old. The poster in his room had lost none of its power. His country needed him.

'No more school and that's final.' Masoud slammed the door as he went out, leaving Soheila and Roya in a shower of plaster.

'You should have left him to me.'

'Why, Mama? Why should you have to put up with all his tempers?'

'Soheila, I have years of experience in handling your

father. It does no good to go at things directly – you have to be a bit roundabout. Flatter him a little. Lead him in the direction you want him to go.'

'That's ridiculous. He's not a child.'

'It might not be right, Soheila, but it's the only way to live with your father.'

Soheila leaned back in her chair, eyes closed.

'What shall I do now, Mama?'

'Just leave it to me. You go to school as if nothing has happened. Tell them that you will resign from the committee and will not take part in any more political activities.'

Soheila jerked forward, eyes fixed on her mother, pleading.

'Mama, I can't do that.'

'I can't help you then.'

'Mama, please!'

'Soheila, you must take my advice. Your father is not a man who is open to reason. Don't push him too far.'

Roya left her daughter sitting at the table and went to join her mother-in-law in the sitting room. She hadn't changed a bit. At eighty-five she was blind but as straight-backed and tight-lipped as ever.

'Well, Roya?' said the old woman, piqued at being left alone, and at hearing the raised voices without being able to catch their meaning.

'Well, Mother?' Roya resented the way her mother-in-law expected to be told everything. Let her ask specific questions if there was something she wanted to know. Roya had invested in more knitting wool, something on which to focus her attention in the long hours she would spend with the old lady. Long silent hours in which the old woman mumbled to herself and sucked at her gums. Knit two, slip two, knit three, pass the slipped stitches over. She could almost pretend the old lady wasn't here. Until she suddenly spoke.

'You see where it has all led.'

'Where what has led, Mother?' Fifty-nine, sixty, sixty-one, sixty-two. She had lost a stitch somewhere. She pulled them all off the needle and began again.

'What are you knitting?'

'A jumper.'

'In June?'

Roya began casting on again. One, two, three, four, five . . .

'All your ridiculous notions.'

'What ridiculous notions?' The question was automatic. Like talking to a child. Fifteen, sixteen, seventeen, eighteen, or was it nineteen? If only the old lady would keep quiet, just for a minute.

'All this silly business. Education. The way they dress. I'm sure my son never gave them such ideas.'

Now her mother-in-law was warming to her subject Roya felt better. She could let her ramble on and concentrate on the pattern.

'That girl should have been married long ago and none of this would have happened. I hope you won't make the same mistake twice. Of course you should have had more children yourself. The devil finds work for idle hands, you know. I never had time on my hands. No time, no devils.'

'Tomorrow I shall take you to the hospital, Mother. I've made an appointment with the physiotherapist.' God worked in strange ways, thought Roya. Rather than a withered arm, how much better would a withered tongue have been. She prayed hastily for forgiveness for such an uncharitable thought and jabbed her needles into the ball of wool.

'I'll fetch your tea, Mother.'

'No need to shout, I'm not deaf.' Mrs Gabayan senior ran her tongue along her gums, savouring the last lingering flavours of the evening meal. Her fingers curled over the arm rests of her chair, tracing the seams in the black plastic.

Roya returned and put the glass of tea on a small table next to the chair.

'It's too low.'

Roya carried through a chair from the kitchen.

'All the sitting room tables are low. It's the fashion,' she explained.

'Fashion!' The old lady sucked her tea noisily through a sugar lump. Roya picked up her knitting.

'And what's all this about Soraya?'

'What about Soraya?'

'About the rape.' The old lady turned her face towards Roya, staring. Roya had to remind herself that she was blind.

'She was raped by some labourers on a building site.'

'How many?'

Roya took out her tape measure. Another half inch of ribbing to go. 'She doesn't know.'

'Her aunt tells me she's very large for her dates. She had an American boyfriend, didn't she?'

Roya ribbed furiously. The discrepancies in Soraya's story would become apparent sooner or later. A baby six weeks early, but a normal size . . . If they ever found out. Please God the child would soon be born and off to a good home and no one any the wiser.

Mrs Gabayan senior picked up another lump of sugar. Balanced it between her lips. Tilted the glass towards her mouth. Sucking in vain.

'It's empty,' she said indignantly.

Roya began on the cable pattern, weaving the stitches round the back, rejoining them. Her whole life was a tangle, certain threads put resolutely behind her and better left that way.

'Rape indeed,' snorted the old woman, crunching the

314

sugar between her gums. 'Why, in my day, a girl would be . . .'

'I'll fetch more tea, Mother,' said Roya hurriedly, throwing her knitting to the floor.

'Do they miss me?' Theresa wrote. 'Do they ask about me?' She thought of going to have a new picture taken to send to them, but her hair was terrible these days. The dye was growing out and she hadn't been able to buy any more. Brown roots more noticeable by the day and her hair limp and straggly in the heat. She was putting on too much weight, and began to be thankful that Fereydoun couldn't see her like this.

Her mother sent a new batch of photographs.

'Everyone's been so kind. I shall soon have to start a rag and bone business,' she wrote.

Theresa was shocked. Her children had never worn clothes that were not new.

Mrs Emani thought they looked nice.

'Is perhaps that you have not chosen them?' she suggested. Theresa thought a lot about this remark during her lazy days. Her children were growing up without her. This baby, she vowed, she would never be parted from. She would have liked to keep it inside her forever. How much she loved Fereydoun! Now that she couldn't see him. She wrote him long passionate letters. She watched Mrs Emani doing her baking on a Tuesday evening and helped parcel up the cakes and buns, pomegranates, tomatoes and hard-boiled eggs, jealously making sure that they were evenly divided between Fereydoun and that woman, Shirin.

Theresa's letters, one for each day of the week, were placed carefully in their numbered envelopes at the bottom of the basket.

* * *

The next day, Fereydoun tore open the packet, ate three buns and two pomegranates, like a schoolboy at a tuck box, and then looked over the rest of the contents. Ignoring the carefully numbered sequence of Theresa's letters he picked out one at random, and read a few lines. If there was as little to write about as she said there was, he wondered why she bothered.

The paper was useful though. On the reverse side he wrote love poems to the Pasdar. And the envelopes served as toilet paper, one for each day of the week, for Fereydoun was regular in his habits.

He didn't write back. What was there to say? He ploughed through the books on Islamic architecture that were brought to him. He even began to imagine that one day these studies might be useful. In Paris. If he were to join Goli there he could create quite an impression with original luxury-style dwellings incorporating an archway here and a minaret there.

'What the hell are you doing? This place stinks enough already.' Masoud Gabayan stormed into the tiny kitchen at the back of the shop. Ali hesitated in the doorway. Zahra clung to the edge of the draining board, vomiting into the sink.

'Get back to your work,' Masoud snapped at Ali. 'What about the customers?'

Ali turned away, back to his mending. There were of course no customers. There hadn't been any for weeks. His worst fears were coming to pass. He seated himself cross-legged in his usual patch of sunlight near the window.

'It must have been something she ate,' said Masoud loudly, following Ali back into the shop. 'But I cannot afford illness among my staff. I have a business to run. If she cannot earn her living, she will have to go.'

316

Zahra staggered back into the room, eyes watering, a handkerchief over her mouth.

Ali thumbed through the pile of carpets until he came to Mrs Emani's. It was time to make a start on that.

The Mullah bowed and took the hand of Mrs Gabayan senior.

'I am honoured to meet you,' he said, and sat down on the end of the settee nearest to her chair.

'It is an honour for me to receive your visit.'

The old lady was clearly impressed. Those were the first civil words Roya had heard from her all day. The rest of her conversation had consisted of complaints about the food, the furniture, the weather and the children.

'Soheila will bring tea,' said Roya.

The Mullah eased himself into a comfortable position, stretching his legs and glancing frequently towards the door. He was so busy these days that he was denied the leisure to contemplate Soheila's charms as frequently as he would have wished.

'Your work continues successfully?' inquired the old lady.

The Mullah's attention was elsewhere. Were those Soheila's footsteps in the corridor? She appeared in the doorway, eyes cast modestly down, bearing the tray of tea. First she placed the Mullah's glass on the low table.

'It is your birthday, Soheila?' asked the Mullah. Soheila looked up then. Just for a second, with a half-smile of acknowledgement.

'Now you are a woman.'

Soheila moved on, a graceful half turn over to her grandmother, back across the room to her mother. The Mullah's eyes never wavered.

'She should be married soon,' croaked the old lady.

Roya clicked her tongue and slopped her tea.

317

'First she must study. Only then can she make a good wife.'

Masoud came in through the door. 'There are husbands,' he said, 'who can better instruct their wives than schoolteachers.'

His old mother lifted her face, brightening at her son's return.

The Mullah nodded. 'It is indeed a privilege for anyone with learning to impart his knowledge to a young and eager mind.'

Roya was not fooled. She had watched the way he looked at her daughter. She dared not say as much to her husband. Masoud had nothing but praise for the Mullah, especially since he'd started his job on the tribunal.

'She should be married soon, Masoudja, before you have another problem on your hands.' The old woman didn't want to be left out of the conversation.

'You're quite right, Mother. It simply remains for Soheila's mother to give her consent. She, it seems, would rather have more shame heaped upon us than admit to the error of her ways.'

Roya felt threatened. Masoud alone she could handle, but an alliance between Masoud and the old lady could, in the end, defeat her.

Theresa Homayoun, in a battered orange taxi, felt her back stick to the seat. She was embarrassed thinking of the wet imprint her thighs would leave when she got out. Forushgah Bezorg was her last hope. She had tried the local Malacouti Supermarket, the kiosks, the store on Takhte Tavous. But she was determined to find some talcum powder and deodorant for Fereydoun. How much he enjoyed such things! He would never understand the personal cost to her of the sale of her brooch. But then that too seemed apt, a selfless token of her love.

318

'I'm sorry, Madam,' said the assistant, 'but we are not allowed to import such things nowadays.'

'But haven't you anything left? Any sort of talc or deodorant would do.'

The assistant rummaged beneath the counter then straightened up, tousled and sweating, holding out one jar of baby powder.

Theresa laughed.

'That's wonderful. How much?'

'It's damaged. I couldn't possibly charge you for it.'

'Yes please, I insist.' Theresa would not accept anything smacking of charity. Not now. Now she no longer looked her best.

Children spilled out of the school entrance, dividing into ever smaller units as they dispersed into the deep troughs of the Mahalleh's alleyways, sluggish in the turgid heat of the late afternoon.

Among them, Fariba and her brothers made their way homewards. The first wild excitement at being let loose from school was soon replaced by a quieter mood in which they kicked at stones, picked at walls and chatted about the day.

But Fariba did not linger. There was supper to cook and the clothes to wash. She hurried past old Daoud's meat shop, raising a mist of angry bluebottles above the stacked cows' heads.

'How's your mother, Fariba?' called out the shopkeeper.

'Much better thank you.'

'Here! Take this,' Daoud yelled after her. Fariba turned back and he thrust a bloody package into her hands.

'Thank you, Agha. Thank you very much.' Fariba broke into a run. Brushing flies off her parcel, she told the others of her good fortune. She would hurry home and light the stove. Cook the meat. What was it? She peeped inside the soggy paper. A cow's hoof! It was wonderful.

But the heat. So much heat, beating down from the sky. Trapped in the narrow alley, bouncing back off the walls and earth.

Two sparrows flew up out of the dust and perched on top of one of the high walls bordering the kucheh. Mussa searched for a stone, threw it at the bird and missed. The sparrows fluttered onto the opposite wall. The children threw more stones.

The birds took off again, untouched. The pebbles landed tap, tap on top of the wall and rebounded to land somewhere on the other side. A furious shout. The sound of feet. A door being opened.

The children giggled and ran. Through the chickens. Towards the bend in the street. Fariba clutching at her chador, her precious parcel. Her schoolbooks an avalanche at her feet. The chickens careered in wild zigzags between the high walls, between Fariba's legs. She fell. A heavy hand on her shoulder. A boot in her back. A harsh command.

'Get up.'

The others out of sight now. Flies humming, scenting blood. Fariba saw only the boots, khaki trousers and leather belts. The butts of the rifles. She looked no higher, shrinking inside her chador, hugging her parcel, heart pounding.

They led her away, one Pasdar uninjured, the other with a handkerchief clutched to his head, blood soaking through the white cotton.

Round the corner of the alleyway a dozen pairs of dark brown eyes watched her go.

Aziz was dozing comfortably with a full stomach when her neighbour came. What else was there to do? Eat, sleep, thumb through some magazines, listen to the endless martial music on the radio, gossip.

Her neighbour from home stared resentfully at the rounded cheeks and glossy hair, the crisp clean sheets, and thought of her own hungry children, playing in the dirt.

'Azizja. Khanum-e-Baniyazdi!' She shook Aziz roughly by the shoulder. 'Aziz. Wake up!'

Aziz's eyelids flickered. She yawned.

'Azizja, I bring bad news.'

'Bad news?' Aziz scrubbed at her eyes with her knuckles and heaved herself into a sitting position. 'Aiee. But it's hot today.'

'Aziz. Please wake up and listen. I have come to tell you that Fariba has been arrested.'

Aziz clenched her hands until the knuckles were the colour of the sheets, the walls, the uniforms. She clutched at the bedspread at her white, calm life. The running water, the peace and the food. A world in which wombs and ovaries were all that mattered.

'Fariba was playing on the way home from school. A whole group of them. They were throwing stones at some birds, they say, and one hit a Pasdar on the ear. Only Fariba was caught. She tripped.'

Aziz leaned back comfortably on her pillows.

'She is only a child. Only ten. They will let her go.'

Her neighbour shrugged. 'Perhaps, perhaps.'

'Where have they taken her?'

'Evin.'

'Evin? Where is that?'

'A long way north. It is a prison.'

A prison! It was more serious than she had thought.

'Oh God. And Hamid? Yes, Hamid will get her released.'

'Hamid!' It was her neighbour's turn to laugh. 'He doesn't want to get involved with the authorities.'

23

This morning I awoke with the sun, stretched and yawned to a background of prayers from the muezzin and the hum of early morning traffic. Then I saw a sight which took my breath away, so striking was the association with my train of thought at the time.

On a certain rooftop there was a woman. The woman, with her skirt hitched up round her waist way beyond what modesty would allow, was trampling a huge vat of tomatoes. Christ left many parables of the grape and the vineyard. Hear, then, one about the tomato and tomato juice. You smile? But to each his own culture.

The woman emerged from the vat stained red up to her thighs as if from some monstrous menstrual flux. You will immediately grasp the significance. Blood-red. Sin. Hell. Damnation. From the waist downwards, such is woman. Above the waist. Ah! How they smile and bare their beautiful bosoms. How they melt your heart with a look. But beware. Do not be taken in by such innocent loveliness.

In sorrow more than anger, I composed the following verses to send to my erring wife. I call them quite simply The Reproaches.

O My Wife, what have I done to thee? Or wherein have I afflicted thee?
Answer me.
I offered you beauty and freedom from care – the beauty of the sunset, air heady with flowers and wine, the purity of the nightingale's song. But your heart was not pure to receive it.
O My Wife, what have I done to thee? Or wherein have I afflicted thee? Answer me.

322

I brought you pleasure and entertainment. A monkey on a chain that danced when you clapped your hands. A songbird in a cage. And in your heart, you scorned such innocent enjoyment.

O My Wife, what have I done to thee? Or wherein have I afflicted thee? Answer me.

I offered you honey and almonds but you turned to me with a face like unfermented wine.

O My Wife, what have I done to thee? Or wherein have I afflicted . . . etc.

I made for you a bed of silk and offered you babies to make your womb leap with joy. But you turned your back on your children, in favour of adulterous pleasure.

O My Wife, what have I done to thee? And wherein have I . . . etc.

I offered you heaven on earth. A lifetime of safety within my house. Shelter within its shuttered confines. And you – what did you do?

O My Wife, what have I done . . . ?

I offered you the Paradise of my love. And you threw dust in my eye and twisted a dagger in my heart.

O My Wife.

At first, Shirin Khaksar assumed that the red-eyed child standing in the doorway was a visitor, but when she glanced up later from her book, the girl was still there, just inside the door. There was no one else in the room at the time. The others were out in the garden, watering the tomato plants.

'You are staying here?' asked Shirin.

'I want to go home.'

Shirin crossed the room and put her arm around Fariba's shoulders.

'I think this will be your bed. Here, next to mine. It's the only free one.' Fariba moved where Shirin led her. She sat on the edge of the bed, the tips of her toes just reaching to the ground.

'You are safe here. No one will hurt you.' Shirin sat down next to the child, took a pen and some paper and began to draw.

'This is a big fat man, selling watermelons. Look, he's parked his cart on a steep hill. Some little boys jump on a Coke tin next to the donkey's head.' Fariba's eyes followed the pencil lines. 'The donkey jumps and the watermelons roll off the cart and down the hill. Everywhere, people are falling over these melons.'

'I would take a melon and run home to my mother.'

'Where is your mother?'

'In hospital.'

'Is she ill?'

'She is expecting a baby.'

'She will be well looked after in hospital.'

'But Khanum, now there is no one to look after my brothers. No one to cook the tea and put them to bed.'

'Soon they will let you go home.'

'Baba will be angry.'

'What is your name?'

'Fariba.'

'Come with me, Fariba. It's not so bad here. I'll show you round. There is a garden, and soon it will be teatime. Are you hungry?'

Fariba nodded.

'The food is good. There will be rice and kebab. Afterwards, perhaps, yoghurt and fruit.'

'If you use so many candles, I will have to lock them up.' Masoud Gabayan stood over the girl, buttoning up his trousers.

Zahra nodded, staring at the ground.

'It's so dark at night,' she murmured without looking at him.

'Yes, but someone might see the light.'

Zahra kept very still, cross-legged, head bowed.

'Why, my wife might learn that you are here, and my wife is a very jealous woman. You wouldn't want her to know, would you?'

* * *

'Mama, what's the matter?' Soheila knelt and put her arms around her mother's waist. 'What's happened now?'

Roya sat rubbing her knuckles into her red eyes; her body was shaking.

'Onions,' she said.

'Oh Mama, you did frighten me.' They laughed and hugged each other.

'You're a good girl, Soheila. Now, let me get on with the tea.' Roya stirred the onions, pausing frequently to sniff and blow her nose.

Soheila looked out of the window. She was happy. Happy that Zeinab was her friend again. Such a silly quarrel it had been. All over a missing pencil. Now everything was alright. She chuckled to see a donkey in the street snuffling in the dustbins while its owner tried vainly to push it on its way.

'You'd better go and say hello to Granny,' said her mother.

Soheila went reluctantly into the sitting room. There sat the old lady, an ominous blackness in the corner of the room.

'Hello Granny, I'm back.'

'And how was school today?'

'The same as every day.'

'Aah, but I suppose you will be married soon.'

'Not yet, Granny. I've still got four more years at school and then I want to go to college.'

'When I was your age I was married.'

'Things are different nowadays.'

'That's where all this trouble comes from. I must speak to your father.'

Soheila laughed, knowing that her mother was on her side.

'Your mother is full of crack-brained notions,' the old lady said, as if reading her thoughts. 'Have you started yet?'

'Started what, Granny?'

'Oh never mind, child. Go and help your mother.'

In Evin prison, Shirin led the way to the shower.

'Have you ever had a shower before, Fariba?'

Fariba shook her head.

'Do you ever go to the hamum?'

'Yes. We have a bath every Pesach.'

'Here, it is the same.'

Fariba copied Shirin as she took off her clothes, laying them neatly in a pile, a small pile of rags. She kept her back turned to the Khanum.

'How old are you, Fariba?'

'Ten.' Fariba wrapped the towel around her. 'But I haven't started yet.'

'Started? Oh, I see. No, you're too young.'

'It is good, because I can't have Baba's babies like Mama does.'

Shirin was a while under the shower before she grasped the meaning of Fariba's last remark.

Later, Fariba sat on the edge of her bed, wearing one of Shirin's blouses and a skirt held up with a wide leather belt.

'I'll get you some clothes that fit properly next time my visitor comes.'

'But these are beautiful.' Fariba fingered the broad gold buckle and the tooled pattern on the leather. Then she put on her chador again.

'We must get you a new veil too.'

'I chew the corners when I'm hungry.' Fariba blushed, her stomach still glowing from the cooked lunch and the many cups of tea.

'What do we do now?' she asked.

'We could do some cleaning.'

'I'd better change.'

'There's no need. Those clothes are quite old, and they will wash.'

'But they are too beautiful to make dirty. What else is there to do?'

'Eat, talk, sit in the sun. Some people read or knit.'

'I don't know how to knit.'

'I'll teach you if you like.'

'Can you teach me other things?'

'What other things?'

'Like school. I'll get behind and the Mo'alem will be angry.'

'Yes, we can do those things too. Maths?'

'I like history and geography and stories.'

'Alright. After we've swept out.'

Fereydoun shambled after the other prisoners, carrying his soap and towel, cursing Theresa for his sagging trousers. They had only been a little tight before. Now they were enormous.

He ignored the other men, having mentally divided them into two categories: those like himself, who were not worth making friends with because they wouldn't have his luck in court, and the others who were a rough lot.

He stripped off and awaited his turn in the shower, his towel round his waist. He had his washing with him, one shirt for each day of the week, three pairs of underpants, seven pairs of socks and his trousers. The trousers would have been better at the dry cleaner's, but he feared that he might never see them again if he risked parting with them. He had found that placing them under his mattress, flat against the concrete floor, got out most of the creases.

Standing in the doorway was Hussein Gabayan, gun on shoulder, enjoying a smoke and a chat. Fereydoun edged closer, wanting to make some witty remark that would distinguish him from the general rabble.

Hussein saw Fereydoun move towards him. Old clever dick. He couldn't stand the type. Fat-pocked thighs and a neck like a bulldog. At least he didn't smell as bad as the others but his obsessive cleanliness was almost as irritating. Street duty, guard duty, hours standing around in court, when, oh when would his true merits be recognized?

Roya's life was never the same again after her mother-in-law came to stay. Mrs Gabayan senior sat, day after day, in the same corner of the living room, like a spider on its web ready to pick up the slightest vibration. Her sticky threads reached into every corner of the flat. Roya feared their threat, not to the blustering creatures that were her son and grandson, but to the delicate butterfly flutterings of her granddaughter.

Roya hardly recognized herself in the mirror these days. She had lost weight and huge purple pouches like bruises deepened under her eyes. She watched the alliance between the Black Widow and her husband, the slow but sure destruction of the delicate network of relationships that she had built up during twenty-two years of marriage. The old lady was poisonous.

Roya carried the after-dinner tea into the sitting room. She dared not leave her husband and his mother alone. The old lady sat drinking in every detail of Masoud's day in court.

'But was adultery proven, Masoudja? Who saw them?'

'Strictly speaking, Mother, it couldn't be proven, but everyone knew they were guilty. You only had to look at them.'

'And the punishment?'

'A hundred lashes.'

Roya saw the old lady's nod of satisfaction. She took out her knitting.

328

'Do you want more tea?' called Soheila from the kitchen.

'Yes please,' Roya called back.

'What else, Masoud? What else?'

'A few executions. Counter-revolutionaries.' Masoud stretched out his legs and cupped his hands behind his head. It was weary work sitting on a hard wooden chair all day. No one seemed to appreciate the discomfort he had to endure. He changed the subject. Executions were becoming boring. 'The Ayatollah has announced a move to reform prostitutes.'

'Not in front of your daughter,' hissed Roya as Soheila came into the room, carrying more tea.

'She should be well versed in such matters with her sister as an example.'

'Let's have no more horror stories tonight,' said Roya. Her eyes pricked and she could hardly see her stitches.

'Rape!' snorted Masoud.

'Your tea, Mama, Grandmother.' Soheila moved round the room, clearing away the empty glasses and placing fresh tea in front of everyone.

'Tell us about rape,' said the Black Widow, feeling for her glass.

'The victim cannot be innocent. She is guilty by default.'

'Guilty for walking down a street?' Roya asked.

'She shouldn't have been there in the first place.'

'Alone and unveiled,' added the old lady.

'The punishment should be the same for victim and rapist. It is well that no one knows about our daughter. The Mullah relies on us to make suitable correction.'

'No punishment can be too severe.' The old lady wagged her finger.

'The child has suffered enough,' said Roya quietly. 'It is no small thing, an unwanted pregnancy and labour and all for nothing.'

329

'If she were my daughter . . .'

'I'll fetch you a biscuit, Mother,' said Roya, getting to her feet and moving noisily between the tables.

'When is she coming home?' demanded Hamid Baniyazdi. He sat by Aziz's hospital bed, watching the nurses in their knee-length dresses and small white caps.

Aziz lay with the bedclothes pulled up to her chin, eyes closed.

'When the baby is born,' said the doctor. 'But first we need your permission. The baby will have to be born by Caesarean. At the same time we will tie her tubes, to prevent any more babies.'

Aziz groaned.

'Another baby would be very dangerous for your wife.'

'What is a man without children?' Hamid whined.

'You already have three sons and two daughters. With this child that makes six!' The doctor held out six fingers.

Hamid shrugged helplessly.

'All you have to do is sign here.' The doctor held out a pen.

'He can't write,' mumbled Aziz.

'Well, all we need then is a thumb print. Just press your thumb here, onto the paper.'

Hamid did as they said, then sat sucking at the blue stain that had signed away his manhood. What was there left for him in life? When they wheeled Aziz away, he left the hospital, wandering in the direction of the bazaar, fearful of meeting anyone he knew. How could he hold his head up? What could he say? How could he look his friends in the eye, he whose wife was barren? It would have been better for Aziz to have a child and die in the attempt. What was a woman, if not a receptacle for man's seed, a vessel to reflect the glory of her husband's most God-like attribute? Yes, Aziz would be better dead than bring this shame upon her family.

* * *

When Roya Gabayan put down the phone, her hands were shaking.

'Who was it?' called the Black Widow.

'Just a wrong number.' Roya went into the kitchen. She needed to be alone. So, Soraya had gone into hospital. And she should have been with her. If only she had been stronger. If only the old lady hadn't come to stay . . .

'Are you having a cup of tea without me?' A black shape materialized in the doorway. It was uncanny the way the old lady moved from room to room. Roya sometimes wondered whether she was blind at all.

'I'm just sitting down, Mother, having a rest.'

The old lady sat opposite, between Roya and the window, her shadow across the table.

'Aren't you going to offer me a cup of tea?'

'No, Mother. I have to catch the post.' Suddenly Roya knew what she must do. Never mind the cost. Paper, string, the little knitted garments from their hiding place in the pantry. Not on the kitchen table, where the old lady might touch them, but behind her, out of reach. Roya lovingly wrapped the small parcel. Silly she knew, but the child would not go empty-handed to the orphanage.

'Are you leaving me alone?' demanded the old lady, suddenly querulous, as Roya clattered out of the flat, down the stairs, out into the street. Into the barrage of heat, sweating now, she ran towards the post office. Up the steps, into the building.

'Bebakshid, Agha. Excuse me please, Khanum.' Roya, usually so patient, elbowed her way towards the dusty counter. She saw her parcel flung carelessly into a sack. The right sack? Would it arrive safely? She hurried home, guilty now about the old lady sitting alone, whining for her tea.

* * *

Soraya Gabayan lay limp and exhausted, her stomach like a soggy sponge, wanting only to sleep. All the months of lying and uncertainty were over, her baby a flash of slippery flesh, a memory of pain.

'You would like some tea?'

She shook her head. Just sleep and a longing for her mother. As she used to sit, when Soraya was ill as a child. A hand to reach out to.

'Mama?' A veiled figure by the bed. Her aunt. For a moment she had almost thought . . .

Masoud Gabayan answered the phone. Roya, her hands covered in flour, stood in the hall, listening. Just a few grunts and then a goodbye

'Who was it? What did they want?' she asked.

But he walked straight past her, into the sitting room. Roya washed her hands, put the biscuits in the oven, then joined them, Masoud and his mother. Plumping up cushions and setting them straight on the shiny plastic.

'I asked who had phoned, Masoud.' Roya tried not to sound too interested. 'Is there something special happening tomorrow? A demonstration perhaps?'

Masoud took out the evening paper.

Roya wondered whether to ring her sister, but she couldn't, not with Masoud within earshot. She pummelled the cushions again, more fiercely this time, and watched them slide around the slippery surface. She let slip all caution.

'Soraya? How is Soraya?'

'Let's strike a bargain. Agree to Soheila's marriage, and you can visit her tomorrow.'

'Was it a boy or a girl?' Roya tried to keep the wobble out of her voice. Not to show him how much it mattered to her.

'It makes no difference.'

'Masoud.' Roya was weeping now. 'I must know. It's my grandchild.'

'It is not your grandchild and Soraya is not my daughter.'

But Roya knew she was a grandmother. She knew also that it was not just Soraya that she wanted to visit. She went into the kitchen and wept.

24

Lulled by the motion of the coach, Soraya Gabayan's head slumped forward until her chin rested on her chest. She woke suddenly as she felt the brown paper parcel slide down her lap, grabbing at it as it edged towards the floor. Her sudden movement woke the baby, whose head turned towards her, nuzzling at her blouse.

Now Soraya unwrapped the parcel and marvelled again over the fragile garments. In the hospital she had already searched it for some message. But there had been nothing, except the love which must have gone into the intricate patterns.

Soraya blamed her mother for the fact that she now sat in the bus with the child on her knee. Had it not been for the parcel she would never have seen her little daughter again. Unable to entrust the gift to anyone, Soraya had gone to the nursery and so become aware of the chaos. She saw the groups of Pasdaran chatting with the nurses, standing arrogantly by while the European staff packed their bags. And she had felt alarm for her baby's safety, had not been able to abandon her to an uncertain future. She had thought up a much better idea for where to take her child.

It was some time after midnight when she climbed off the bus in South Tehran. On one arm, her baby, in the other hand a small suitcase. The air had the thick sticky feel of a cooling cake, the stars were bright. The pavements grilled the soles of her feet.

Hungry and thirsty, Soraya made her way stiffly towards a food stall. Squatting down on her suitcase, a piece of bread balanced on top of the baby on her knee, she blew on a glass of tea.

'Miss Gabayan?' came a man's voice.

Soraya did not look up.

'Miss Gabayan?' The voice was louder now, right in her ear. She nodded now, tearing off strips of nan and dunking them in the sweet tea.

'You have your baby?' Hamid Baniyazdi squatted on the pavement next to her, happy to have someone to talk to, now that his wife was no longer a wife, his home no longer a home. 'Boy or girl?'

'Girl.'

'Aaah.' Now Hamid understood why the girl was there alone, why there was no one to meet her. 'If it were a boy, Agha Gabayan would have met you,' he said.

Soraya drained her glass as fast as she could and stood up.

'I'll get you a taxi.'

'No thank you.'

'Carry your bag?'

Soraya shook her head, held out a few rials and hurried away as fast as she could, over the outstretched legs of sleeping bodies, through the goats and hens, out at last into the main south-north thoroughfare.

She walked half a mile, the baby and suitcase becoming heavier by the minute. The streets were deserted. She felt quite confident though, a mother with a two-day-old baby. She was not even disturbed when she turned a corner and saw a group of men coming towards her. Pasdaran maybe, in combat jackets and ragtag uniform. With some sixty thousand groups patrolling the streets these days it was hard to tell.

They stopped as they came near, blocking the way.

'Excuse me, gentlemen, I'm looking for a taxi.'

Without street lighting, Hussein hadn't recognized his

sister, but as soon as he heard the voice he knew who it was. She must be mad to have brought the child to town. He shrank to the back of the group and waited to see what would happen.

Someone mimicked what Soraya had said in a high falsetto. The others laughed, closing in around her. Soraya put down the suitcase and tightened her hold of the baby.

'And where might you be going to, young lady, all alone at this time of night?'

'Home.' The mention of her father's name would have been sufficient protection, but she could not use it. Not now.

'Well, well. And your husband? Where is your husband?'

Soraya looked round the circles of faces, leering in the faint glow of their cigarettes. A hand reached out and pulled her chador away, to reveal the white cotton blouse and full skirt.

Hussein felt close to panic. Any one of his friends might recognize Soraya now. He thanked God that the night was dark.

His friend Akbar snatched the baby from Soraya. The brief flare of a match lit up the fair hair and the bright blue eyes. The baby turned towards the Pasdar, making little sucking motions with her mouth.

'It thinks you're a woman, Akbar.' They all laughed. Soraya pulled her chador back over her head. Headlights shone down the street.

'A taxi,' she said, holding out her hands for the child. Akbar turned and ran into the narrow street behind him, holding the baby like a rugby ball. Soraya ran too, grabbing at his arms and shirt.

Then they were all after her. She lost her chador in the scrum. 'Foreigner's whore,' they laughed, holding the child high out of reach, tossing it from one to another.

Hussein leaned against the wall and watched. There was no harm in the game, it was all good fun, the sort of thing he used to do at home with a toy to tease his sisters.

Breathless and sobbing, Soraya ran from one to another. Each time she stopped, exhausted, they held the child out. 'Come and get it . . .!'

She was running again when she tripped on a doorstep and fell.

One of the young men flung himself on top of her. Hussein dragged him away. This was no longer a harmless game.

He helped Soraya sit up. 'Are you alright?' He had acted on instinct, not thinking.

'You know her?' asked Akbar.

'It is my sister.'

They handed over the baby, embarrassed now.

'It was just a bit of fun, Hussein. No harm done, eh?' They shuffled from foot to foot, not knowing quite what to say.

'Go on,' he said. 'I'll catch you up.' He sat, his arms round Soraya and the baby.

'It's lucky you came along just then, Hussein.' She wept.

Hamid Baniyazdi sat on the kerb and tried to work out what was going on. A young lady like Miss Gabayan walking the streets unaccompanied? Mr Gabayan announcing neither the marriage nor the birth of his first grandchild? There was something fishy here.

Hussein caught up with his friends, walking in silence, an evening's fun turned sour.

'What are you going to do?'

Hussein shrugged, hands in his pockets, sullen.

'We ought to report her.'

337

'For what?' Hussein stopped and faced them, daring them to go on.

'Come on, Hussein, don't be so naïve. She should be publicly tried and sentenced.'

'She's my sister.' Hussein had never felt so miserable.

'You know what it could do to your career?'

Hussein nodded, and as his feelings of pity subsided, he began to feel anger towards Soraya. Let her mess up her own life, but not his as well!

'Who is the father?'

'She was raped. Some building labourers, on her way to college.' Hussein avoided his friends' gaze. 'It was broad daylight. Lunch-time.'

'Come on, Hussein – a baby like that! It could only have been a ferangi.'

'But what would they do to her?'

'Oh the usual. But it would look better for you if you were to report her yourself. You know, show your devotion to the cause.'

Soraya walked unsteadily in a northerly direction. She hadn't been able to find her suitcase. She kept close to shop fronts, away from the pavement's edge, through the town centre, past shop windows in which dummies sported chadors. Further north the shops gave way to flats, then the flats gave way to houses with high-walled gardens. Up the long, long slope of the mountains, seeing now the peaks in the first light of dawn.

From the east came the streaks of a garish sunrise. In front of her a church tower gleamed white among the trees. Birds sang loudly in the Mission garden. Soraya forced herself to hurry. Through the pointed archway, close to the wall in the black shadows of the cloisters. She left her shoes by the gate and moved silently over the flagstones, praying that the baby would not wake and cry.

But where to leave her child? The air was cold. She tried the church door. The handle turned. Inside, all was quiet.

Soraya took off her chador and doubled and redoubled the thin material to provide some sort of bed. She wedged the baby between a pile of hymnbooks and the poor box, and still she did not leave – not until she heard the flush of a toilet and saw the gleam of an electric light flash across the flowerbeds.

Then she was gone. Down the hill, down the street towards home. Mother. Hearing in her mind the frightened wail of a new-born baby.

Aziz, holding her baby, stood at the top of the flight of steps leading from the hospital, reluctant now to leave the place that had been her home for the last two months. Clinging to the hem of her chador was a toddler of about eighteen months. A beautiful little girl with glowing skin and thick curly hair, staring wide-eyed at the traffic and bustle of the street.

'Come, Shahnaz!' Aziz took her hand. Ten days after the delivery of her daughter, Aziz was feeling fitter than she could ever remember, in spite of the Caesarean and the sterilization – at the thought she almost lost her poise. But soon it wouldn't matter. Soon she would be in Israel. It was all arranged. And in Israel there would be no shame, no stigma.

She tugged at the child's arm. Shahnaz looked up at the stranger who was her mother. Her home was the hospital, the nurses in white, four meals a day and a bath at bedtime. She hung back, away from the heat, the noise, the dust.

Aziz inhaled the fumes, heard the street cries, felt the heat of the sun on her head and was anxious to be gone. Israel beckoned. Her children. Her home.

Shahnaz wept with fear, face buried in her mother's

chador. Aziz moved slowly down the steps, holding her new baby. She lingered in the sunshine, saw the light glinting on pyramids of golden pomegranates stacked on the pavement.

A girl came up to her, a girl in a red-fringed shawl, tugging at her sleeve, asking for money. Aziz was pleased. No one had ever asked her for money before.

She crossed the road, the dusty maidan, into the maze of alleyways. 'Good day!' How pleasant to be recognized, to show off the new baby. 'Salamat!' How nice to see old friends, neighbours who had shared hard times.

'A girl? Ah, never mind – perhaps next time.' Aziz smiled to herself, knowing there would not be a next time, relieved and yet . . . But in Israel it was going to be different.

Nearly home, trembling now with excitement, Aziz took a deep breath, pushed the door of the compound open.

The children playing round the tap looked up, suspicious of the tall plump stranger, the dimple-kneed toddler. Then recognition.

'Mama,' shrieked one of the boys. Now they were all round her, her sons, tugging at the bundle in her arms.

'Is it you, Mama?'

Aziz took from her pockets the biscuits she had been hoarding. The children fell upon them, starving.

'Who's there?' called out an old woman standing in the doorway of Aziz's room, shading her eyes against the light.

'Sister? My sister . . .'

The two women hurried towards each other, faces bright with the joy of greeting.

'The baby?' asked Aziz's sister.

'A girl.'

Her sister's face lost all hope. She turned away.

340

'More shame you have brought us,' she said. 'Not even your child is a cause for celebration.'

'Sister, do not say that.' Aziz grabbed her sleeve. 'Would you not rather be me than . . . than you now?'

'I would rather be dead.'

Aziz sat on her doorstep, suddenly weary. She watched her sister waddle behind the bulk of her belly, back to the tap, the endless futile rinsing. Then she stood up, pulling Shahnaz after her, sickened by the smell of her home. Fariba would never have let the room get like this.

'Sister,' she called out. 'Sister, how is Fariba?'

Her sister did not look up, did not answer.

'Sister . . . ?' Aziz watched the water slop over the edge of the bowl into the endlessly thirsty dust.

'Today,' said her sister without looking up, 'today she goes on trial . . .'

'Hamid, where is Hamid? He is with her? Her own father?'

'Is that likely? He hasn't been seen since.' Her sister laughed bitterly and stared at Aziz's stomach. 'What reason has he for coming home any more?'

Aziz turned and ran, ignoring the screams of Shahnaz, the tiny baby wailing in her arms. Through the alleyways, into the street, a taxi.

'Where?' asked the driver.

Aziz stared. She'd never been in a taxi before. Didn't know where she was going, only that she must see Fariba, must find her.

The driver clicked his tongue against his teeth. Rolled his eyes, gazed up to heaven. God deliver him from all women.

'The prison,' suggested Aziz through the fold of her chador, shrinking back into her seat, the baby sucking at her breast.

* * *

341

Roya Gabayan took no notice of the first gentle knock at her door. Someone passing on the stairs, the swing of a shopping bag, or the tack of a broom against the skirting board of a neighbouring flat. Then it came again, slightly louder, and a whispered 'Mama!' through the letterbox.

Roya wrenched at the lock and chain, dragged open the door and pulled Soraya inside, into her arms, weeping and laughing. Easing her daughter's face against her breasts. Burying her lips in the long soft hair. Feeling the crust of blood on her temple, holding her at arms' length, peering, touching, satisfied that there was no real damage. Then back into her arms again, squeezing and weeping.

Then Roya tried to release her daughter, needing to talk now, but Soraya stayed slumped against her mother, eyes closed, face grey with exhaustion. Half carrying her child who was now a mother, Roya staggered into the kitchen, into a chair, cradling Soraya on her knee. Soraya sobbed weakly, her face buried in her mother's neck. Roya sang softly, swaying gently in time to the music until, like a baby herself, Soraya slept.

Then a dark shape moved between the two women and the sun, casting its shadow. Cold and ominous. An arm reached out, feeling its way from Soraya's shoulder up along her neck, to her bare head.

'Without so much as a chador!' The old woman smacked her gums with satisfaction, her worst fears confirmed.

Roya turned her back, putting herself between her daughter and the Black Widow. The movement woke Soraya. Roya wanted to get her away, along the corridor to Soheila's bedroom, into Soheila's bed.

Soraya lay there now, aware of the quiet movements of her mother about the room. The warm, wet sponge dabbing gently at the dried blood. A child again. Waking. Sleeping. Mama watchful at her bedside. A cup of tea, hot and sweet, placed in her sleepy hand. A plate of cakes. Dates and oranges. The smell of hot bread.

'What name did you say?' asked the taxi driver.

'Fariba Baniyazdi.' Aziz shrank back into the taxi, out of sight of the gaunt walls of Qasr Prison, while the driver inquired at the gate.

'Inja nist. He said try the Alavieh School.'

Aziz nodded, anxious to be gone.

'Twelve toman seventy-five it is already,' said the driver, looking suspiciously at Aziz.

'Khube. Let us go to the Madresseh.' For she had money in her pocket. Money they had given her in hospital to buy food and clothing for her family, to get everyone ready to go to Israel. Back across the city centre, snarled up with traffic, every minute an age. What if she were too late? What if she missed her? And there was so much to tell Fariba about how she had to collect the tickets and how they would leave on the big silver plane. The baby was sweating, restless in the heat of the metal car. Aziz wondered if it would be quicker and cooler walking, only she didn't know where to go.

More people piled into the taxi, wedging her in a tight sandwich in the middle of the back seat.

'You don't mind, Khanum? Only a slight detour and we can drop these good people on the way.'

Aziz sat listening to the driver telling them about her daughter. They looked at her pityingly while the dial clicked up the fare, twenty-five toman thirty-two cents, clonk, thirty-three, clonk . . .

Now the taxi sped up a side street and screeched to a halt. 'Here we are.' The driver pointed up the alleyway opposite. Aziz looked about in disbelief.

She fumbled inside her clothing for the money, wrapped in a handkerchief, tucked inside her vest, soggy with milk. She counted out the money slowly and carefully

343

on her knee – each note, each coin, while the driver tapped impatiently on the steering wheel.

Theresa Homayoun sat under the mulberry bush in Mrs Emani's garden, humming to herself. 'The mulberry bush, the mulberry bush. Here we go round . . .' But the only thing that was round was her stomach. And the berries, fat purple lozenges full of juice that fell and burst on the ground like bloodstains. She started to giggle. What she had just read in the paper had made her laugh. That anyone would dare, in the Islamic Republic! Would claim to be God! Only a foreigner could get away with it. She read the article a second time.

'FOREIGN PILOT COMMITTED TO MENTAL ASYLUM' ran the headline.

The Manager of the Hotel Alexander the Great was greatly alarmed yesterday morning by the behaviour of one of his guests. Summoned to the rooftop by anxious staff, he found the gentleman stripped to his underpants, teetering on the parapet some six storeys above the street.

The man was flinging his breakfast (of toast and fried herring) into the street below, shouting all the while: 'God is Great.' When asked what he was doing, the man replied: 'Feeding the five thousand.'

The Manager was quite rightly alarmed as there were no more than twenty people in the street below at the time. A doctor, summoned to the scene, inquired of the patient his name. The reply was 'I am who am', which caused the doctor some concern. It was not grammatical, certainly not what one would have expected from an educated man.

The doctor concluded that the man was mad. He was removed by ambulance, despite his repeated requests to have an aeroplane put at his disposal so as to 'return to his Father, who is in heaven'.

At lunchtime, Hussein Gabayan was instructed to report to the Mullah Afsharzadeh, down at the Alavieh School. Hussein walked briskly, proud of the shadow which walked beside him, gun over shoulder, cap askew at a jaunty angle.

He wondered what the summons meant. He hoped, he prayed, just as he had been hoping and praying all these weeks since the formation of the New Revolutionary Guard. To be a real soldier of Islam at last! A real war, that's what he'd like to see. A Crusade. Militant Islam. Guns, glory and Paradise! He'd seen it all in the cinema.

When he was shown into the Mullah's office, and saw his father already sitting there, Hussein's thoughts immediately turned to his sister. His cheeks burned with shame.

'You have deceived me,' said the Mullah. He placed a report on his desk. '"Rape," you said. "Pity the child, she has suffered enough," you said. And it was all lies! God forgive us all. And even now, Hussein, the report was not made by you. Had you no thought of where your duty lay?'

Hussein hung his head, avoiding his father's eyes, wondering which of his friends had given him away.

'Now the matter must be put right. Sin must be punished. The case must go before the courts and justice must be seen to be done.' The Mullah fiddled with his pen, wove it through the fingers of his right hand, round and back again.

'Father.' Hussein spoke on the spur of the moment, wanting to exonerate himself from any blame. 'If I have not spoken before, it is because I have thought and prayed much about this matter. It seems to me' – Hussein cast about in his mind, seeking inspiration, blurting out the first thing that came into his head – 'that we should constitute a Family Court among ourselves. There have been precedents. This is a family affair. We should take action ourselves.'

The Mullah was clearly impressed. 'The idea does you credit. "Let not compassion move you,"' he quoted,

'". . . in a matter prescribed by God." And to show my faith in the rightful outcome of this sad business, and to protect your younger daughter from further contamination, I am prepared to marry her. Today.'

A knock on the door indicated it was time for the Mullah to return to court. 'And you, Agha Gabayan, are excused from further duties until such time as your family affairs are sorted out.'

When the Mullah had left, Masoud walked over to the window and stood with his back to his son, looking down on the teeming alleyways. Mothers, sisters, brothers, fathers, making their way towards the court. This was something that must be avoided at all costs. A public trial of Soraya. His first-born. He prayed to God to give him strength for the task that lay before him. That God would guide his judgement. And his hand. Masoud leaned heavily on the dusty window-sill and wept.

Hussein despised himself for the silly weakness that had prompted him to defend his sister last night. She deserved whatever she got. A child by that American – he'd kill him with his bare hands if he could, and feel the full weight of the law behind him. He couldn't blame his sister though, not entirely. Everyone knew that women were weak and foolish. They needed protection. His father must bear a large portion of guilt.

Hussein looked up to see his father's shoulders shaking. His father, who should be strong! He put his arm round the older man and led him from the room.

In a temperature aspiring towards one hundred and three degrees, Mrs Emani scurried from shop to shop with her string shopping bag. It was midday, but she made no concession to the heat, she simply became a little dustier than usual. She was even overpaying in her haste, but it didn't worry her.

Tonight, Theresa would have tomatoes for her tea. Sweet juicy tomatoes. All that goodness for the baby!

In the bus, Mrs Emani took out the unfinished matinée jacket. Time for two more rows before the carpet shop.

Fariba was surprised to see so many grown-ups in the schoolroom. She was led to the front row, though she preferred the back, where she was less likely to attract the teacher's attention.

She looked around before she sat down. Mama! Mama, with the tiny bundle on her knee that was her new brother or sister. The prayers, the indictment meant nothing. Mama was there. Mama looking so well. Fariba would have liked to sing (only it was forbidden) or dance (only it was forbidden too). There could be no more trouble now that Mama was home.

'Mama is here,' she whispered to the guard sitting in the chair next to her.

'Ssh!' he whispered back, fingers to lips.

Fariba thought of home. A home transformed now Mama was back. Mussa and the boys, how were they? And Shahnaz? Which page would they be up to in their textbooks at school? Would she ever catch up again? She would ask that nice Khanum, her friend, who knew so much about maths and poetry and everything. And all those stories! Haji Baba the man was called, such a boaster, so clever. Even Baba would be amused.

The thought of her father cast a slight shadow on her mood. Fariba turned peering about the court. No, Baba was not there.

Fariba watched a sunbeam spangle the dusty air. It came from somewhere behind her, lighting her new shoes (well, the Khanum's shoes) in a small spotlight. She twisted in her seat and craned her neck. There was a small window, high up, near the roof.

The guard tapped her on the shoulder and turned her

to face the long table where the Mullah sat. How long they talked, and how boring it all was. She looked down. The sunbeam was still there, thick and solid, a staff of light. Fariba poked it with her fingers. Nothing! Her hand went right through and the light shone now on the back of her hand.

Fariba looked round, caught her mother's eye, pointed to the dancing light. Had Mama seen it too? Fariba leaned forward and cupped her hands trying to imprison the small bright circle. There it was, shining on her palms, and the light on the floor was gone. She laughed with delight.

Then a hand on her shoulder. Fariba looked up to share her joy with the guard, but he frowned and pointed towards the table. Fariba sighed and wrapped her chador closely around her face. Underneath it her fingers felt their way along the chain the lady had given her that morning. Such a beautiful chain, thin and golden with one stone suspended from the centre.

A diamond, the lady said it was. She said it would sparkle in the sun, but there was no sun in the small cell of their new prison. Fariba much preferred the other place. And the food had been better there as well.

She felt the many-mirrored surface. The sharp edges dug into her fingertips. The lady said that a diamond was so hard that it would cut glass, only there had been no glass in their window, only bars. There were glasses here, on the table in front of the Mullah. Empty tea-glasses. Perhaps it would cut those. Just to look at the glasses made Fariba feel thirsty, and bored. She yawned loudly. Shuffled about on her chair.

'Is it lunchtime?' she asked the guard. 'I'm hungry.'

Fariba could tell from the way Mama was holding the baby that she was giving it her breast under her veil. Strange though, she hadn't heard it cry. Perhaps it was sick and weak like poor little Shahnaz had once been.

She stood up, to walk over to Mama and see for herself. As the guard grabbed her shoulders, pulling her back into her chair, his hand became entangled in the chain. The chain tightened then snapped.

The next minute, Fariba saw the stone lying on the floor in the little pool of light.

'It sparkles. It does!' she cried with delight.

Then someone took it away, her glistening stone. Hers!

'It's mine, give it back. It was a present,' Fariba called out. But they kept it there on the table and called her a thief. Then Mama was next to her, a quick hug, Fariba clutching at her Mama's arm as she was led away.

'We will go to Israel, Fariba,' her mother called after her. 'It's all arranged. I'm going now to collect the tickets.'

'When will we go, Mama, when?' Fariba called back over her shoulder. 'Will it be tonight?'

Roya Gabayan was chopping up meat for the evening meal. It was tough, but would make a tasty stew. The Black Widow sat at the table. She knew blood was in the air; her nostrils twitched and she slavered in anticipation.

'With onions and cinnamon, Roya? Don't forget the cinnamon!'

Roya did not chop the meat on the kitchen table as usual, but on the cupboard so that she had her back to the old woman. She faced the mountains instead, lifting her eyes in joyful thanks that Soraya was safely home.

And the little garments had been just right, Soraya said. Like an angel the baby had looked in them. Roya was already worrying about the time when the child would grow out of them. Her granddaughter.

She had been weak and wrong to send Soraya away. A baby was not an object that could be hidden. It would all come out in the end, she was sure of it. If they had been open about the pregnancy from the start, she would have

349

had her own little granddaughter with her now. After all, these things happened all the time. She'd read about them in magazines.

Roya wiped her hands on her apron.

'Where are you going now?' quavered the old hag.

Roya shut the door behind her. Across the hall, along the corridor, into Soheila's bedroom. There was Soraya, still asleep with the bruises turning yellow down the side of her face. Roya smiled, reassured. Nothing healed as well as sleep. She tiptoed out of the bedroom, back to the kitchen.

'The devil finds work for idle hands.' The old woman shuffled her fingers along the table edge.

Roya looked down the street. Oh God – Masoud and Hussein were coming home. So early. She didn't want them back, not while Soraya was sleeping and the meal not yet ready.

She sawed hastily at the red flesh, catching her finger with the sharp knife. The cut was clean and deep. There was no pain, no blood, at first. Then it welled up, dripping on to the cupboard, and the nerves of her fingertip screamed. She pinched the jagged edges of the cut together with the thumb and forefinger of her right hand.

Masoud kicked open the kitchen door.

'Where's Soraya?' he demanded.

'Asleep.' Roya wound a paper tissue around her finger and watched the blood soak through, red against the bright yellow, in a widening circle.

'Hah, Masoudja, is that you?' The old woman turned to face her son's voice.

Then Soheila and Hussein were there, struggling in the doorway, Soheila fighting to get free.

'Mama, I won't do it. Don't let them.'

'Masoud, what is going on? Soheila should be at school.'

'This afternoon she is marrying the Mullah, that's why she's here.'

'Over my dead body, Masoud.' Roya pushed Soheila behind her, into the angle of the kitchen cupboards.

The old woman cackled. She enjoyed a scene. She twisted her head in the direction of each sound, anxious to miss nothing.

Fariba Baniyazdi stood on her mattress and tried to reach the window bars. She grasped the sill with both hands, scrabbling at the stone wall with her bare feet, until her nails were torn and bleeding. If only she could see out she might be in time to catch a glimpse of Mama, walking down the street with the baby. Boy or girl? She hadn't time to ask.

She fell back on to the bed, her face flushed with effort. She had passed that nice Khanum in the corridor. Her suitcase was still here. She hoped she'd be back soon.

Then Fariba remembered the necklace. What would the Khanum say? Would she be angry? But it wasn't her fault. The chain had been broken, she could still feel the place on her neck where it had dug in before it snapped. They'd taken it away. Called her a thief.

But the lady would put everything right. She was that sort of lady. Like a princess. Beautiful, all in black, her hair brushed and shining and tiny jewels in her ears. Fariba longed for her to come back, her Khanum.

It was late afternoon when she heard a key turn in the lock. Fariba panicked. She looked round for somewhere to hide but there was nowhere, the mattresses on the floor were the only furnishings. She burrowed underneath, a small hump in the angle of the wall, and lay quite still.

Shirin Khaksar returned to the furnace of her cell. So. It had happened at last. Yet, in spite of the condemnation

351

of the court, she had lived according to her conscience, and whatever she had done she had thought at the time to be right.

But the child! What had she done? And where was she? How could she have forgotten her? Shirin saw the hump in the corner and gently pulled back the mattress.

'Fariba?' She eased out the whimpering child and held her on her knee.

'Well, Fariba? How did it go?' Shirin stroked the curly black hair, wet with sweat and tears, and hummed softly.

'Shall I tell you a story?'

Fariba shook her head.

'What's the matter, Fariba?'

'They took it away.'

'What?'

'The necklace. They said I was a thief.'

'The necklace doesn't matter.'

'But it sparkled. The stone sparkled, just like you said it would. Like a thousand tiny mirrors in the sunshine.'

'Don't weep over the necklace, Fariba. Have this one instead.' Shirin unclasped the gold chain round her own neck and fastened it on Fariba.

'You're not angry with me?'

'No, of course I'm not.'

Fariba flung her arms round Shirin's neck and kissed her.

'Mama was there.'

'And how was Mama?' Shirin found that she felt jealous.

'She looked, well, *beautiful*, Khanum.'

'Did you understand what was going on in there?'

'It was very boring. But Mama was feeding the baby.'

'Was it a boy or a girl?'

'I don't know, but do you know what she said?'

'Shall I guess?'

352

'You'll never guess, not as long as you live, Khanum. We are going to Israel!'

'To Israel!'

Fariba smiled. Her eyes shone. Then she looked troubled.

'Khanum, they won't go without me, will they?'

'Oh no, your Mama would never do that.'

'Have you been to Israel?'

'No.'

'Shall I write and tell you all about it when I get there?'

'I'd like that. You must write to me and send me lots of pictures.'

'We will be very rich, I think. Mama and Shahnaz will never be sick again.'

'What will you do, Fariba?'

'I shall be a doctor.'

'That means a lot of hard work.'

'Will you help me?'

'Of course I will.'

'Then we'd better start now.'

25

The Elburz Mountains shimmered hazily in tones of muted orange and russet. Evening stirred the city into a last frenzy of activity before the all-enveloping chador of the night.

Theresa still sat in the garden under the mulberry tree, her feet on a stool, a mirror in her hand. She was studying her hair and wondered when her mother would send the bottle of peroxide she had asked for. How could she possibly visit Fereydoun looking like this? Brown roots, split silver ends, she looked terrible. Yet she'd never felt better in her life. She put down the mirror, settled comfortably back into the chair, and watched the panorama of the mountains. The baby stirred gently, reassuringly. Soon Mrs Emani would be back to cook the supper, and she would smell the richness of frying meat and cinnamon.

In his cell, Fereydoun laid down his pen. It was too dark to see properly. Soon it would be suppertime, then sleep. He folded away his drawings, quite pleased with the day's work. A desirable residence, conforming to every aspect of Islam in both proportion and propriety. Toilet appropriately positioned. The windows – pointed Moghul arches – guaranteed to funnel every syllable from the muezzin into the living area, providing, of course, that the double-glazed windows were open and the air-conditioning turned off. The house would create a sensation in Hollywood . . . or Paris. Perhaps it would be a good advertisement for his work if he were to live in a similar house himself. Theresa would love it.

He thought of Theresa in the velvety darkness of twilight. She floated, dismembered in his mind, the curve of back and thigh, a shoulder, a breast, like a jigsaw he couldn't quite put together. Even her face escaped him. Thick dark lashes, blonde hair a golden waterfall, but he couldn't put her together.

Key in the lock. Fereydoun turned to see who was bringing his supper? Would it be, could it be Hussein? An old man plonked a tin bowl on the floor. Fereydoun sniffed at the food and put it down again. He took out one of Theresa's letters, and on the back began drafting a poem to his slim, pale guard.

Aziz Baniyazdi had left the courtroom happy that Fariba looked so well and cheerful, with more colour in her cheeks than she had ever seen before. Such a pretty child with her cheeks filled out, her hair brushed and shining.

Aziz strolled in the late afternoon, her baby asleep, money in her pocket. Life was good. She stopped at a stall to buy kebab, squatting down and chewing at the edge of the pavement, she watched the people go by.

A volley of shots made her jump. The stall-holder pointed at his head and laughed. Aziz sank back against the wall, finished the skewer of meat and wiped her fingers and mouth with the corner of her new chador. Merci Agha. And sauntered on.

Not home, she decided. She wouldn't go home just yet. She was enjoying herself. She would go via the Social Work Office and see if the tickets and visas were ready. They had told her in hospital that everything was as good as settled. Best to call now before they forgot about her.

It was a long walk. No need for a taxi now there was no hurry. Aziz stopped at a roadside kiosk, feeding her baby while she leafed through photographs and magazines. A glass of chai and a chat. Walked on, the air cooler, thick and heavy with fumes and dust.

At last, the familiar streets of the south. Across the maidan, down an alley. The Social Work Office was shut. And not just shut for the night. Boards nailed over the windows, a large padlock on the door.

Aziz turned away, suddenly bowed and weary, like an old woman. Towards home. She had been away too long. Come to expect too much. The children would be anxious. Hungry. And Hamid? Would Hamid be there tonight? Her steps became a slow, reluctant trudge, feet dragging through the litter.

Soraya Gabayan woke as the front door slammed. She heard the heavy footsteps, then voices from the kitchen. It was good to be home again. She lay for a moment savouring the feeling. Soheila's voice? Hussein's? Her father? She got out of bed and dressed quickly, regretting the loss of her suitcase and the carefully chosen presents.

Her appearance at the kitchen door caused a deathly silence.

'What is it?' cackled the Black Widow. 'What has happened?'

'Soheilaja, it's good to see you.' Soraya crossed the kitchen and hugged her sister.

'What's happened? Oh, nothing's happened. Only that she has shamed us by walking the streets of Tehran with her baby for all to see!' Masoud yanked the girls apart and forced them to sit down.

Four women, round a kitchen table. Three generations. Two men standing over them. A domestic ensemble.

The crescendo of heavy footsteps in the corridor. Bolts flung back. The door kicked open.

'Wait here,' Shirin whispered to Fariba.

356

A hasty consultation, the rings slipped off Shirin's fingers, bracelet and ear-rings, a quick rummage in her suitcase to produce a red silk scarf.

Fariba lay on the bed, drowsy in the heat, the tales of Haji Baba and Israel a happy swirling mist in her mind.

'What are you doing, Khanum?'

'Fariba, I want you to wear this.' Shirin tied the scarf over Fariba's eyes. 'No peeping now! Hold my hand.'

'Where are we going?'

'Outside.'

'Why can't I look?'

'It's a surprise.'

'There are soldiers with us?'

'In this place there are always soldiers.'

'What's the surprise? Is it Mama? Is it the aeroplane?'

'I'm not telling you.'

Hussein Gabayan wondered how much longer his father was going to dither about. He didn't believe he'd ever do it. He wouldn't dare.

Impatiently, Hussein snatched the revolver from his father. He'd never pulled the trigger of a revolver before either and he wasn't prepared for its sudden violence. The kick. The smell. The jerk of Soraya's body. The backlash of skull and brains which splattered the front of his imitation combat jacket. Then the incredible silence. It seemed to last forever.

Until a car horn blared loudly in the street. Then Masoud moved. He hoisted Soheila out of her chair. Led her away. She walked stiffly. Like a puppet. Arms dangling, eyes blank. Hussein followed like a page boy, holding up the end of her chador, which drifted behind her down the stairs.

'What's happened? Where's everybody going?' The old woman leaned forward, fingers clamped to the table edge. Then they crept, crab-like, up against the hard point of

Roya's elbow. Back towards the left now, and the soft heaviness of Soraya's arm. Through the strands of her hair. Over the cold plastic table cloth. A moist stickiness on her fingertips. Mrs Gabayan senior raised her hand towards her face. Her nostrils twitched. Blood!

'Well, well, daughter! The wages of sin, eh?'

There was no answer. Roya too had gone.

'I can't hear my footsteps any more, Khanum. We must be outside.'

'That's right, Fariba.'

'Khanum, I can hear an aeroplane, have they gone without me?'

'There are always planes in the sky. That one is going east, towards Japan.'

'How do you know?'

'It's heading away from the sunset.'

'Why have we stopped?'

'We have to wait here a minute.'

'Why does your voice sound funny? Khanum – you're hurting my hand. You're squeezing too hard.'

'I'm sorry, Fariba.'

'Khanum, I don't want to play this game. It isn't fun any more. I'm going to take the scarf off.'

'Fariba, don't!' Shirin stepped towards the child, struggling to keep Fariba's hands away from the red scarf, her body a shield against the first round of bullets.

As the echo of guns died away, Fariba heard a sound more disturbing.

'That plane, Khanum! Where's that plane going to?'

But there was no answer. Fariba ripped off the blindfold.

'Mama? Oh Mama!' Fariba opened her mouth to scream.

* * *

358

'They've bungled it again,' chuckled Fereydoun, a spoon of rice halfway to his mouth, as he heard the second volley of shots.

Mrs Emani knelt in the back row of the church, her shopping bag nicely lumpy against her calf. She prayed for Jamshid, dreaming of the day when he would be a priest. With his fair hair and in one of those lovely dark green vestments, he would look so handsome . . .

The altar boy rang the bell, recalling Mrs Emani's attention to her devotions.

'Lord have mercy.'
'Lord have mercy.'
'Christ have mercy.'
'Christ have mercy.'

'She hasn't cleaned up, Hussein! I can hear the flies.' The Black Widow still sat at the table. In the dark, though she didn't know it.

Hussein picked up a chador off the hook behind the kitchen door and, without looking, threw it over Soraya's head and shoulders.

'I haven't had my tea yet,' whined the old lady. 'I'm hungry.'

'I'll put the kettle on, Grandmother.'

'But there was meat with cinnamon and onions.'

'I can't cook, Grandmother, but I can make good tea.'

The old woman leant back, reassured by the sounds. Running water, the hiss of the gas, a match being struck, the hum of water heating.

'So, your sister is married?'

'Yes, Grandmother.' Hussein stood looking at his own reflection in the window.

'Where's your mother?'

'I don't know.'

'She should have tidied up before she went out.'

'Oh, she'll do that later.' Hussein wondered where his mother could possibly be this late at night. He found some bread in the bin, a small lump of goat's cheese in the fridge, some plates and knives.

'There's not enough room on the table,' he said.

The old lady leaned forward and with surprising strength pushed Soraya out of the way.

The Mullah Afsharzadeh spread his prayer rug and knelt, facing Mecca. He indicated to his wife that she should sit behind him. Out of sight.

He knelt and turned his thoughts towards heaven, towards his God. But where was God? Tonight, God hid his face. His soul aspired towards the infinite but remained earthbound; his body trembled with anticipation. The Mullah's knees were locked by arthritis. He gestured to his wife.

Soheila, wife of the Mullah, came closer. Her eyes were swollen. She bent down and felt the terrible weight of her husband, the smell of his fusty robes. His breath rank and his beard harsh against her cheek.

Ten links to the chain. Don't try to tell me that is mere coincidence! Ten 'Thou shalt nots' shackle me to the tree. It was a tree which fashioned the cross on which hung the Saviour of the World. Arbor una nobilis. And the chain is necessary if I am to endure this suffering. Even Christ, you know, was tempted to come down from the cross. 'Take this chalice from me.' His very words. But it was the nails. The nails that held him there. So it is with me. Chained to my destiny. My tree. My cross.

I must confess to a certain degree of discomfort. A chafing of the ankles as my manacles slacken by the day. And why do they slacken? I tell you: 'Blessed are they that hunger and thirst for righteousness' sake.'

We are all, you see, hungry for the wrong sort of food.

A T-bone steak. Black Forest Gateau. Or even a crumb of affection. To differing degrees I accept guilt in every case. But especially the latter has been my downfall. I have yearned for the love of my mother. My wife. And see where it has led me.

But that way madness lies.

Come to me and I will give you food for your souls. There is, you see, an answer to all this. A simple answer, but so profound it may not be uttered aloud. I will write it for you. A simple four-letter word. Here in the dust with my finger.

Now. Straight line down, through a right-angle. Along. There! A perfect L.

Followed by a circle. Without beginning. Without end. Let us call it eternity.

Now for the next. Oh God, give me strength. How can I go through with this? Whose face between her forks presageth snow, but underneath is sulphur and the pit . . . Slant down into the moist, delicate, hair-softened angle. Back up the smoothness of a thigh.

Quickly, quickly. The final letter before my strength gives out. Such a strong letter this. Two sturdy right-angles, reinforced by a centre bar.

Ah! Consummatum est. But there is one further task which I must undertake. Such a revelation cannot remain here in the dust to be trampled by profane feet. I must summon assistance. Come hither, friend! Yes, you. You with the dustpan and brush. Come nearer.

Now my friend, gather the grains of this message together. Sweep them gently inside this envelope and make sure that it is delivered. To the Ayatollah himself.

The service over, Mrs Emani picked up her shopping bag, crossed herself with Holy Water and tucked her rug under her arm. What a treat to have the rug back. She would put it next to Theresa's bed. It would be so nice

361

for her to have something soft for her feet when she got up to feed her baby in the night.

Out through the church door, and there was the priest, holding in his arms, of all things, a baby!

The streets were deserted. It was night-time. Who in their right minds would be outside now?

Roya was searching for her grandchild. In the bus station and the bazaar, in alleyways and doorways, she looked among the sleeping beggars. The thin wail of a newborn baby went straight to her heart. 'God, oh God, please do not let me be too late.' She prayed for forgiveness. She had been weak and now she was paying the price. She was a woman. She should have stood by her own flesh and blood.

Like one possessed, Roya staggered from street to street, and the Pasdaran stood aside to let her pass.

The children were fed and asleep. How easy to slip back into the familiar routine! Aziz sat by the tap in the centre of the yard, in the faint glow of the stars, for how could she sleep tonight?

The other women avoided her. Disaster enough she had brought on them all, now that she was no longer a woman. Aziz dragged nappies backwards and forwards through the sludgy water. Such lovely nappies they had been only that morning. New nappies. Shining white.

And Aziz knew that years hence she would still be there. There was no Israel. No Paradise. Not for her. She should have known better. And now there would be no more babies. She had no husband, not any more. She was no longer a wife. Aziz shivered and envied Fariba.

Mrs Emani got out of the taxi. It had been so kind of the Father to find her a taxi. She hadn't quite liked to say

362

that she couldn't really afford it, now that there were so many mouths to feed.

She squatted at the edge of the road, cradling the golden-haired infant in one arm, while with the other she fumbled in her handbag for the key. She wouldn't knock. Theresa might be resting. Rest was so important for her, for the sake of her baby.

Mrs Emani could hardly believe her luck. A daughter and two babies! A lifetime of servitude awaited her. And she would be a willing, such a willing slave.

Mrs Emani shuffled awkwardly through the front door. It was suddenly too narrow for herself, the baby and the bulging shopping bag.

'You're late,' called Theresa. 'I'm starving!'

Mrs Emani smiled as she switched on the light in the hall. So wonderful her life had become.

The taxi driver drove away. He wasn't being dishonest he told himself. If the old bag didn't remember to take her rug with her, that was her fault. A good rug too by the look of it. It would fetch a few toman in the bazaar.

It was midnight when Masoud burst into the kitchen. 'Look,' he shouted, grinning from ear to ear, holding a white bloodstained banner before him.

'What is it, Masoudja? What's going on?' His mother plonked her tea glass down on the clotted surface.

'Allah be praised, Mother, I have one daughter who does me credit.'

Hussein, leaning against the kitchen cupboard, grunted with satisfaction. He lit a cigarette.

'But what has happened, Masoudja, won't somebody tell me what's going on?' The old lady pulled herself to her feet and groped towards her son.

'Look, Mother, look!' Masoud thrust the cloth at her. 'Soheila has not disgraced us on her wedding night.'

363

The old woman seized the cloth. Sniffed at it like a dog. Whirling round the kitchen, Masoud tripped over the body of Soraya.

'Why's *that* still there?'

Hussein shrugged. 'Mother's gone out.'

Father and son manoeuvred the corpse under the table. Out of the way.

Then Hussein turned on the radio full blast, and the kitchen rocked to the tune of a popular hymn. Hussein didn't know the words. He didn't know the words to any hymn. But he sang at the top of his voice. La, la la.

Masoud took his old mother in his arms and capered about the kitchen. One, two, three, hop, one, two, three. Faster and faster. Dizzy with the speed. The bloodstained cloth crushed between them. Offering thanks to God, the Compassionate, the Merciful.

Fiction in Paladin

The Businessman: A Tale of Terror   £2.95   ☐
Thomas M. Disch

'Each of the sixty short chapters of THE BUSINESSMAN is a *tour de force* of polished, distanced, sly narrative art . . . always the vision of America stays with us: melancholic, subversive and perfectly put . . . In this vision lies the terror of THE BUSINESSMAN'
Times Literary Supplement

'An entertaining nightmare out of Thomas Berger and Stephen King'
Time

Filthy English   £2.95   ☐
Jonathan Meades

'Incest and lily-boys, loose livers and ruched red anal compulsives, rape, murder and literary looting . . . Meades tosses off quips, cracks and crossword clues, stirs up the smut and stuffs in the erudition, pokes you in the ribs and prods you in the kidneys (as in Renal, home of Irene and Albert) . . . a delicious treat (full of fruit and nuts) for the vile and filthy mind to savour'
Time Out

Dancing with Mermaids   £2.95   ☐
Miles Gibson

'An excellent, imaginative comic tale . . . an original and wholly entertaining fiction . . . extremely funny and curiously touching'
Cosmopolitan

'The impact of the early Ian McEwan or Martin Amis, electrifying, a dazzler'
Financial Times

'It is as if Milk Wood had burst forth with those obscene-looking blossoms one finds in sweaty tropical palm houses . . . murder and mayhem decked out in fantastic and erotic prose'
The Times

To order direct from the publisher just tick the titles you want and fill in the order form.   **PF1**

Original Fiction in Paladin

Paper Thin   £2.95 ☐
Philip First
From the author of THE GREAT PERVADER: a wonderfully original
collection of stories about madness, love, passion, violence, sex and
humour.

Don Quixote   £2.95 ☐
Kathy Acker
From the author of BLOOD AND GUTS IN HIGH SCHOOL: a
visionary collage–novel in which Don Quixote is a woman on an
intractable quest; a late twentieth-century LEVIATHAN; a stingingly
powerful and definitely unique novel.

All these books are available at your local bookshop or newsagent, or can be ordered direct from the publisher.

To order direct from the publishers just tick the titles you want and fill in the form below.

Name _____

Address _____

_____

Send to:
Paladin Cash Sales
PO Box 11, Falmouth, Cornwall TR10 9EN.

Please enclose remittance to the value of the cover price plus:

UK 60p for the first book, 25p for the second book plus 15p per copy for each additional book ordered to a maximum charge of £1.90.

BFPO 60p for the first book, 25p for the second book plus 15p per copy for the next 7 books, thereafter 9p per book.

Overseas including Eire £1.25 for the first book, 75p for second book and 28p for each additional book.

Paladin Books reserve the right to show new retail prices on covers, which may differ from those previously advertised in the text or elsewhere.